'You're out of here!'

Dan's wide hand shot out. He seized Elly by the arm and marched her firmly towards the door.

Elly had only enough time to swipe her purse from the coffee table and grab her coat from the back of her chair before he ushered her out of the room.

'I don't know what kind of game you're playing, and I don't care. You're leaving, lady.'

'But don't you want to—'

Before she could get out the rest of her sentence, she found herself standing alone in the cold ocean mist on Madge's lemon-bright porch. After the door slammed behind her, she could still feel the pressure of Dan's strong fingers on her arm and his palm on her backside. The nerve of the man. He'd thrown her out!

Then the implication of what had just happened hit her. A triumphant grin spread slowly across her lips.

She had found her missing prince!

THE COLTONS

The Raven's Assignment
by Kasey Michaels

ᕍ ᙮ ᙭

THE COLTONS

Welcome to Black Arrow, the birthplace of a proud, passionate branch of the Colton family, of men and women who would risk everything for love, family and honour.

Jesse Colton: As a special government agent, danger comes with the job. But protecting breathtaking Samantha Cosgrove—and his heart—could prove to be his toughest assignment ever.

Samantha Cosgrove: The sweet, idealistic campaign manager has stumbled upon a troubling secret. Only Jesse Colton can help her discover the truth—and unlock the passion hidden inside her.

Gloria WhiteBear: Will the secret past of this Coltons' matriarch come back to haunt her grandchildren?

Sky Colton: Jesse's hardworking younger sister is becoming famous for her original jewellery. But life has a very different design in store for this independent woman.

Available in October 2003 from Silhouette Desire.

Ride the Thunder
by Lindsay McKenna
(*Morgan's Mercenaries*)
and
Plain Jane MacAllister
by Joan Elliott Pickart
(*The Baby Bet: MacAllister's Gifts*)

The Secret Baby Bond
by Cindy Gerard
and
Cinderella's Convenient Husband
by Katherine Garbera
(*Dynasties: The Connellys*)

The Secret Prince
by Kathryn Jensen
and
The Raven's Assignment
by Kasey Michaels
(*The Coltons*)

The Secret Prince
KATHRYN JENSEN

The Raven's Assignment
KASEY MICHAELS

SILHOUETTE® DESIRE™

*Silhouette, Silhouette Desire and Colophon
are registered trademarks of Harlequin Books S.A.,
used under licence.*

*First published in Great Britain 2003
Silhouette Books, Eton House, 18-24 Paradise Road,
Richmond, Surrey TW9 1SR*

The publisher acknowledges the copyright holders of the
individual works as follows:

The Secret Prince © Kathryn Pearce 2002
The Raven's Assignment © Harlequin S.A. 2002

*Special thanks and acknowledgement are given to Kasey Michaels
for her contribution to The Coltons series.*

ISBN 0 373 04881 5

51-1003

*Printed and bound in Spain
by Litografia Rosés S.A., Barcelona*

THE SECRET PRINCE

by
Kathryn Jensen

KATHRYN JENSEN

has written many novels for young readers as well as for adults. She speed walks, works out with weights and enjoys ballroom dancing for exercise, stress reduction and pleasure. Her children are now grown. She lives in Maryland with her writing companion—Sunny, a loveable terrier-mix adopted from a shelter.

Having worked as a hospital switchboard operator, department store sales assistant, bank clerk and primary school teacher, Kathryn now splits her days between writing her own books and teaching fiction writing at two local colleges and through a correspondence course. She enjoys helping new writers get a start and speaks 'at the drop of a hat' at writers' conferences, libraries and schools across the country.

One

"**Y**ou're mine, lady." Daniel Eastwood tossed his jeans on top of the sweatshirt already in the sand and fixed his dark eyes on her. "Giving me the cold shoulder won't keep me away."

She was even more beautiful this morning than she'd been the day before…or the one before that. The muscles angling across his taut stomach and lean thighs tensed, primed for action. He rolled his wide shoulders in anticipation.

Three long running strides, and he dove into the chill waves of the Atlantic. She yielded, as always, to his fierce strokes. Her cool fingers supported him, beckoned him to deeper waters, challenged him. He could feel her strength in each liquid gray-green surge. He swam exactly half a mile along the deserted beach before flip-kicking around to slice back through the icy foam, back toward where he had started, directly below the pastel bungalows of the Haven.

Dan had sustained an intimate relationship with the sea since the first day he had seen her. The school field trip to Ocean City had carried him a good three hours by bus from the grim streets of south Baltimore, a world away. Never had he forgotten the sense of awe, respect, and fascination he felt that day—a city kid, standing on that endless stretch of pale sand, so much water all in one place. Water that seemed to breathe with its own movement and the motions of living things hidden beneath it. And all that clean air hitting him in the face, filling his lungs, it made him feel strong and new inside. Although he had to return to the city with his classmates that day, he had never forgotten the ocean's beauty or wanted to live anywhere but beside her.

As soon as he was old enough, he had returned to take a summer job as a lifeguard. And each June after that, with the exception of those four he had spent with the marines, he had been drawn back to her as surely as the tide is pulled by the moon. He never lost sight of her capricious temperament, though. The unpredictable squalls. Sudden drops just off shore that hadn't been there days before. Riptides that could seize a strong swimmer, drag him out to frigid depths, and rob him of his will to ever breathe again. He loved her beauty and power, despite her faults.

As he turned his head to draw a final breath that would carry him the last four strokes of his morning regime, he glimpsed a woman standing beside his clothes, her hand held delicately above her eyes to shade them from the early-morning sun. She gave the impression of having come for him, not just someone idly watching a lone swimmer brave fifty-degree water.

"What the devil," he muttered, swallowing a mouthful of salt water in his distraction. His people knew not to disturb him at this time of day. That is, if any of them were in the office this early. Setting his feet down, he stood in chest-deep water, the sand sucking and scraping beneath the pads of his feet as he studied her.

Not a local. He would have recognized her this time of year with all the tourists gone. She was tall for a woman, maybe up to his chin, which would make her about five-nine. Her hair was russet streaked with pink-gold highlights from the dawn sky, pulled back in a prim knot at the nape of her neck. Her dark-green business suit seemed absurd beachwear. Tan leather pumps dangled from one crooked finger. Her mouth was pulled into an annoyed pout. The tiny grains of sand sifting between the threads of her pantyhose probably weren't helping her mood.

But as soon as he started up the slope out of the water, her expression changed. The water line crept teasingly down his chest, not yet revealing the presence or lack of a bathing suit. Her eyes widened with alarm. He smiled, kept on coming, and soon the upper edge of his flesh-molding Speedo showed above the white spume.

Immediately, her lips lifted in a weak smile of relief.

Dan chuckled to himself. What he would have given to have been swimming in the buff that morning, just to watch the shock in her pretty eyes.

A nippy breeze off the water hit him, and the sudden cold took his breath away. "Throw me that towel!" he called to her.

She scowled as if she hadn't at first heard him over the grating, gurgling rush of the waves against the sand. Looking around, she focused on a generous pile of terrycloth near his clothing and scooped it up. "Isn't November a little extreme for swimming in Maryland?"

"Not for me." He couldn't resist. "I'm naturally hot-blooded."

She rolled her eyes and tossed the towel at him. "Oh please—"

"Seriously. My body temperature runs two degrees above normal. Always has. I draw the line, though, at breaking through ice for my morning constitutional."

"Limits are good." Her eyes sparkled with humor.

Elly forced herself to look past the near-naked man toward the softly glowing horizon. She tried to remember the reason she was standing on a beach in the middle of winter in her stocking feet. But Dan Eastwood was very difficult to stop looking at. No male she'd ever personally met possessed a body like *that*. Wide, muscled swimmer's shoulders, a rock-hard stomach, and hips that slimmed to strong, efficient kicking levers. But she hadn't come to flirt with the owner of the Haven. Her mission was much more important than that and, she reminded herself, time was of the essence.

"You're Daniel Robert Eastwood?" she asked, risking another glance his way. God, he was gorgeous!

"I'm Eastwood. And you?"

He was drying off his beautifully muscled chest, his long, strong arms—the towel dropped lower—his *everywhere*. She looked away, tiny beads of sweat springing up beneath her hairline despite the frigid air. "I'm Elizabeth Anderson. I need to ask you a few questions, if you can spare me ten minutes."

He frowned. "If you're selling hotel supplies, you'll

need to see my business partner, Kevin Hunter. He takes care of all the ordering. His office is in the main building."

"I've already spoken with Mr. Hunter. He told me where you'd be."

"He did, did he?" She liked the way his dark eyes flashed at her, suggesting he wasn't at all displeased with his partner's decision.

With a sudden jolt, Elly realized that she had been running the tip of her tongue across her upper lip and she stopped herself. He might read the gesture as an appreciation of his near-nakedness, which of course it was. But it was crucial that she keep her mind on the business at hand. A lot of people, very important people—not the least of which was her father—were depending on her.

As Dan tugged his sweatshirt down over his head, he snuck a good peek. She looked slim and healthy, though a little on the pale side, as if her work rarely took her out into the sunshine and she didn't take much time off for outdoor recreation. Her pleated skirt was short, revealing elegant, long legs. Her breasts…hard to tell. All he could make out was a promising swell beneath the ultra-conservative suit jacket. Pity it wasn't August. She'd have been hard put not to strip down under Ocean City's blazing sun.

"Suppose we walk up to my house," he suggested. "You can tell me what this is all about."

"Why don't you get yourself dressed, Mr. Eastwood? I'll meet you back at your office."

"That's not convenient." He started walking away from her, up the sloping beach. A moment later, he heard her scurrying behind him in the sand, and he smiled to himself.

"Why isn't it convenient?" she called out.

"I have a nine o'clock. No telling how long the meeting might last. Ever heard of making appointments, Miss Anderson?"

"There isn't time. I need to speak with you right away."

Dan stopped and turned to face her. The urgency in her tone signaled trouble. "Maybe we'd better settle this right here. What's the big crisis?"

She sighed and gazed thoughtfully along the windswept beach then turned back to study his face with an odd intensity.

"Talk fast," he prompted. Pretty soon his fingers were going to fall off from the cold. After that, who knew what would be next.

"All right then," she snapped, giving him an irritated look. "I am a professional genealogist. I work for my father's company, and we've been hired to verify the ancestors and descendants of a gentleman, now deceased. There's a possibility you might be related to his family."

He laughed. "That's it?"

"That's it," she said. "All I need to do is ask you a few simple questions, then I'll be out of your hair." She tipped her head to observe him. "Your lips are turning blue. I suppose it's all right if we talk at your place, since it's so cold outside."

"Thank you." He stepped up onto the boardwalk that ran over a mile along the shore. Most of the structures at the far end of the driftwood-gray planks were high-rise condominiums and hotels. But here, in the older part of town, along with the arcades, snack shacks and amusement park rides, were a few of the older-style beach bungalows that had survived the ocean's violent mood swings. Four years ago when Hurricane Evelyn had swept away entire blocks of the low wooden structures, Dan had seen the opportunity he'd been waiting for. He was out of the Corps, had earned his degree in business on the GI Bill and saved up a nest egg. He was looking for an investment that would keep him close to his beloved beach.

He and his best friend Kevin put together a proposal to buy the ruined property. They raised the level of the land by bringing in tons of fill, built protective man-made dunes, then erected sturdy, smaller versions of the original bungalows—twenty-five of them in a cluster. The Haven evolved into a far more successful business than either of them had expected. Dan couldn't help feeling proud of what they'd accomplished.

But now that most of the hard work had been done, the days often ran together. The off-season was particularly lonely. After Labor Day, the tourists disappeared, including most of the dateable women. But here was pert, intriguing Elizabeth Anderson with her burnished locks, long legs, and baffling need to interrogate him. He toyed with the tempting idea of canceling his nine o'clock to spend the morning with her...if he could find a way to stretch her promised ten minutes to a few hours.

"So tell me about my mystery family." He opened the door to the first house they came to and waved her inside.

"We don't know that they *are* your family," she cautioned. "Not yet. That's why I need to talk to you."

"So shoot." He tossed the damp towel on the arm of the tan leather sofa and she followed it with a look of female disapproval for his casual housekeeping.

"What are your mother's and father's full names?"

"My mother is Margaret Jennings Eastwood. She goes by Madge. My father, I never knew. His name was Carl Eastwood. He died shortly after I was born."

She nodded, sliding a small pad of paper and pen from her purse. Elizabeth wrote a few notes. "And the date of your birth?"

He told her.

"That makes you, let's see…thirty-two?" He nodded. "Your mother's current address and phone number?" she asked smoothly.

He stopped halfway into the bedroom and turned to face her, suddenly suspicious. "Why do you need to know that?"

"I'm sure she'll be as interested as you are in your shared heritage," she said with a brilliant smile. But her eyes shifted away from his before she'd finished speaking. He wondered if she might be concealing something he should know before giving her more information.

"If you need to speak with my mother, I'll take you to her. What else do you need from *me*?"

She looked vaguely disappointed, but glanced down at her pad. Her tongue did its little lip-flick thing again. "Well…where were you born, Mr. Eastwood?"

"It's Dan. In Baltimore, Mercy Hospital."

She blinked, checked something she'd written a few pages back, then nodded. He sensed she was holding her breath as she asked the next question. "And have you always lived in Baltimore?"

"Until I graduated from high school. Then I enlisted in the Marine Corps. After that I took up permanent residence in Ocean City. We've been here ever since."

A subtle blink of her eyes told him he must have given her a piece of information she thought valuable.

That troubled him. He didn't like being kept in the dark.

"Do you have any siblings?" she continued.

"No."

"Not even half brothers or sisters by another father?"

Dan scowled, even more uneasy at the intimate turn of her questions. "What are you implying, Miss Anderson?"

"My friends call me Elly." She beamed at him—all hazel-eyed innocence. Something tightened pleasantly in his stomach, and he couldn't help smiling back despite his growing suspicion that she was setting some kind of trap for him. "It's a simple question, really," she continued. "These days, many families include step-kids, half siblings...yours, mine, and ours.... Women *are* allowed to marry more than once, you know."

"My mother never remarried," he stated quickly.

"I see."

Dan wished he could get a look at what she was writing. Her pen was in constant motion now, scratching out far more than the few words of each of his responses. The sense that his privacy was being invaded in some mystifying way that he couldn't yet understand became almost overwhelming.

"I have to change and get to that meeting," he grumbled. "Unless you're willing to be straight with me about what you're really up to, Miss Anderson, this is the end of our discussion."

Looking disheartened, she flipped the little book shut then shoved it and the pen into her shoulder bag. "I'm afraid, for the time being, anything more than what I've already told you is confidential."

"Then you'd better leave," he said gruffly. He told himself he was being an idiot, shaking off the prettiest thing that had crossed his beach in months. She looked as good indoors as she had outside in the salty air. If anything, her eyes seemed brighter, more alive than before—as if she was excited by something she had just learned.

But the meeting with his contractor really was important. And even as his libido urged him to get her phone number, his brain was warning him to distance himself from her. She was pure trouble, although what variety he hadn't as yet figured out.

"I'll let you know if I can tell you anything more," she promised coolly then stuck out her hand to shake as if determined to conclude their conversation with a professional gesture, even if it had begun under less than businesslike conditions.

"Next time, maybe you'll join me for a swim," he suggested as he opened the door for her.

She laughed. "In November? Don't hold your breath."

Too bad, he thought as he stood alone in his living room a moment later, the knob still in his hand. *I'd love to be the one to warm you up after a winter dip.*

Elly sat in her car gripping the steering wheel, trying to compose herself. Her father would be furious with her for not getting everything out of Daniel Eastwood they so desperately needed. But things had started out badly. She'd nearly keeled over when he came up out of the water—all gleaming muscles and smooth, bronzed skin. A classic vision of Neptune in his younger years, sans trident. That skimpy red Speedo hadn't left much to the imagination. Not much at all!

She felt a hot flush across her cheeks and brow and let out a yip of frustration. She wasn't usually flustered by men. In fact, she'd become pretty much immune to these feelings from choice. It was her defense against getting involved. Involvement meant intimacy, and intimacy meant...

A flash of dark memory rocked her without warning. Suddenly, she could hear and see everything as it had been that night. The high-pitched cry in the night...her father's frantic shouts into the telephone...the wretched look of helplessness on his face. And finally, her mother's unmoving body glimpsed through the half-open bedroom doorway seconds before sirens shattered the silence in the little house.

Just as quickly as the horrible vision had struck, it passed, leaving Elly trembling, her body moist with sweat, her heart pounding erratically in her chest. She covered her eyes with her palms and drew in deep, calming breaths. "It's over. It's over," she whispered until the fear slowly subsided and the pressure in her chest lessened and her brain cleared so that she could think again. Where had she been? What had she been thinking when...

Yes, she reminded herself, *Dan Eastwood.*

She opened her eyes and focused on the long line of gray-green surf on the other side of the sand from where she was parked. She could do this. *She could do this!*

Eastwood. Even if he hadn't refused to answer any more questions, it would be torture to go back and attempt to grill him further. As long as those dark eyes rested on her, Elly knew her mind would wander to that scene on the beach and she'd be incapable of focusing on her job, and—Lord, help her—she might even fall apart as she had just now, only right in front of him. And she couldn't bear that.

The real problem was, although she'd verified several basic points of their investigation she still didn't have enough information to prove he was the one they were looking for.

She looked at her watch. Within a few hours, she'd have to call her father in Elbia with an update. They both knew that if she failed to find the person they were looking for within twenty-four hours, all hell was going to break loose in the international press. The London tabloid that somehow had been leaked information from the palace would reveal a scandal that might threaten the Elbian crown. And Anderson Genealogical Research would earn a very big, very black mark for breaching their own right-to-privacy rule, even if it hadn't been their fault.

Now what was she going to do?

Worrying her bottom lip between her teeth, Elly slid her notebook computer off the passenger seat and into her lap. She flipped open the screen, booted up and summoned the correct file. From memory, she added the information Eastwood had just given her. She had found his name and address through an Internet search, but his mother's phone number and address hadn't come up, probably because she didn't have an e-mail address and her phone number was unlisted.

However, Eastwood had let slip that his mother lived somewhere in the area. "We've been here ever since..." *We,* not I. And he'd offered to take Elly to her, so the woman couldn't be far away.

Elly finished typing her notes then grabbed her purse and locked the car behind her. Neighbors were always a great help in instances such as this, she thought with renewed hope. That was where she'd start.

Elly stood on the top step of the tidy yellow bungalow, straightened her suit jacket, put on a friendly smile, and knocked. It was only a moment before the door opened.

"Yes?" A short, middle-aged woman with blond hair stepped into the opening and gave her a curious smile.

"Margaret Eastwood?" Elly asked.

"Yes, hon." Her accent was pure Bal'morese.

"I was just speaking with your son and—"

The woman's face lit up. "You're a friend of Dan's?"

"Well, not exactly a friend. You see, I was looking for you, but I found Dan's name first and—"

"Come in and tell me why he sent you over." Margaret beamed at her. "This is one of the nicest things about the Haven. A gated community, they call it. You can feel safe chatting with folks, not like in the old neighborhood where we had to be so very careful who we let into the house."

"Well, yes, of course," Elly agreed, feeling just a little guilty, for she was about to become a most unwelcome intruder in this woman's life.

As Elly stepped into the cozy colonial-furnished living room, she focused on a collection of antique glass bottles arranged on shelves in a bay window, then on a display of photographs on top of an upright piano. There were several of a little boy at different ages, babyhood through toddler, then at various school ages. Elly sniffed the air, distracted by a delicious aroma. "Something smells wonderful."

"Gingerbread," Margaret said. "I always make old-fashioned New England gingerbread in the fall. It reminds me of home, and Danny loves it."

"Then you're not from around here?"

"Oh my goodness, no. But Maryland is my home now. I've been here all of my adult life. Sit down, I'll bring you a cup of coffee and a warm slice."

Elly turned around to protest but Margaret was gone.

"You said you've lived here all of your adult life?" she shouted toward the kitchen door.

"In Maryland, not Ocean City. We lived in Baltimore while Dan was young. But he turned into such a beach bum after a few summers of lifeguarding down here. After he was discharged from the service, he wanted me to move down here with him while he attended the community college. Later, he and his friend bought this land and built these cute little cottages." She was beaming proudly as she walked back into the room, holding a tray laden with coffee mugs and plates of fresh gingerbread topped with mountains of whipped cream. "Danny also runs a summer camp for city boys and girls."

"I didn't know that," Elly admitted.

"Oh yes. He feels very strongly about giving inner-city children a few weeks off the streets, to let them see a different world from their troubled neighborhoods."

Elly accepted a steaming mug of coffee and a dessert plate with a second twinge of guilt. She didn't want to deceive this woman who was being so hospitable to her. "Mrs. Eastwood, I have to confess that Dan didn't actually send me over to talk with you."

"Oh?" She looked disappointed.

"I've been hired by a European family to fill in a

missing branch on their family tree. The von Austerands. Do you recognize the name?''

Elly watched as the woman's face grayed and her
fingers pinched nervously at the napkin in her lap.
''No.''

''They're like the Windsors of England. They are
the royal family of a small country that borders on
Austria. Elbia.''

''I think you'd better leave,'' Madge said tightly.

But Elly was determined. She continued choosing
her words carefully. ''We have reason to believe that
a young American woman had a brief romantic liaison
with the young king of that country thirty-three years
ago, before he married. There is a chance that she was
carrying his child when they parted, but if so, she disappeared before the baby was born. Would you know
anything about this, Mrs. Eastwood?''

Dan's mother firmly set her plate on the coffee table
and turned her face toward the rainbow of glass in the
window. ''My husband was an American. His name
was Carl Eastwood, and he died before Dan was a year
old,'' she pronounced tightly.

Carl Eastwood. There it was again, the name Dan
had used. Carl with a C according to the documents
she'd already dug up. Could it be a coincidence that
the young king's name had been Karl? His Royal Highness Karl von Austerand had died just a few years ago,
and now his son Jacob wore his crown. Jacob had always been thought to be the king's sole heir, until evidence of a secret love affair turned up in a routine
cataloguing of the family's papers only days ago. Days
which now felt to Elly like weeks and months of frantic
searching.

"I wouldn't know about affairs or kings or illegitimate royal babies," Madge said sharply.

Elly's heart beat faster despite the woman's denial. Something in her pale eyes told Elly this was a woman unaccustomed to lying, who was desperately trying to do just that.

"I understand how difficult this must be for you," Elly said softly, setting aside her own coffee and fragrant gingerbread to reach across the space between the two chairs and pat the other woman's arm. "But if you can just give me a little more information, please."

Madge's chest rose and fell with labored breaths. She stiffened and leaned back into her chair, her hands gripping the arms. Her features contorted into sharp folds, as if she was trying to work out a difficult puzzle. "Go," she whispered hoarsely. "Get out of my house."

Elly sighed inwardly. She respected the woman's right to privacy, but if she didn't get to the truth soon, both Madge and her son would find themselves in a terrible fix. This was no time for cat-and-mouse games. A simple statement from the woman would save days they didn't have for a full public records' investigation. She'd already picked up and lost two reporters on her way from Connecticut to Baltimore. They might show up at any moment—then it would be out of her hands, if her theory about Dan Eastwood was right. She decided to try a different angle.

"Mrs. Eastwood, I'm not trying to upset you. But in cases where relationships have broken up, the children often *want* to know about their lost family members. Don't you think Dan would like to learn who his real father is?" She was bluffing, just a little, for she wasn't one-hundred-percent certain of all the facts. But if it worked she would know for sure.

Madge's mouth flew wide on a horrified gasp. "My son doesn't need to know—"

Her words stilled in the air as the front door clicked shut and footsteps approached the sitting room from the hall. Both women turned to face the doorway.

Dan Eastwood looked around the corner, his dark eyes glittering dangerously. Even at a distance, Elly could see the thin blue vein throbbing at his temple and the tense cut of his mouth. "I don't need to know *what,* Mother?"

Elly's heart felt as if it were being squeezed by a cold, hard hand. She crossed her fingertips over her chest and swallowed. The warning rumble of Dan's voice sent icy prickles down her spine.

She glanced quickly at Madge, whose expression had altered with amazing speed from a stubborn glare to a helpless pucker. "Oh, dear. I guess I shouldn't have let this young woman in. She told me she was your *girlfriend,* Danny."

Elly gasped in outrage and shot to her feet. The woman wasn't as guileless as she appeared. "I never said that! Mrs. Eastwood, you know that I never implied my visit was—" She let out a frustrated wail. Between his mother and a stranger, who was the man likely to believe? "Never mind. I came alone because I felt your mom might feel less self-conscious speaking to me without your being here."

Dan quirked one skeptical, dark brow at her.

"Honest. I didn't mean any harm."

"I told you I would *bring you* around if necessary!" Dan snapped, then turned to his distraught-looking mother. "I don't know how she found you. I'm sorry. Now, ladies, what is it I *don't* need to know?"

Madge firmly pressed her lips together.

"Then *you* tell me," he stated, swiveling back to Elly.

"At the moment, there may or may not be anything to tell." She was doing her best to be discreet. But Dan was making things harder by the minute, and Madge seemed incapable of saying anything to either stop the truth from coming out or to set facts straight. Elly stood to face him. "It's important that I find out if your mother was ever in Europe…specifically, in Paris."

Dan looked from the woman he'd fantasized about less than an hour earlier, to his mother. He read a level of anxiety in Madge's eyes he had never seen before. "What's going on here, Mom?"

"She's upsetting me," Madge whimpered. "Make her leave."

Dan ground out words between clenched teeth, fighting to hang on to his temper. "She's going to leave as soon as she explains what the hell she's fishing for!"

As infuriating as Elly was, his body still reacted with disturbing warmth to her presence. It was impossible to keep his eyes off her pretty, animated face…or her hands, which kept moving from twin perches on her hips to tug nervously at her blouse's neckline or tuck themselves away when she folded her arms over her chest. Which was another issue entirely…her enticingly lovely, perfectly proportioned chest. She'd evidently left off her jacket for this visit, which offered a much nicer view. Someone help him!

"Why does it matter whether or not my mother ever was in Europe?" he had the presence of mind to demand.

Elly took a deep breath and stepped toward him, praying the right words would come to her. "Papers have recently come to light that indicate a young American woman named Margaret Jennings spent a year abroad, as a student in Paris. That was your maiden name. Right, Mrs. Eastwood?"

Dan answered for her. "Yes, and her junior year she attended the Sorbonne. You told me you did, Mom."

Madge closed her eyes but acknowledged nothing.

Elly held her breath and asked, "Was it during that year that you met a young man named—"

"I met Carl Eastwood there, yes!" Madge snapped, pushing herself up from her armchair with startling energy. "We married, and nine months later Dan was born. But Carl died very young." Tears filled her eyes and she wiped at them with the sleeve of her dress.

Dan frowned, looking more puzzled than ever. "I thought you and Dad hooked up in Baltimore."

"No. No, it was in a little village outside of Paris." Madge sniffled and looked away from her son. "Years later, I heard the church burned down. Probably destroyed all its records too."

Elly opened her mouth to tell the woman she knew that was a lie, but at the last second thought better of it since her six-foot-plus son stood by ready to defend his mother's honor.

"Go on," Dan growled, his too-perceptive gaze locked onto Elly's face. "What were you about to say?"

She swallowed over a sandpaper-dry spot in her throat. "There is no record of a marriage, that's true." She hesitated, but the look on Dan's face told her she must finish what she'd begun, regardless of how he took the news. "There is no record…because there has never been a Carl Eastwood in your mother's life. And there never was a marriage.''

''All right, you're out of here!'' Dan's wide hand shot out. He seized Elly by the arm and marched her firmly toward the door.

She had only enough time to swipe her purse from the coffee table and grab her coat from the back of her chair before he ushered her out of the room.

''I don't know what kind of game you're playing, and I don't care. You're leaving, lady.''

''But don't you want to—''

Before she could get out the rest of her sentence, she found herself standing alone in the cold ocean mist on Madge's lemon-bright porch. She could still feel the pressure of Dan's strong fingers on her arm and his palm on her backside after the door slammed behind her. The nerve of the man. He'd thrown her out!

Then the implication of what had just happened hit her. A triumphant grin spread slowly across her lips.

She had found her missing prince!

TWO

Elly bounced in anticipation on the edge of the hotel bed, her ear pressed to the telephone receiver. Someone had gone to find her father to take her call. She'd never seen the castle in person, but photographs of Der Kristallenpalast, the famous crystal palace, revealed an immense, turreted structure of pale, lustrous marble and hundreds of richly appointed rooms. Frank Anderson could easily be half a mile from the nearest phone.

His unmistakable smoker's voice suddenly rasped across the line. "It's about time. What do you have?"

"It's a boy!" she cried.

"The old king had a *son* with the Jennings girl?"

Elly grinned, enjoying her moment of triumph. "That *girl* is now in her fifties, goes by Madge and is being really stubborn about admitting that she had a royal fling thirty-some years ago."

"Understandable," he grumbled. "She married

now? Not wanting her husband to know about her past?''

''No,'' Elly admitted with a sigh. ''But she's sticking to a story about an American husband who died young. I'm certain she made him up for her son's benefit.''

''But you're sure about this young man?''

She hesitated barely a heartbeat. ''Yes. Dad, he even looks like Jacob. And the photos of Karl when he was young could be Daniel Eastwood today. They have the same dark hair and strong, angular features, although Eastwood's eyes are dark brown, not blue.''

''That could easily come from the mother's side. Good. I'll tell Jacob.''

''Do we have enough to prove legally he's the old king's son, though?'' she asked. She trusted her intuition and the facts she'd uncovered, but the law was another thing.

''Karl was studying at the Sorbonne the same time as Margaret Jennings, according to the school's records. He kept her love letters to him and her farewell note. A handwriting expert can make quick work of comparing this woman's handwriting with that of the person who wrote those letters. There are other documents as well.''

Elly was so excited she could barely speak. But she was also deeply moved by the drama revealed by the decades-old letters they'd found. Those must have been desperate times for a young prince, soon to become king, and his frightened mistress. Had Karl even known that the girl he'd fallen in love with but could never marry carried his child? Nothing they'd found to this date mentioned her pregnancy. How very sad, Elly thought, if the man had died never knowing he had another son.

But now, years later, wonderful things might come of this discovery for Dan and his mother. Not that they deserved it, Elly thought ruefully, tossing her out the way they'd done. But imagine discovering a brother you never knew existed! And a royal one at that!

"What now?" Elly asked her father breathlessly.

"Jacob's advisors told me this morning that if you found the woman and she had a child by the king, they'd want both of them brought over on the first possible plane."

She frowned. "Why?"

"Damage control. They believe that with the pair here in Elbia, the press will have a harder time getting to them. There are also some touchy legal issues to be ironed out, the sooner the better from the crown's perspective."

Elly's mind whirled, and she felt short of breath. "Eastwood doesn't even believe me. How will I get him on a plane to Europe? Dad, this isn't our job. All we agreed to do was verify historical records. We're not private investigators."

"Elizabeth." His chastising papa-bear growl ended in a soft cough. She hated that he smoked. But since her mother had died there had been no one, including herself, who could talk sense to the man about his health or anything else.

"Well, we're not!" she insisted.

"We have no choice at this point. The king blames us for the leak. He's absolutely convinced that no one in his court would peddle such volatile news to the press. Now we have to do what we can to save a bad situation. And—" He balked.

"There's more bad news?" She didn't want to think about one more complication.

"Consider the many implications of this discovery, Elly. There is enormous wealth at stake. Even an illegitimate child might demand a portion of his father's fortune. And what about the mother? As far as we know, she has never been compensated for her pregnancy or given any financial help in raising the boy."

Elly rolled her eyes to the motel room's chalky ceiling. The packet of letters her father had only recently discovered hidden behind a panel in an ancient armoire had turned into a modern Pandora's box. In addition to the love notes, signed "adoringly, Margaret," other letters, returned from the United States as undeliverable, indicated that over the next ten years Karl had tried to locate his lost love, but failed. Perhaps it was just his beloved Margaret he searched for. Or maybe he feared the existence of a child and knew the danger an illegitimate offspring, older by several months than his son by the queen, would pose to his dynasty.

"Get them on a plane," Elly repeated dully, shaking her head. "Short of kidnapping mother and son, I'm not sure how I'll manage that."

"We don't have much time," Frank reminded her. "If I were that young man or his mother, I'd want to find a good place to hide out for a while. The press will eat them alive."

Elly shook her head. "Something tells me this guy isn't the type to run away from anything."

"Elizabeth," her father whispered hoarsely, sounding increasingly worried, "if this explodes in our faces, our professional reputation will be destroyed. We might as well give up the business. *Do you understand?*"

She swallowed. It was that bad then. "I'll bring them to you," she promised. "Somehow."

Dan was thirty minutes late for his appointment with the contractor, mostly because he had other things on his mind. His thoughts boomeranged back and forth between memories of manhandling an attractive redhead out his mother's door, his hand placed strategically on her pretty rump, and the less enjoyable knowledge that he'd probably never see Elly Anderson again.

Luckily, the contractor was still in his office. They negotiated a few terms, signed the contract. Within a week the storm damage to the bungalows closest to the shoreline would be repaired. One less thing to worry about.

Dan drove back toward the Haven along Ocean Avenue and turned into the parking lot. A flash of crimson hair in the sunlight caught his eye. Setting the parking brake on his SUV, he squinted through the windshield into the wintry glare. A man and a woman stood where the lot met the sandy boardwalk.

Elly's elegant legs appeared even longer whenever the wind flipped up the hem of her skirt. Her hair, lifting free of confining pins, swirled in russet waves around her face as she talked to Kevin and occasionally lifted a hand to hold flaming wisps out of her eyes.

"What's that woman up to now?" he muttered, heaving himself up out of the car.

Dear old Kev wore that deer-staring-into-headlights expression common to men confronted by a pretty woman. Dan only hoped his friend hadn't said anything to encourage Elly's snooping. He jogged across the parking lot toward them.

"I thought we agreed you were through with this nonsense!" Dan shouted into the wind.

Elly turned to observe him, her eyes far too enticing to cool his simmering blood. Simmering because he was furious with her but also because she looked so deliciously disheveled with the wind tugging at her skirt and hair, and teasing open the collar of her jacket to reveal a sliver of flesh at the top of her breast.

She planted her feet firmly and straightened her spine to meet him. "We need to talk, Mr. Eastwood."

"Isn't that where we started this morning?"

Kevin looked from one to the other of them with a puzzled expression then backed off two steps. "I don't know what this is about, but I'll let you two hash things out. Got work to do."

To Dan's surprise, Elly didn't so much as blink or make any move that might be construed as retreat. "I need you and Mrs. Eastwood on a plane for Europe," she stated. "Tonight at the latest."

He laughed. "You're not only wrong about my mother, you're insane!"

"No," she said solemnly, "I'm not. Not on either account. I have evidence. Please listen to me. If you don't, both of you are going to be hurt far more than you can imagine."

There was something fervent and beyond argument in her tone. This was a woman who believed in what she said. For the first time Dan felt deep in his gut that Elizabeth Anderson wasn't flinging idle fairy tales at him or working some kind of confidence game. He remembered the look on his mother's face earlier that day. Madge had been afraid—not of lies, but of the *truth*. And that terrified him.

He looked at his watch. "It's getting close to lunch time. Are you hungry?"

Elly gave him a guarded look. "Famished," she admitted. "No time for breakfast this morning. Why?"

"Let's get a table at Kirby's. We can talk this out over crab cakes."

Kirby's, one of the most popular seafood restaurants on Ocean Avenue, was nearly deserted during off season. They sat in a fifties-style red vinyl booth and Dan ordered two steaming crab cake platters piled high with salty French fries, little paper cups of sweet coleslaw on the side.

Elly poured a stream of rich ketchup over her fries and dug in hungrily. Dan ate more slowly than usual, watching her. He was aware of her thin ankles crossed beneath the table, visible through the space between his bench and the table top. When he lifted his eyes they fixed with fascination on her animated lips as she relished the crunchy potatoes and fat crab cake with its savory Old Bay seasonings perfuming the room around them.

He found it impossible to hold onto his irritation with her. But he *was* curious and more than a little suspicious of her motives for wanting to whisk him off to another continent. "So tell me about this proof. And why the urgency to get me out of the country?"

"I know you feel I'm intruding," she began, spearing another fry with her fork and shaking it at him in schoolmarm fashion, "and I don't like being put in the position of having to accuse anyone of lying about their past but—"

"But that's precisely what you are doing, isn't it?" he asked in a low voice.

Elly pursed her lips and studied him for a long moment, as if searching for diplomatic words. "People can be very creative about their past, if they are afraid. A woman has to be particularly careful. And a single mom *always* has to explain herself to others. No doubt your mother felt that a dead husband was easier for people to accept than the truth."

"And that truth is?" He might be willing to believe her. *Might.* But not without one hell of an explanation.

Elly continued with obvious caution as she pulled a manila envelope from the briefcase on the bench beside her. "I have photocopies of letters found on the von Austerand family's property. There now is little doubt that the ones signed *Margaret* were written by your mother, but we can verify that as soon as she is in Elbia."

She put up a hand to stop him from interrupting. "We believe your mother fell deeply in love with Karl von Austerand the year she studied in Paris. She probably believed they would marry, but he wasn't completely honest with her. He was engaged to another woman of royal blood. And he was the crown prince, soon to become King of Elbia.

"Karl was attending the college under an assumed name to avoid publicity. When Madge discovered they could never wed, she ran home to America—probably just after learning she was pregnant. Instead of returning to her parents' home in Massachusetts, she found a place to live in Baltimore and hid her shame by inventing a husband. The move probably was intended to elude Karl, too. Perhaps she feared what he might do if he discovered their child. *You.*"

Dan could feel the heat rising from his chest to his throat. He glared at the folder resting on the table beneath her hand. "This is very difficult to believe," he said tightly.

Elly slowly shook her head. "I'm sorry. See for yourself."

He couldn't move, was barely capable of breathing. Still furious with Elly, he was nevertheless increasingly fearful that what she claimed might be true. She didn't have to tell him how drastically his life would change if it was.

And what about Madge's quiet existence? She hated confrontation. She had always favored a life without complications. Any shattered love affair and unwanted baby were as complicated as life got. Unless the father of your baby was a man whose family's status rivaled that of the royals of England or Monaco—people with unlimited wealth and power, who could never escape their celebrity or stay off the front page of grocery-store gossip rags for long.

Elly rested her warm hand over his on the tabletop. "This must be a shock to you. You've grown up believing one thing, and here I am telling you everything is different. I'm sorry. Truly, I am." Her eyes shone with sincerity and compassion. "I would have preferred to let your mother keep her secret. But it's out of my hands now. Others have found out, so you both needed to know."

He couldn't utter a word. His lips felt as stiff as if he'd climbed from a December ocean.

"Take your time reading while you finish eating," she offered. "Then let me know what you think." Her accent was flavored with New England. Maple-syrup sweet, with a touch of Yankee logic. He would have liked to get to know her better, a whole lot better. She seemed a nice person, in addition to being so easy on the eyes. But it appeared that more pressing matters were on deck.

Dan took a bite of his cooling crab cake and chewed without tasting anything, then studied her as she sipped her cola. "There's a lot riding on this, isn't there? I mean, aside from being hounded by the press."

She slanted him a look that would have done the Mona Lisa proud. "There might be."

Dan slipped a thin stack of photocopies from the envelope. He scanned the first report quickly:

Daniel Robert Jennings. Born August 20, 1970. Verified location of birth: Baltimore, Maryland. Birth certificate on record. Mother: Margaret Jennings. No father listed. Name of mother and child legally changed three months later: Eastwood. Reason given: marriage to Carl Eastwood. No Carl Eastwood match through public records. Internet search unsuccessful. Social Security source reports no matches for location and dates given. Results: Suspect fictitious name.

There were other reports, which he read hastily, his pulse throbbing in his temple, his mouth going stone dry…

Margaret Jennings, scholarship student at the Sorbonne, 1969-1970. Superior student. Dropped out of school 3/70. Reason given: personal.

Frigid droplets of sweat skittered down the back of his neck. He stared at the next page's remarks: "Love letters signed 'your adoring Margaret,' no envelopes." There were even photocopies of two of the letters. He tried not to think about the passion and longing behind the words, which seemed far too personal to be read by other than the two people involved. But he needed only to glance at the handwriting to know it was amazingly similar to Madge's flowery style. Then there was another notation:

Letters from His Royal Highness Karl von Auster-and to one Margaret Jennings in the United States, dated 1970 (3), 1972 (2), 1973, 1975, 1976 and 1980—all returned as undeliverable.

"Well?" Elly asked, glancing up at him from her empty plate.

He smiled weakly. "I imagine Karl's legitimate son might be a little nervous about this discovery of yours."

"More than nervous. Particularly since you were born before he was."

"Ouch."

"It gets worse," she assured him. "Somebody in the palace leaked rumors of the affair. A reporter and his photographer are hot on your trail. They were following me, but I shook them off in Baltimore. It's only luck that I found you before they did."

Dan no longer felt hungry. He pushed his plate away. Visions of TV cameras, reporters armed with microphones and endless telephone calls from pushy media hawks flooded his imagination. For an instant he tried to tell himself that it might be a good thing—free publicity for the Haven and his City Kids program.

A second later, reality smacked him upside his head. It wouldn't be his property or his favorite charity that would get all the attention. It would be Madge and the past she'd tried so hard to hide from him, from her friends and neighbors, from the world. This would kill her.

He stared numbly at Elly across the table. "We didn't ask for this."

"I know. But I promise you, my father and I had nothing to do with letting your mother's past become public knowledge. And now we'll do everything we can to help both you and Madge weather the storm."

"What do you intend to do? Wave a magic wand and make us disappear?"

She gave him another one of those delicious enigmatic smiles. "Something like that."

Elly was relieved when Dan told her he would agree to go with her to Elbia. But convincing his mother to evacuate her comfy cottage was, at first, a struggle. Then came the first phone call from a *Washington Star* reporter.

Apparently the British press who had first been leaked the information had contacted several American newspapers in their search for the missing prince of Elbia. The *Star* put a team on the story and soon it was clear that the prying phone calls were destined to become even more harassing visits. Madge was so horrified at the prospect of her home being invaded she reluctantly agreed to the trip.

With help from the Elbian embassy, Elly booked all three of them on the Concorde for that night. On their way from the Eastern Shore of Maryland to Dulles Airport in Washington, D.C., they somehow picked up two carloads of reporters. "It's all right," Elly assured a frightened Madge, "as long as we keep moving, they can't get to you. And State Department security is waiting for us at the airport.''

The limousine she had ordered raced the two black sedans through twisting roadways approaching the international terminals, then the three of them were led to a lounge where security guards kept the press at bay while they waited to board the plane. Soon, a State Department courier arrived with passports for Dan and his mother, and minutes later they were herded onto the immense jet without being accosted. She felt like giving a victory cheer. But as the sleek, tipped-nose Concorde took off with a gentle rumble into the night, Elly sensed they'd only temporarily eluded their troubles.

The seating on the Concorde felt far more spacious than that on most commercial flights. Elly had never flown on the famous French-built jet that only the elite of the world could afford. Two roomy seats were positioned on either side of the aisle, and the service was impeccably attentive. Madge and Dan sat on one side. Elly was on the opposite side of the aisle, at the window seat, while the place beside her remained empty.

After they'd taken off into the night, Elly closed her eyes for a moment. Exhaustion overcame her. She felt weightless; her mind drifted. Back to another time in her life. A time when there had been more than just two Andersons. Elly, Dad…Mom. She felt herself being sucked back in time as she pictured her mother's face smiling down at her. Elly fought the memories, struggled to escape from the images that kept her from finding peace in her own life. Her heart began to race. Her breaths came in short, shallow puffs as the muscles in her chest constricted. Resisting was futile…

''It's going to be all right, Elly,'' her mother had

promised when Elly became concerned that her baby brother might come at night while Elly slept. Then she'd miss all the excitement. "It's all planned. The doctor will meet me at the hospital on the date you and I wrote on the calendar. Remember? I'll have an operation called a cesarean section to take the baby from my tummy. You'll be able to see him minutes after he's born, then you and I will fight over who gets to cuddle him."

They'd laughed together over that. Her father had told Elly that, at twelve years of age, she was almost old enough to be a little mother herself, at least in some cultures in other parts of the world. Even before the baby's seventh month of gestation, she had begun to feel her little brother in her arms, to sense a growing protectiveness of him and know that they would be a wonderful family together—the four of them.

Then the half sleep she'd sunk into on the plane dragged her deeper into darker memories. Of *that* night.

Again she was tortured by Patricia Anderson's agonized screams and her father's shouts for help to the 911 operator. When she'd tried to go to her mother, Frank had blocked her from the bedroom, shouting frantically at her that she couldn't go in, shoving her back into her own room as if she were being punished for a crime she didn't understand.

Blue and red lights flashed in the street outside her window. She'd watched two paramedics rush into the house while the driver pulled a gurney from the ambulance. "She will be okay," she whispered to herself. "Daddy said so." But minutes passed and the ambulance still sat there. Soon Elly knew, without being told, that when they did bring her mother out it wouldn't be to take her to the hospital.

Elly heard a whimper and something moist trickled down her cheeks. She twisted violently in her seat, felt the heaviness in her chest pressing relentlessly, then sensed a warm hand settling on her shoulder.

"Are you all right?" It wasn't her mother's voice, as she'd so often imagined at the end of her worst attacks. This voice had a deeper, stronger timbre. "Elly?"

She blinked her eyes open and took a moment to orient herself to an adult world, lights dim along a slender, shining cabin. Her throat burned, and her temples throbbed hotly. Turning her head, she looked up at Dan who had crossed the aisle to sit in the vacant seat beside her.

"You were having a bad dream," he murmured.

"Was I?" The break between the past and the present seemed liquid, as if she still might float back into the pain and experience it all over again.

Dan took her hand between his and rested it on his knee. "Want to tell me about it? If you share a dream, you can keep it from coming back, you know." He smiled at her.

"Not this one." She shivered then swallowed twice, trying to ease the roughness in her throat, trying to calm her drumming heartbeat. Horrid sounds still reverberated in her head. The awful coldness of death clutched at her. "This one's a keeper, whether I want it or not."

Dan frowned. "A bad one, huh?"

"The worst." She would have let it go at that. But his quiet compassion and steady gaze beckoned her to say more. She had a sudden intuitive flash that she and

Dan shared something—pasts that would haunt them
and remain with them all of their lives. "It's not fantasy," she explained. "It's like an instant replay of
something that really happened."

"Like a soldier having a flashback of battle?"

"Something like that." Elly drew herself up in the
seat, still trembling, and glanced across at Madge. She
was fast asleep. "You're really good to her," she whispered.

"Why shouldn't I be? She's my mother."

"Some people don't appreciate what they have, the
sacrifices their parents make for them."

"I guess that's true," he agreed slowly, encouraging
her with his steady gaze. "Aren't you good to your
mother?"

Her eyes closed. She shuddered.

"I'm sorry," Dan whispered. "That was far too personal." He took a deep breath. "I suppose I felt justified, since you've dug up so much about me. I know
nothing of you, except that you work for your father."

She shrugged, feeling a little calmer at the sound of
his mellow voice. "There's not a lot to tell. I was
twelve years old. My parents had tried for years to have
a second child. They were overjoyed when it looked
as if my mother would carry to full term." Her voice
was flat, without the emotion she held so carefully
within her. "Mom died in childbirth. My baby brother
didn't make it either."

"That's terrible." He squeezed her hand. "It must
have taken a long time to get over that." Then their
eyes met and he knew. "Or maybe you never have."

She looked away from his too-perceptive gaze. The
thick-glassed window to her left was black. No moon.
But fat, white stars shone through the night over the

endless Atlantic Ocean. She felt Dan's thumb drawing comforting circles over the back of her hand.

Suddenly, Elly found herself talking. Pushing out words without taking a breath, baring her soul as she'd never done with anyone in her life. She couldn't imagine why everything should tumble out of her at this moment, in front of this man. Perhaps because she foresaw pain and a struggle coming his way. Or maybe it was because they would soon go their separate ways. Sharing the agony of her past and fears of the future with this man who was passing so briefly through her life was as devoid of threat as confiding in a wall.

As she let the words flow, telling him of the night she had lost her mother forever and her father for many months to his grief, Dan's arm came around her, as if to shield her from her own memories.

"My dad just stopped functioning after my mother died. He didn't go to work. He didn't eat enough to keep a person alive. He started smoking again, and he drank quite a lot, I think. He spent a lot of time away—most of every day and always the nights. He wouldn't mention her name. We didn't talk."

Dan stared at her, his eyes hard and dark with concern. "That was when you most needed him."

She sighed. "Yes, but I can't blame him for distancing himself from me. If you ever saw my mother's college graduation photo, you'd think that I could be her twin. It just hurt Dad too much to look at me, and think about her."

"That's no excuse for neglecting a child," he snapped.

She squeezed her eyes shut. "You can't understand how it was." She swallowed. Dare she go on? Dare she tell him the rest, the part that still controlled her future and wouldn't let her move on with her own life? But now that she'd opened her soul to him it seemed impossible to stop the flood of feelings.

"Years later," she whispered, "Dad told me what had happened that night. My mother had an enlarged heart. They'd known that since I was born and had elected to do a C-section. Her doctor had advised another C-section to take the stress off delivering her second baby. When she went into labor early, her heart couldn't take it, and the baby died of asphyxiation before the medics could arrive." She swallowed three times before she was able to look at him again. Tears clung to her eyelashes.

"I'm so sorry, Elly."

She nodded, plunging on. "Dad insisted that I get a complete physical a few years later. He didn't seem surprised when they found I'd inherited my mother's heart problem, it was just a little larger than it should have been. Nothing easily fixed, just something to live cautiously with.

"From that day, I decided never to have children of my own. I love kids, I really do," she insisted, her heart breaking even as she said the words. "But I can't risk my life the way my mother did."

"Death in childbirth is a very rare thing these days," Dan commented gently. "Chances are, if she'd been able to reach a hospital, she'd have been all right. You shouldn't—"

Elly pulled her hand away from him. "Don't tell me what I should or shouldn't do!" she snapped. Not wanting to alarm the sleeping passengers around them, she choked back the sob that swelled inside her. The words came out in breathless gulps. *"Don't...lecture...me!"*

"I'm not, Elly," he whispered. "I'm just trying to state a medical reality. All sorts of advances have been made in the last ten or more years. Odds are that if you really want a baby, you could have one without complications."

She glared at him. "Odds. Chances. Do you really believe that adding one more child to this earth is worth the risk to me or any other woman whose body isn't strong enough?"

He didn't answer.

She let out a long breath, feeling strangely better for the release of emotions. She thought more clearly now about her past choices.

Over the years, she'd had a few male friends—mostly kept at arm's length with no physical relationship involved. A few she'd slept with, but only after first being sure they lacked all desire to settle down and start a family, then guaranteeing she couldn't become pregnant with them. She had stayed on the Pill during those limited months in a relationship and, because she'd never given her heart, she hadn't regretted when they'd moved on to other women. The last breakup had been heart-wrenching, though. Sam had been a good person and she'd grown intensely fond of him. His only crime was that he'd changed his mind. He had decided he wanted to be a husband and father instead of a boyfriend.

In the year since then Elly had let no one into her life. But sitting beside her now was a man who was as much temptation as any woman could handle. More than *she* could, she feared. Instinctively, she gauged the level of her reaction to him, and knew that the passion centered in the core of her being was new and real and strong. He had touched something in her no other man before him had been capable of, although they'd known each other only hours.

"What about you?" she asked quickly. "Why aren't you married?" A tiny part of her hoped that his answer would be an echo of her own. *I don't want kids.*

"I suppose at first I was too involved with other facets of my life," he admitted. "The marines—that didn't seem a time for settling down. I was stationed all over the place. Then I went to college on the GI Bill and earned my degree. After that I needed time to start my business. I've always wanted a family, but now that it seems the right time, the right woman doesn't seem to be around."

She cringed inside. Well, there it was. He was looking for a life-mate, a mother for his unborn children. *And I am definitely not her,* she thought with an irrational twinge of sadness. Yet Elly was still profoundly attracted to him. He set off tickly sensations in parts of her body she had forgotten existed.

Dan squeezed her softly around the shoulders and she looked up into his concerned gaze. "Feeling better?"

"Yes," she admitted half-heartedly. "I'll be fine. Thank you for lending your shoulder." She patted the damp fabric of his blazer.

He glanced back at his own seat across the aisle. Madge had repositioned herself, lifting her legs to rest them across his cushion. Like many of the other passengers, she was asleep.

"Mind if I stay here for a while?"

Elly nodded. "No problem. She'll need her strength when we get to Elbia."

They talked through most of the night, keeping the conversation light. It was as if they both understood that much of what they'd already shared was too personal for people who had just met. But somehow, Elly thought, it had been the right time to speak of such things.

The jet landed at Orly, outside Paris, soon after dawn. The reporters who had tailed them to Dulles hadn't been able to keep up with them at the Concorde's pace, even if they had managed to find another flight on a traditional plane. But they must have alerted their cohorts, for the paparazzi jostled each other for position at the concourse entrance.

"Oh dear," Madge whimpered, "how will we ever get past them?"

Elly pointed to a cluster of French gendarmes looking over the disembarking passengers. "Looks like the palace has been in touch with authorities here. Let's go." She took Madge's arm and led her forward. Dan followed close behind.

The security team whisked them into a car that veered quickly away to a private runway. A high-speed helicopter marked with the von Austerand royal crest lifted them away and, just two hours later, Elly drew a sharp breath at the sight of the Crystal Palace as they flew over the mountains separating Austria from Elbia. Below, and surrounding the magnificent towers and crenellated parapets, was the storybook city of the same name whose history reached back into medieval times.

Madge uttered a cry of delight at the sight. "How beautiful." Tears filled her eyes. She looked sadly at her son and shouted over the roar of the rotors above them. "Do you hate me, Danny, for keeping this from you all these years?"

He patted her arm and shook his head vehemently. "You gave me a warm, safe childhood," he yelled back, smiling. But as soon as his mother turned back to the view, his expression tightened.

Elly spoke directly into his ear. "What's wrong?"

"Later," he mouthed.

She nodded, guessing his thoughts. Madge hadn't kept a royal upbringing and a title from her son. Tradition and politics had done that. She would never have been allowed to bring her child to this magnificent place. The appearance of Karl's mistress and illegitimate son would have been an insult to the queen. At most, Elly suspected, Karl might have offered to pay for the baby's care and for Madge's silence. Dan's mother must have understood this. She had chosen not to be found by him. She had turned her back on her lover's charity...or bribe, whichever it might be.

Elly grasped these truths with an intuitive sense shared by all females. When fate conspired against a woman, her pride was all that saved her, if she was to survive at all. And now Elly knew she must do whatever she could to protect both Madge and Dan, for, in a way, she was responsible for their troubles. If she and her father hadn't unwittingly revealed information to the wrong person, the press wouldn't even now be on their trail.

Three

It was at dinner that night, in one of the castle's more intimate dining halls, that Elly finally met the royal family. She and her father had walked together from their rooms in a separate wing of the castle. They found Dan and Madge already there with a dozen other guests, standing with cocktails in hand. Elly accepted a glass of white wine from a steward, crossed the room to join them and introduced her father to mother and son.

"Who are all these other people?" Dan asked.

Frank looked around, then back to Dan. "Jacob's court, and his political, financial and cultural advisors. They're here to check you out and decide what to do about you." He gave Dan a wry smile and lifted his glass in an ironic toast. "Not to put any pressure on you, my boy."

Dan scanned the room warily. The muscles in his

neck stood out in taut relief above his shirt collar. "Why don't they come right out and say what they're thinking?"

"They don't know what to think yet," Elly said softly. "You're a wild card. No one knows whether you'll threaten Jacob's rule, demand a fortune for yourself and your mother or just prove to be an embarrassment."

"I already told you I don't want anything!" Dan snapped.

Elly wondered if he was really that irritated with the Elbians or just in a bad mood for any of a number of reasons—like being forced to fly halfway around the world at a few hours' notice. She turned to Madge, who was sipping delicately from a crystal stem. "What about you, Mrs. Eastwood? What do you want out of all this?"

"I want to go home," she said solemnly, then closed her lips tightly and looked away.

Elly imagined the woman did miss the cozy safety of her little bungalow. The palace was intimidating with its hundreds of rooms full of priceless antique furnishings and exquisite art collections. It was like living in the Louvre. "Maybe you'll feel differently once you meet the king and queen," she said encouragingly.

"They are gracious and fair people," Frank put in.

Madge nodded her willingness to give them a chance, but she still looked uneasy.

Dan observed his mother with obvious concern. He looked no more convinced of the royal pair's good will than she did.

Elly wished she could think of a way to steer him toward a more receptive frame of mind for meeting his half brother. But before she could say anything else, the immense gilded doors at the far end of the room swung wide. An attendant in full livery stepped through. He stood as straight and silent as one of the palace guards while conversation hushed and the roomful of guests turned to face him.

"Announcing Their Royal Highnesses, King Jacob von Austerand and Queen Allison..." There followed a long list of formal titles for the royal couple. Elly's heart beat in triple time, and a thrill rushed through her as Elbia's young rulers entered the room.

Jacob was strikingly handsome in a stoic way. He didn't appear to be the type of man to smile very often, but when he did, Elly imagined he'd light up any woman's heart. His hair was a glistening ebony, and his eyes flashed midnight blue.

As to his queen, Elly had never seen a more beautiful woman. The young American who had married Jacob wore her pale-blond hair coiled softly on top of her head, anchored with a crown that would never be mistaken for the rhinestone-studded ornaments worn by hometown beauty queens. White diamonds blazed upon gold in an intricate filigree pattern. Elly vaguely remembered TV news clips about the couple—how the young prince had caused constitutional upheaval in his little country when he had insisted on wedding a commoner, and an American on top of that. But somehow the two of them had weathered the political storm, and they seemed at peace in their marriage now.

Queen Allison smiled sweetly at her guests, lavishing attention on each person in the room as her fingertips rested lightly on the back of her husband's extended hand.

As Jacob and his queen crossed the room, the king's gaze swept impatiently across faces until they settled on Dan's. A sharp questioning look blazed across his eyes but was quickly obscured by an official smile.

He stopped in front of the four of them—Elly, Frank, Dan and Madge. They performed the traditional bows and curtseys as they'd been instructed to do by the palace's protocol officer. Dan's bow, Elly noticed, was no more than a slight forward tilt of his body, and he wasn't smiling. The distrust between the two men was uncomfortably evident.

Elly's heart raced with apprehension as her father made the introductions.

"You had a pleasant journey?" Jacob asked politely.

Dan gave a stiff nod. "Uneventful."

"I've been told you had company on your way to the airport," Allison commented, her voice softly soothing. "I hope the reporters didn't frighten you, Mrs. Eastwood." She looked with compassion toward Madge.

Dan spoke before his mother could answer. "A lot of commotion over nothing, if you ask me."

"Really?" Jacob's perfect English was accented with harsh Germanic tones and clipped consonants. "You think that claiming a monarch as your father is a small thing then?"

Dan shifted his shoulders and met Jacob's hostile stare with equal intensity. "Look, Your Highness, less than forty-eight hours ago, I was taking my morning swim and planning my work day, oblivious to the existence of this postage stamp of a country. I didn't ask for this, and I'm not *claiming* anything. It's other people who are all in a lather about this situation, not me."

Elly held her breath as Jacob studied his half brother through blue-black eyes that sparked with displeasure. All conversation in the room had ceased. She suspected

Jacob had the authority to do whatever he pleased within the confines of his little kingdom, and perhaps beyond it. A man with that much power could be dangerous.

The young king turned abruptly to Madge. "Is it true that you were my father's mistress?" Tact, apparently, was not one of Jacob's strong points.

Madge blushed, and her hand shook, spilling a little of her wine.

"Now hold on!" Dan barked, his face flaring red with anger.

The queen's hand moved almost imperceptibly up her husband's arm in a cautionary gesture. Jacob shot a quick look out of the corner of his eyes at her, and she lifted a brow.

"I'm sorry," Jacob said awkwardly. "I'm being far too direct. It's just that we've all been turned on end by this discovery. My subjects worry about their 'postage stamp of a country,' as you put it." He shot Dan a cold look. "They need to be reassured that their government isn't in danger of—"

Dan laughed out loud. "What the hell do they think I'm going to do? Storm the castle?"

Jacob did not smile. "You can't possibly comprehend the seriousness of this situation."

Dan bristled. "And I don't think you understand what your interference might do to *my* business! Not to mention to my mother's privacy."

Elly shot a quick look at Madge, whose lips were compressed in a pale line. Allison's hand moved away from her husband's arm and she looked apologetically into Elly's eyes, as if to say, *I'm sorry. This is something I cannot interfere with.* Even Elly's father seemed unwilling to risk intruding on the brothers' heated debate.

Sucking in a quick breath, Elly stepped between the two men. "Arguing isn't going to do any good," she stated firmly.

They glowered over her head at each other, and she was struck again by the remarkable resemblance between the two men. Couldn't they see it for themselves? They shared a father's blood! Didn't that count for anything?

"Listen," she tried again, "maybe a formal dinner isn't the place for this discussion. It seems to me that you're both saying the same thing—neither of you likes the situation. Your Highness," she said turning to Jacob, "I don't know Daniel Eastwood that well. But it appears to me that he only wants to be left alone. He isn't looking for profit from these unexpected circumstances."

Elly's gaze shifted to Dan. "Put yourself in Jacob's shoes. It's natural for this to be a difficult time for any family. But the von Austerands have a lot to lose if things aren't handled the right way."

"What you mean by *the right way* is that you think the past should be hushed up. I'm not sure that's fair to everyone involved." Dan glanced meaningfully toward his mother.

Madge shook her head nervously. "Please. I don't want a lot of fuss on my account."

"Giving you the credit you're due for having raised a son on your own isn't making a fuss," Frank said in a gentler version of his customary raspy voice.

"You act as if this is my or my mother's fault," Dan growled, his face glowing with fury. He lunged forward, pushing Elly aside to get closer to Jacob.

Immediately, two burly bodyguards moved in from shadowy corners of the room. Jacob waved them off with a look of annoyance.

"Go on," he said. "You might as well get if off your chest."

Elly found herself holding her breath. She forced down a gulp of air and prayed the two of them wouldn't kill each other before the night was through.

Dan faced his brother, matching his aggressive hands-on-hips, chin-shot-up stance. "My mother didn't ask to be burdened with a baby. If there is blame, it should go to your father for deceiving a young girl and leaving her pregnant!"

"I'll thank you not to speak of my father with disrespect when he cannot be here to defend himself!" Jacob snapped.

"The fact that he's *dead* doesn't change what he did!" Dan insisted. "He took advantage of a young woman's innocence. No woman should feel compelled to bear a child she doesn't want."

Elly's heart caught in her throat. Could he possibly realize how closely his statement echoed her own feelings?

Jacob's cold glare shifted subtly to a thin smile. "Interesting," he murmured. "You are arguing against your own existence. But you *do* exist, Mr. Eastwood, and I venture to say that a man in your position, who feels as strongly as you do about a wrong done to someone he loves, will exact a punishment. I know I would." The harsh gleam in Jacob's dark eyes left no doubt about that. "I would want retribution for my mother. *Tell me, sir, that you do not!*"

The tension in the room was as thick as a New England coastal fog. Elly reached out to touch Dan's arm at the same moment Allison rested her fingertips on the king's clenched hand, raised threateningly before him.

"Please," Elly said softly, "let's eat. We're all tired and hungry, and that can't improve our tempers. Later, you two can agree on a more private setting to discuss this."

Allison gave her an appreciative blink of her blue eyes then stated with regal firmness, "I agree. We will have our dinner now, Jacob. Let's give reason a chance to prevail."

Elly waited on pins and needles all the next morning, fearful that one of the brothers had surely murdered the other by then. Except there were those bodyguards, who likely wouldn't stand by while Dan decked Jacob. So she revised her imagination's view of events. Dan was either nursing serious wounds or was chained in the tower. Or both.

Despite its emotional beginning, the meal the previous night had been magnificent—seven courses of heaven. But Elly would have enjoyed it far more without the suffocating tension in the hall. Conversation was kept intentionally light. Nothing more important than plans for cross-country skiing or shopping trips were discussed. The evening ended with an invitation for Dan to meet with Jacob in his private office the following morning. No one else was asked to be present.

At a little after noon, a knock sounded on Elly's door. She dove for it and opened it to find Dan in an agitated state. "He wants me to sign *documents!*" he growled, rushing past her and into the bedchamber.

Elly scowled at him. "Documents? What kind?"

"Legal statements drawn up by his royal lawyers,

saying that I'm not related to him or his family in any way.''

She gasped. "But that's a lie!"

''Exactly. I told him I wouldn't do it.'' Dan paced the room like a caged beast.

Elly thought for a moment. "I'm sure Jacob is just trying to find a way to outwit the press. That would be to both your advantages.''

"I know, but I can't do what my mother has done all of these years—deny the past.'' He let out a long groan of exasperation. ''Besides, the woman deserves something for all she went through because of that man.''

''You mean Karl, your father,'' Elly said softly.

"My father!'' He laughed wildly, shaking his head. "A pompous, spoiled aristocratic teenager, no doubt. Probably spawned dozens of little Karls all over Europe.''

"I don't believe so,'' Elly said, coming to his side. She could feel his hurt, his anger, as if his emotion seeped into her pores from the air between them. But she sensed his turbulent state wasn't all on behalf of Madge. He himself must have felt betrayed. "I expect your father wanted very much to find you and your mother.''

He rounded on her, eyes ablaze. "Why? To bribe her to silence?''

"I don't think so,'' Elly said slowly. "I've read the letters he wrote to her during the years after she left Paris, when he was trying to contact her. They are beautiful, tender love letters, begging her forgiveness, asking her to reveal to him where she had gone so that he could help her.''

"Then he knew of my existence?''

Elly hesitated. "We're not sure. He might have guessed. Madge didn't tell him why she was leaving him, other than to say that she'd discovered his true identity and knew they couldn't remain together."

"The bastard broke her heart!" Dan snapped. As she looked up at him, a blue vein throbbed at his temple. His eyes were hot and glistening with tears he was too proud to shed.

He glared at the stone wall to his right and, for an instant, she could imagine a rage and frustration so great he might throw a fist at the cold, gray marble.

Elly's heart went out to Dan. She stepped in front of him and brought her hands up to frame both sides of his strong jaw. "I know Karl hurt her," she whispered. "It was wrong that he deceived her. But I believe from all I've read of his correspondence that he deeply loved your mother and only wanted to hold on to her for as long as he was able. Eventually, his duty to the crown dictated his marriage to the woman betrothed to him. He had no choice, Dan. Not at that time, before the rules were challenged by his own son, Jacob."

Dan gripped her wrists as if to pull them away from his face, but his eyes met hers and something sharp and quick and piercing passed between them that transcended his bitterness. In a single motion, he stepped forward, backing Elly into the wall. She felt the cool curve of each stone from her hips to her shoulder blades.

Elly knew before his mouth covered hers that he was going to kiss her unless she struggled or cried out for him to release her. And she would do neither because she had wanted him since the moment they had met and now the need had intensified to a white heat that defied common sense as well as her own secret fears.

His hands found their way to her breasts through the bodice of her dress. They kneaded her pliant flesh and raised her nipples to hard peaks that pressed through the fabric. She felt her insides go liquid. A welcome heat pulsed through her body.

He didn't ask her permission. It was as if he understood the surge of desire rushing through her body, which fed his own. His mouth lifted from hers. Gasping for breath she curled her fingers through the short hairs at the nape of his neck and nibbled hungrily at the spot on his throat where the muscles angled along his shoulder.

She luxuriated in the sensation of his hands moving over her, through clothing, then beneath. Her flesh prickled and danced at his touch. She glanced down to see that the buttons at the front of her dress had come open, and she sensed that he was waiting just these few seconds to see if she might protest. When she didn't, he snapped the front clasp of her bra between thumb and finger, and it parted to expose her breasts.

As he bowed to touch a nipple with the tip of his tongue she arched toward him, asking for more. He complied, drawing the soft flesh into his mouth, warming her with his tongue, teasing the erect brown tip with the sharp edges of his teeth. Her fingers bit gloriously into his shoulders, and she dropped her head back against the stone.

He grasped her hand urgently in his. "Touch me."

Unsure of what he wanted at first, she let him guide her hand down the length of his body. Beneath the zipper of his pants she felt his strength, his hardness.

"I know it's too soon," he growled. "But I need you to know how much I want you, Elly."

Too soon? She thought dizzily. *Or has it been far, far too long?*

It seemed as if all of her life she'd waited for a man who could come this close to making her forget all the hurt and loss and heartache of the day she'd lost both mother and infant brother. And the emptiness of her own childless future.

The emotional connection had been there between them from the start, she now realized. She understood his turmoil, believed in him, wanted to comfort him in this difficult time of his life. And maybe she even wanted his strength and comfort for herself. Maybe she could trust him enough to accept those gifts from him. He was right, she reluctantly admitted; they'd known each other only a handful of days. But she pushed that knowledge aside, refusing to let rational thoughts dictate her actions this one time.

Elly kissed Dan with fierce abandon, pressing her hand against his hardness.

He let out a low moan at the parting of their lips. "Don't do that again unless you—" Interrupting him by pressing her mouth over his, she put more pressure behind her hand. He gasped for breath. "—mean it."

She let her lips part, silently inviting him to deepen their kiss. They touched tongues. His hands slid possessively up beneath her skirt. Through the thin silk of her panties, he touched her.

Then the one thing she most dreaded happened.

As if something mechanical inside of her suddenly shut down, she felt nothing where all the warmth had been. Then the nothing turned cold and frightening. Her mother's swollen face flashed before her, then the image of a tiny casket lying beside a larger one. The old terror seized her, turning every sweet impulse into lethal temptation. Elly's body stiffened in Dan's arms.

"What?" he asked.

"I can't," she whispered, the words catching in her throat. Her eyes burned, and she squeezed them closed and wished with all her heart that she could find the strength to give herself to this wonderful man. "I want to, but I can't."

"I can protect you, Elly."

"No. You're right. It's too soon." It would always be too soon for her.

He was silent for a long moment. Then he opened his arms and stepped away from her. The disappointment in his handsome face broke her heart. She'd have given anything to please him and to satisfy the longing within herself.

Elly slumped against the wall, feeling lost, inadequate, chilled.

"Do you want to talk about it?" he asked.

What good would that do? All she could say was what had already been said. She shook her head. "I'm sorry. I wasn't trying to be a tease or lead you on."

"I know," he whispered, touching her cheek with his fingertips. "When the time is right...when the person is right, it will happen."

She gazed up at him desolately. "You really think so?"

He smiled. "I do. I'd just really like that someone to be me, Elly."

Four

As a man accustomed to an active life, Dan had found only two methods of achieving the physical release his body required on a regular basis. The first was by working out, usually by swimming. But lifting weights was acceptable when the weather was so terrible he couldn't bear plunging into frigid water. The other was through sex.

The second was harder to come by because there wasn't always an available partner. And as the years moved along he found himself less and less inclined to be intimate when he didn't feel an emotional as well as a physical connection with a woman. As luck would have it, he'd felt both with Elly, fiercely so. But she hadn't been able to give herself to him, and the frustration he suffered as a result was unnerving.

He didn't blame her at all. He sensed her need was as great as his, if not greater. He felt confident he could help her, if only he could break through the emotional barrier she'd lived behind for so long. How he'd go about that without forcing her, though, he had no idea. And force was definitely out of the question.

Meanwhile, there was the problem of his growing restlessness and hunger for physical action. He missed his early-morning swims, and he thought constantly of Elly, her sweet kisses and lovely breasts. He decided he'd have to settle for a good hard run to work off his body's mounting tension.

He had packed running shorts, a T-shirt, athletic shoes and socks. Even though it was winter and snow from the last storm stood in low heaps throughout the garden and on street corners, most of the streets themselves were bare. Besides, he was accustomed to running barelegged on the beach even during the coldest months. He jogged out through the open gates of the Crystal Palace, giving the guard a wave as he left to make sure the man would recognize him and let him in when he returned.

For the first mile he felt stiff, and every stride required intense labor. His breathing was tight. His pores began to sweat in response to the exertion. Somewhere in the middle of the second mile, the muscles in his thighs and hips loosened, and his arms began to pump smoothly at his sides like well-maintained machine parts. His shoulders and neck felt relaxed. He moved with the automatic grace of an athlete.

Dan looped through the quaint medieval streets of Elbia, the only real city in the tiny country by the same name. If a visitor didn't know better, Dan mused, that person might assume he'd either been transported back in time by hundreds of years, or else this was an immense amusement park that had been built to resemble a historical period. But Elly had told him a little of the amazing history of Elbia, which had survived two modern wars and many ancient ones. As he ran faster, harder, he marveled at colorful shops that might have been kept by the great-grandfathers of present owners, not yet open for the day, and the homes with their sturdy stucco-and-stone walls and charming peaked tile roofs.

He set each foot carefully, stride after long stride, on the rounded cobbles, concentrating on working his body, less and less aware of the carved wooden signs dangling from chains over the sidewalks and the flashes of color from shop windows. It was Elly's sweet face that floated before him. She was a lovely enigma, a challenge and a troubled soul. Yet, as difficult as it was to overcome her fears and win her trust, he sensed the effort would be well worth it to a man. If only he had the patience to hold out that long.

Then a disturbing thought came to him.

She was clearly attracted to him, and they had been well on their way to making love the night before. But why was she so willing to be with him if she was really so terrified of having children and she knew that he wanted them? Was it because she had known from the day she'd waved him down on the beach in Ocean City that he was the son of a king? Because she figured he was marked to inherit thousands, possibly millions?

Even more alarming was his own longing for her despite her having made it clear she would never agree to have children. He felt he was a fair man, willing to make compromises. He no longer expected to find the perfect woman—the ideal blend of intelligence, sexuality, gentleness, beauty and practicality. But the decision to create a family, to have babies or remain childless, was a make-or-break point in the classic bargain struck between a man and a woman, at least as far as he was concerned.

At this time in his life, when he should have been seriously focusing on the woman capable of and willing to be the mother of his children, he should have walked away from Elizabeth Anderson. Instead, he hungered for her.

Feeling more and more off balance, Dan swung back along the outer edges of the city as the streets began to come alive with people opening their shops or seeking their morning coffee and fresh roll before heading for work. The palace gates came into view. Something had changed. He slowed at the unexpected sight before him.

A cluster of men and women armed with cameras, microphones and compact tape recorders slung over shoulders milled around outside the main gate. A man with a TV camera propped on one shoulder was shooting between the iron bars, which had been shut. One guard stood alertly inside the massive metal grille, another outside, watching the cameraman warily.

Dan came to an abrupt stop, hesitated a moment, then slowly approached the group. The outside guard saw him just as Dan was about to raise his hand to signal he had returned. Before he could do or say anything, the soldier broke through the crowd and came swiftly to Dan's side.

"This way, please sir," he said in heavily accented English.

With a hand on Dan's shoulder blade, the guard pushed him between camera-whirring, question-shouting reporters. The other guard already had cracked open the gate. With a sudden lunge Dan and his escort were through it and into the safety of the courtyard. The disappointed paparazzi were left outside, still shouting, clicking and whirring.

"What the hell is going on?" Dan gasped for breath.

"We were hoping, sir, that you would return before they arrived."

"You knew this would happen?"

"It wasn't unexpected, sir."

Dan shook his head and allowed them to usher him through the towering central doors into the great hall where Jacob stood between Elly and his queen. All three turned toward him with worried expressions. Jacob's bloomed into anger at the sight of his half brother.

"*Where* have you been?" Elly asked breathlessly.

Dan shrugged. "Out for a run. Is that a crime in this country?"

Jacob took a step forward, glowering at him. "It was a foolish thing to do. We might have found a way to send them away if they hadn't seen you. Now there is no hope of denying your presence in Elbia."

"I came here to work out a solution to this mess," Dan growled. "I'm not hiding from anyone."

"Not very well you're not!" Jacob snapped.

Elly stepped between the two men. "This isn't helping. Stop arguing, please."

The young king stared coldly at her as if shocked by her continued interruptions. Elly felt chilly sweat rise across the nape of her neck. What had she been thinking, talking to him that way? If Jacob sent her away, she'd be unable to right their mistakes and rebuild her father's company's reputation. Then there came an even darker thought: *She'd never see Daniel Eastwood again.*

Allison sighed. "Jacob, please, she's only trying to help. And your brother doesn't yet understand how it is here...how we must live in the public eye." She smiled adoringly at him, and Jacob visibly relaxed a notch.

"I'm beginning to get the idea," Dan muttered, "and I can't say that I like it. I needed to work out. You don't seem to have a convenient ocean, so I thought a run through—"

"In the first level below ground, there is a gymnasium with every sort of equipment you might require," Jacob said. "All you had to do was ask."

Dan observed him, trying to figure out what made the two of them go at each other's throats this way whenever they were in the same room. Did all brothers do this at one time or another? Battling like two male lions competing for dominance in the pride? Maybe because they had grown up apart, not meeting until they were adults, they had to fight their way through this stage of their relationship now? Whatever the reason, he resented Jacob for interfering in his life and for ordering him around.

"Don't you ever feel you just have to break free, Your Highness?" Dan asked in a low voice. "Don't you ever yearn to get the hell out of these stone walls?"

For a long moment, Jacob just stared at him, and neither woman dared speak. Then Jacob's lips barely moved. "Nearly every day of my life. *Nearly every day.*"

Dan was stunned. His brother was human after all, and perhaps more like him than either of them had guessed.

Allison's hand reached out and touched her husband's arm. She turned to smile faintly at Dan. "We both look forward to the quiet days when the international press corps is off covering other people's lives in other countries. That happens so seldom. We rarely can travel outside Elbia without at least a small contingent of reporters."

Dan met Jacob's eyes. There was no softening in them, but there was a flash of longing for solitude and peace that he could understand only too well. If they had just been two ordinary guys back in Ocean City, Jacob would match him stroke by stroke in the chilly Atlantic along a deserted beach at dawn. But here in his royal world he would never know the luxury of privacy.

"I'm sorry if I've caused a stir," Dan said sincerely. "I didn't mean to."

Jacob gave him a brief nod of acknowledgment. "What's done is done." He started to turn away. "Let's adjourn to my office. My PR officer is meeting us there, and we can discuss a statement to placate the press."

Dan looked down at his sweaty T-shirt and brought the bottom edge up to wipe the sweat from his face. "I'd like to change first, if that's all right."

"Certainly," Jacob said.

Dan started toward the stairs leading to the upper chambers, but Jacob called after him. "I should mention that I've conferred with my advisors, and I can offer you a monetary settlement for publicly renouncing the throne. Since lying to the public is something you disdain, this will enable you still to claim my father as yours, but will get you off the hook since you say you don't want anything to do with the von Austerands and Elbia. You can sign the agreement today if you like.''

Dan froze, mid step. He turned and looked at Elly, whose face had turned ashen, as if she knew what his reaction would be before he did. She blinked once at him, urging caution and restraint, he supposed.

But he wasn't in the mood for tiptoeing around issues or for doing something just because it was a convenient solution for his brother. He rounded slowly to face Jacob across the expanse of pale gray marble, his hand gripping the carved banister.

''Listen,'' he said slowly, ''I may be just a city kid who fought his way to making good in a small way. I may not live in a castle or have a title or be able to live in your grand manner, Jacob. But I am proud of who I am. Not because I have a king's blood in me. Just because I'm me.''

Jacob's eyes darkened to blue-black chips of obsidian, but he said nothing.

''I resent you treating me like an intruder and trying to buy me off.'' Dan paused long enough to let his last words sink in and make sure Jacob was listening to the rest. ''I won't sign your document or accept a penny from you.''

Less than an hour later, Dan stood at a casement window, his mood still dark as he looked over the formal gardens behind the castle. Paths looped through dormant winter shrubs as dusk fell. Nearly hidden by tall evergreen hedges was a glass-walled gazebo. Still within the castle walls but barely visible from where he stood was the helicopter pad where they'd landed earlier that day.

He pinched the bridge of his nose between thumb

and forefinger, trying to erase the growing tension he felt in a tight band across his forehead. He was worried about a lot of things, including the incident in Elly's room. The memory of their embrace still erupted in little simmering pools of heat in unexpected places within his body.

But now he thought again about Madge. She seemed to blame herself for the current complications in his life. Although they'd initially arrived in the royal city without fanfare or any sign of reporters, it had been only a very short while before the press figured out where their quarry was hiding. Since then his mother had appeared more and more nervous.

Dan didn't understand all this fuss over a love affair that had ended decades ago, but Elly assured him the public's interest would be high enough to spur on greedy tabloid stringers and photo jocks. For now, though, the castle seemed a peaceful enough place. He stared down at the rose bushes, dormant for the winter, and imagined how beautiful they would be in full bloom, come the spring. And the snow-covered mountains hovering behind a purplish haze in the distance...how magnificent this land and this immense structure that surrounded him were! It was hard to believe a castle had been his father's home, which made the place Dan's own ancestral home. That would take some getting used to.

"What are you thinking?"

He turned at the gentle sound of Elly's voice. "About destiny, I suppose."

"Destiny?" She pursed her lips and frowned. "Why is that?"

"I look around this amazing place where I've never been. Yet somehow it feels familiar to me." He wiggled an eyebrow at her, going for a lighter tone than he felt. "Spooky, huh?"

"Definitely." She came up beside him and peered through the narrow opening in the stone wall.

The glass pane had an antique, wavy appearance that made it appear he was viewing the world through water. At the time the palace had been built, he supposed, there must have been no glass at all to cover windows, then the place would have been very drafty indeed. Centuries had seen the structure modernized—electricity installed in the main wings, plumbing added. But it still felt richly gripped by the past.

He thought about his father, whom he'd never met, standing on this very spot. And his grandfather...then the men of his family for many generations before.

"You said the von Austerands have been in power for five hundred years?"

"About," she said. "They wrestled this tiny kingdom from the Holy Roman Empire back in the sixteenth century. Somehow they've managed to hold on to it through wars and power struggles."

"Amazing," he breathed, "to be part of that."

"Yes." She looked up at him with shining eyes.

Later, he was never quite sure what came over him at that moment. Perhaps it was merely the romantic influence of history, or the idea of being a healthy male descended from a long line of conquerors. It was true that Elly was gazing up at him as if he really was the prince they claimed him to be. For whatever the reason, history or hormones, he felt compelled to conquer her.

She was so close to him already that all he had to do was drop an arm around her waist and curl her into his chest. Her sultry hazel eyes flashed at him, her lips parting in surprise. He quickly bent down to touch his mouth to hers. Her lips quivered then tensed. He lightly teased them to life again with his own.

When he lifted his head, she rested her cheek against his chest. "I thought we weren't going to do this."

"That was your decision. Let's just say, as much as I'd like to honor your wishes, milady, I'm having a real hard time keeping my distance."

She said nothing.

"Elly, maybe now isn't the time, with all that's going on and understanding as I do that you have issues of your own to deal with. But I just want you to know, I'd give half my kingdom to sleep with you."

She laughed at him and shook her head. "You don't have a kingdom to give away, unless you count the Haven. Anyway, I wouldn't talk like that in front of Jacob or anyone in his court. They'll think you're out to overthrow the crown."

"I wouldn't want the job if they offered it," he stated, touching the soft curls framing her face. They looked like burnished copper in the late-afternoon light. The strands felt warm to his touch. "I like my life the way it is…with one exception. Children. And one special woman to make them with." And it would be nice, awfully nice, if she could be as pretty and warm and appealing as Elizabeth Anderson, he mused.

Elly shivered in his arms as if she'd heard his thoughts.

"Why are you so uncomfortable with any mention of my wanting a family?"

"You know why," she said tightly.

"Two people don't have to choose names for their offspring just because they've kissed once or twice."

"Of course not," she agreed with a nervous laugh. But her pretty eyes skittered away from his.

"And we wouldn't have to reserve a church if I were to touch you like this." He curved his palm around her cheek, then let it drift down her flushed throat to rest just above her breast.

"Absolutely not," she murmured huskily, bringing her glance back to his with steamy intensity.

Dan subconsciously listened for footsteps down the corridors. None echoed against the stone.

He lowered his head slowly and touched his lips to hers again, deepening the kiss, tasting her honeyed mouth, trying not to think too hard about where this delicious moment might be headed. Or how soon she would stop him. When he stroked the back of his fingers down the side of her breast she lifted her arms around his neck, and he hoped against hope that she wouldn't make him release her this time.

"We want different things," she whispered.

"Do we really?" he asked, observing her with a tense smile. "Right now, there's only one that comes to mind."

"I don't mean *that*. I mean, the desired result is different. You want a family, I don't."

He moved her back from him just the few inches necessary to study her expression. "Two things, woman," he said. "First, this is the twenty-first century. We have something called birth control. Two people can sleep together without getting pregnant." He tapped a finger over her lips when she started to protest. "Secondly, maybe I don't consider you wife-and-mother material. Ever thought of that, sweet Elly? Maybe I just want to roll around with you on that big, canopied bed in my suite because you're a beautiful woman who turns me on. End of story."

She stared up at him, a frown furrowing her brow.

He didn't know if she believed him or even if he believed himself. What did it matter? He wanted to touch every imaginable spot on her body. If nothing but pure pleasure came of their intimacy, then that might not be such a terrible thing. It had been a long time since a woman had moved him this way. In fact, he couldn't recall when, if ever, that time had been.

"I've only known you for a few days," she murmured. "I don't sleep with strangers or—"

He pressed his lips over hers, refusing to hear generic objections. If she was going to turn him down, she'd have to do it honestly. "Just tell me you don't want to sleep with me," he said as his mouth left hers. "I'll never bring it up again."

"Liar."

"Try me."

She was silent in his arms. He smiled. Good.

At last she spoke carefully. "I'm not saying that you don't get me a little—" she hesitated "—a little *provoked* in a rather enjoyable way. I just don't want to rush into anything and disappoint either of us."

He put on a wounded expression for her. "You think you'd be disappointed after making love with me?" He caressed her throat then drew his fingertips slowly down her shoulder, along her arm, until they finally wove between hers.

She shivered, looking confused. "That's not what I meant. I just wouldn't want to hurt you, Dan, if things got serious."

"Why don't you let me worry about that? I'm pretty good at taking care of myself. If growing up in Baltimore didn't teach me that, the marines sure did."

Elly blinked up at him, and all she could think was, *But what about me? Who is going to take care of me*

when I can't live up to what you want? Because Daniel
Eastwood, despite his flirting and insistence that he was
just interested in a good time, was ultimately a man
who would find one woman to marry and have kids
with. Probably lots of them. And when he found that
woman, none of his lovers before her would matter.
Including Elizabeth Anderson.

The realization sent an oppressive wave of sadness
over her. To be able to be that woman would be wonderful. But it was her fate to be the woman left behind,
for she could never give him a child, or at least be sure
that she would be there to raise their baby with him.
Aside from her own physical impairment and fear of
death, she couldn't bear the thought of causing any
man she cared for the grief her father had suffered.

"It's better that we not get involved," she said hastily, then desperately searched for excuses. She could
only come up with a lame, "You know, with all that's
going to be happening in the next few weeks."

The earthy brown of his eyes intensified, and she
saw something in them she hadn't noticed before and
couldn't define. Determination? Patience? Or just pure
stubbornness? Was he reacting to her refusal as if it
was a challenge? By telling him they couldn't possibly
become involved, while letting him know that she was
tempted, had she inadvertently waved a red flag before
the man?

"Really," she whispered, moving herself out of his
arms, "it's much better if we keep this on a professional level."

Elly stood outside the door to Dan's chamber in the
castle the next day and knocked a third time. There
was no answer. Something told her that he wasn't in-

side ignoring her. The room behind the closed door felt empty.

She felt awful for putting Dan through so much. By bringing him to Elbia Elly had meant to make things easier for everyone. But now everything seemed worse. More confusing, more complex than ever. There was so much to settle between Jacob and Dan...and so much to untangle between Dan and herself. For although she'd tried to return their relationship to one based purely on her professional capacity, she wasn't convinced that was possible. Not when he looked at her the way he did.

Now she tried to think where he might have gone. He would naturally seek water, a beach, when he was troubled and felt trapped. Probably the Adriatic was closest. But that was hundreds of miles away.

If not an ocean, then at least the out-of-doors, and that could only mean the garden since Jacob had ordered all of them to remain within the castle grounds until further notice.

Stopping at her own room only long enough to grab her coat, she ran through soaring stone hallways of an ancient wing of the castle lit by amber electric sconces and down a rear stairwell to a door she hoped would bring her directly into the gardens. There was one at last, of heavy oak studded with iron bolts. A modern deadbolt had replaced whatever older latch had been there, and she turned the lock then tugged on the weighty door. It creaked open and sunlight poured through, forcing her to squint into its winter brilliance.

Stepping outside, she shaded her face with one hand and gave her eyes a chance to adjust to the sun. She breathed in air scented with mountains, pine and an astonishing absence of petroleum residue. Although cars were not banned in Elbia, it was easy to get around the city and countryside by bicycle or on the little red buses that cheerfully plied the hilly streets, and few residents bothered with the expense of buying an automobile.

She walked down a brick path through the rose garden. The bushes were little more than dry sticks, neatly pruned to encourage a fresh burst of flowers come warm weather. Further on was a formal English-style garden of hedges, smartly clipped to resemble whimsical creatures and clever geometric designs. She went on and came to another area where a gazebo grown over with ivy sat at the center of converging paths. A shadow moved behind frosty panes of glass. Cautiously, she approached, still unable to make out who might be inside.

When she was only a few feet from the door, the figure turned as if it had seen her. She froze, not daring to come closer. It was Dan, she was sure of it. The width of his shoulders and dark hair could only have belonged to one of the two brothers. And she remembered Dan had been wearing a deep blue shirt. He opened the door for her.

"Join me?" he said, stepping aside to let her in.

She climbed the steps and moved past him as he shut the door behind them. It was still cold but being out of the wind helped. The sun shining through the glass provided natural solar warmth.

Elly took her hands out of her coat pockets and rubbed them together as she studied his expression. "Are you all right?"

"Of course I'm all right," he muttered irritably. "Why shouldn't I be?"

"That was quite a scene between you and Jacob yesterday. And then, there's been the stuff happening between us. I hope I haven't hurt your feelings.''

"I don't know what he expects," Dan mumbled, ignoring the second part of her statement as he scraped the sole of one shoe against the dark green floor boards. "No, I take that back. I do know all too well what he expects." He narrowed his eyes and glared at her. "Jacob believes he can have everything his way, because that's how it's always been for him."

Elly decided maybe Dan's tactic was best. They would simply ignore their attraction and address other issues. She shook her head. "I don't think so. He may come off as arrogant and stubborn, but he's not an unreasonable man. My dad and I talked with him after you left yesterday. He desperately wants to protect his people and his crown, but he also wants to find a way to do the right thing by you and Madge. This isn't your average family, you know. Things become a bit more complicated when you're sovereign over a country." She tried out a weak smile on him.

"Right," he agreed dryly.

Elly stepped closer, feeling an energy between them dragging her even nearer. We're the moon and the tide, she thought. She resisted but only with great effort.

"Look," she whispered, "I know you have your pride. But don't punish your mother because of it. And don't be blind to all the good that can come of this."

"*What* good?" he snapped.

She sighed. Why was it so difficult for men to accept a gift without attaching an ulterior motive to it? "What if you accept Jacob's settlement on behalf of your City Kids beach program? Let your mom do what she wishes with her share. Or, if she won't take it, invest it for her so that if she ever needs the money for medical care or assisted-living arrangements, she'll have it.''

He glared at the toes of his shoes but said nothing.

She continued quickly, gratified that he was, at least, listening to her. "You don't have to take a penny for yourself, Dan. But those kids you care so much about…they could really benefit. How many more of them each summer could you bring to Ocean City with Jacob's help? What about constructing extra lodging space near the Haven? Or a special educational center where your campers could experiment with computers or learn technical skills that might help them get jobs some day? The possibilities for good are endless with enough funds.''

Dan lifted troubled eyes to her face. "I'll think about it.''

"Promise?''

"Promise." He lifted one corner of his lips in a half smile.

She sensed that he meant it, that he'd gotten her message. But the way his eyes had deepened to a richer color and seemed suddenly alive with hot sparks also told her that he had put aside questions of pride, money and summer camp for considerations of a much more elemental nature. Elly's heartbeat quickened. Suddenly she found breathing a struggle.

"Wh-what are you thinking?" she stammered.

He tipped his head to one side and focused on her all the more closely. "That you feel as deeply about children as I do, only you try not to show it.''

She swallowed. "I just hate to see great opportunities go to waste.''

"No, it's more than that." His gaze was crisply perceptive. He stepped up to her. "You want kids of your own, don't you? Deep down, I mean, beyond all the fear and sad memories, you *want* them.''

A solid knot grew in her throat. The beginnings of tears prickled behind her lashes. "We can't have everything we want. Sometimes we just have to settle for what's best for us…what's safe.''

"So there *are* regrets," he said, hitting too close to home. "How will you deal with those regrets later on, Elly? What happens when you are forty years old, fifty or sixty, and your dad is gone and it's just you? Will you look back on these barren years and be content? Or will you ache for the children and grandchildren other women have?''

She turned sharply away from him and blinked back fat tears. "Stop that! Not everyone is meant to be a parent. I *like* my independence. I enjoy being—" How was she ever going to finish that sentence? *Alone? I like being alone?* That wasn't true. As a child she had thrived on being part of a family. She would have welcomed two, three, six brothers and sisters, if only she could have kept her mother too.

"You like being what, Elly?" He moved to within inches of her, and she jerked backward but had nowhere to go. The glass walls of the gazebo curved around behind her.

"I like…not having to *worry* about other people," she blurted out. "With children, I'd be fussing over them all the time, afraid they'd be struck down by disease, hit by a car or beaten up by school bullies. I'd be a *horrible* mother.''

His hand lifted to twist a strand of her red hair. "I think you'd make a wonderful mother. There are, you know, no guarantees in life. Whenever we want something that's very important to us, we must give up something in return. And when things don't work out as we wish, we have to go on with life.''

Elly's lips trembled. Tears spilled down her cheeks, but she dashed them away with the back of her hand. ''Don't do this to me, Dan. Don't make me feel self-ish.''

''That's not what I want you to feel.''

She choked on a sob. ''What then?''

He moved forward and took her in his arms. The warmth was incredible. ''I just want you to be sure of what you really want or don't want. Regret is the bitterest of pills.''

She swallowed, staring helplessly up at him as he held her. ''I've often wondered if she knew.''

''She?'' He looked confused.

''My mother. I've tried putting myself in her place. I wonder if she understood the risks of her heart condition, if she'd been warned by her doctor that even a C-section would be dangerous, but she never said anything about it to me...maybe not even to my father. She wanted a second baby so badly, but for a long time she just couldn't seem to get pregnant again. Then several years passed and my parents stopped talking about another child.''

''They'd given up?'' he guessed.

''Or maybe that was when the doctor told her that it would be too risky to try again,'' she whispered against his chest. Why was it so much easier to speak of these things, these terribly sad things, while Dan was holding her like this? ''I just miss her so very much.''

It was impossible to stop crying now. Elly wept openly and Dan held her, letting her mourn the woman who had brought her into the world, allowing her to cleanse her heart of the bitterness and grief that kept her from loving fully and openly. He didn't try to stop her tears, didn't tell her that everything would be all right or that she would forget her mother's sacrifice. And she silently thanked him for that small, precious gift of silence, of compassion.

When the tears finally stopped, Elly felt lighter of spirit.

Dan didn't speak now. He just ran the pad of his wide thumb beneath each of her eyes in turn, wiping away the moisture as she gazed up at him. He wasn't smiling and he wasn't frowning. His expression was one of concentration on an important task. So she didn't see the kiss coming until his mouth had pressed gently but firmly over hers.

She savored the melting sensation of their lips. Emotions burst from her as if reborn from within a dead soul. A whirl of feelings wrapped around her—so heady, so potent that her knees almost buckled beneath her.

As if knowing this, Dan tightened his arms around her, supporting her against his body as his kiss deepened. The world spun. The gazebo's windows swam before her eyes, glittering in winter sunlight. The air felt suddenly thinner, finer, easier to breathe and she was no longer aware of chill beyond the warm circle of Dan's arms. The darkness of the past receded.

Elly's breasts pressed against the curve of his muscled abdomen. She could feel each ridge, each toned band made taut by miles of swimming. Her jacket had fallen open, and he wore no coat. She was sure he was as aware of her body as she was of his. It seemed as if they'd escaped to a world of their own—apart from family, the castle's immense staff, the press who would continue to hound Dan now that they'd found him.

He had spoken to her heart, and his words might not solve all of her problems, but they had healed a small part of her and brought new hope to her life. He was right, of course. She wasn't guaranteeing herself a long, healthy life by avoiding the single potential danger of childbirth. She was simply avoiding life at its richest. And one day, very likely, she would regret her decision. But in the meantime, it was all she could do to consider being close to a man whose masculinity she could even now feel pulsing between them.

Elly kissed him back, deeply, allowing her lips to part welcomingly for him. A small sigh of contentment escaped from her soul. Clinging to him she delighted in the way his hands smoothed upward along her ribs beneath her jacket. His palms pressed against the sides of her breasts through her clothing, and her nipples tingled in anticipation.

It had been so long, so very long since she'd felt desire for a man's touch. And now it seemed as if no man would do but this one. Daniel Eastwood. No less than a prince.

The fierce passion in his eyes told her that he was no longer thinking of anything but the signals their bodies were sending each other. A longing filled Elly to feel him inside her, even if only this one time. The need crowded out all caution, all warnings of consequences.

Dan drew her along with him as he backed up, then sat on a wooden bench. Pulling her down onto his lap he pressed his cheek against the V of her blouse collar then turned his head to kiss the sensitive valley between her breasts.

Elly sucked in a ragged breath, let her head drop back and soaked up every delicious sensation as his lips slipped lower. With one thumb he hooked a bra cup, tugging it down to expose her breast. Cool air tingled against her exposed flesh. He ran the pad of one finger around then across her nipple, and she thought she'd rocket through the glass roof.

"Oh!" She gulped to catch her breath. "Oh, Dan!"

When his mouth closed over her nipple and ravenously feasted, Elly felt a sudden rush of heat between her thighs. She lifted off his lap with a soft gasp of pleasure. His hand took advantage of the new opening and slid between her legs, smoothing upward but stopping short of touching her where the heat had centered most torridly.

She silently begged him not to stop, wanted to ask him to use his strong fingers to stroke and probe her, prolonging the fire building within her body. But she couldn't put her needs into words. And unless she could give him what he wanted in return, she believed it wasn't right to accept the intimacy he was offering her.

Her head fell forward against his strong shoulder and she pressed one palm gently, reluctantly against his chest in a Stop signal. His hand immediately moved back down to neutral territory on her knee. His lips released her breast and he looked questioningly up at her.

"I won't hurt you," he whispered. "I won't let anything happen to you, Elly. Trust me."

With all her heart she wanted to. Her body's hunger called out for him, but the past inevitably crept in over the warmth and desire again. She squeezed her eyes shut.

"I'm sorry...so very sorry," she murmured.

"Sh-sh-sh," he said, soothingly. "It's all right."

It wasn't all right, not by a long shot, she thought. "I can't keep letting things get out of control. I swear, I'm not trying to torment you, Dan. It's just that…that…" She lost it then and broke into tears. "It's just so hard."

"I know," he whispered, holding her, rocking her as his hand stroked the back of her head.

Elly knew he couldn't possibly understand the war being waged inside her between her natural passion and her fears. She hardly understood it herself.

He held her tighter, touching his lips to her damp cheek, bathing it in comforting warmth that never seemed to sink into the rest of her. "It's not important. You're safe with me, Elly. We won't do this again. It's not worth putting you through the agony."

She felt her body finally relax against his, sheltered in his arms.

He spoke softly to her. "If that's what you want, we'll just be friends. Okay?"

It wasn't what she wanted, but it was what she supposed she must settle for. "Okay," she agreed, lapsing into post-sob hiccups. Then she did feel safe, more so than ever in her life.

Five

Friends, Dan thought bitterly each day whenever he saw Elly. It wasn't at all what he had wanted, and he didn't know if he could be only that to her. Being holed up in the castle with her made it all the more difficult, for there was no place to escape to.

Ten days after they had arrived in Elbia, neither his relationship with Elly nor the one with Jacob looked any better. Elly kept her distance, and Jacob barely offered him a nod when they happened to pass in a hallway. Dan was pretty sure his brother was avoiding both him and Madge at mealtimes. They'd met formally two more times, but Dan still refused to sign anything, as he remained uncertain that he should be the one to make a decision for his mother. Madge still insisted that she wanted nothing from Karl's estate.

He thought he understood her reluctance to make her liaison with the monarch official. After all, once it was put in writing that Dan was Karl von Austerand's illegitimate son, Madge's indiscretion would be there for all the world to see and comment on. And he knew how much that would hurt her. Then there was the notoriety that the scandal would bring to the Haven. He was torn, wishing he knew what was best for everyone.

A good part of the reason he felt unable to think clearly was Elly. He believed that she felt something special for him, and that she wanted him as much as he wanted her. It frustrated him to no end that he'd promised to stop pursuing her—but what else could he have done when she obviously was in such pain whenever they came close to intimacy?

Every time he saw her it became more and more a test of his will not to touch her. The temptation was nearly impossible to ignore. He began to wonder if his imagination was playing tricks on him. How could she have felt so very different in his arms than any other woman? How could the simple appearance of the woman in a room send his heart reeling and his libido into overdrive?

The castle, as immense as it was, no longer felt big enough to contain the two of them. He grew frantic to break free—to swim, to run up mountainsides and down into valleys, to expend some of the pent-up energy being shut up with Elly had built inside him. But Jacob was insistent that no one leave the castle grounds, and as much as he hated giving in to his brother's rules, he supposed they had little alternative.

One morning, ten days after they'd arrived in Elbia, Dan spent two hours in Jacob's gym, running on the treadmill then lifting weights. No matter what he did, he couldn't exhaust himself or stop thinking about Elly.

Then she walked into the gym dressed in hot-pink biking shorts and a matching sports bra—and he rolled his eyes in desperation as his body reacted to her sexy outfit.

"Mind if I join you?" she asked pertly. "I'm going stir crazy."

"Like everyone else in this damn castle," he muttered. "I don't understand the point of this siege mentality. We can't avoid the press forever. What are we waiting for?"

"Jacob's advisors are hoping the paparazzi's fascination with you and Madge will wear out if we're patient enough."

He shook his head. "I wonder…"

Dan lifted a forty-pound dumbbell from the rack and curled it with one hand for another ten repetitions. He watched his biceps swell then relax with each flexing of his arm, but he wasn't paying much attention to the exercise. His mind was on Elly. She looked adorable in her workout gear, so close in design and coverage to underwear. He remembered with intense clarity touching her breasts, now so sparsely covered. He remembered kissing them. A lick of flame swept through him, and he had to put down the dumbbell and take a steadying breath.

"Try to be patient," Elly said encouragingly. "Not even the staff can leave the castle grounds without being accosted by a dozen reporters. We might as well enjoy our captivity in luxury." She smiled at him, as if to gently chide him for his complaints.

He shrugged good-naturedly. "I guess this isn't exactly on a level with being thrown into the dungeon."

"Hardly. Which is another reason why I have to exercise. I've never eaten such amazing food. It's just too delicious to turn down." Elly blinked up at him as she strode over to a stationary bicycle and climbed on. "I stooped to seconds last night," she confessed. "And did you have any of that yummy chocolate torte?"

He shook his head. "I don't have the sweet tooth you seem to have." But he could certainly do with a nibble on her throat right now, he thought without a trace of guilt. Dan slung a towel around his neck and leaned against a wall as he watched her start to pedal.

"Are you finished with your workout?" she asked.

"I suppose. Don't feel a whole lot better for it. I need to get outside…and I don't mean for a stroll in the garden." A thought suddenly struck him. "You said the staff can't get out without being harassed?"

"That's right. One of the groundskeepers told me that every time he comes or leaves, he's bombarded with questions." She laughed. "He just tells the reporters he never sees any of us, doesn't know a thing."

"But he comes and goes," Dan repeated.

"Well, yes, he has a family in the town and needs to get home to them. But if it were you or me—"

"But that's just the point!" Dan interrupted her, his spirits soaring at an idea. "The paparazzi are only interested in the royals, me or Madge…or anyone who is willing to talk about what's happening inside the castle. If a gardener or maid or cook doesn't have information they can use, they don't care how many times they come and go from the castle."

Elly squinted at him suspiciously. "So?"

"So maybe another groundskeeper will leave by the back gate this afternoon."

Understanding brightened her face. "Dan, you wouldn't…"

"Want to come along?" He sensed, even as he said the words that he was inviting trouble.

Elly laughed. "There's absolutely no way both of us could slip out unnoticed."

"Not exactly unnoticed. Would you prefer to be a cook or a maid?"

She gave him a skeptical smile, but he could tell she was as excited as he was at the prospect of escaping, if only for a short while, from their confinement. "I'll go talk to the cook. She seems a cheery soul. Maybe she'll lend me something from one of her assistants."

Less than an hour later, Elly met Dan inside the door that led from the kitchen on the ground floor out into the gardens.

"Now, you do keep your head down and don't speak a word *auf englisch* while they're in hearing," Cook advised Elly as she helped her on with a white kitchen smock. "You just keep saying, *'Entschuldigung! Ich wisse nichts.'*"

"That means, Excuse me! I know nothing," Elly explained to Dan.

"What about me?" Dan asked. He had already borrowed some old clothing from Cook's husband, the royal family's head gardener.

"Let the *Fraulein* do the talking," Cook said bluntly. "Your *Deutsch ist* lousy."

Dan laughed, not taking offense. "I don't care as long as I get to see something outside of these stone walls."

"Here," Cook said, pressing a mesh shopping bag stuffed with paper-wrapped parcels on Dan, "you may get hungry. I've sent word to the guards on the rear gate that you'll be coming. They will let you out and watch for your return.''

"Thank you," Elly said gratefully. ''You've been great. You won't get into trouble for helping us, will you?''

Cook winked at her. "The king, he used to lick my cooking spoons as a little boy. He would never be angry with his *Tante* Anna.''

As they approached the back gate, Dan felt the tension building in his shoulders and neck. It was so warm that they really didn't need coats, yet their simple locally made garments made them look their parts as a groundsman and cook's assistant.

There seemed to be just as many reporters attached to the rear gate as there had been at the main entrance. As soon as the guard let them through the iron grille a flurry of excitement ran through their ranks. Several started barking into cell phones, alerting others that prey was afoot.

But Elly played her role impeccably. Murmuring a few guttural words in German as Cook had instructed she jutted out her chin, dropped her glance and headed down the road in a stiff stride, all business. Dan stayed close by her side, glowering at the reporters who tossed out hopeful questions. He pulled his cap lower over his eyes and tried to look as bored and unintelligent as possible.

By the time they'd gone a hundred yards down the road, their followers had dismissed them as unlikely sources of information and returned to their positions outside the gates.

Elly laughed out loud as soon as they were out of hearing. "We did it! We actually fooled them!''

''You should take all the credit. If I'd opened my

mouth they would have known immediately that I was an American.'' He looked appreciatively at her. She was glowing, and he felt a shared enthusiasm for the day that spread out before them.

The weather was balmy for winter. The sun shone brightly, chasing away the chill and melting the last traces of snow that lingered among the roots of road-side shrubs.

''I feel positively giddy with freedom!'' she cried. ''Where will we go? What will we do? How about a stroll around the city?'' Her eyes sparkled.

Dan grimaced. ''I'm afraid that would increase our chances of being caught. Someone in town will know we're not really from the castle staff.''

She stopped walking and frowned. ''What then?''

''The lake,'' he said. ''I could see a corner of it from my window, and it doesn't look as if it's that far. A mile or so.''

''Good. By the time we get there, I'll be hungry enough for lunch, and we can see what Cook has packed for us.'' She peered curiously at the mesh bag.

Dan set a crisp walking pace, and Elly seemed to have no trouble keeping up. Color filled her cheeks as they strode away from town, past cottages and into a wooded area that reminded him of tales from his child-hood—Little Red Riding Hood, Hansel and Gretel. He felt free and young and daring, and having Elly at his side made the outing even more delicious.

The knowledge that nothing could happen between them seemed less painful here. They could be friends, as she wanted, and share an outing without feeling compelled to be anything more. He felt in a very rea-sonable, mature mood at the moment.

By the time the trees opened out into a clearing and

he could see a ribbon of blue water before them, his body felt energized from the exercise. He was pleasantly aware of Elly's slim figure beside him, and of her breathing which was quicker and deeper from the walking. But he felt satisfied that he could enjoy her presence without becoming aroused. This is good, he thought.

"Hungry?" she asked.

"If you are, we can eat first."

"First?" She looked around as if trying to assess alternatives, given the deserted woods surrounding them. A worry line creased her forehead.

"I thought we might go for a swim," he suggested.

"You're kidding, in the middle of winter?" She laughed, then went on before he could respond. "Oh, I forgot, you're the one with the elevated body temperature who swims in oceans in November."

He grinned. "Feel this." He took her hand and walked her down to the edge of the water.

She humored him and bent down to touch her fingertips to the water's softly lapping wavelets. Her expression changed from wariness to amazement. "It's warm. Why?"

"Fed by a thermal spring. Cook's husband told me about it while he was dressing me. It stays the same temperature year round." And with the sun beaming down on them, it didn't seem too cold to shed clothing that now felt much too heavy for the day.

"I can't swim very well," Elly objected. "And I don't have a bathing suit."

He winked at her. "You have a natural one."

"Oh, no!" She laughed at him. "Skinny dipping alone might be one thing but not—"

"Not with me looking on with lust in my heart?" he teased her.

"Something like that." Her pretty eyes skittered away from his.

"You wore that stretchy little athletic bra and bike shorts this morning. Didn't cover anything more than undies. Swim in your underwear."

She gazed longingly out over the crystal-blue water. "It does look refreshing," she admitted, "after all that exercise."

"Go for it," he encouraged her, already shrugging out of his jacket and starting to unbutton the gardener's flannel shirt. He stripped down to his hip-hugging briefs.

Elly hesitated only a moment longer. Then, with one final cautious look around her, as if to make sure no one was watching, she tore off her coat then the white cotton smock. She still looked a little nervous, but her eyes gleamed at the water and she ran barefoot toward it shouting at him, "I'll beat you in!"

"Oh no you won't!" he yelled, even as he raced toward the water's edge, flashed past her and dove, slicing through the mirror surface at a shallow angle. The water glided over his flesh, supporting him with less buoyancy than his lady the ocean but still gently lifting him so that he could skim up to the surface with little effort. He broke through with a splash and stood on the silty bottom, looking around for Elly.

She had walked in and stood with the water up to her waist. "This is marvelous! It felt cool near the edge, but there's a current of warmth right where I'm standing. Must be from the spring."

He nodded, pretending to listen to her words, but far more interested in the view—her pert breasts rising seductively above her bra, her slim waist, her eyes shining at him.

"Could you swim well enough to make it up the shore to that floating log?" he asked, pointing a hundred feet or so up the beach.

"Probably. I can manage a decent doggie paddle," she admitted, "and a slow crawl. I took summer swimming classes at the Y when I was a teenager."

"Let's go then." He started out slowly, giving her time to get used to the feel of the water around her body, then he let her set the pace. She had a nice, compact stroke, although he suspected she'd tire quickly, not being used to swimming any distance or often. He liked the way she seemed to feel comfortable in the water, turning her face into it for two good strokes before swiveling her head to the right for a breath.

They reversed direction and came back to where they had started. When she stood up, Elly looked toward the woods.

"Still worried about Peeping Toms?" he teased.

"I thought I saw something move near those trees."

Dan looked but could see nothing. He came behind her, wrapped his arms around her and gave her a quick, reassuring hug. When she lifted her head he gave her a light kiss on the lips over her shoulder, then quickly backed off. "More likely a deer or a fox than a person," he said, "this time of year."

She nodded and blew out a soft breath. "It's amazing. I'm not the least bit cold, even though it's winter. But I am starving."

"Let's eat then."

Out of the water they pulled on their coats then sat on the mossy bank. The sun was warm and Elly felt strangely at ease, sitting with Dan wearing only underclothes beneath their jackets, eating thick country sandwiches of Emmentaler cheese, spicy bratwurst sausage and mustard, nibbling on pickles and washing it all down with white wine Dan had uncorked for them. It seemed Cook had thought of everything.

As she finished her sandwich and brushed the crumbs from her fingers and lap she couldn't help laughing softly to herself. Dan turned to look at her. "What?"

"I feel like a high-school kid, sneaking out for a secret date with a boy."

"Skinny dipped at the beach with the boys, did you?" He was grinning and she accommodated him by blushing.

"No. I was boringly shy, I'm afraid. It's taken me this long to pull a stunt like this."

"But you still drew the line," he said, tipping his head in the direction of her modest beige bra and panties, peeking out from beneath her coat.

"The remainders of my conservative youth." She shook her head and smiled but couldn't help letting her eyes shift to the opening of his jacket and the well-defined shape within Dan's briefs.

His body in the water that day had been just as breathtaking as on that first day she'd seen him. Above the low line of his navy-blue briefs his stomach was hard and flat. A reddish brown smattering of hair rose across it and patterned out wider and darker to almost black across his muscled chest. His shoulders were beautifully formed—sleek, muscled, shaped by hundreds of strokes along the Haven's beach.

She suddenly wanted him to lie down over her, to press his muscled torso over her breasts and hips and let her feel all of him. She wanted this desperately, and with an urgency that felt overpowering. And she wondered where this passion had sprung from when she'd already decided they would never make love.

Yes, she'd been attracted to him from the start, but it had been the kind of attraction she had been able to control. Or maybe it was only that Dan *allowed* her that sense of control. Perhaps the feelings she felt now were a result of sharing their daring escape plan and successfully pulling it off. They were conspirators! Stripping down to swim together and dining on the pebbly beach, laughing at the foolish press they'd so easily tricked…it was all part of a game they'd created. Like naughty children. It was innocent fun.

Or was it? she wondered. Despite their intent to remain just friends, a fragile intimacy had intruded. She was increasingly aware of their provocative state of undress, and of the tempting impulses passing between them.

"I wonder how often we could do it?" Dan mused aloud.

Elly's eyes flew wide open and she stared at him. "Do *what?*" He couldn't be saying what she was thinking.

"Perform our vanishing act."

"Oh, I don't know." She laughed nervously and started to pack sandwich wrappers and leftover pickles back into the string bag. "I suppose they'd catch on after a while."

"We could do this again tomorrow," he suggested. "It's a whole lot better than being cooped up inside the palace, waiting for Jacob and his advisors to come up with their next strategy for dealing with me." He hesitated, then scowled into the distance. "You don't think they'd do anything as drastic as they did in the old days?''

"The old days?"

"Well, in medieval times if you had a rival for the throne, you got rid of him. Classic solution—lock him away. Or poison the poor guy, or just order him killed in his sleep.''

Elly laughed, throwing back her head. "You do have a wild imagination. Jacob may come off pretty strong sometimes, but I don't think he'd stoop to murdering his own brother, or anyone else for that matter.''

"Hold it right there,'' Dan said, staring intently at her exposed throat.

She froze, thinking he meant to brush a wandering bug from her skin. Instead he leaned across and touched his lips to the sensitive sweep of flesh beneath her chin.

"I've been wanting to do that all day,'' he said in a low voice that sent ripples of heat through her. Then he pulled back and sat tensely, looking away.

She was trembling. She was adrift. Why, she asked herself, was she denying herself this wonderful man's companionship? Because of an irrational fear or a real danger to her life? She wished there was some-one…anyone she could talk to who would understand and help her sort out her life.

A mother, she thought sadly. That was who she needed so very badly right now. Her own mother. She would have had the answers. She would have explained why a woman puts her life in a man's hands whenever she enters into intimacy with him. Trust between two people, it was such a fragile thing.

In the distance, an almost indistinguishable sound

shattered her thoughts. She looked up and around. "What was that?"

"I didn't hear anything." Dan leaned toward her as if he was going to kiss her again.

She braced an outstretched palm between them, holding him away so that she could listen. There it was again—a soft growl, as if from a small irritated terrier. She narrowed her eyes and studied the nearby woods, but could see nothing. When the sound came again, it seemed to be coming from the other side of the lake.

"I heard it that time," Dan said. "Could be an animal upset that we've intruded on its home."

Elly nodded. Perhaps. "We should leave," she said. Something told her that whatever had made the strange sound wasn't as harmless as your garden-variety squirrel or groundhog. Anything larger, and she didn't want to meet it.

The next morning Dan awoke to an angry pounding on his door. He squinted at the travel alarm beside his bed and groaned when he saw that it wasn't yet 8:00 a.m. Since there had been no urgency in rising while staying at the castle, he'd grown accustomed to sleeping in. Later that day, with or without Elly, he'd promised himself another excursion to the lake. His mood felt so much improved over the days before.

"Come in," he growled, tugging on the bedclothes to cover his naked hips.

"Get up and get dressed!" a voice ordered smartly.

He scowled as Elly bounded across the chamber, tossing a newspaper onto a chair. She flung open the doors to the armoire on the far side of the room. "And put something decent on. Jacob's in a snit and we're in deep trouble."

"He is? We are?" He sat up in bed trying to make sense of her words. "What's happened now?"

"I found out what that growling noise at the lake was yesterday."

Now he was intrigued. "Yes?"

"You know the sound a thirty-five-millimeter camera makes when it auto-winds?"

The flesh at the back of his neck prickled. "Someone was taking pictures of us at the lake."

"Right." She tossed a pair of khaki pants and a blue oxford shirt onto the bed. "Where is your underwear?"

"I'll take care of my own underwear, thank you." He flung off the covers and she hastily averted her eyes. He would have found the gesture amusing if he wasn't so damn furious. Grabbing the sheet off the bed, he wrapped it around his waist. "How do you know that's what it was?"

"Because of this." She picked up the newspaper she'd brought into the room and pitched it at him. It was a British tabloid. He unfolded it. A full third of the front page displayed a grainy photo of Elly and himself standing in the water. It had been taken at the exact moment he'd given her that companionable peck on the lips. The caption read: The Prince and his Playmate (details, page 3).

"Good grief, how did a photographer get close enough to—"

"Telephoto lens, no doubt," Elly muttered. "He must have either followed us from the castle without our seeing him or he just happened on us then took up a position on the far shore of the lake. You can tell by the angle."

"I see." He handed her the paper with a sinking feeling in his gut. From a drawer he pulled out a clean

T-shirt and briefs, then took his clothes into the bathroom. "So I take it His Highness has seen that paper."

"Yup, and he's furious."

Dan finished buttoning his shirt, tucked in the tails and ran his belt through the loops as he strode back into the bedchamber. "What are we supposed to do about it?"

"I'm not sure, but I expect the first move in such situations is called Facing the Music."

Elly held herself rigidly and let Jacob's outraged words sweep over her. Then she repeated what she'd already told him once before that morning. "No matter how it looks, nothing happened. Besides, it wasn't our fault. We were careful. We just didn't know anyone was there."

But one fact remained, and Elly knew it. By deliberately disobeying Jacob's orders that they remain on the grounds, they had given the press a fresh supply of gossip to weave into all sorts of shocking stories.

"Careful?" Jacob fumed. He thrust two more newspapers across the table at them.

The German journalists were even more inventive than the English. And the French press was having a field day with what they had billed as *le scandale royal*. A photo showed Dan and Elly sitting on the beach, eating their lunch. Beneath the photo, which had obviously been altered, was an easily translatable French subtitle: Unidentified Lover of the New Prince Bares It All. The photo had been touched up, removing the bra Elly had never taken off and supplying her with another woman's breasts.

Dan watched Elly go stone-white as she stared in horror at the photo. Tears trembled at the corners of her eyes. He felt awful for her. This was so much worse for her than for him. "This is a blatant invasion of privacy!" he growled. "Can't anything be done?"

"You took it upon yourselves to disrobe in a public place." Jacob glared at him accusingly. "If the photographer had broken into the castle that would be another thing."

"But I told you, we weren't *doing* anything," Elly said weakly, looking at Allison who had just entered the room. "We just went for a swim, decently covered, then ate lunch on the beach."

Allison shook her head in sympathy. But before she could speak her husband jumped in. "The point is, it doesn't appear to the observer that all was innocent. Even if the photographer altered the print, the fact remains...the two of your were frolicking in a secluded lake with next to nothing on!"

"Oh, don't be a prude, dear," Allison said with a sigh, shocking Elly with her casual tone. "You remember what being in love was like." She gave her husband a secretive look. Elly suspected the royal couple was still very much in love from the responding glimmer of a smile from Jacob. "Besides, you can't honestly expect everyone to remain shut up in the palace indefinitely. That's no solution."

"With a little more time, everything would have settled down," Jacob grumbled.

"With a little more time, the paparazzi would have dug up more stories about your father's playboy years," Dan snapped. "I don't see what good is being done by our being here at all."

The two men glared at each other.

The gulf between the two brothers was clearly widening. Elly wished there was something she could do to help them work together, but she feared it was already too late for that.

Six

Elly hid her deepest and most personal rage and humiliation from Dan. She had decided before she told him about the newspaper photos that her reaction was crucial to his. If she let him know how hurt she'd been, that would only make him all the angrier. And right now the only thing that would save them all was clear thinking.

But she couldn't totally ignore her own fears: her fear that her father's business, and therefore he himself, would be irreparably damaged by the new scandal she and Dan had unwittingly instigated, and then there was her fear for her own future. She no longer believed she could remain alone all of her life. Yet the thought of being with other men, men who didn't want a family, felt far less appealing than spending long, loving days with Dan, whose warmth, generosity and passion came so naturally to him. She longed to play a role in his

life, but couldn't begin to figure out how. Then there
was the worry, eating away at her, that by bringing Dan
to Elbia she hadn't brought two brothers together, she
had started a war. And she now had escalated that war
by sneaking off with Dan against his brother's orders.

The day after word of their woodland tryst broke,
the royal press secretary delivered copies of newspapers from a dozen countries, including the U.S., to the
dining room. Although most were the sleazy, gossip
rags that harassed movie stars and politicians, a few
respected publications showed the same embarrassing
photographs on inside pages. The articles were short,
sketchy and less accusatory. Still, she felt nauseated
seeing herself and Dan in such intimate poses, for all
the world to view. And it wasn't as if they'd done
anything wrong! she kept reminding herself. She'd
been discreet, revealing no more than a modest bathing
suit would, and they'd shared no more than a kiss.

Elly sighed and stopped walking on her way back
from the empty dining room where she'd had just juice
and a bagel for a late breakfast. She looked out a window into the garden. Madge and Frank were sitting on
a stone bench in a sunny spot, looking cozy in their
warm jackets. Madge took a photograph from her coat
pocket and showed it to him. He smiled and nodded,
and seemed to be commenting on it. She assumed it
was a picture of Dan as a child. One proud parent sharing memories with another. That was nice. At least two
people in this castle were getting along, she thought
ruefully.

The sound of voices came to Elly from the end of
the long hallway hung with rich tapestries. Elly looked
up to see Allison heading her way, little Prince Cray
holding her hand, a nurse carrying baby Kristina. Elly

smiled at the little group. What a joy to have two little ones as beautiful and cheerful as these two. What she wouldn't give to be brave enough to…

She cut off the thought…the wish…the dream that could never be.

Elly put on a smile for the children. "Well, hello! How are you two doing today?"

"Great!" Cray chirped. "I talked on the terror-phone."

Elly laughed. "You mean, the *telephone.*"

"Actually, he can be a bit of a terror on the phone," Allison said with a sigh. "When it rings in the nursery, he races us for it and wants to do all the talking himself." She patted her son affectionately on the head. "We're heading back to the nursery. Would you like to come along?"

Elly involuntarily tightened inside. But she couldn't resist. "I'd like that. May I?" she asked, offering to take the baby.

Kristina held out her pudgy little arms and gurgled at her. The nurse handed her over.

"She's so beautiful." Elly stroked the tiny, soft head and its blond curls.

"We think so," Allison murmured, love shining in her eyes. She tousled her son's hair, so as not to leave him out, and he grinned mischievously up at her. Then Allison turned to Elly with a different expression entirely. "I'm sorry you're having such a difficult time with the press. It isn't fair that your privacy should be invaded this way. Dan seems like a nice man too. It can't be easy for him."

"It's not," Elly said solemnly. "He must feel so very helpless, and he's a man used to action. You

know, seeing a problem then doing something to resolve it. This time his hands are tied.''

"Dealing with the public through a voracious press
has been the hardest thing for me to adjust to,'' Allison
admitted. "I've only been in Elbia and married to
Jacob for less than two years, you see. Before then, the
only contact I had with a newspaper was writing an-
nouncements for children's story hours at the library in
the community events column.''

Elly didn't want to say that she was aware the birth
of their son had preceded the couple's marriage, but
the lovely American's marriage to the bachelor prince
of Elbia had been a lead story in newspapers and magazines everywhere. Their wedding had been the focus
of TV and radio talk shows, and the ceremony itself
had been telecast by satellite all over the world. Now
that she had met Allison in person, she wondered how
this woman, no older than herself, had survived those
unbelievably stressful days.

But now Allison seemed both content with her sur-
roundings and comfortable with her role as Jacob's
queen. Elly noticed that the staff, though respectful of
her, never seemed nervous around or fearful of their
mistress. Allison never ordered them about but quietly
asked for their help when she needed it and always
thanked them afterwards. There was no question that
their queen was beloved by her subjects.

"How do you live with the prying and lack of privacy, day in and day out?'' Elly asked. "I think I'd go
mad.''

"It's not often this bad,'' Allison admitted as they
continued walking. "Usually, we're very open with the
journalists, and they respect the times we ask to be left
alone. It's only when we travel that things sometimes

get a little rough.'' She reached out to touch her daughter's cheek in a protective gesture.

"How much longer will my swimming escapade prolong their interest?"

Allison smiled at her. "Good grief, it's not as if you were totally nude, skinny dipping with the entire football squad!" She laughed merrily, making light of the situation, and Elly instantly felt better. "Oh, who can say. A couple of weeks? Maybe longer, it depends. Sad to say, if there were a terrible disaster somewhere in the world or a popular celebrity died, most of them would rush off to cover the new story and forget all about you."

"I don't know if anyone can stand another two weeks shut up here. It's so unfair to the rest of you, suffering for my mistake."

Allison shrugged. "We'll make do. Have you seen Dan today? How is he taking things now? Any calmer?"

"I haven't dared search him out." Elly shook her head. "Last I saw him, he was brooding and looking unapproachable."

"Typical male."

Elly grinned. "A lot like his brother, is he?"

"Mirror image. It's spooky when I watch them together. If they could only accept each other and work together."

"That's just what I've been thinking," Elly admitted. "But it may be hopeless."

"Give them time," Allison advised. "They have a lot to work out."

Elly knew that was true. Just as she and Dan had a lot to resolve, which was something she'd been trying desperately to ignore. Emotions left unspoken, feelings too fragile to put into words, hopes that might come crashing down and shatter at the mere whisper of the truth.

She tucked her thoughts away within her heart, not yet ready to admit to them. After all, there was a good chance Dan would never speak to her again after this latest incident.

Two days earlier, Dan had been so angry he didn't dare stay in the same room with anyone. He checked on Madge in her room and apologized for embarrassing her.

'She had seemed more amused than upset by the photos, as if relieved that the spotlight had shifted away from her indiscretions and had now turned to the younger generation's.

"It won't happen again," he assured her.

She didn't comment on that. "Elizabeth seems a very nice girl," she said. "I didn't like her very much at first, but I suppose she was just doing her job."

He blinked at his mother. Was this her way of saying she *approved* of Elly? He left without asking for clarification. Too much was already on his mind. Too many decisions had to be made, and quickly.

On the third day, he woke up with a clear head and a few ideas. He dressed and, before he'd had breakfast, found his way to the press secretary's office and asked for the morning's newspapers. They were just as he suspected they'd be. Each still carried a risqué photo of him and Elly, some from slightly different angles, as if the photographer had moved along the bank of the lake, snapping away. The captions were more outrageous than ever and featured stories to match. He asked to borrow the papers for a short while and marched off with them wedged under one arm.

It was only eight o'clock, but he knocked firmly on Elly's door and when he heard a sleepy, "Come in," he let himself in.

"Oh," she said, "I was hoping it was one of Allison's marvelous clairvoyant servants with coffee."

"Coffee can wait," he said briskly and tossed the stack of papers down on her bed.

She gazed at them dejectedly, turning a shade paler. "I don't think I can stomach any more of this."

"Look at them," he ordered.

She scowled. "This is cruel and unusual punishment, particularly this early in the morning. Besides, you're the one who suggested we go for a swim. In fact, if it wasn't for me, we'd have both been caught on film for posterity with—"

"With our posteriors showing, I know. But look at the damn papers."

She groaned. "You are an impossible man."

"I know." He grinned at her. "Now pay attention, I'm going to quiz you in a minute."

Elly sat up in bed and pulled the stack of newsprint into her lap. Today the photos seemed a little smaller, taking up space on inside rather than front pages. Apparently, shots of less clarity had been saved to be run later. Anyone looking at the pictures would assume from the attitudes and nearness of the man and woman in the photo that they were lovers. Even at a distance, the way she and Dan were looking at each other revealed an intimate connection and a longing that, for all the viewer knew, might have been satisfied moments after the picture had been shot.

"What do you see?" Dan asked her.

"Good grief, need you ask?"

"What do you see?" he repeated.

"Two lovers," she groaned.

"Maybe, but look at the caption."

She grimaced but read it aloud. "The Secret Prince and His Mysterious Lover."

"And the story?"

"Do I have to?" Elly wailed.

"Read the first three paragraphs of this one." He pushed a New York daily at her.

She read to herself then looked up at him. "It's total fantasy. Ludicrous. They have no idea what they're talking about. This part about your challenging Jacob for the throne is complete—"

"Rubbish, I know." He sat on the bed beside her. "And so are the stories in the Chicago *Journal* and the LA *News* and the London *Express*. In every single paper, reporters are trying to weave stories from rumors. They have no facts upon which to base their speculations."

"Good!" She shoved the noxious tabloids off her lap.

"No," he said slowly, "not good. Not yet." He gave her a devilish grin.

She frowned at him. "You're scaring me. The last scheme that warped mind of yours cooked up got us into worse trouble!"

He ignored her concern. "I was awake most of the night thinking about this mess. And it occurred to me that we're tackling the problem all wrong. Hiding out only makes my presence more intriguing. And covering up the facts of my mother's liaison with Karl only makes the story seem more lurid and mysterious than it really is. And people love mysteries."

"Almost as much as they love gossip about the rich," Elly said.

"Right. So it's my theory that Jacob should hold a press conference. Go public with everything we know, as soon as possible. Let them take pictures of all of us and ask whatever questions they feel like asking. Get it all out into the air."

"And what about us? What about those pictures of you and me in compromising non-attire?"

"The truth, again."

Elly looked doubtful. And in a way he was lying to her on this one count, because he wasn't going to tell the world that what they saw in those photos was exactly what he had been feeling. He had wanted to make passionate love to Elly. He had wanted to strip off that dripping bra and tear away her nearly useless panties and see all of her and have all of her. The pictures hadn't lied about what was in his heart, although they had misrepresented what they'd eventually not done.

"The truth is," he continued, "we were feeling stir crazy after being trapped inside the castle for days and decided to break out and go for a walk. The swimming was on a whim, and the kiss was between friends and never went any further than that. They can believe it or not. The key is, after things ease up and Jacob and I work out our relationship, which could be just a matter of a few days, I'll be returning to Maryland and you'll be going your own way. Then no one will have anything to whisper about."

Elly looked at him, wide-eyed, as if turning his words over in her mind. "That's true," she murmured, tossing back the bedclothes and standing up beside the bed. "It will be over." She sounded more than a little sad at the thought, but he couldn't be sure that he wasn't reading his own feelings into her words.

"So what do you say we take my plan to Jacob?" he asked.

She shook her head and paced away from him. "He flew to Vienna yesterday…some sort of economic meeting with heads of state from a handful of other European countries. But I think he's supposed to be back tomorrow afternoon."

"Good, we'll hold down the fort until then and fine-tune my plan."

He caught her looking at him, and there was a tenderness in her expression that took him by surprise. "What are you thinking?" he asked softly.

She reached out slowly, as if some inner spirit had possessed her and she was no longer in control of her actions. Her fingertips brushed the short hairs in front of his ear. "You'll make a wonderful father."

He laughed, not understanding. "Huh?"

"You never stay angry, and you work out problems. Your children will feel secure, knowing you will be fair and not blame them for their mistakes. And they'll understand that you will always be there for them, to help them solve their problems. Pretty important dad stuff."

His eyes latched onto hers. A woman who understood a man's need to be gentle, lenient, fair and protective of his children was rare indeed. But there was also his need to know her, completely. He wanted to touch her mind, understand the demons that stood in the way of her trusting him, and find a way to work around them. He ached to bring her peace.

Then somehow, all those charitable feelings took a sudden, unexpected twist, and he found himself overcome by a primitive male urge to seize her and make love to her despite her earlier rejections. He hated himself for feeling that way, for even considering taking her against her will. But the primal hunger was there beneath the civilized man, as it was in every male. The heat in his loins grew and a pounding in his head blocked out rational thought. The muscles in his arms ached, and even as he looked down at her he could feel what it would be like to seize her and possess her as he had in a thousand dreams.

The only thing that separates us from animals is our ability to choose not to act, he reminded himself, fiercely holding back.

"What's wrong?" she asked, stepping closer to him and studying his expression with concern as her fingertips grazed his cheek. Her nightgown clung to her slim body, revealing too much, or not enough...he couldn't decide.

Had he spoken out loud? "Nothing," he said, turning away from her. Then something made him change his mind. "Damn it, Elly, it *wasn't* nothing."

He gripped her shoulders, and her still-raised hand dropped from his cheek to his chest as her mouth opened in surprise. "I've wanted you since the day we met. I've let you know how deeply you move me, how special I think you are. But you hold me at arm's length then turn me away. If you feel nothing for me, just say so. I won't bother you again."

She stared up at him, her lower lip trembling. "Dan, please. You know it's not like that."

"How is it then?" he demanded, fighting the impulse to throw her down on the bed. "You know I won't let you get pregnant if that's not what you want. Don't you trust me?"

''I do...'' She began to sob as her eyes filled with tears. ''Of course I trust you. I just. I *can't*...don't you see?'' She couldn't get the words out for her gulping sobs.

''No, I don't see, obviously. Here is a man who wants the woman standing before him, and a woman who is so in need of a good man in her life she quivers when he comes too close. *We want the same thing, Elly!*''

''No! No, we don't!'' She shook her head violently, trying to step away. But he held her firmly by the arms, not allowing her to retreat. ''We've gone over this before. It's not just about now, this minute, this hour in our lives...it's about the future. I know what my limits are, and I've learned to accept them. I'll never be able to give you what you want, a child. Perhaps more than one. Let's not fool ourselves.'' She stared up at him, her eyes shimmering pools. ''Please. If I can be strong enough to walk away from you, feeling as close to you as I do right now, you can certainly be strong enough to *let* me walk away.''

With a lump in his throat he released her, but only to let her move two steps away from him before grabbing her hand and tugging her back to face him. He stepped up to within inches of her. ''I'm not that strong.''

She shook her head, tears clinging to her lashes. ''Oh, Dan.''

He cradled her against his chest. ''Let's not try to map out our entire lives in one night. Life never turns out as we expect anyway, does it?''

She moved her head again, more softly, less frantically, her lips brushing the fabric of his shirt. ''No, it doesn't.''

"So, Miss Anderson, tell me this…" He took a deep breath, risking all. "For the next few hours, do you think we could give each other what we most desire just *at this moment* and not think about the past or about some time years down the line?"

She didn't answer immediately, and a white-hot stab of fear shot through him. Then her whisper soothed him. "I'd like to try."

His heart soared and, to his consternation, his body responded with energy. If she felt his hardness between them, she gave no indication, unless the slightly amused tilt of her smile was for that reason.

Dan slowly lowered his head and kissed her deeply, holding back none of his passion. Before, he'd never been sure that she felt as much for him as he felt for her. But now the commitment seemed equal. They were partners in an act of love, neither one aggressor or victim, seducer or seduced. They stood on even ground and that pleased him. Their pact made it possible for him to forget, for the time being, the family he might have to wait longer for or never have. And their agreement apparently made it possible for her to make love with him without guilt for depriving him of his dream or threatening her life.

They would keep each other safe and they would pleasure each other, and to hell with anything else.

Her lips opened willingly to his. As he moved his hands over her body he gave silent thanks for having picked up his wallet when he'd left his room an hour earlier. For there was the key to Elly, the condom he would willingly wear to reassure her that she was safe with him.

In fact there was more than one in there. Who knew what had possessed him to jam two long strips into the thin leather tri-fold, but he'd been in a rush while packing and perhaps he'd had a momentary crazed vision of dark-eyed foreign women throwing themselves at him as he stepped off the plane in Paris, so there they were. He was just glad he had ample protection because he had a feeling they might need every one of them.

He pulled three foil packets from his wallet and placed them in clear view on the night table. Elly blushed as her eyes rested on them.

''You're beautiful when you're embarrassed,'' he whispered. ''Let's see if we can embarrass you some more.''

She looked up at him with a slightly dazed expression as he kissed her again and slipped the straps of her nightgown off her shoulders and down her arms. The garment slid from her body to the floor in a puddle of pale silk. She wore nothing beneath it and, although he'd known that would be so, the sight of her completely nude before him ripped the breath from his lungs. In the words of his city kids, she was awesome.

He sensed she had averted her eyes, and he lifted his gaze to her face and gently nudged her chin with his knuckles to make her look at him. ''Don't be ashamed of what we're doing.''

''I'm not…I'm—'' Her eyes blazed and her cheeks flushed a lovely dark color. ''I feel freed, I feel wonderful.'' She hesitated, looking suddenly shy again. ''Do you suppose we could even up the odds a little?'' Her eyes swept slowly down his shirt front to his pants.

He laughed, delighted with her. ''Yes, ma'am.'' He couldn't remember ever getting undressed quite as fast as he did that day. Within seconds he'd flung belt, pants, shirt, underclothes, shoes and socks into a heap.

He remembered thinking that first day they'd met on the beach that he'd have loved to have been swimming naked, just to see her expression. Now he received his reward for waiting. Her eyes were wide, glassy, and she kept passing the tip of her tongue over her lips as if they were parched by desert heat. Her hands clasped in front of her, and she tipped her head to one side, observing him critically, as if he were sculpture in a museum.

"So what's the verdict?" He stepped toward her.

"Not bad. Not bad at all." A smile teased the corners of her lips.

"That's all I get? A not bad?" he growled then grabbed her.

They fell onto the bed and Elly could no longer keep up her smug act. Her heart was pounding in her breast. Every nerve in her body tingled with anticipation. For the first time in her life, she was with a man who was about to make love to her, and the dark side of life seemed miles away. She thought of nothing but opening her body to Dan.

She kept her eyes open when he kissed her. She didn't want to miss a thing, and the sight of Dan was glorious, for he was sleek and muscled, and every angle and curve of his body was pure masculine poetry. When he lifted one arm to curl it around her and bring her closer to his chest, the muscles in his shoulder and biceps bunched just as they had when he stroked through the ocean. When he moved her into his chest, she lifted a finger to trace the conformation that might have been carved by a master sculptor. She marveled at each pale blue vein, each tiny mole, each sinew that swelled across his wide chest.

"You are amazing," she whispered. But when she

looked up, the cocky grin she imagined she'd find on his lips wasn't there. They were tightly pressed together as if he was concentrating on a matter of grave importance. And his eyes blazed. His gaze never seemed to move from her face, but she knew he was studying her entire body. The intensity made her shiver.

"Don't be afraid," he said.

"I'm not. I'm just waiting."

"Not for long." Now he did smile, but it was as much a warning as a promise of pleasure. It said, *Hold on tight, woman, here we go.*

He moved over her, supporting himself on one forearm while he caressed the soft swell of her hip. The muscles in her limbs grew rigid but in a most pleasant way. He smoothed his fingertips down the outside of her thigh then up the inside, toward the pulsing lips of her womanhood. Elly lifted herself to meet them, and he found her and pressed softly inward until she let out a little gasp of delight. His touch grew firmer, centering around her most sensitive area, circling, stroking, raising golden tongues of fire within her. Her head spun. Her limbs ached as she locked them against his body, and his fingers continued to work their magic.

She felt as if something snapped within her, something that was supposed to break—a bond, a chain tying her to the past. At a sudden rush of heat, she opened her mouth on a scream of ecstasy, but Dan cut it off with a plunging kiss. Delicious sensations burst through her with the brilliance of fireworks—dazzling, surprising her with their intensity. And all this from the mere touch of his hand.

Elly was aware of Dan shifting on the bed beside her, heard the sound of tearing foil and almost immediately he returned to her. She didn't have to look to know he had kept his promise. Nevertheless, he took her hand and gently guided it down along his body and folded her fingers around his sheathed shaft to reassure her.

"I know," she whispered. "I know."

He was over her now, sweeping her hair away from her face with both hands as he held his upper body over her on his elbows. Their hips pressed together. She felt the heaviness of his masculinity, the warm furriness of him against the tops of her thighs. Slowly she lifted her knees, parted herself and wrapped her legs around his hips to welcome him.

He only had to raise his own hips and move upward an inch to find her. Then with no effort at all, he entered her, filling her, it seemed, completely. The world hummed around her and her eyes closed on the blissful sensation of completion. As a woman, as a lover, as the giver of tenderness and passion that she had always longed to be.

But that blissful moment of peace lasted only seconds, for then Dan was moving within her, raising her with him to undreamed-of heights, cupping his palms beneath her bottom and lifting her hips to meet his thrusts as he delved deeper and deeper within her until she was sure there could be no more room for him. And Elly tightened around him, bursting with honeyed answer to his perfectly timed strokes, and she turned her face into the wiry fur of his chest and let out a smothered whimper of ecstasy that seemed to roll on forever.

At last Dan arched his body above hers, his eyes tightly shut, his face contorted in agonizing pleasure, as he pressed hard into her with a low groan of male satisfaction. He fell in exhaustion upon her, and she wrapped herself around him, holding him within her for as long as the silvery forever of one morning allowed.

Seven

Conversation around the breakfast table the following morning seemed distant and insignificant to Elly. Another day had passed but an invisible, golden thread still stretched between herself and Dan—and though no one in the dining room could see it, she knew it was there. A unique connection held her to the beautiful man who sat across the table from her.

Dan ate quickly, barely looking at her during the meal except for a single meaningful glance when no one else was looking. Then he excused himself and left the room. Shortly afterward, Elly bid her father, Madge, and Allison good bye for the rest of the day, saying she had work to finish and would spend the day at it, probably skipping lunch. Her father gave her a puzzled look but said nothing.

Elly was back in her room for only half an hour before Dan appeared, as she somehow knew he would.

The previous day, after they had parted, had been busy for both, and there had been no time when they could be alone.

Dan followed his own best advice: he focused on the moment. These precious few hours when Elly was his. If he just concentrated on the way she made him feel, he could forget about the mad twist of fate life had dealt him. Forget about the press and the public hysteria, which might do all sorts of damage to the Haven. Forget about how humiliating all of this was for his mother. Forget that each minute he held Elly might be their last together and certainly brought them closer to the time they must part.

He made love to her immediately on joining her in her room, then two more times during the long, lazy hours of the day in between conversations that covered everything from their childhoods to hopes for their careers, favorite colors, and most-beloved music, foods, and books. Then, at last, Elly looked up at him with smiling, misty eyes and said the abhorrent words, "We have to go down for dinner."

"Can't we ring for room service?" he begged.

"This isn't a hotel. Besides, I think someone might suspect something. Particularly after our much-publicized romp in the lake."

"Oh that." He groaned then pulled her close and whispered softly into her ear. "When we're together, all the bad stuff goes away. Doesn't it?"

"Yes. All of it," she murmured with a touch of amazement in her sweet voice.

His heart melted at the sincerity in her voice, for he knew the "bad stuff" for her had been very black indeed, the fear that had been her mother's unintended legacy to her. It seemed a miracle that she'd been able to leave those fears behind, at last, to be with him and him alone. No one else had been able to give her that. He felt empowered, as if he'd been singled out to perform this special task in her life.

"Come on," she said, leaving the bed to pull him to his feet. "Put some clothes on. With any luck, Jacob will have returned and you can explain your master plan to him."

Dan frowned. "Do you think he'll even listen? He hasn't exactly been a loving and compassionate brother."

She gave him a semi-severe look. "I haven't seen you falling over backward to please him either. There's definitely a family gene that leans toward stubbornness."

"You think so?"

"I know so. Now, dress!"

Dan took his place at the heavy wooden trestle table across from Allison with her two children on either side of her. Jacob had indeed returned and was at the head of the table, with his family to his right. Dan sat to his left, then came Elly, then Madge, with Frank Anderson sitting across from her.

Although seated beside Dan, Elly felt as if he was miles from her after the intimacy of the day and the night before. She cast him a longing look but snapped her eyes down to her plate when she felt her father's curious gaze on her.

Allison made small talk, asking how Jacob's trip had gone and he responded with vague observations. He looked distracted, and Elly saw him glance more than once at Dan, as if he wanted to say something but couldn't find the right words. Dan shot his brother worried looks, as if he too was searching for the right words. Tension slowly filled the room, like hot water being poured from a steaming pitcher.

Meanwhile a magnificent meal was being served. Each course was presented by Cook's competent kitchen staff. Elly was beginning to recognize them and learn their names. Rachel was very young, born in Elbia. She wore her hair in braids, looped up beneath a white cap. Friedrich was a tall, gaunt-looking man with gray hair and a stern demeanor that softened whenever his eyes came to rest on the little prince and princess. He had come from Vienna over thirty years ago to serve the von Austerand family. Maria was a dark, middle-aged Italian woman, chief assistant to Cook, who prepared many of the meals herself but insisted on overseeing the service to the family.

The other dining-room attendants rotated, according to the meal, but usually Elly recognized them. She studied a new man. He moved carefully about the room, ladling soup from a gilded porcelain tureen. Unlike the regulars, when he stood between two diners he served to the guest on his right then to the one on his left, rather than moving around the table to always serve toward the right as, she'd noticed, was convention. She glanced at Maria to see if she'd caught the minor slip in protocol, but she was turning back toward the kitchen.

It seemed an unimportant detail to Elly, yet something about the man felt not quite right to her. She turned toward Dan and found his gaze steadily on her. Frowning, she slid her eyes in the direction of the server, then gave Dan a questioning quirk of one eyebrow.

He followed her line of sight, watched the man for a moment, then shrugged.

He was right, it was probably nothing, she told herself. A hurried replacement by an inexperienced waiter. She turned her attention back to the conversation at the table.

Cray was babbling happily about his day's activities, everything from his adventures with learning to talk on the telephone to telling his father, the king, about his finger-painting exploits. "It was gooey and slippery, and all over the paper and table and floor and me!" he cried with delight. "Green and red and blue *everywhere!*" He waved his hands in the air to demonstrate the degree of delightful messiness he'd created. Everyone one at the table congratulated Cray on his artistic efforts.

As his mother was inviting all guests to come to the nursery for a viewing of his first exhibition, a motion just barely caught the corner of Elly's eye. She turned her head to follow it.

The new server stood beside the tall mahogany buffet along one side of the room, across from the little prince and princess. As Elly watched, he turned as though to shield something in his hand from view, and she heard a soft click.

Her breath caught in her throat. *What was he doing? What was he holding that he didn't want anyone to see?*

She reached out to touch Dan on the shoulder, but apparently he'd also been watching the man. Dan shot to his feet, knocking his chair backward with a crash to the floor. To the other guests' amazement, he launched himself across the room and, before the server could react, Dan had tackled the man and pinned him to the floor.

"Call your security!" he bellowed at Jacob.

The king didn't need to say a word. Three burly guards appeared within seconds in the dining room. Elly suspected cameras hidden somewhere in the room had caught the struggle.

There was pandemonium as Jacob jumped to his feet, Cray shouted out questions, Kristina started to cry and Frank Anderson glared in confusion at Dan as if he'd committed an act of terrorism. Elly could only stand by until things sorted themselves out.

Two of the guards relieved Dan of his prisoner while a third smoothly placed his body between the intruder and the royal family. Jacob, she'd noticed, had instinctively moved in front of Allison and the children, as if to shield them.

One of the guards removed a small, black object from inside the folds of the intruder's white smock.

"Is that a gun?" Madge gasped.

The guard held a miniature camera up for Jacob to see.

"I'm a respected member of the press!" the man shouted in English. An American, Elly thought with a sinking feeling in her stomach. This isn't good. "We have freedom of speech in my country—and that's personal property!"

Dan stood close by, glaring at the man. "You don't have the right to break into a man's home or terrorize his family, you idiot!"

But the guards were already dragging the man through a door and, in another minute, a shocked silence hung over those remaining in the dining room.

"Oh my," Madge breathed, pressing a hand to her heart.

"Are you all right?" Elly asked.

"Yes, I'm fine. It's the little ones I'm worried about." She looked at Cray and Kristina, the prince clinging to his mother's skirt, the baby in her arms.

"It's all right now," Allison said to her children comfortingly. "The stranger is gone now. I think we need some quiet time." She looked meaningfully at Jacob. He nodded. "Let's go have a story in your nursery. We'll ask Cook very nicely to bring our dessert to us there, for a special treat." The third guard automatically accompanied the queen and her children out of the dining room.

"I think I'll go to my room too," Madge murmured, looking shaken despite her denial. "I have a headache."

"That was quite a shock," Elly said. "You should rest for a while. Do you feel steady enough on your feet?"

"I'll manage," she said, but her smile seemed wobbly.

"I'll walk her back to her room," Frank said quickly, giving Dan a reassuring look.

Elly, Dan and Jacob were the only ones left in the room along with the disarray of a half-finished meal. Dan righted his chair. No one spoke for a long while, then it was Jacob who finally sat down heavily at the head of the table and looked up at the two Americans.

"That shouldn't have happened." He sighed. "Thank you."

"For what?" Dan asked simply. "It was just another reporter with a camera."

"It might have been something else." Jacob gave

his brother a long, grim look. "If that had been a gun, the guards would have spotted it and come in, but in the few extra seconds he could have gotten off a shot."

"Elly saw him first but I was closest to him. No big deal."

"But you put your life in jeopardy for my family," Jacob insisted. "For all you knew he could have shot or stabbed you to get to me, or to my wife and babies. You didn't hesitate. I will never forget this. Never." He stared hard at Dan with an electric intensity that crackled around them.

Elly could feel the testosterone level in the room rise. This was male bonding at its best. She would have smiled if the circumstances had been different. "What will happen to the man?" she asked.

Jacob shrugged. "Not much. We'll hold him for a few days, put the fear of God in him. His newspaper will protest. The U.S. Embassy will appeal to us. Then we'll allow your government officials to escort him out of the country." He gave her a funny look. "Did you expect me to lock him away in the dungeon for eternity?"

She laughed. "Something like that, I suppose. Your Highness—" she hesitated "—this has to stop."

"Yes," he agreed. He looked at Dan. "I respect your reasons for not wanting to release your claim to my father's name...*our* father's name. And I understand why you won't accept a financial settlement. In your shoes, I would feel much the same way." Maria stepped gingerly into the room, but Jacob waved her off. "That leaves us in an awkward situation, though. I don't know what to do now."

"I have an idea," Dan said, slowly lowering himself

into the chair nearest Jacob's. "I thought of it yesterday and wanted to talk to you then, but you weren't here."

Jacob nodded. "Go on."

Elly crossed her fingers for Dan. Jacob was listening with guarded interest, but there was no guarantee he'd agree to Dan's strategy.

"Maybe we've been going at this all wrong," Dan started. "By trying to hide the truth and giving the press no facts at all, we've only made them more intrigued with the possibilities. They smell scandal and won't let up until the story seems no longer interesting to them. As long as we remain silent, they'll invent new and provocative stories to suit their readers' curiosity."

"Let me understand this…you think we should find a way to *bore* them?" Jacob gave a weary smile. "Difficult to do, brother, for people like us. We announce a vacation to Australia, and it becomes a mission of political importance. When Allison purchased a new bed for Cray, half the mothers in Europe bought the same brand for their toddlers."

"Not bore them…*defuse* them. Call a press conference, make it open to anyone. We'll issue a joint statement saying that you and I are in complete accord. I'm thrilled to have found my father's family, and you're overjoyed to have located your long-lost brother."

Jacob rolled his eyes. "Laying it on a little thick, aren't we?"

Dan shrugged. "We have to put a positive spin on this. I'll accept the monetary settlement, but it will be on behalf of my mother, for her future care, and for my City Kids program. That portion will be used to build and support a year-round camp for kids at risk who need to be pulled off the street and given a safe place to be for a while.''

Jacob looked interested. ''And what about the throne? You are older than I by several months. By rights, even though my father and your mother weren't married, you are the first heir.''

Dan shook his head. ''I wouldn't want your job for anything, bro'.''

Elly smiled at the slang, which also brought a wry twitch to Jacob's lips.

''There are some definite advantages,'' Jacob said, lifting a hand to indicate the grandeur of this single room among the hundreds of richly appointed rooms in the castle.

''This wouldn't make me happy,'' Dan said. He shot a look at Elly, and she blushed. ''Other things are much more important to me. I'll sign a release relinquishing all rights to my royal status. If the Duke of Windsor could do it, so can I.''

Jacob's eyes remained steadily on Dan, as if reassessing him. ''And there is nothing else you ask?''

''Not a blamed thing.''

Elly felt so proud of Dan. She stepped to his side and touched him on the arm to tell him so.

''It's a good plan, but I think we can improve on it,'' Jacob mused, leaning back into his chair and spearing a piece of asparagus with his fork. ''We will have the press conference and announce everything just as you have suggested. But—'' he pointed the fork tines at Dan for emphasis ''—the announcement will be made at a grand ball, in your and your mother's honor.''

Dan looked worried. ''I don't think that's necess—''

''Humor me,'' Jacob said, straightening in his chair.

"I don't often get a chance to outwit our aggressive brothers in the paparazzi. If we are to convince them that I am welcoming the cherished lost branch of my family, then we must make a grand show of it. As you've said…a positive spin to beat all positive spins."

Elly grinned. "I think it will work, Dan. Really."

Jacob looked as if he was enjoying the game. "Instead of a rivalry, they will witness brothers helping each other and celebrating their finding each other. Then, to further distract the press, we will invite so many celebrities they won't know who to focus on. The truth about my father's long-ago affair and Daniel Eastwood's birth will seem far less interesting to them."

Dan looked thoughtful. Then he turned to Elly with a questioning look.

"Go for it," she said. But she couldn't help adding wickedly, "Although I can't imagine shooting pictures of you if Tom Cruise were in the room."

"Thanks," Dan said dryly. He turned back to his brother. "Make a note not to invite Mr. Cruise."

As soon as the announcement of the ball was made, Allison requested the services of her favorite seamstress.

"It must be wonderful to have someone who can make anything you want to wear," Elly commented wistfully as she sat in the nursery playing with Kristina the day the dressmaker arrived.

"It's actually a very practical and cost-effective arrangement," Allison said. She was chasing Cray around the room with a hair brush in hand. He was at the stage where he didn't like to be fussed over, and hair brushing was the worst sort of torture as far as he was concerned. "I know many women of the aristocracy who wouldn't wear anything less than couturier. Helena knows my taste exactly and will make me a one-of-a-kind gown or traveling suit for a fraction of the cost of a Parisian design.''

Elly laughed. ''You watch your clothing budget that closely? Why, with all the money floating around this place?''

Allison shrugged. ''Habit, I suppose. For a long time I had to pinch pennies just to support myself and Cray on a librarian's income. That was before his father came back into our lives. But I also think it's obscene to spend a fortune on clothing when the money could go toward helping people who really need it.''

Elly looked with admiration at the young American who had so recently become queen of the little country. She had grace, goodness and beauty. ''I think that's wonderful,'' she murmured. ''So what is Helena making for you this time?''

''Nothing, actually,'' Allison replied, winking at Helena as the woman unpacked her measuring tapes, notepad and swatches of fabric. ''She's come to fit you.''

''Me?''

''I doubt you came prepared with formal wear, given your hasty escape from the States.''

''That's true, but—''

''And with the paparazzi still guarding the castle gates, it's impractical for you to consider going into town to shop for a dress. Of course, if you really insist, we could airlift you in the helicopter to Vienna, but that's just as expensive as Paris these days.''

''Oh, no!'' Elly protested. ''I don't want to put you to any trouble. Frankly, I hadn't even thought of a dress. I'm just glad that Jacob and Dan seem to be working together now instead of fighting.''

"I am too," Allison admitted, finally tackling Cray and bringing him kicking and squirming into her lap.

After a while, Gretchen, the children's nurse, relieved the two women of the little ones so that they could concentrate on a gown for Elly. She chose a pale green silk to compliment her red hair, with cream-colored lace trim. After admiring Allison's closet-full of gowns with full, bouffant skirts, she worked out a very different, fitted design with Helena that started in a strapless bodice, clung to her waist and hips, then tapered to the floor in the back. In the front, the skirt was cut nearly as high as her knees to reveal her shapely legs. It was a sophisticated, sensual style that made her feel as elegant as any princess.

In a separate wing of the castle, Jacob met with Dan to discuss the details of their statement to the press. Dan listened to the wording Jacob's secretary had drafted and read aloud to them, his fingers peaked before his lips in concentration. Three other advisors, a woman and two men, also listened in, taking notes, looking terribly serious. The tension in the room was thick, and no one spoke until the reading was finished.

Then, in the silence, everyone looked at Jacob for a reaction. "I have no objection to anything there," he said slowly. "I believe we've covered it all—the surrender of claim on the throne, the compensation...which I hope is sufficient?" He turned to Dan.

"It's more than generous. I didn't expect that much."

"No more than your mother deserves," Jacob said, his voice sounding husky with emotion. "I'm just sorry that it comes so late to her. As to your share for the children's program, I wanted to add more than we'd initially discussed. By creating an annuity for your City Kids, you'll be able to operate freely for a longer period of time. I expect it will become self-perpetuating.''

Dan was moved. "Thank you for thinking of that. I wouldn't have."

Jacob nodded, looking satisfied. "Does anyone have any objections or problems with the draft?"

His advisors closed their notebooks and the gaunt, gray-haired one cleared his throat. "*Nein,* Your Highness.''

"Then print it up in final form, will you, Wilhelm? We'll get on with plans for the ball."

Dan sat with Jacob through the remaining meetings of the day at the king's invitation, although he felt of little use. Still, it seemed to be something Jacob wanted him to do—as if he was trying to include Dan in this official part of his life to make up for their earlier quarrels. As he heard Jacob negotiate with his cabinet, then his household staff, and finally with his social secretaries each element of the next few weeks' activities, he found himself more and more amazed by how hard Jacob worked and how sharply he focused on details. And through it all, Jacob listened attentively to suggestions and never dismissed anyone's ideas as without worth. He was a fair, generous and intelligent ruler, and Dan began to feel pride growing inside for this brother he'd never known he had.

As the night of the ball approached, excitement mounted in the castle. Elly felt it in the kitchens as Cook organized her army of assistants, some of them gifted chefs in their own right. A menu was designed and vast quantities of ingredients ordered. Supplies arrived daily and were added to the immense walk-in refrigeration units in the castle's cellar. Wines were delivered by the case. And as the day neared, the fresh vegetables and meats came by the truckload.

Then there were the candles, by the hundreds, placed in sconces high on the stone walls of the immense ballroom. Banners were brought out of storage and cleaned to be ready for hanging. Flags of the attending nations were mounted in long rows leading from the castle gate through the courtyard and up to the front entry. Tables seemed to sprout from nowhere and were positioned along with chairs below the raised dais where the royal family would be seated. Elly's heart raced with anticipation.

And every night, Dan came to her room. They lay together on her bed and discussed the day's events. They laughed at the antics of the little prince and princess, and admired Jacob and Allison for their grace in handling what could have become an endless battle with the paparazzi. But after the talk and laughter, they made long, delicious love.

The one thing they never discussed was the future, for it was still forbidden ground. Nothing that Elly could see had changed in Dan's desire to have a family or her need not to have one. Although she thought about offering to adopt a baby with him, she sensed that this would be a terrible disappointment to a man who was capable of producing his own children. At times she felt so inadequate that she cried silently into her pillow after he had fallen asleep. When all was said and done, she knew that if the brothers' plan worked it would mean the end of her relationship with Dan. For leaving Elbia would mean losing Dan to his future bride, the mother of his children, whoever she might be.

Eight

The night of the ball, the castle was ablaze with lights, and the delectable aromas of a hundred different foods wafted from the kitchens and through the halls. Dan and Elly had discussed the evening's escort arrangements. Elly had told Dan he should really accompany his mother and she would enter the grand ballroom on her father's arm.

"But I get the first waltz," he had insisted.

"Definitely…well, unless Tom shows up…" Her eyes twinkled mischievously.

"Cruise?"

"You got it."

He laughed at her. "Deal."

But when he left his room dressed in the tuxedo Jacob had lent him, since they were nearly identical in size, he turned down the hallway toward Madge's room and saw two figures leaving it.

"Hey there, you stealing my girl?" he shouted, laughing.

"Sure thing, what you gonna do about it?" Frank Anderson retorted. He grinned at Madge. "Doesn't this young man of yours have a date of his own?"

"I know we discussed going together, Danny," she said coyly. "But Frank thought it might be nice if you two children went as a couple, then we could…"

"I get the picture," Dan grumbled, as if disappointed, although he definitely was not. "This is a setup."

Frank shrugged. "You two seem to be spending a lot of time together." He gave Dan a long look, as if for the first time considering the younger man's intentions toward his daughter. "We thought you and Elly might appreciate making your entrance together, if only to stir up the press one last time."

Dan hesitated, feeling awkward. "I hope you don't have a problem with my seeing your daughter, sir. She's a wonderful woman, and I have only the best intentions toward her."

"No problem," Frank said gruffly. He offered his arm to Madge and she slipped her hand through the crook. "I just don't want to see Elly get hurt. You wouldn't do anything to harm her, I know. Would you, son?"

There was grit underlying the man's polite tone, and his pale eyes hardened for just an instant. Dan suspected Madge, who was preoccupied with arranging the folds of her gown, wasn't in a position to see them. But he read Anderson's look as a warning.

"I would never do anything to hurt Elly," Dan stated firmly, meeting her father's gaze. "Never."

Frank nodded and his smile returned, all signs of a

storm gone. "I was sure that was the case. Why don't you go fetch her now? She must be anxious to join the party."

"Yes, sir, I will." Dan stood in the middle of the long stone corridor and watched his mother and Frank walk away, chatting amicably. The excitement for the evening had left him. He felt a chill through his bones as he replayed Elly's father's words.

Frank hadn't threatened him by any stretch of imagination. What he'd done was merely place a sobering thought before him. Which was that, just by encouraging Elly's affections, he was laying the foundation for breaking her heart. Because they both knew that, as hard as she'd tried to deal with her fears, ultimately nothing had changed. Their relationship existed only on a day-to-day basis. No commitment to the future existed.

Feeling far less festive, Dan walked slowly along the guest wing and stopped in front of Elly's door. The same door he'd entered with his spirits joyfully sailing many nights before this one. Now the ship of his heart was dragging the bottom of a dark cove, and he had to haul himself up out of the depths of his depression to put on a smile when he knocked on Elly's door. He wouldn't say anything to her about his discussion with her father. That would only upset her, and he wanted the little time they had left together to be happy. He could at least give her sweet memories.

He knocked.

"Come on in, Dad!" she called through the door.

"It's not Dad," he responded, forcing cheer into his tone. He stepped inside. "The senior branches of our families have run off without us. We'll just have to—"

He broke off, stunned then mesmerized by the vision before him.

For the next two minutes, Dan felt incapable of speech. He barely breathed and nearly tripped over his own feet. Elly stood shimmering in the light from a tall antique bronze floor lamp. The pale green of her dress appeared as light as sea foam, and the gleam of her red hair, piled loosely on top of her head, might have been a flame for the fire it ignited in his loins. A gold choker clasped around her throat was centered by an outrageously large emerald.

"Lord but you're beautiful, woman."

She smiled. "That's the sort of reaction I like from a man. What were you saying?"

"Your father and my mother have run off to the ball together. I'm to escort you." He moved closer and gave her a playful leer. "Lucky me."

She ducked away from his reaching hands. "We don't have time for that now," she said, laughing.

"I just want to feel the fabric."

"Right."

"Honest."

"I think we'd better save all that feeling stuff for later. Jacob expects us downstairs for the receiving line at exactly eight o'clock, and it's— Oh my gosh, it's seven-forty-five now!"

Elly snatched a silk shawl from the back of a chair, gave her hair one final glance in the mirror, and whisked past Dan. He dove in front of her to swing the door open a fraction of a second ahead of her. Shutting it behind him, he quickly caught up with her to offer his arm.

"Slow down." He laughed and patted her hand where it rested on the ebony sleeve of his jacket.

"Nothing's going to happen until we get there. They won't even open the castle gates to guests until eight."

"I'm just worried about what will happen once the press arrives. You and Jacob seem so sure that everything will be fine, but isn't this like inviting foxes into the hen house?"

"You think they will find some way to use the ball to make things even worse for Jacob?"

"Or for you. Yes, it could happen. There always seems to be an angle they can manipulate to create the appearance of scandal."

Dan frowned. "I've wondered about that too. But we've come this far and there's no turning back with over five hundred guests about to fill the ballroom."

From the far end of the corridor, bright lights flickered and glowed, and an orchestra played. Elly drew a deep breath and entered the immense hall on Dan's arm. She knew she should have been praying that everything would work out that night as planned. Instead, she felt a deep sadness because, if all did go well, this night would mark the end of everything the two of them had shared. It was one thing to sleep with Dan for a few days or even weeks, secure in the knowledge that she couldn't become pregnant because they were being careful each and every time. It was another to remain in a long-term relationship that he might try to alter to meet his desire for a family. He was single-minded and stubborn enough a man to think he might succeed.

Elly's heart fluttered with emotion as they crossed the ballroom toward the royal couple of Elbia, bedecked in jewels and formal regalia. She tried to focus on the next few hours, which would be so important to all of them.

Jacob wore the legendary von Austerand crown, and Allison a diamond-and-sapphire necklace that set her eyes sparkling. But all Elly could think as she took step after step toward them was that the man at her own side, whose arm she now leaned on, the same man who had wrapped his arms around her in passion, would soon leave her. She almost wished the brothers' plan would fail, compelling Dan and her to stay shut up in the castle another week...a month...an eternity. But she knew that was foolishness. Nothing she could do would delay their inevitable parting.

Conversely, she had never felt as close to any man as she felt to Dan. Letting him go would be the most difficult and painful thing she'd ever done.

When they at last stopped in front of the royal couple, Elly curtsied to Allison and Dan made a real bow to his brother. "Looks like you have a good turnout," Dan commented to Jacob, keeping his voice low.

"Indeed." Jacob lifted one coal-black eyebrow. "The question now is, will they be satisfied with the show we have to offer them?"

Dan took his place in the receiving line to Jacob's left, and Elly stood beside Dan. She looked around the vast hall but couldn't find her father or Dan's mother among the guests slowly entering through the three sets of soaring doors at the far end. She hoped that Madge hadn't succumbed to last-minute jitters and decided not to come. On the other hand, her father could be very persuasive when he wanted to be. She would leave that worry to him.

"By the way," Jacob said, slanting a mysterious glance at his queen, "we've discovered the culprit who leaked news of our brotherhood to the press."

"You have?" Dan asked, suddenly alert.

Elly leaned forward to listen. Whoever it was, she was sure Jacob would fire him or her immediately for such a serious breach of trust.

"Yes," Allison said solemnly, although her eyes twinkled as if she were secretly amused. "It seems that Cray's fascination with telephones is to blame. Gretchen told me that she was changing the baby one day when the phone rang and Cray picked it up. She didn't think anything of it at the time, believing he was talking to me or Jacob."

"Apparently, the switchboard operator had meant to connect a reporter to our public relations office, but in error rang the nursery," Jacob explained. "Cray launched into one of his usual chummy conversations that encompass everything from what he had for breakfast to parroting things he's overheard his parents talking about."

Allison rolled her eyes in motherly exasperation. "Gretchen remembers him saying something about his daddy having a big brother in America. But by the time she took the phone from him the caller had hung up. Whoever it was, he must have rushed straight off to chase down more leads."

Elly laughed out loud. "Oh no!" She looked at Dan, who was shaking his head in amazement.

"True," Allison said. "I think we're going to have to monitor the young man's calls until he learns that gossiping to strangers is different from talking with family members."

A burst of motion erupted near the immense central doors, interrupting the group's shared amusement. A dozen photographers broke through a line of dignified couples who had been approaching the dais. They rushed across the ballroom, cameras clutched in front of them, brushing roughly between guests who stared with irritation at them. Elly looked on helplessly as Jacob's security team closed ranks in front of the receiving line.

"Nein!" Jacob said, his voice sharp. "Let them through."

"They can wait until the formal announcement," Dan suggested gruffly.

"No. We might as well let them take their shots."

Elly stood nervously at Dan's side as the paparazzi's cameras flashed and whirred, and some of them shouted questions at the king and his brother. Jacob answered in a controlled voice for both of them. "It's only fair that we wait until everyone is here, gentlemen and ladies of the press. If any questions aren't answered when I make my statement, you'll have time to ask then."

Dan stood stiffly and nodded his agreement.

Elly scanned the room and finally spotted her father leading Madge their way. She caught his eye and shook her head subtly, warning him off. She didn't want Madge to be caught in the barrage of camera-wielding reporters.

Then her gaze skipped to a newly arrived party—a famous Italian actress and her movie-producer husband, accompanied by an entourage of three other couples. One man she recognized as a British soccer champion, another an American actor who had just won an academy award. The women with them looked so familiar, she was certain she must have seen them in recent movies. An idea struck her.

"Oh!" she cried out excitedly, tugging on Dan's arm. "Isn't that Maria Stanza!"

In a single wave of motion the photographers swiveled in the direction Elly was pointing. A second later, the entire press corps was dashing across the room, dodging past less notable guests to reach their new quarry. Flashes exploded, questions were shouted, but they were all aimed at someone other than the royals.

Allison glanced down the line toward Elly and smiled appreciatively. Jacob's expression hadn't altered, but his vivid blue eyes appeared relieved.

"Very smooth," Dan commented in her ear, giving her a quick squeeze.

Elly grinned. It looked as if Miss Stanza was enjoying the attention, and her friends were getting some welcome publicity as well.

After the receiving line disbanded, the guests danced to an orchestra that alternated Viennese waltzes with classic love songs and modern tunes. The press was kept busy recording the images and words of distinguished politicians, sports figures, and entertainment industry stars. It was ten o'clock before Elly knew it, then the music stopped and Jacob stood on the dais to make his speech.

The crowd's chatter gradually hushed and everyone looked up at the young king.

Jacob welcomed everyone in German, then in French, and finally in English, which was the language in which he chose to make his statement:

"Ladies and gentleman, I thank you for your attendance," he said solemnly. "I intend to keep this very short. Most of the information you require for your articles is contained in the detailed press release that you are about to receive. It includes a complete history of my father's relationship with a lovely woman by the name of Margaret Eastwood, before his marriage to my mother. This relationship had been kept a secret by my father and Ms. Eastwood in order to protect all involved parties. My mother never knew of it, and neither did I until recently.''

Jacob drew a deep breath and looked around the silent room. ''It is with great pride that I welcome my brother Daniel Eastwood to our country. He has become a friend to me personally and to my family during his stay with us. We value him as a strong addition to our family.''

Hushed voices rose from the crowd as guests looked at one another in surprise. But Jacob didn't pause.

''Although Daniel has a right to claim the throne of Elbia as his own, being the older of my father's only two children, he has elected to pass that right to me. For that I am grateful, I wish to continue serving my people as their king. Daniel has in no way been forced to this decision, and has asked nothing for himself. But it is only fair that his mother be compensated for the years she spent raising my father's son, my brother, on her own. And I believe my brother himself should receive some benefit as well.''

Elly glanced at Dan. He seemed to be concentrating very hard on Jacob's words. She caught a worried look in his eyes.

''What's wrong?'' she whispered.

''He's changed the speech we agreed on. I'm not sure what he's up to.''

Elly felt a warning chill climb her spine. Would Jacob dare to double-cross Dan in some way? If so, before all of these people there would be little Dan could do about it.

Jacob continued. ''My brother is a man of pride and many talents, not the least of which is the talent to share with the less fortunate. He would have left Elbia with nothing for himself, with only a small grant for his favorite charity. But I have decided that that is not enough."

Dan's face flushed, and Elly was sure he was about to protest, but a quick devilish smile from Jacob seemed to confuse him long enough to make him hesitate and say nothing for the moment.

"The crown has decided to give a sum of three million dollars to City Kids beach program in the form of an annuity in Daniel Eastwood's name. The interest earned by this annuity will enable the program to thrive independently of future donations. In effect, it will be self-perpetuating beyond the life of its founder."

Elly swallowed. She had never expected such a generous settlement, and when she turned to see Dan's reaction she could see how moved he was. The redness of his face had faded, but now he seemed in shock.

After the applause of the crowd died down, Jacob continued in a strong and calm voice. "There is, however, one more wrong that must be righted. An endowment of honor that cannot be ignored. I'm sure my father would have wanted to do this himself, if he were alive today…so it remains to me." Jacob's and Dan's eyes met. The first giving nothing away to the second. "My brother, though we did not share the same mother, might have been a king but for his fairness and generosity. If he is not to be king, he can be no less than a prince. Certainly not in my family's eyes. Therefore, I hereby endow Daniel Robert Eastwood with the honorary title of Prince of the Realm."

The room stood in stunned silence for two entire seconds, then broke into applause and shouts of "Long live Prince Daniel!" Champagne circulated on trays around the room, music played and guests laughed and shouted in approval. In the mayhem, Dan turned to Jacob.

"You couldn't leave well enough alone, could you?" he grumbled.

"It wouldn't have been right, *mein Bruder*," Jacob said.

Dan nodded. "You know, I'll never live this prince thing down back on the streets of Baltimore."

"I expect not." Jacob smiled. "All the more pleasure for me to have given you the title."

"Some brother you are."

"And you!" Jacob responded, slapping him soundly on the back.

The night was a dazzling success after that. An hour later, most of the press suddenly departed, rushing to file their stories with their papers and magazines, hoping to get a jump on their rivals. Although they might rearrange facts to spice up their stories, Jacob and his advisors seemed satisfied that the final outcome would be relatively tame. Besides, there had been bigger game afoot in the form of the celebrities they'd photographed and interviewed. With only so much space in each publication, it seemed a sure thing that Maria Stanza's rumored affair with her chauffeur would attract far more attention than Jacob's peaceful welcome of his brother.

The evening flew past in a whirl of color, music and laughter once the paparazzi had departed. The guests began to relax and enjoy one another's company. Old friendships were renewed; new ones begun. Although English was spoken by nearly everyone and Elly was comfortable speaking with people from all over Europe, there were snatches of a dozen other languages to be heard among the guests. Laughter and dance were the universal languages, though, and she found herself to be a popular partner. For nearly two hours she danced every dance with some of the most charming men of all ages she could ever hope to meet.

But not one of them made her heart sing as it did when Dan's eyes met hers across the vast, crystal chandeliered room and his hand rose toward her at the first strains of the Blue Danube waltz, inviting her to join him. They met in the middle of ballroom, and he lifted her right hand delicately in his left, placed his right palm at the small of her back, and smiled down at her.

Her heart melted as they circled the room. Suddenly, it seemed the hundreds of guests around them simply evaporated into the air, and she was floating, the soles of her satin slippers barely whisking across floor. The pale green silk of her gown swooshed around her ankles. His wide tuxedoed shoulders leaned into each turn as they spun. Ceiling-high mirrors flashed past them. Marble walls seemed to dissolve into sugary-white clouds. It was a night for fantasies, a night when nothing could go wrong.

"You're not a bad dancer, Mr. Eastwood," she teased. "For a swimmer, that is."

"You're no stumbling Jane yourself." His dark eyes studied her approvingly, then he gave her a sexy smile. "For a nosy little bookworm, that is."

She pouted at him. "Does that mean I'm forgiven for intruding on your peaceful beach-town existence?"

"Forgiven totally," he murmured. "And then some."

She felt herself blushing at the intensity of his gaze as they whirled to the romantic strains of the violins. "What does that mean?"

"I'll be eternally grateful to you for bringing me and

Jacob together. He's a great man, and I expect we will become close friends over the years.''

''I'm glad everything has worked out between the two of you.'' And she meant it wholeheartedly.

''There's more,'' he said, his voice lowering solemnly. ''I'm thankful I've had the chance to know you, Elly. We're very different people, and learning about each other hasn't been easy at times. But I'll never forget the special moments we've shared.''

''Like this one?'' she whispered, her voice trembling.

''Like this one. Yes.'' Then he held her closer, and they spun faster and faster until she was laughing from the sheer joy of being held in his arms and being part of these precious seconds in both of their lives.

It was after two a.m. when Elly walked to her room by herself, thinking about the night. She had left while Dan was still busy talking to Jacob because she wanted time to herself.

This is it, she thought. The end of a romance that had been fated to last no longer than a brief affair. There remained no reason for her to linger in Elbia. She didn't need her father's reminders during the evening that they had other jobs waiting for them at home. Jobs that had been hastily put aside until the missing von Austerand heir could be found. Well, now he had been found, and there was nothing more for her to do here...or in Ocean City to which Dan would be returning.

''Elly.''

She turned at the sound of her name echoing through the long passageway, and her heart swelled. She couldn't look at Dan, though. Her eyes fell to the stone floor, filling with tears. *Oh, damn,* she thought.

"What's wrong?" he asked, striding quickly along the corridor to join her. "The evening went very well, I thought."

"I'm happy that you and Jacob have reconciled your differences. Now it should be safe for you and your mother to return home."

"Then why the tears? It's us, isn't it?"

She nodded. "I should…*we* should never have gotten involved, knowing how different we are. Now it will be a hundred times harder to say good bye."

"Do we really have to say good bye?" he asked, tenderly touching a wide finger to her damp cheek. His eyes were too gentle, too full of emotion for her to meet them for more than a second.

"Yes," she said bravely. "We do. And you know why, so please don't ask for another round of explanations."

"You're everything I've ever wanted in a woman," he said forcefully.

"Everything except one."

"You might change your mind. With time."

She shook her head. "No. I've always known I would never have babies. It's part of who I am—this too-big heart. Just like my mother's." She gazed tearfully up at him. "I love kids, though, and if you ever consider adopting…well, maybe—"

The look on his face stopped the words that clogged up in her throat.

"I realize there are kids without parents and homes." He was angry now. She could hear it in his tone, which chilled her. "I try to help a lot of those kids, in my own way. But I want my own children too. Adoption isn't for me.''

She searched frantically for an area of compromise. ''Maybe a surrogate mother. Your genes would still—''

''Are you crazy, Elly?'' He seized her by the shoulders and shook her hard. ''Why would I want to impregnate another woman when I have you?''

She shrunk from his grasp. ''You don't *have* me. That's just it,'' she whispered hoarsely. ''Not if you intend to use me to produce your progeny like a living test tube.'' She ducked away from him when he tried to reach for her again.

''Elly, we can't just throw away these last few weeks. We've shared too much.''

''I'm not throwing them away!'' she shouted through her tears. ''I just want you to leave me alone. I can't do it! Don't you understand? I just can't do it, Dan!''

Sobbing, she broke for her door, shouldered it open then ran into her room. She didn't remember hearing the door close but it did, with the dull thud of finality a moment after she hit the bed at a run. Burying her face in a pillow, she wept bitterly. Mourning the loss of the only man she'd ever truly loved, mourning the loss of the children she might have had, if she'd had a normal heart and been strong enough, brave enough.

For a long time, she thought she was alone in the room, then she felt the bed ease down under the weight of someone sitting beside her.

''Don't say it,'' she choked out over the tears. ''It won't make any difference.''

''Say what?''

Had she guessed wrong? If so she was about to make a worse fool of herself. "Don't say that you love me."

"All right. I won't say it. And you needn't say it either."

"Yes," she said. "It's better that way."

He took a deep breath. "Will you at least take some time to think about your decision?"

"I've had plenty of time—years. Nothing has changed or ever will."

"Come with me to Maryland," Dan begged. "We can talk more."

She shook her head, fraught with pain. "There's no use prolonging the inevitable. It will be easier if I put you…put *us* behind me."

Dan wrapped his arms around her. "I promise, Elly. I won't let anything bad happen to you."

She pushed him away and glared into his eyes. "And you think my father wanted something *bad* to happen to my mother? He couldn't protect her when her heart gave out. How do you propose to protect me?"

He looked down at his hands in desperation. They both knew the answer. The only way he could shield her from her worst fear was by swearing they would never have a child together, and that was something he was unwilling to do. He'd never give up. He'd argue them both to exhaustion.

Her heart felt heavy in her chest, and hot, and her breaths came in shallow tugs as she took in the look of disappointment on his face. Even so, it couldn't outweigh her own regrets.

"So, this is the way we say our farewells?" he asked.

She reached out and touched his cheek, then laid her palm along the strong line of his jaw. "I'd rather say goodbye in a different way, if you still have—". Her eyes strayed to the bedside table drawer. "That is, if you still want to."

He nodded soberly. "I couldn't let you go any other way, Elly."

And she let him take her in his arms, believing beyond doubt that he would keep his word and hold her safe this one last time before they parted forever.

His gentleness moved her. Wherever Dan touched her, he touched with reverence and, although he never said the words, love was written in every caress, in every kiss, in every movement of his body over hers.

As Elly kissed him, she told herself over and over again, This is the last time I will ever feel this man's body next to mine, his weight on me, his power within me.

She cherished every second, branded her mind with each passionate touch of his hands, his lips. He slid his chest down over her breasts, and she closed her eyes and concentrated on the lovely rough texture of the curled hairs over the sensitive flesh of her nipples.

The heaviness and firm promise of his masculinity pressed against her thighs, and she gently lifted one leg to nudge him. Dan moaned softly, gripped her hand and guided it downward then wrapped her fingers around himself. She stroked him, memorizing the contours that mimicked velvet-over-fist hardness, and she ached to feel him inside her.

Still lower he moved until his lips grazed her breast, then teased first one then the other dark saucer of nipple to a tight, hard peak between the sharp edges of his teeth. She pressed herself upward against his mouth, wanting to remember even the muted twinges of pain along with the seething pleasure.

Elly gripped him harder, even as his hand slid between her thighs and found her warm center. Although she had been ready and eager for him from the moment he joined her on the bed, and he must have sensed as much, he slowly caressed her, at first with only the very tips of his fingers, then with more urgency, moving the length of his long fingers within her. Her eyes shot wide open as flames rushed through her and she clung to him, unsure she could survive another second yet greedy for more. Wave after wave of delicious heat seized her and she writhed with pleasure and called out his name, begging him not to stop. Ever. Ever.

Then his hands parted her thighs and she eagerly took him into her, savoring, dying with the fullness of him as he slid in and out of her, hitting all the most deliciously sensitive spots with each passage, driving her mad with ecstasy. And she knew there would never be another man like this one. Dan. Who had touched her so deeply but would soon leave her. So that when he at last thrust himself fully deep into her, filling her, completing her, and she knew from the iron tension of every muscle in his body that he was nearing the final moments before his own climax, she held on and wouldn't let herself release wholly until she could no longer control the crescendo of her passion. Then she gave herself over utterly to him, and they soared together, each one nourished by the other's rapture.

Dan reluctantly left Elly's bed, just long enough to dispose of the protection he'd worn. His body felt satisfyingly spent, but his heart was in shreds. Even as he'd made love to her, he'd been in agony. The knowledge that this was the end of all they'd been to each other, rather than the beginning of a long and happy life together, tore him apart. And so he wasn't thinking about what he was doing as he removed the condom, but something felt strange, and it occurred to him that he should pay attention. He thought he could feel the pad of his own finger against his thumb, where latex should have been.

He looked down.

It wasn't a large tear, but it was badly placed, near the tip of the sheath, and it seemed certain that the opening was large enough to have leaked. A hollow, gritty feeling settled in his stomach, and he felt a sudden lurch of desperation before he reminded himself of how slim the odds were that anything could have happened as a result of one unprotected incident.

He looked back through the open bathroom doorway to the bed where Elly lay, entwined in white sheets, her eyes closed, a sweet smile on her lips. He should tell her. But was there really any point in frightening her for no reason? This had been their last time, and it should be perfect for her. She was leaving him, and all he wanted was to let their good byes this night be as sweet as possible.

Let it be, a voice from inside whispered. And so, he did.

Nine

Elly woke to find Dan still beside her in the bed. For a moment, her heart soared as she reached out to stroke the fine, dark hairs in front of his ear. She rested her chin on the firm muscles of his shoulder and pressed her lips lightly to the side of his neck, now sexily rough with new whiskers.

She would miss this intimacy...miss Dan in any setting or context more than she could say. But it was clear he needed the family he had dreamt of for so long, and she was only in the way. There had never been any getting around that.

The tightness in her chest grew to a suffocating ache. Tears filled her eyes, blurring her vision of his long, strong body tangled in the sheets. She slowly lifted her hand away from his face and turned away to roll out of bed. The ache turned to a crushing pain that made it nearly impossible for her to straighten up or breathe as she walked into the bathroom. Grabbing blindly at a strip of toilet paper she dabbed at her eyes and choked back sobs, wishing for strength.

Leaving Dan…oh, how was she ever going to do it!

Furious with herself for breaking down, Elly tossed the soggy tissue at the little wastebasket beside the toilet and missed. She bent to scoop it up and, this time from a squat, placed it there, her eyes focusing hazily on a filmy object beside her tear-damp tissue.

Something was wrong.

She couldn't have said what, at first. The condom was an amorphous shape, just a lump really. But it suddenly appeared to her to have *two* open ends, which was, of course, impossible. She lifted it gingerly from the basket, thinking to prove her eyes were playing tricks on her. But when the thin layer of material lay in her palm, she could see a finger-width tear, and her heart felt as if it had stopped.

"No," she breathed. "Oh please, no."

Perhaps the thing had torn as Dan removed it? Yes, that must be it. If it had happened while they'd been making love and he'd realized the problem, he would have told her. She swallowed, staring down at her hand.

Or would he? What if it had torn and he'd known it then done nothing about it? He had been inside her when he'd climaxed. The condom would have been useless. Her stomach churned, and she pressed a hand to her abdomen, her head whirling.

Then a worse thought occurred to her, as if there could be anything worse than carrying the seed of her own demise within her. What if Dan had intentionally sabotaged his own protection?

He had often said that he was sure she'd adjust to

motherhood if she only let herself stop worrying. Might he have decided to impregnate her, believing she'd then be forced to accept her condition and have his baby?

If he had tricked her or intentionally deceived her, she could never forgive him. If his crime had been less, and he simply hadn't realized until he'd removed the condom that anything was wrong, he was still at fault. She had a right to know.

Elly dropped the useless thing back into the basket and slowly stood up. She felt dizzy, and the space behind her eyes burned hot with anger then ice-cold from terror. So many emotions boiled within her she didn't know if she'd be able to speak.

Hold on, she cautioned herself. *First, find out how much he knows.* At the very least he must have seen the hole, for he couldn't have removed it without noticing.

She walked stiffly back into the bedchamber, took her robe from the bedpost, slipped her arms into it and tied it tightly around her waist.

Dan rolled over and smiled at her. It took him a moment to realize that Elly was not smiling back. In fact, she looked downright grim, worse than grim...close to exploding. "What?" he asked.

"I want to know what happened last night," she said evenly, though he thought he heard the beginnings of tears behind her words.

He slid up in the bed, pushed a pillow behind his head and tested one of his best boyish grins on her. "I had hoped you would remember. My ego is shattered."

"Damn your ego, Daniel Eastwood!" she spat. "Tell me when it happened—before, during or after we made love."

His heart felt as if she was gripping it in her cold

little hand, and squeezing the life out of it. "What do you mean, *before?*"

"Then you know about the hole. Did you intentionally tear the condom we used last night?"

He was shocked. "Of course, I didn't. Why would I—" But the condemnation in her eyes said it all. "You seriously believe I would try to impregnate you against your will?"

"I don't know—you seem to want that family of yours awfully badly. How far would you go to have things your way?"

"Not that far. Never!" he roared, tossing back the bedcovers. "And I resent your implying—"

"I'm not implying anything," she interrupted, her voice snapping like a tempest-tossed arctic wave. "I'm accusing you straight out, Daniel."

"Well, you're wrong. I would never intentionally hurt you or force you to do anything you didn't want to do." He found his briefs on the floor and pulled them on. How could she even think…? Well, he had kept the truth from her, so he supposed she might assume the worst. "I didn't realize it was damaged until it was too late."

"And when was too late? Before or after you climaxed inside me?"

He held back his rage as best he could, but his face felt on fire and his fists clenched spastically at his sides. He wanted to hit something. Not *her,* but something. To break things and watch them splinter. To work out his fury in a physical way, because, damn it to hell, words certainly weren't getting through to her.

"It was too late *after* we'd made love and I was disposing of the condom!" he roared.

She blinked at him suspiciously. "You didn't realize it was torn until then?"

"No. Don't you think I would have stopped?"

"I don't know. Would you have?"

"Yes!" he bellowed without hesitation. He stepped toward her, but she backed away, suddenly looking frightened. "Listen, there was nothing I could do about it last night. Telling you then would only have upset you and—"

"And you don't think I'm upset now?"

He shook his head, at a loss for what to say to her. He was making a worse mess of this, but she wasn't making things any easier on him. "I don't think it's as bad as you might believe. The odds are so small. Where are you in your cycle?"

"Near the end," she admitted. "My period should start in just a few days."

"There. It's even better than I thought." He was trying to speak in a calming tone, but he still wanted to shout at her that she was panicking for no reason. "Let's not spoil last night by fighting."

She sighed, gnawed at her bottom lip and looked away from him. A tear slipped from beneath her eyelashes. "I just wish it didn't have to end this way."

He moved cautiously toward her. "It doesn't have to."

She squeezed her eyes shut and shook her head, looking miserable. "It does. It really does. I couldn't stand wondering if whatever we chose for protection on any given night had worked. Nothing is foolproof. Last night should be enough evidence of that."

"No guarantees," he murmured, his heart aching. "Not in any part of life." Of course he'd always known that. But now he couldn't even imagine the family he'd once hoped for. Because no woman other than Elly would ever feel right to him as the mother of his children.

Elly lifted a shoulder in silent agreement. No guarantees.

"How soon will you leave Elbia?" he asked.

"As soon as possible. Work is waiting for me back home. I expect my father will stay to finalize the job here."

"Let me know when you have made plans for your flight," he said woodenly. "I'll want to see you off."

She didn't answer. And two days later when she stepped into the helicopter on the pad behind the palace, there was only her father to see her off because she wanted it that way. She couldn't have survived a farewell scene with Dan. She barely survived the flight home as it was.

Elly waited one week before working up enough nerve to take the test. For all that time she argued against her instincts. Dan was right; the odds were that nothing at all had happened and she was letting her imagination run away with her. But she had to know.

On her first attempt, she was so nervous she dropped the paper strip in the toilet bowl, invalidating the test. On her second try, her hand was shaking so badly she nearly dropped it again. Somehow she managed to hold onto the test strip long enough to get a reading. Then she dropped it because it was positive.

Her entire body trembled as if she'd been plunged into a winter sea. Her stomach lurched, spasmed, then tightened into a knot so hard she had to grab for the edge of the sink and gasp for breath. She forced herself to do a third test, just to be sure. It turned out the same way.

She was pregnant.

Elly didn't want this. This wasn't how her life was supposed to turn out. She had been perfectly happy without children. After all, some women weren't meant to be mothers. And she was one of them. If her mother had been satisfied having one child, she would most probably have lived a long life.

But if your mother had made the same choice that you made before you met Dan, a voice murmured in her ear, *you would never have been born.*

Elly sank to the bathroom floor and sat staring at the test slip.

A life. That was what this was all about. There was a life inside her, just as, at one time, she had been a tiny life inside her own mother. Her mother had cherished her and brought her into the world.

What would she do with this life Dan had given her? What could she do? She dropped her face into her hands and wept.

Dan returned to Ocean City with a sense that his world had been turned upside down, soundly shaken until all the reliable habits had clinked out like loose change to the ground, then stood back on its feet to face a totally new and foreign landscape. He no longer knew how to function.

While in Elbia, he'd longed to return to the Haven, to his turf, to daily swims up the shore and to his plans for City Kids. But figuring in all his dreams, he now realized, had been Elly. Standing on the beach and handing him a towel as her eyes grew huge when he strode out of the water. Walking around inside his house, as relaxed and at home as she'd been with him in Elbia. Curled up in his arms in his bed. She was always there, in his mind and in his heart.

But no longer in reality.

The first week he was home, he concentrated on work—contacting his banker to arrange for the trust department to manage the royal annuity, putting his Realtor to work hunting up additional property to add to the Haven for his City Kids camp, bringing Kevin up to date on the many changes that would have to be made.

They were going to need a larger, full-time staff, including camp counselors, and they'd add a cafeteria and cook with helpers. These were all things that would have wildly excited him at any other time. But they seemed empty gestures without Elly.

Then there were Jacob, Allison and their two precious children. He had a brother now, a sister-in-law, and he was an uncle! He was so very proud of Jacob and all he'd done for his little country. Jacob had been generous to him, personally, but had also helped so many unfortunate people outside the family through the royal charities.

Aside from all that, he envied Jacob. Not for his vast wealth or for the power of his title. He envied his brother for the love his family bestowed on him daily, without reserve. And he wished with all his soul that Elly had been able to give him that kind of unlimited love…for he had believed he was capable of loving her, if only she would let him.

At the end of a week, his pain and disappointment had gnawed a hole through his heart so immense that he no longer feared her rejection. He had to talk to her, had to hear her voice even if all she did was send him away again.

He found the business card she'd given him on the day they'd met and punched in the long-distance number for Anderson Genealogical Research. An answering machine picked up, Frank's gravelly voice: "Your call is very important to us. Please leave your name, time of call and phone number so that we can—"

Dan hung up. His brow was sweating and his hand shook as he set the receiver down. An hour later, he tried once more. Again there was the machine. The following day, he called three times. And the next day three more times. Finally, he left a message: "It's me, Elly. Call. We have to talk." But four days later Elly hadn't called him back.

He was desperate, fuming and raw from her silent rebuffs. She had obviously put their affair behind her, but he could not forget. Slowly the thought came to him. A family was what he'd always wanted, yes. But if it came to choosing between having Elly and having babies with another woman, he knew of only one answer.

It must be Elly.

Perhaps it was too late, but perhaps not. He picked up the phone to make one last call. Long distance, to Elbia.

Jacob seemed happy to hear from him. "So have you already begun construction of your additions?" he teased, knowing how excited Dan had been to start work on his new project.

"Let's just say the ball is rolling but it has a long way to go. The reason I called was to see if Frank Anderson is still there. I've been trying to reach him through his office, but all I get is a machine."

"He's here," Jacob said. "I can have him call you."

"Good," Dan said. "I have to ask him for a favor."

"Oh? You need some additional research on your family?"

"No, I need to ask for his daughter's hand in marriage."

He could hear Jacob half choking, half laughing at the other end of the line. "You see," Jacob sputtered, "I knew something was up between you two. I wish you all the happiness."

"Wish me luck first. I'm not at all sure Frank will be happy about this. And Elly will need some high-power convincing."

"Then, good luck. And if there's anything I can do to help—"

"I'll call," Dan finished for him. But he knew, in his heart, that everything rested on him alone.

Later that day, Frank called, and it was clear that Jacob had prepared him for Dan's question. Dan had been justified in his concern. The man sounded none too pleased with Dan's intentions. "Of course I would give my blessing to anyone who loved Elly, and whom she loved as well," he muttered sternly. "I could see she had a certain affection for you. But it's my understanding that she has chosen not to pursue the relationship."

"Because of her mother," Dan said as gently as he could while still getting straight to the point. "Not because of anything that happened between us. She fears childbirth and knows I've always wanted children."

For what seemed a long time, Frank didn't respond. Dan wondered if he'd lost the connection, but before he could ask if Elly's father was still on the line, the older man began to speak in a low, troubled voice. "There's something you should know, if she hasn't already told you. Elly can never have kids of her own."

Dan frowned into the receiver. Something in the way Frank had phrased that last sentence made him suspicious. "Was that her decision or yours?"

"It's mutual," Frank snapped. "When we found out she had the same heart defect as her mother, we had a serious talk, she and I."

Dan winced, almost sure he could guess what was coming. "And you told her that you couldn't bear losing her the way you had lost her mother, is that it?"

"More or less. But it wasn't just what I wanted. She had been traumatized by her mother's death. And medically, it just didn't make sense for her ever to take the same risk, knowing what we knew."

Dan wondered how much pressure Frank had intentionally or unintentionally put on his daughter to remain childless. First by neglecting her when she'd most needed his comfort and support. Then, after he'd assuaged his grief, by drumming into her how much like her mother she was.

"I love my daughter and don't want to lose her," Frank continued defensively. "There's nothing wrong with that."

"And I love your daughter and I don't want to lose her either. So I'm willing to put aside my dream of a family to be with her." Dan paused, feeling angry and frustrated. "Is that all right with you, or have you also told her she shouldn't marry under any circumstances?"

"Taking that risk is up to her," Frank said coldly.

So that was it. All of her young life, her father had warned her about the dangers of men, marriage and having babies. And she had the death of her mother to prove him right.

"Someday you'll have to let her go, Frank. She's a grown woman now, not yours to keep. If she doesn't come to be with me, it will be with another man who won't love her as much or take as good care of her as I will."

The silence was worse than almost anything the man could have said. Dan guessed the man's blessing would not be forthcoming.

"Frank, at least talk to her for me. Ask her to return my calls, or I'll have to do this my own way. She'll resent your holding her back once she makes up her mind to live her own life."

"I know you mean well," Frank choked out. "I feel badly that I wasn't there for her when she needed me. But I'm here now and I will support whatever she wants. If that's to remain childless, that's what it will be, though." He hesitated. "I've been talking to your mother, and she says you're dead set to have kids. I expect that's what sent Elly heading for the hills."

"It probably is. But will you just put in a word for me? Encourage her to let me come up to Connecticut and talk to her."

"I'll do what I can," Frank promised.

"Whatever she says, I'll honor," Dan agreed. "All I'm asking for is one last chance."

Elly paced the floor, furious with her father. First he'd come home and, instead of pitching in with all the work that had to be done, he was off sightseeing with Madge, who had appeared at the airport on his arm, to Elly's shock. Then he'd taken Elly aside to tell her what a good man Dan Eastwood was. And it was clear that either Dan, his mother or both of them had gotten to her father, big-time.

She hadn't even been able to decide yet what she would do about the baby she carried. If the little life growing inside her could have been donated, like a spare kidney, to a woman who desperately wanted a child, she might have done it in the first few days after she'd discovered she was pregnant. But by the time she'd known for two weeks, she'd begun to wonder what this very new person inside of her would grow up to look like. And that had been her downfall.

Would he or she have Dan's dark hair, or her own red? Would their baby have his tall, strong build, or her more delicate bone structure? If she gave the child away, she would never know. And to give the child away, she'd have first to give birth to it, which was the reason she hadn't wanted to get pregnant in the first place.

Why couldn't life be easy!

She swung around at the sound of a car door slamming in her driveway. The Anderson Genealogy offices were located in the bottom floor of the house she shared with her father. She was upstairs in her bedroom and, when she looked out the window, a car with rental plates was sitting in the driveway. Dammit, it was *him*.

Elly raced downstairs, finger-combing her hair as she went, despite her intention not to let Dan in the house. She ran her tongue over her lips and tried to recall if she had put on makeup that day, then told herself to knock it off because she didn't care what she looked like when all she was going to say to Daniel Eastwood was, "Sorry you made this long trip. I don't want to talk to you. Good bye."

The doorbell rang. She stopped dead in the middle

of the office, unable to move a step closer to the door. He knocked on the door. She touched a hand to her chest and tried to breathe deeply, slowly, like a sane person. He pounded on the door. She began hyperventilating.

"Elly! I know you're in there. I ran into your father at the end of the street and he said so. Open up!"

No! she voiced the word, but nothing came out.

"I'm not going to stand out here forever, and I'm not turning around to go back to Maryland without having my say. Now open up or I'll let myself in the hard way."

She looked down at her hands. They were shaking so hard they looked blurry. "Coming," she whispered hoarsely.

She twisted the lock button in the middle of the knob and opened the door. Stepping back, she bowed her head so she wouldn't have to look at Dan as he moved past her into the room.

She sensed that he had stopped in front of her and, when she lifted her gaze by a few inches, there were the toes of his shoes facing her bare feet. "Say what you have to say," she said quietly, still not daring to meet his eyes.

He reached out and drew her roughly into his arms. "Elly, you're more important to me than anything in this world. Anything."

She buried her face in his chest and breathed in the scent of him. "You're saying that you've given up your dream of a family?"

"No, I'm ready to consider two a family. You and me. That's all I need to be happy. I love you, Elly, and I know you love me. That's got to be enough for us."

He sounded desperate and angry and determined…and she loved him for all those reasons.

But he didn't know yet what she knew. And she would have to tell him. "I can't…can't marry you until…"

"Until what?"

Until I decide if I'll keep your child or— No, she couldn't do that. She would never be able to reject Dan's baby. Which left only one alternative. To let it grow and thrive in her and not give it up. And for the first time it struck her that this little life didn't seem at all an intrusion. It felt a part of her, something that was meant to be, that had always been fated to be brought into the world, against all odds, on the strength alone of one man's wish for a family. And strangely enough, she felt okay with that, to be part of a larger picture of life. Not to be, as she'd feared she'd become in marriage, the victim of a man's design to fulfill his role as populator of the planet. She would share in a miracle, and happily so.

She looked up at Dan for the first time. "I can't marry you until…until you ask me," she whispered.

He stared down at her, looking like the most befuddled male on the planet. "What?"

"You're talking all around the issue. You never really asked if I would marry you."

"Good grief." He lowered his head to touch foreheads with her. "All right, woman." He knelt before her on one knee and produced a small box from his coat pocket. "I came prepared."

"I see you did."

"Elly, I love you for being you, with all your beauty, your intelligence, your kindness and your fears. I want you in my life. Anything else isn't worth losing you over. Will you marry me?''

"I won't take away your dream of having children," she said slowly.

His face fell. "Oh, Elly...please don't say—"

"Because I think a family is that important to you, a real family. So yes, I will marry you, Daniel Eastwood."

He frowned up at her. "Not to spoil the happiest day of my life, but I don't understand your answer. Are you saying that you will marry me and try to have a baby with me despite your heart problem?"

"I won't have to try very hard." She spread her hand over her stomach.

His eyes widened. "No. You aren't. We—"

"—made a baby the last time we made love."

"Then why didn't you call and tell—" He broke off, understanding showing in his eyes. "You still didn't want it when you found out. You were considering not telling me."

"I was," she admitted, touching his face tenderly. "I'm sorry, but I was. And I thought about every possible way I could avoid motherhood, until I had to face it. Then I remembered how much my mother loved me and how often she told me I was her most precious gift. I suddenly knew that if my little brother had been born, he would have given her just as much joy. Of course she knew the risks, but she took them anyway. I suppose all of life is a risk, isn't it?"

"You're still scared, aren't you?" he asked, kissing her gently on the lips.

"Yes." She lifted her chin another notch. "But I'll do everything I need to do to protect the baby and myself. God willing, we'll have a healthy baby."

He held her for a very long time before speaking again. "Would you have called and told me all this if I hadn't come up here?"

She pressed her cheek against his chest and thought for a moment. "I don't know. I think so. But I'm very happy you told me that you wanted me for myself, not as just a means to a family. It made the decision so much nicer."

Ten

—

Dan and Elly's wedding was in the spring, before Elly started to show too much. As Allison adored weddings and felt a special closeness to Elly and Dan, who had fallen in love in Elbia, Der Kristallenpalast was offered as the setting for their wedding, as it had been for many others of the king's and queen's family members and close friends before. And Daniel Eastwood, Prince of the Realm, was definitely considered family now.

Frank beamed with obvious pride as his daughter walked down the flower-strewn aisle of the castle's chapel at his side. But Dan thought he saw another emotion in the older man's eyes. Perhaps sadness at losing his only child? Or was it a lingering touch of the fear he had instilled in Elly all of those years?

It gave him an uneasy moment, but he quickly pushed all doubts aside at the happy smile on his beautiful bride's lips.

Kevin, his best man, nudged him in the ribs. "You lucky dog, you," he muttered under his breath.

"I know," Dan said. "How well I know."

He gazed out over the pews. In the very front row was his mother. She had never looked more contented. Already she was talking about her grandson, for they'd had a first sonogram and knew that Elly carried a boy baby. The two women had immediately begun picking out little blue baseball suits, rough-and-tumble teddy bears and other toys the child would be incapable of playing with for a good two years after his birth.

Everyone seemed pleased that they were marrying, but no one could have been happier than Dan himself.

Although their honeymoon might have been anywhere in the world, they chose to spend a week in Elbia, the most romantic place in the world, according to Elly. After they returned to Ocean City, they immediately began work on the City Kids project. Elly still did some genealogical research for her father, via the Internet, then sent him results by e-mail. She enjoyed the work, which helped him but also gave her something interesting to do while waiting for the birth of their son.

She wasn't without worry as her due date neared, but Dan was always there to reassure her. They had found the best obstetrician for their needs—a woman who specialized in difficult pregnancies. She had put Elly on a restricted activity schedule during the final two months, but allowed her a walk along the beach each morning while Dan swam.

As they woke up to each new day together, Dan thanked the powers that be for the chance he'd been given to keep Elly in his life, and to start a family too.

It was as much as he'd ever dreamed of having, and far more than he had believed he'd ever possess.

It was an ordinary morning three weeks before Elly was to enter the hospital for the C-section that had been carefully arranged to deliver their baby without undue stress on Elly's heart. Waking slowly, she lay blissfully in the warm bed, then looked down at her left hand. Her wedding ring felt strangely tight, and the flesh around it seemed puffy, swollen. She frowned, but was distracted by an unusually strong stirring within her womb. Elly smiled, pleased to feel the baby so active, and reached out for Dan.

He moved beneath her hand. "Hmmm?"

"Wake up," she whispered. "Your son is doing jumping jacks in here." She brought his hand over to her belly.

Dan immediately rolled over and grinned as he pressed his palm against the firm mound of his wife's stomach. "He certainly is. This kid will be ready for the Olympic swim team before he's three."

Elly laughed, then winced at a sudden sharp twinge low in her back followed by a tight sensation in her chest.

"What is it?" Dan asked, immediately concerned.

She laughed again. "Nothing. I must have just slept at a funny angle. My back hurt for a moment, but now it's gone."

"You're sure?" He looked worried.

"Of course, silly." She started to move out from under the sheet. "I'll just get up and stretch, and—oh my!"

"Elly!" Dan threw off the bed covers and leaped across the bed to catch her as she teetered forward, clutching her swollen stomach. "What's wrong?"

"I don't know…I…" She gasped for breath, then smothered a cry as another pain twisted her insides and left her dizzy and helpless. "Doctor Shelton said…said everything was fine. Three more weeks to go but—"

"But what?"

"These feel like—" she gasped again, unable to catch her breath now, droplets of sweat popping out on her brow "—these feel like…like—"

"Contractions?" Dan asked.

"Y-yes." She lowered herself back onto the bed with Dan's help. Tears trickled from her eyes. The pain was bad, and her heart was racing. She could breathe a little better now, seated, but only in shallow, rapid intakes. She stared across the room into the mirror over the dresser. Her features were puffy and pink, and suddenly it was no longer her own face looking back at her. It was her mother's face, the day before she'd died. And then Elly remembered how her mother's hands had swollen too, just like hers, so much so that she'd had to remove her rings that final day of her life. "Oh, please, no—" she wailed.

"Elly…Elly?" Dan cried, but his voice sounded distant and all she could concentrate on was her body's struggle to deliver a baby that wasn't supposed to come, not this way, not with her heart pulsing out of control and working so hard, not without the professional help she needed to bring this child into the world.

Desperately she tried to calm her heart, tried to think only of the things she must do to make sure Dan's son was born strong and healthy, no matter what might happen to her. She was terribly dizzy. The room became a blur. If she could just hold on long enough for the baby to be delivered, to draw its own first breath, then the rest she could accept.

Please let my baby live, she prayed. *Please don't take both of us from this wonderful man!*

She looked up into Dan's panic-stricken face, swimming hazily before her, and reached out to touch it. But her fingertips brushed air and fell to her side as a deep voice bellowed out in terror.

Dan grappled for the bedside phone, then was dialing 911, even as his roar of denial still echoed in the bedroom. This couldn't be happening, he thought desperately. Had Frank been right all along? Had he jeopardized Elly's life by encouraging her to keep their baby? But she had come to want it just as much as he, and now he wouldn't let history repeat itself. Dan refused to let fate take this woman from him.

The emergency operator spoke calmly, asking all the right questions.

"How soon will the ambulance get here?" Dan demanded, one hand pressed over Elly's stomach, as if he could physically hold her to this earth.

"They're on their way now, sir. Stay on the line with me. Tell me how she's doing."

He looked quickly at Elly. Her face had drained of all color. "She's unconscious."

"Is she still breathing, sir?"

He lowered his ear to her lips and felt a delicate wisp of breath. "Yes. But her heart…I don't know how much of this she can take. The baby was starting to come. Tell me what to do!" he shouted into the phone.

"Just wait there with her, sir. Watch for the ambulance."

He stared frantically at the clock, then at Elly. Seconds ticked past. He couldn't bear just sitting here while her life and the life of their baby rested in the balance. How many minutes did they have?

"Call the hospital," Dan barked. "Tell them we're on our way."

"But sir, the medics will be…" The woman's words drifted emptily away.

He had a bad feeling. What if it took them twenty minutes…thirty minutes or more to get there? How long did it take for a woman with an over-stressed heart or a baby deprived of oxygen to lose their lives? Ten minutes might be too long. And the Haven was just about that far from All Saints Hospital.

He dropped the receiver back into the cradle, spun around and scooped Elly's limp body up off the bed. "Hold on, darling," he whispered in her ear. "It's not going to happen that way again. I promise."

It seemed to Elly that she was in two bodies at the same time—her own and Dan's. Or perhaps not, maybe she had become part of everyone and everything that surrounded her. She could feel the awful pressure in her back and stomach, more intensely than ever, and her heart wasn't behaving well at all. But the pain felt somehow remote, as if someone else had taken the burden of it from her.

She wasn't looking down on herself, as people who experienced near-death moments often reported. She was everywhere, all at once: on their bed at home, being lifted in Dan's warm arms, watching the two of them from the perspective of the bungalow as he carried her at a run to his car. It was as if she became part of him at that moment. She could hear his heart thudding steadily, pounding with a fury within his chest through her cheek. And although her eyes were shut, she felt as if she was seeing through his eyes as he drove, and she knew where he was taking her, to the hospital.

Then they were driving very fast, and she could see the car as clearly as if she'd been standing on the street corner watching it flash past. A horn was blaring, like an off-key siren, and they were weaving through traffic, screeching around corners, running red lights.

And all the while Dan never stopped talking to her. "You're not going to leave me, Elly. I won't let you. You're mine and you're staying on this earth until it's your time. This baby is going to be born, and you need to stay here and be his mother. Do you hear me, darling? And your husband can't live without you, so don't you even think of giving up."

Even as the car squealed to a stop and he was throwing open the driver's door and racing around the outside to open her door and scoop her limp body up off the seat, he was shouting at her, claiming her, stealing her from death's ravenous jaws and dragging her back to the living.

A woman's voice said, "We'll take her now. It's all right, sir."

"I'm staying with her," Dan insisted.

But suddenly his arms were no longer supporting her, and the cool surface of a gurney came up beneath her. A nurse and orderly were wheeling her away, dashing through shining doors and running down a long polished corridor.

"No! I need to stay with her!" Dan shouted, but he sounded distant now and she wanted to beg them to let him be with her, but nothing came from her throat. She was desperate to see him, to tell him how much she loved him, for it might be her last chance.

There was a sharp jab in her arm and a moment later her eyes flew open. Suddenly, she was one person again: Elly. And the pain in her stomach became hers again, and more severe than ever. But Elly smiled up at the nurse and through trembling lips said, "Whatever you have to do, save my son." She grasped the woman's hand. "Do you hear me? Whatever it takes, give that man out there his little boy." And there was no longer any fear.

Dan glared at the formidable steel doors separating him from Elly. He paced the hall, glared, paced. When he could stand no more, he bolted through the right-hand door, but there was a woman the size of a Cadillac on the other side, and she thrust herself forward, backing him out of the trauma room before he could even get a glimpse of Elly.

"Now you just mind your manners," she said to him. "You can only get in the way in there, and you'll be wanting those doctors with your wife to keep all their attention on her."

"She needs me! What if she's—"

"What she needs is the kind of help they can give her," she assured him, her voice softening now that she had shoved him down into a chair and he didn't appear to be getting up again. "You did your job, Daddy. You got her here. I understand you broke the last record at Indy coming cross-town. Let them do what they can. I'll be back in a few minutes to tell you how she's doing. I promise."

He nodded but couldn't say a word of thanks. His throat was so dry he was unable to swallow, his eyes burned with tears he knew he'd never be able to shed. If he lost her now...

Dan dropped his head into his hands and prayed for all he was worth that the woman he loved would still be on this earth an hour from now. He didn't dare ask for another day.

The light was bright and joyous and beckoning. Elly knew it would be wonderful to see even before she opened her eyes, for she could feel its soothing warmth on her closed eyelids. Her heart was at rest, and her body felt as light as the air blowing softly around her. She had never been happier or more at peace.

"Elly?" a voice called to her. It was him. Dan.

She smiled to herself, remembering how he'd looked the last time she'd seen him. He had been so handsome, his dark eyes fixed on her intently, his hair still all mussed from sleep. Yet she would have spared him the pain she had seen etched in the lines around his strong mouth and across his forehead. Then she had looked up at him from the bed they'd moved her to, smiled and asked, "Have you seen your son yet?"

The man had broken down and wept as he clutched her to him.

"Elly, are you awake, darling?" he asked now.

Slowly she opened her eyes. Behind him was the sunny yellow hospital room bursting with flowers. The blooms had come from all around the world. The biggest arrangement of pale pink roses had arrived yesterday with a card embossed with the royal crest of Elbia. All the nurses had come to stare in amazement at it. There had been delicate orchids from her father and Madge. And dozens of bouquets from strangers in Hawaii, England, Canada and as far away as Australia, from well-wishers who had read about the Secret Prince and his bride's brush with death on the way to the hospital. The couple and their new baby were the toast of the tabloids now.

Dan bent down and kissed Elly softly on the lips. "The doctor says you can go home today." He was grinning, his brown eyes rich with happiness.

"Really?"

"Really. He says you're doing just fine. You do feel strong enough, don't you? We can insist you stay another day if you like."

"Oh no," she said quickly. "I want to go home."

"Good, the nursery supervisor says we have to take Dan Junior before he breaks through the bassinette."

She laughed, delighted with her two men. "He's kicking out the end of it?"

"He's a pretty big boy with a lot of energy. No wonder you had a tough time with him." His smile dimmed slightly. "Elly, I know at one time I went on about having a lot of kids. But I never want to come this close to losing you again. This is it for us. I've decided that three is plenty. And you already know I was happy to call two a family."

She touched the side of his face, shaved smooth for the first time in days. "I know, my love. I know. But the doctor says that what happened the other day wasn't related to my heart at all."

Dan squinted at her. "He's sure? What was it then?"

"The symptoms of an anxiety attack are almost identical to those of a coronary seizure. I guess when I saw that my hands and face were swelling up like my mother's had just before her heart attack, I believed the worst. My breathing all but shut down. I couldn't get enough oxygen, and that made me dizzy and, finally, I lost consciousness. Once I came out of it with the help of a mild tranquilizer, I could deliver the baby normally.''

"All the same, you scared the hell out of me.''

She stretched up to kiss him softly on the cheek. "Doc says it's possible I might never have another episode like that again, but if I do, there are simple medications I can take to control the symptoms, so that things don't get out of hand.''

"That's wonderful.''

"I think so, especially since I've been thinking I might want another baby.''

He studied her with amazement for a long minute, then drew her into his arms. "Only if we get one hundred percent clearance from the experts. Even then, I think I'd move you into a room here from six months on, just to be on the safe side.''

She laughed at him. "You fuss over me too much. I feel stronger than I've ever felt.''

"Good thing too,'' a voice called from the doorway over a sudden explosive wail. "Because this little tiger is ready for a five-course meal and, if you don't provide it, there will be heaven to pay!''

Dan and Elly turned to see their son kicking up a storm in the arms of a petite nursery attendant. Elly laughed at the woman's amused expression. "I hear DJ is giving all of you fits down in the nursery.''

"He's a joy,'' the woman said, smiling down at the baby as she handed him over to his father. "It's just that he gets ornery when he's hungry.''

"Just like his daddy,'' Elly said, her heart melting as she watched the expression on Dan's face soften with love for his son as he cradled the tiny bundle in his strong arms.

"I never get ornery," he protested mildly, his attention fixed totally on the squirming, squalling baby. "Never," he whispered in the baby's tiny ear, then kissed the soft red fuzz on top of his little head.

DJ stopped crying and looked up into the man's face. Elly's heart soared at the picture they made together—father and son. Her husband and her son. Life was perfect.

The nurse smiled as she turned to leave. "I'll be back for him in twenty minutes."

"May we keep him here in the room with us?" Elly asked.

"You're sure you feel strong enough, Mrs. Eastwood?"

"For him, yes. Please?"

"Sure. I'll let them know in the nursery."

"You don't have to do this," Dan said. "You should get your rest while you can. We'll be leaving for home in a few hours."

"I want to," Elly said. "I've been waiting all my life for this, and I didn't even know it. Now that I have both of you here with me, I'm not letting either of you out of my sight."

"Bad news," he said, watching as Elly parted the bodice of her gown to prepare to nurse the baby, "one of us has to go to work and the other will eventually need to go to school."

She sighed. "Party pooper."

As Dan bent down to place his son in Elly's arms then watched him hungrily seek out her nipple, his heart swelled with love and gratitude. He hadn't stopped thanking whatever invisible force had allowed him to keep Elly and see his son born healthy. He expected it would be a long time before he was able to accept their presence in his life as routine.

Sitting on the bed beside them, he curled his arm around Elly's shoulders and kissed her lightly on the brow. She was beautiful, she was his, and she'd given him the most precious gift any woman could give a man. He wanted to hand her the world, but the Haven would have to do. That and all the love he could give her, both in his heart and in the bed they would again share as soon as she felt ready.

"I love you, Elly," he whispered, nearly overcome with emotion.

"And I, you," she said, turning her soft hazel eyes up to gaze at him happily.

Then he kissed her on the lips and she returned his kiss with an energy that made him suspect it wouldn't be long before she invited him to join her in the passion they'd discovered halfway around the world, in a magical place called Elbia.

* * * * *

THE RAVEN'S ASSIGNMENT
by
Kasey Michaels

THE COLTONS

ARE BACK!

The Coltons—
When this most talked about dynasty is
threatened, only family, privilege and the power
of love can protect them!

Look out for these wonderful spin-off stories:

WHITE DOVE'S PROMISE by Stella Bagwell
August 2003 - Silhouette Special Edition

THE COYOTE'S CRY by Jackie Merritt
September 2003 - Silhouette Special Edition

WILLOW IN BLOOM by Victoria Pade
October 2003 - Silhouette Special Edition

A COLTON FAMILY CHRISTMAS
by Judy Christenberry, Linda Turner
and Carolyn Zane
November 2003 - Silhouette Books 3 in1

SKY FULL OF PROMISE by Teresa Southwick
THE WOLF'S SURRENDER by Sandra Steffen
December 2003 - Silhouette Desire

THE COLTONS: BLACK ARROW

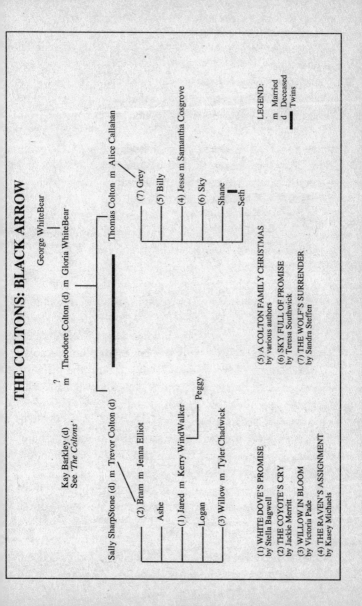

George WhiteBear

? m Theodore Colton (d) m Gloria WhiteBear

Thomas Colton m Alice Callahan

(7) Grey

(5) Billy

(4) Jesse m Samantha Cosgrove

(6) Sky

Shane

Seth

Kay Barkley (d)
See 'The Coltons'

Sally SharpStone (d) m Trevor Colton (d)

(2) Bram m Jenna Elliot

Ashe

(1) Jared m Kerry WindWalker

Peggy

Logan

(3) Willow m Tyler Chadwick

(1) WHITE DOVE'S PROMISE
by Stella Bagwell

(2) THE COYOTE'S CRY
by Jackie Merritt

(3) WILLOW IN BLOOM
by Victoria Pade

(4) THE RAVEN'S ASSIGNMENT
by Kasey Michaels

(5) A COLTON FAMILY CHRISTMAS
by various authors

(6) SKY FULL OF PROMISE
by Teresa Southwick

(7) THE WOLF'S SURRENDER
by Sandra Steffen

LEGEND:

m Married
d Deceased
─ Twins

KASEY MICHAELS

is the *New York Times* and *USA TODAY* bestselling author of more than sixty books. She has won the Romance Writers of America RITA® Award and the *Romantic Times* Career Achievement Award for her historical romances set in the Regency era, and also writes contemporary romances for Silhouette Books.

To Julie Barrett, who has the patience of a saint.

Chapter One

*P*OTUS *is on the move.*

"Copy that."

"Copy what, Sean? It's a little late for activity from the residence, isn't it?" Jesse Colton asked, looking up from the page he'd been reading as he walked through the West Wing toward the doors and what was left of his evening.

"Nothing, Jesse," Sean said, no longer talking into his shirt collar. "POTUS is on the move. It's nearly midnight, so he's on the way to the main kitchen, probably. FLOTUS keeps stashing the residence fridge with apples and pears. POTUS wants coconut-cream pie."

"I wonder what the American Heart Association would have to say about President's sweet tooth," Jesse said, perching on a corner of Sean's desk just inside the main vestibule. As jobs went, Sean's was pretty cushy—but guarding the West Wing was also pretty boring. "And the loyal opposition would probably start demanding monthly cholesterol checks."

"Yes, but with us all sworn to fall on our swords rather than play tattletale, I guess POTUS is safe, both from the AHA and FLOTUS."

Jesse looked at the small, boxy screen on Sean's desk, a constantly updated listing showing the location of the first family. Sure enough, POTUS, better known as President Jackson Coates, now showed in the main kitchen, with FLOTUS still in the second-floor residence, probably sound asleep. "POTUS. President of the United States. FLOTUS, first lady of the etcetera, etcetera. The acronyms ought to sound more presidential, don't you think?"

"I'll mention it at tomorrow's meeting of the Proper Presidential Acronym Committee—that would be P-PAC, of course," Sean said, shaking his head. Sean was the perfect Secret Service agent; his hair was neatly clipped, his suit neatly pressed, and his smile neatly neutral. "What do you have there, Jesse?"

Jesse looked down at the now-closed manila folder. "This? Personal stuff. Don't worry, I'm not planning to remove state secrets on your watch, and sell them to the tabloids. I mean, how much could they pay for a headline like POTUS Caught in Coconut-Cream Orgy."

"That's a relief. So, what do you have there?"

Jesse grinned. "That's it, Sean, trust nobody."

"No, seriously. You were frowning. Frowning over personal stuff is never a good thing."

Jesse opened the folder and looked at the single sheet

inside. "My family seems to have inherited a house in Georgetown."

"And this is bad news? Georgetown? Cushy address. Oh, wait a minute. Does it come with fifty years of back taxes they all want you to pay because you're getting rich here at the White House, feeding from the public trough?"

"Not quite, no," Jesse said, knowing that if Sean knew the whole truth, he'd probably fall off his chair. "The place has been rented out for about sixty years now. I'm just trying to figure out a way to explain to the Senate Ethics Committee how I, a lowly public servant, came to be part owner of the Chekagovian embassy."

"You're kidding," Sean said, grabbing for the folder, which Jesse quickly raised beyond his reach. "Is that legal? I mean, for a member of the president's staff to own part of a foreign consulate?"

"I probably own a third of the garage, Sean. There's a bunch of us who each own a small chunk of the place. The whole Colton tribe, as we call ourselves when we're being facetious, inherited it. But I'll admit, it is dicey. I mean, if we have a slow news week, who knows what could happen if this gets out. So I guess I have to tell…somebody."

"Chief of staff?"

Jesse blew out a quick breath. "Might as well start at the top." He slid the folder back into his briefcase and stood up. "Luckily, he went home at a decent hour, so it will have to wait. Besides, I need to do a little more digging into the deed, all that legal stuff, to be sure of my facts. See you tomorrow, Sean."

"See you, Mr. Moneybags, Mr. I-Own-Part-of-Georgetown," Sean called after him, then said, "Hey, wait! I forgot something."

"You never forget anything, Sean," Jesse said, slowly walking back to the desk. "You just want to pump me for more information."

"Not me. The more you know the less you want to know, that's my byword. No, seriously," he said, rooting through some messages on his desk. "This came in late, after your secretary left. Now where in hell— ah, got it."

He handed Jesse a "while you were out" memo.

Jesse frowned at the unfamiliar name as he read the memo. "Urgent? You did see that part of the message, right, Sean? The *urgent* part?"

"Hey, everything's urgent around here. The message arrived via the main switchboard, after being routed to the OEOB first, and then a couple of other places, which is probably how I ended up with it."

"The Old Executive Office Building? I haven't worked there in months."

"Well, guess not everyone knows you've been bumped up to a big-deal office in the West Wing. You should have taken an ad. Most do."

"Funny, Sean," Jesse said, heading out once more, this time frowning over the pink memo. "Samantha Cosgrove. Urgent. Now, who the hell is Samantha Cosgrove?"

Samantha Cosgrove, all the long blond hair and petitely formed five feet four inches of her, sat behind her desk, staring daggers at her telephone.

She hadn't gone on her coffee break with Bettyann. She had turned down lunch with Rita.

She hadn't left her desk all day. She was starving, and her stomach had begun to growl, she was nervous, and she was beginning to get angry.

Okay, so she'd been angry at one o'clock. It was now quarter to five. Now she was incensed.

Bettyann, the staff secretary, stuck her head inside the small office. "I'm heading out now, Samantha. Dinner at the golden arches? My treat."

"No thanks, Bettyann," Samantha said, pretending an interest in a pile of campaign literature that was about as exciting as the Weather Channel on a calm, clear day across America.

That's what the latest slogan was all about: a calm, clear-minded, new day across America. Vote for Senator Mark Phillips for President. *Bor-ring*. Surely somebody, somewhere, could come up with something better than that?

"You sure, Sam? You haven't eaten anything all day, except for that cupcake you stole from Rita. Her only satisfaction is that it had been sitting on her desk for two days, and had to be very, very stale."

"It was," Samantha said, sighing. "Okay, I'm going home. The world will keep on turning without me if I go home. But no thanks to the golden arches, Bettyann. I can hear leftover stuffed peppers calling my name."

"Right. See you here tomorrow."

"See me here, will she?" Samantha grumbled about a half hour later, grimacing as she shoved work into her briefcase. "Why not. Where else would I be?"

She grabbed her light, full-length burgundy raincoat

and followed a few other stragglers into the elevator once she'd looked through the outgoing mail, first checking to be sure nobody saw her.

Once outside, Samantha turned right and headed toward the White House on foot.

She had seen photographs of Jesse Colton, so she knew what he looked like: about six feet tall, short black hair, dark eyes. Sort of mysterious-looking, even primal.

"Okay, so he's a hunk," Samantha muttered to herself as she pulled up her hood, because it had begun to drizzle. Even in the rain, she loved living in Washington, D.C.

She'd been back in town for two years, because it took at least two years for a presidential candidate like Senator Mark Phillips to float test balloons to see if anyone would vote for him, pretend for months that he wasn't interested in running, announce the setting up of an informal Phillips for President Committee, talk to the money people, promise everybody everything, and then finally announce his formal candidacy.

Now, with the primaries beginning soon in New Hampshire, the Committee to Elect Mark Phillips had gone into full swing, had gone public, and Samantha was working hard.

She just needed to know if she was working hard for the right man.

Jesse Colton might work in the West Wing now, as she'd been informed, but she already knew he still had to walk to his old parking space, in a parking garage some distance away. It was easier to get into the West

Wing than it was to get a better parking place near the White House.

He drove a black sedan, nondescript, yet somehow classy. He arrived at the parking garage by seven o'clock in the morning, six days a week, and could leave again anywhere between five o'clock and midnight.

She knew, because she'd watched him for five long, worrisome days before making the call yesterday. The call that hadn't been returned today.

"Not stalking, Samantha, watching," she assured herself tightly as she quickly joined some other people as if she belonged with them, and then stepped into the parking garage, out of the drizzle that was rapidly turning into a downpour. "There's a difference."

The difference, she decided two hours later, was that stalkers probably planned better. Maybe even brought a peanut butter and jelly sandwich and a thermos of piping-hot coffee with them.

She'd finally given in and jogged to a small local restaurant to grab a take-out hot dog and a soda, along with a bag of potato chips, then jogged all the way back to breathe a sigh of relief when she saw the black sedan still in its assigned parking spot.

It was nine o'clock and she had begun fantasizing about peanut butter and jelly sandwiches again, when she finally saw him.

She thought it was him. She could be delirious from lack of food, but she was ninety-nine percent sure the man walking toward her was Jesse Colton.

When he clicked something on his key chain and the black sedan's lights went on, she was sure.

Stepping out from behind her second home—the concrete pillar—she said, "Jesse Colton? If I could have a minute of your time, please?"

He kept walking. "Call my office."

"I did."

"Did you leave a message?"

"I did. For you to call me. You didn't."

"Now there's a clue," he said, opening the rear door of the sedan and throwing his briefcase inside. "It's late. If you want an interview, go through the press secretary's office."

"I don't want an interview," she said, walking toward him. "I'm not a reporter."

"Darn. And I'll bet you're not this generation's Deep Throat, either, ready to tell me deep dark secrets, or Mr. White, who was going to let me know that Mr. Green did it, in the library, with the rope. I don't get any luck."

He had opened his car door and slid inside, but before he could close the door again, Samantha was there, her body between the door and the car.

"Are you always an ass?" she asked him, shaking her head so that her hood slipped off. She reached beneath her collar and freed her long blond hair, let some of the thick curls spill onto her shoulders.

She wasn't dumb. She was blond, fairly pretty, and had fabulous legs. She had yet to meet a single man in D.C. who had found her unattractive.

"Am I being propositioned?" Jesse asked, and his smile was a little too amused for Samantha's comfort.

"No!" she said, backing up a pace. Which was a bad move, but she realized that too late.

"Pity," he said, then reached out and closed the door. But then he rolled down the window. "You're Samantha Cosgrove, right?"

She bent down, looked in the window. "You knew that?"

"Oh yeah, I knew that. Blond, pretty and tenacious as a bulldog. I had you checked out."

"Why?"

"Because you want to talk to me. Do you have any idea how many people want to talk to me, Samantha Cosgrove, now that I'm in the West Wing?"

"Oh, aren't we popular. I'm so impressed."

"I'll bet you are. I know I am," he said, flashing her that whiter-than-white smile again.

She wanted to bang him over the head with her briefcase. Instead, she turned her back and began walking away.

"Hungry?" he asked, backing up the sedan so that he was beside her once more.

"Only if I could find a way to make your entrails appetizing," she said, and kept walking.

He kept backing up. "Ah, don't go away mad, Samantha. I was going to call you."

"When? Christmas?"

"No, I go home to Oklahoma for Christmas. Tomorrow. I was going to call you tomorrow. First I had to check you out."

"Did I pass?" she asked, interested, but she kept walking. The man set her teeth on edge.

"Well, let's see what I've got. Daughter of megarich parents residing in Connecticut after living here for decades. One brother, younger, still in college. Freshman,

I believe. One sister, older, a literary agent. Juliet, right? Mommy does charity work and belongs to all the right social groups. Daddy's a lawyer, and personal friends with and a large contributor to the presidential primary campaign for Senator Mark Phillips, who is personally endorsed by my boss, the current president. Graduated with honors, double major, in both journalism and political science. Very nice, Samantha. *Cum laude.* Even nicer. Senior staffer on Phillips's committee. Hardworking, clean-living, good cook, lousy dancer—"

"I am not a lousy dancer! I'm a very *good* dancer," Samantha protested hotly, stopping so that she could turn, glare at him.

"And here I thought you weren't listening. Okay, good dancer, although that wasn't in my report. So, you want to go get something to eat, and then prove to me that you're really a good dancer?"

"I wouldn't dance with you for all the tea in—"

"You did say *urgent,*" he interrupted.

"Are you always this arrogant?"

"No, it comes with the White House credentials. Honest. You can look at the job description. It's right there—once cleared to work in the West Wing and given a blue badge, arrogance is mandatory. Red badge? Orange badge? I spit on red and orange badges."

"You're insane," Samantha said, but then she laughed. She couldn't help herself. "Really. Insane."

"But I'm buying. How about a New York strip, since you look ready to bite something. Baked potato dripping in sour cream. A good bottle of white zinfandel? You look like a white-zinfandel drinker to me.''

''I like merlot.''

''So much for my source. I'll have to order her head chopped off in the morning. So, are you getting in, or are you just going to take the Metro home and eat those leftover filled peppers?''

''How did you—oh my God. It's true. You people know *everything*. You had someone in my house? Going through my refrigerator?''

''Nothing that illegal. But Brenda—she's my secretary—did happen to stop in at Senator Phillips's election headquarters late this afternoon. She told me someone named Bettyann would have given out your shoe size if anyone asked. Brenda also told me that you're blond and a looker. She was right. Now, come on. Get in.''

Samantha threw up her hands. ''Why not. I deserve a free steak after you invaded my privacy that way. You *are* buying, you know.''

''I wouldn't have it any other way,'' he said once she was in the passenger seat, her briefcase on the floor.

''Neither would I,'' she said, arranging her oversize raincoat across her legs. He didn't deserve to see her legs. ''And then we'll talk?''

''And then we'll talk. Promise,'' he said, slipping the car into Drive and heading out of the parking deck. ''But first we eat. I don't know about you, but I'm starving.''

''I can relate,'' Samantha said, hoping her stomach wouldn't growl before she could feed it.

*   *   *

Finding an empty table in any half-decent restaurant close to the White House was darn near impossible, anytime day or night, but as they approached one of the best ones, Samantha told him to pull up out front at the valet service area.

"Much as I'd like to tell you I'm even smarter than my personnel file says I am, I didn't know you were going to be lying in wait for me in the parking lot, or that you'd agree to come to dinner with me. That said, I don't have reservations."

"That's all right. Just pull over."

He did, and the valet opened the passenger-side door. Samantha accepted the hand she was offered, and said, "Good evening, Anthony. It's good to see you again."

"And it's wonderful to see you again, Ms. Cosgrove," Anthony the valet said, guiding her under the canopy and out of the rain.

"I guess I'm just supposed to schlep it on my own," Jesse grumbled to himself as Anthony and his large black golf umbrella didn't move from the canopy again.

He got out, tossed his keys to Anthony, and found himself following Samantha inside the dimly lit foyer of the restaurant known for its old boys' club decor and aged steaks.

She was already standing in front of the podium, with an Anthony look-alike holding her raincoat over his arm, and speaking fluent Italian with the maître d'.

A few more Italian phrases, some sharp snapping of the fingers by the maître d', and they were being escorted past the line of diners waiting to be seated and to a prime table. Jesse was pretty sure he recognized a representative from Pennsylvania in the line, as well as a second assistant undersecretary of state.

"How'd you do that?" he asked once they were seated.

"So much for your thorough research. I was raised in the District, remember, before Dad decided to relocate in Connecticut. I've known Anthony and his family for years, since my father and mother first began coming here," she told him as she spread her napkin in her lap.

Then she leaned forward and said with an unholy grin on her lovely, patrician face, "You see, Mr. Colton? Badges? I don't need no steenkin' badges."

If he were less a man of the world, Jesse would have believed he fell in love with Samantha Cosgrove the moment the words were out of her mouth.

Instead, he threw back his head and laughed, and banished any other thoughts as unprofessional. And definitely personally dangerous.

They were handed oversize menus, leather-clad, and Jesse watched as Samantha frowned over hers.

She was so blond. So sleek. So High Society.

And he was the part Comanche nobody from Black Arrow, Oklahoma.

Man. Who would have thunk it.

"I think I want two of everything," she said at last, smiling at him overtop the menu. "Is that all right?"

"That depends. How good are you at washing dishes?"

"Ah, the woefully underpaid public servant," Samantha said, closing the menu and placing it beside her cutlery so that she could fold her hands on the tabletop. "Do you like it?"

"Being a public servant, or being underpaid?" he asked, closing his own menu.

"No, seriously, do you like it? I mean, I get chills, just thinking about the West Wing. The Oval Office. All that power, all in one place."

"And the doughnuts ain't bad," Jesse said, grinning.

She sat back. "All right, so I'm not immune to the idea that you work in the West Wing. It's heady. How did you get there, anyway?"

"Hard work, determination, knowing the right people—all that good stuff."

"Will you please be serious. I mean, I know you started in the Secret Service."

"Not much of a secret, is it?" he commented, trying to look upset. "And then I moved on to the NSA—National Security Agency."

"Yes, and from there to the West Wing. One of the president's trusted advisers. I don't remember reading that you stopped a bullet for him, or anything like that."

"No, nothing that dramatic. Let's just say I'm ambitious, and that, yes, I did know the right people, and that I was in the right place at the right time. When the president's second term is over, and your guy's in the Oval Office, I'll head back to the NSA. I'm only on loan, you know. That was the deal."

"You won't want to be part of Phillips's staff?"

"I won't be asked. Same party, Samantha, but each man comes in with his own people. And, frankly, I think I'll be glad. The NSA is where I really want to be. I'm not all that political. I'd rather think I'm serving my country, not just the current administration. Since the president agreed, and really wants more of an outsider's opinion on national security, we're fine. This was, hell, this was an ego thing as much as anything else. But enough about me. Why do you want to be part of Phillips's staff?''

The waiter approached, and they both gave their orders, then were silent as the wine—compliments of the owner—was opened and poured.

"Nice touch, even if I am going to have to pay for it. We're not allowed to accept gifts, you know. Still, I could get used to this," Jesse said, sipping the wine. "So, Samantha, are you going to tell me? Why do you want to be part of Phillips's staff?"

"Because he's right for America," Samantha said, and then she grimaced. "Okay, okay, the truth. Not that he isn't right for America. He's a wonderful man. But to get the chance to walk into the West Wing? Stand inside the Oval Office? Be even a small piece of the power behind the man in that office? You've admitted it, so I can say it. Who wouldn't want that?"

"True, true. Fifteen-hour days, constant emergencies, news leaks, congressmen who need their hands held. It's great."

"You're just saying that. I don't think you'd ever be anywhere you didn't want to be."

Jesse didn't answer her. He just lifted his glass in salute and took another sip of wine as the waiter placed large bowls of salad in front of them.

Oh, he liked this woman. He really, really liked her.

And she was correct. He was right where he wanted to be. Across the table from a very interesting woman.

By the time they'd finished their steaks, Jesse was feeling pretty mellow.

Mellow enough to ask a question he probably shouldn't have asked.

"Have you ever been to the Chekagovian embassy?" he asked, because it seemed as if she'd been everywhere else in the District, and most parts of Virginia. She knew everybody, probably through her parents or Senator Phillips, and had been invited to all the right parties.

Samantha sat back and rolled her eyes. "Oh, the Chekagovian embassy! Isn't it beautiful?"

"I don't know. I've never seen it." That much was true. He'd only gotten the fax from the local law firm yesterday, and was still trying to grasp the idea that he and his relatives owned the pricey mansion…and the rest of it.

"You've never seen it? Oh, you have to see it. I mean, I've never been inside, but from the outside? The grounds are magnificent, just for starters. I was there for a photo op with the senator's wife, but we didn't get to go inside. Gorgeous gardens, with flowers all over—"

"I've heard that. Gardens, with flowers in them. Very unique."

"Don't be funny," she said, then waited until their plates were cleared from the table. "And it's not just the gardens. The mansion is truly extraordinary. Federal style. Wonderful old redbrick. A million windows. Exterior wood all painted creamy white, and definitely handcrafted by experts. It's...it's a slice of American history. Really.''

"And it serves as the Chekagovian embassy."

She nodded. "That's what happened to so many of the best old houses. It's the price we pay for being the center of the political world. Of course, if we weren't, who knows what would have happened to those lovely old mansions.''

"They'd never have been built.''

"Good point. I hadn't thought of that. Anyway, I'd love to get inside that place, just for a look around. Why did you mention it?''

Jesse drew back, knowing he'd probably already said too much. "Oh, no real reason. I'd just heard it was a...a nice place.''

Her gorgeous blue eyes narrowed. "Liar.''

"I beg your pardon," he said as the waiter poured coffee for them. "I never lie.''

"Oh, the new millennium's George Washington. You cannot tell a lie. This city hasn't seen another one like him, until you, of course. I'm so impressed. Really.''

"All right, all right," Jesse said, holding out his hands. "But only because you dragged it out of me at fork-point.''

"I did not," she told him. "That was next.''

Jesse laughed. He didn't know if the good food had made him feel so comfortable, or the good wine...or the great company. What he did know was that if he didn't soon tell someone what he'd learned in that fax, he was probably going to burst. Just like a little kid with good news.

"First I have to swear you to secrecy," he told her.

"Certainly," she said, then held up her right hand. "I, Samantha Cosgrove, do solemnly swear that I won't breathe a word of what Jesse Colton is about to tell me, so help me spit. There. Is that good enough?"

"Pretty good. Although I'll still have to kill you once you know everything."

"That seems only fair. You were Secret Service. Does that mean you could kill me with a rubber band or pencil sharpener?"

"We don't do those anymore. Now we use Post-it notes. I'm hell with a Post-it note."

"I'll bet you are. Now, come on, tell me. What do I want to know about the Chekagovian embassy?"

"That I own it?" he said, raising his eyebrows.

"That you...that you...oh, you fibber you. You *own* it? Well, that makes us even. I own the Washington Monument. Oh, and we rent out the Lincoln Memorial. Tax reasons, you know."

He smiled, shook his head. "I know, it's hard to believe, but I own it. Really. Well, I own some of it."

"Some of it," she repeated, spooning three sugars into her coffee.

"Hey, easy on the sugar."

"Never mind me. You'd better take yours black, because I think you've had too much wine, and you'll need to sober up before you drive home."

"You think I'm handing you a line?" he asked, tipping his head to one side as he looked at her. God, she had a wise mouth. He loved to hear her talk. He'd love more to shut her up...with his own mouth.

"If you are, I have to admit I've never heard this

particular one before tonight. So, if I promise to be good, and not laugh too hard, why don't you tell me *why* you own part of the mansion?''

"That would take until tomorrow morning," Jesse said, wincing. "So we'll leave that for another time, if that's all right with you."

"There's going to be another time?"

"If you want, yes. But it's getting late, and I've got a six-thirty meeting at the White House. So…"

"So I should tell you my reason for contacting you in the first place? For…for stalking you?"

"What a good idea," he said, grinning. "You can tell me part of it, the way I told you part of mine, and then we'll go on from there. If you want to."

"I shouldn't. You're much, much too sure of yourself, Jesse Colton."

"It's a failing, I agree. So? Do we have a deal?"

She nodded. "We have a deal. But not here, there are too many ears. Pay the check, and I'll tell you once you drive me home. At the curb, Colton—I'm not inviting you into my house. Agreed?"

He eased his wallet from his slacks pocket and pulled out a credit card. "Agreed. Spoilsport."

They left the restaurant after Samantha was kissed on both cheeks by the maître d', two interchangeable Anthonys and a plump woman who came out from the kitchen, wiping her hands on an apron as she called out, "Bella! Sweet Bella!"

"Are you this popular in all the District restaurants? If so, I think ours could be a beautiful relationship, at least until my credit card maxes out."

"I'll bet everyone in every gym in town knows

you," she said as he tried to open the car door for her, only to be beaten out by Anthony Number One.

When he slid in behind the wheel, he said, "Actually, they know me at most of the museums. I'm big on museums."

"I wouldn't have guessed that," she said as he pulled away from the curb. "Head toward Dupont Circle, and I'll give you directions from there."

Fifteen minutes later he pulled the sedan over to the curb in front of an old redbrick town house. "Apartment?" he asked, looking at the well-kept building.

"Mom and Dad's place, for when they come to the city. We never sold it. Juliet doesn't stay here, not that she's ever in town, but I'm the younger daughter, and part of my permission to come here to work hinged on my agreeing to stay at the old homestead. Mom's a worrywart," she told him, fishing in her purse for her key and not finding it. "Now, remember that sworn-to-secrecy stuff?"

"Hope to spit," he said, turning off the ignition, knowing the windows would fog up within minutes. But if he didn't turn off the ignition, the chances were lower that he'd be invited in for a nightcap. Hope to spit, yes. And hope springs eternal—that was Jesse's motto, or at least it was since meeting Samantha Cosgrove.

She took a deep breath, then stared through the rapidly steaming-up windshield, her fingers nervously opening and closing the snap on her purse. "I have fairly varied duties at campaign headquarters. I handle press releases sometimes, organize fund-raisers, help write some of the lesser important speeches. Even lick stamps if we're shorthanded. I do everything.''

"All right," Jesse said, and that's all he said, because he could tell that Samantha was nervous and still might change her mind about talking to him.

"In the course of my...duties," she went on after a moment, her cheeks pale in the light of a strong street-lamp across the way, "I learned a few names. More than a few names. I learned yours, for instance.''

"But not my whereabouts, because you tried to reach me through the OEOB.''

"I used an old directory," she said with a wave of her hand. "That doesn't matter. What matters is that you have a reputation, Jesse.''

"Whatever it is, I didn't do it," he said, then winced. "Sorry. It was getting a little tense in here. I thought I'd try to lighten the mood.''

"That's all right. I'm not saying this very well. This is embarrassing, because I'm usually very good with words. But you do have a reputation, Jesse. For honesty. For being a straight shooter. For being intensely loyal and definitely trustworthy.''

"Now I'm embarrassed.''

She shifted on the seat, turning to face him. "Last week," she began, then closed her eyes for a moment before looking at him again. "Oh, this is so hard.''

"Just say it fast, Samantha," he advised her, taking her hand in his. Her fingers were icy cold, nearly bloodless. He didn't know what was wrong, but whatever it was, she wasn't only worried, she was scared.

"All right. Last week, Thursday, I think, I...I was licking stamps. I mean, not really licking stamps, but I was there late, and there was mail to go out, and since I was there and had no plans, I stayed to do it."

Jesse's radar switched on. Mail. Mail leaving a senator's campaign office. The possibilities were endless. "Go on," he urged when she stopped speaking.

"I can't. I can't do this. Senator Phillips has been so good to me. And my father? He adores the man. They were in the army together. I mean, I used to call him Uncle Mark. I still do, in private."

"Samantha, sorry, but you can't stop here. What was in the mail?"

"Outgoing mail," she clarified, then sighed. "It had to be a mistake. I mean, he wouldn't do anything wrong, I know he wouldn't."

"What was in the mail?" Jesse repeated, squeezing her fingers.

"Something...something that shouldn't even have been in there, in the campaign office," she said quietly, pulling her hand free. "You know he chairs the Senate Ways and Means Committee, and they deal with some very sensitive material..."

"Money, Samantha. They deal with a lot of money. In Washington, money equals power, and power equals money. Now, one more time, Samantha. What was in the mail?"

"Tomorrow," she said quickly, one hand on the door handle. "Come to the office tomorrow evening. Around seven. Everybody else should be gone. I...I'll show you then."

"You didn't send it out?"

She shook her head. "No. I couldn't. I'm sure that

information should never have been released. I shouldn't even have *seen* it.''

"Did you also save the envelope?" Jesse asked, thinking ahead.

"Yes. That's how I got to see the contents. The envelope wasn't sealed correctly and the glue was all gone. I wanted to tape it shut but couldn't find any tape—sometimes our office is a real mess—so I slipped everything out of the envelope to put it into a new one and I saw…I saw…" Her voice was so quiet he had to lean over to hear her above the sound of rain pelting the roof of the sedan. "I'll…I'll show you everything."

She opened the car door, then turned back, grabbed his arm. "But you can't tell anybody. Not until we know exactly what's going on. I mean, it was the senator's mail, but that doesn't mean that he—"

"We'll talk about it tomorrow, Samantha," Jesse said, putting his hand over hers. "It's probably nothing."

"That's what I think. It's nothing. Just a…a mistake. Good night."

And then she was gone, running through the rain to the steps of the town house. She knocked, and a few moments later a uniformed maid opened the door, spilling mellow yellow light out onto the brick sidewalk.

"Nice work if you can get it," Jesse muttered, putting the car in gear to head home to a sleepless night.

Chapter Two

At ten o'clock the next morning, Jesse passed by the well-dressed secretary who held the door open for him, and into the large, teak-paneled law office of Rand Colton, oldest son of former Senator Joseph Colton.

His relatives. Amazing. A whole, huge branch of the family Jesse and his family hadn't known existed until a few short weeks ago. The wealthy, socially and politically prominent branch of the family, about as far away from Oklahoma and Black Arrow as a person could get.

He'd seen photographs of Senator Colton, read stories of the scandal and murders and near tragedies that had nearly torn the California family apart.

He'd run several Colton names through the Internet, read the microfiche newspaper articles at the library, and had come to the conclusion that the last thing these people needed was for another problem to rear its ugly head, both privately and for public consumption.

The public had consumed plenty already, with the murder attempts on the former senator by both his business partner and his supposed wife.

That had been the double whammy, that his wife had been the victim of amnesia for ten years while her twin sister, a convicted murderer, had impersonated her, taken her place in Joe Colton's house, Joe Colton's bed.

Bizarre.

It was the stuff of tabloids, made for TV docudramas, all that sleazy stuff. Except it all had happened to good people.

But all of that was over, in the past. Problems solved, lives mended, the future bright.

Until these latest revelations that, thankfully, were still hiding under the press's radar. Until, if the information Jesse had received thus far was correct, it had been learned that his grandmother had been the legal wife of Joe Colton's father, Teddy. The *only* legal wife of Joe Colton's father.

Making Senator Joseph Colton the bastard born on the wrong side of the blanket. Oh yeah, the tabloids would gobble it up if they knew. One thing Jesse wanted to make very clear to the senator's son was that nobody in the Oklahoma branch of the Coltons planned to go public with anything. Ever.

"Jesse," Rand Colton said, walking around from behind his desk, his right hand extended in greeting. "Or should I say, *cousin?*"

Jesse took the man's hand in his, felt the dry warmth and solid strength he hadn't expected to find in the grip of a lawyer. "Jesse's fine," he said, then took a seat on a chair that was part of a small conversational gathering of chairs and couch on one side of the large office. "Are we really sure?"

"You've spoken to your family?" Rand asked, lowering his six-foot-two-inch frame into the facing chair.

"Yes, when I went home after my grandmother's funeral. I couldn't be there in July, as I was traveling in Europe with the president, but I finally got there. They've been having some pretty interesting times in Black Arrow."

"Thanks to my uncle, yes," Rand said, shaking his head, then looking toward the now-open door. "Is there something wrong, Sylvia?"

"Oh, no sir, Mr. Colton. I only wondered if you and Mr. Colton might like some coffee," the secretary said.

"Coffee?" Rand asked, looking at Jesse.

"Sure," he answered, and turned to smile at the secretary. "I take it black, thank you."

"Oh, no trouble, Mr. Colton," Sylvia gushed, and Jesse saw a slight flush in her cheeks. "Really. It's absolutely no trouble at all."

As the secretary turned to exit, and nearly collided with the doorjamb, Rand said, "Do you always have that impact on women? I doubt I'll get any coffee at all. You'll probably get coffee *and* doughnuts."

Jesse settled himself in his chair once more, and grinned. "It's my Comanche blood, I suppose. Some women find that exciting."

"I find that Comanche blood interesting, frankly," Rand said, crossing one long leg over the other. "From everything I've learned about Teddy Colton—our mutual paternal grandfather—he was a heavy drinker, a social climber, a pompous ass—and a world-class bigot.''

''I really wouldn't know,'' Jesse said, resting his arms on the chair. ''But I've seen early photographs of my grandmother just before she went to Reno to get a job that would allow her to send money home to her parents, and she was a beautiful woman. I mean, truly beautiful. He probably couldn't help himself.''

''I can believe that. I can also believe that Teddy met her and married her—before his society marriage to my grandmother. My paternal granddaddy, a bigamist. It's still mind-boggling. Have you seen the documentation?''

Jesse nodded. ''On my visit home, yes. I brought the deed and marriage license back with me so I could look into the matter here. Although why Gloria—my grandmother—never told her sons the full truth is still beyond me.''

''Pride,'' Rand said with a slight nod of his head. ''The way I've heard it, thanks to my father, is that when she realized she was pregnant and contacted Teddy, it was to learn that my grandmother was also pregnant. She could have raised one hell of a stink but she didn't. She just went home to raise her twin sons on her own. I admire her greatly. A simple woman with real class and a giving heart. Teddy, on the other hand, didn't trust her.''

''Never measure others by the length of your own lodgepole, as my great-grandfather would say. Teddy would have used information like that as a hammer, and so he felt sure Gloria would, as well. But she never did.''

"And she never took a penny from the trust Teddy set up in her name," Rand said, "or from the house he put into the trust for her. The Chekagovian embassy. I've already asked the lawyers who handle the trust to request that the embassy be vacated, and that's well in hand."

"I can't believe we can evict the Chekagovians," Jesse said with a smile.

"We didn't have to. It seems the embassy was already in the process of being emptied in favor of a newer building closer to the Capitol. It should be entirely vacant by the end of next week. I'll make sure you have keys waiting for you at the lawyers' office, as I'm sure you'll want to see the place. I know I would. Say, next Friday?"

Jesse lowered his eyelids, thinking that Samantha would be pleased when he told her he could take her on a tour of the estate. Nothing like turning this entire thing into a dating opportunity. He blinked, ordered his mind to concentrate on the matters at hand.

"Thank you. And about the trust? I'm still having a hard time getting my mind wrapped around that number. Ten million dollars?"

"Rounded down, yes. Sixty years of interest is a lot of interest, especially when the stock market began taking off—and especially when the trust was handled well enough to get out of that market and into safer funds while it was still high," Rand said, grinning. "And imagine. If my uncle Graham hadn't gotten greedy, nobody might have known about any of this."

"Yes, how did that happen?"

Rand and Jesse both stood up as Sylvia entered, carrying a tray holding a small pot, two cups and saucers and one plate of doughnuts. "Thank you, Sylvia. Sylvia?" Rand prompted as his secretary continued to stare at Jesse.

"Thank you, Sylvia," Jesse said, and the secretary blushed again, then backed her way out of the room.

"Truly amazing. I believe it's called charisma, Jesse," Rand said as he sat down once more. "Living in this town, you ought to run for office. You'd certainly get the female vote, if Sylvia's any indication."

"I'll keep that in mind," Jesse said, then took a bite of the glazed doughnut he'd selected.

"Anyway," Rand said, picking up his coffee cup, "it was Graham, my father's brother, who contacted our lawyers here in some desperation, wanting to sell up anything that might be left of their father and mother's estate."

"Yes, I remember the name now. Graham. The younger brother?"

"That's him. Graham earns plenty working for my dad, but money just runs through his fingers, so he was looking for another way to make a quick buck. The way I heard it, some junior law clerk, God knows why, mentioned the Georgetown mansion. Never should have happened because my grandfather had apparently explicitly demanded the estate be kept private unless the inquisitor had the deed in hand. Anyway, the clerk was disciplined, although I'm rather glad he made the mistake, if not happy how Graham reacted to learning of your grandmother's existence. He went ballistic, thinking about the money and the possible scandal."

"So you don't mind any of this?"

Rand shook his head. "The money simply isn't an issue. As for the scandal? It's ancient history. Besides, if the news had come out years ago, when Dad was running for the Senate, I imagine his handlers would have put a hell of a spin on it. Who knows, he could have ended up as president."

Jesse laughed, as did Rand. "My family met your father in Black Arrow. They were very impressed with him. Even my great-grandfather, and let me tell you, the old boy isn't an easy sell."

"Dad's good at impressing people. It comes naturally to him, probably because he's a good man. I wish I could say the same for Graham."

"He's the one who hired somebody to find the marriage license, birth certificates, the deed to the Georgetown mansion, and destroy them? The same guy who ordered the town hall burnt down?"

"Not to mention the break-ins at the newspaper office and your late grandmother's feed and grain store, yes. Busy, busy, busy. Although Graham swears he never told his hireling to do any of that. No violence, he told the guy, or so he says. Just to find the papers and destroy them, as if destroying evidence and robbing a family of its just inheritance were forgivable. But that's Graham. He sees things his own way. Luckily, the documents were always in a locked box in your grandmother's bedroom."

"And the lawyers here have verified everything from the original deed for the Georgetown property to the marriage license," Jesse said, perhaps a bit too sternly.

"Your whole branch of the Colton family is quite legitimate. You can rest assured that nobody on our side of the family is going to oppose your claim in any way."

"Thank you. And I can tell you that no one on our side of the family is going to look this gift horse in the mouth, or try to profit from a sad situation by going public with it."

Rand seemed relieved by his last statement. "Sounds like we've agreed, then. Good, and I thank you. So, what do you and your family plan to do with the estate? With all that money?"

Jesse grinned, looked quite boyish for a moment. "We haven't the faintest damn idea, cousin."

Samantha ate at her desk, some quite wonderful beef sandwiches left over from the Sunday roast.

She knew the meat was good; it had been a nearly perfect rump roast she'd prepared with garlic mashed potatoes and freshly steamed broccoli. Rose, the live-in maid, who was a full-time student and the only staff Samantha would allow her mother to put in the house, had sworn it tasted like ambrosia. Samantha had agreed.

Yet, today, it tasted like cardboard.

She lifted the top piece of bread and stared at the meat, lettuce and mayonnaise. Nope. Not cardboard.

"Damn," she said, closing the sandwich once more and putting it back down on the desk.

"Something wrong?" Bettyann entered the office and put some papers down on Samantha's desk, then deposited her rounded rump there as well.

"Nothing I'd want the media alerted for," Samantha

said, and watched as Bettyann blushed to the roots of her dyed blond hair.

"What…what does that mean?" the secretary asked, looking so guilty Samantha was surprised to not see the woman's hand stuck wrist-deep in a cookie jar.

"It means, Bettyann, that someone was here yesterday, asking questions about me, and you answered them."

"I did? What did I say?"

Samantha shook her head. Some things just weren't worth the effort. "Nothing, forget it."

"No, really," Bettyann said, standing up once more, and leaning her hands on the desktop. "Did I say something I shouldn't have said? And who did I say it to?"

"I'm not sure. Some secretary. Do you remember someone asking questions about me?"

Bettyann shook her head. "No. I do remember someone—a woman—coming in here yesterday, asking questions about everyone. You know, run-of-the-mill gossip. What it's like to work here, how are the bosses—stuff like that. I thought she was thinking of applying for the job we advertised last week. You know, sort of feeling us out without actually handing us a résumé? Why? Was it a reporter? Oh, cripes, Samantha, please tell me it wasn't a reporter."

"It wasn't a reporter," Samantha assured her. "Still, Bettyann, in the future, please try not to be so helpful to strangers, okay?"

"No, not okay. I shouldn't have said anything. I'm really, really sorry."

"I know. But we're getting closer and closer to New Hampshire, Bettyann, and the magnifying glass is being applied everywhere, including this office. I've been working on a memo directed to all staff, concerning questions that may come into the office. A sort of protocol to follow. I should have done it sooner.''

Bettyann grinned. ''Oh, good, it's your fault. I knew it wasn't my fault.''

''Spoken like a true politician. Get out of here,'' Samantha said on a laugh, and watched as Bettyann, hips exaggeratedly wiggling, left the office.

Once the secretary was gone, Samantha rewrapped her half-eaten sandwich and shoved it back into the navy-blue thermal bag she'd brought from home. Maybe she'd be hungry later, although she doubted it.

After Jesse Colton showed up, and looked at the papers locked in her bottom drawer? Maybe then she'd eat. Or she'd never be able to eat again.

Three hours later, while considering designs for a new series of campaign buttons, Samantha looked up at a knock on her opened office door.

She put down the buttons and stood up, then walked around the desk to give the well-dressed brunette a hug. ''Aunt Joan, what brings you to the salt mines?''

Mrs. Mark Phillips bestowed an air kiss on Samantha, then stepped back to look around the cluttered office. ''Oh, my. Time to get the bulldozers in here again, my dear,'' she said as Samantha quickly moved a stack of files from the only other chair and motioned for the senator's wife to sit down.

Joan Phillips was in her early fifties, but good genes and even better plastic surgery had her looking like a well-preserved forty. Or less.

Dark hair, marvelous blue eyes, skin the consistency of cream. A figure that flattered her designer suits. Jewels glittering on her hands and at her throat and ears, but discreetly, and half of them heirlooms that whispered rather than screamed "old money." A cultured voice, the ability to look adoringly at her husband as he made the same stump speech for the fiftieth time.

In short, Joan Phillips was the perfect candidate's wife.

Joan bent down and picked up the "Calm Day Across America" advertisement proposal Samantha had fashioned into an airplane and soared across the office...which was about as far as she thought it should go.

"Is this an editorial comment, or were you just playing?" the senator's wife asked, unfolding the makeshift airplane and reading the copy.

Samantha smiled. "I'll let you decide after you read it, okay?"

"Well, that must have taken at least two seconds of thought," Joan Phillips said after a moment, and then she refolded the page, sent it soaring toward the most distant corner of the room. "Did they come up with anything better than that, I most sincerely hope?"

"I've narrowed it down to two, yes, and I'll send those over for you and the senator to make the final decision. Or would you like to see them now?"

"No, no, not now. There's plenty of time for that when Mark and I are alone. I don't want to make up my mind without his input."

"Okay," Samantha said, wishing she didn't feel so nervous. Clumsy. All those bad things she always felt when in the presence of the neatly put-together Mrs. Mark Phillips.

It had always been that way, since she'd been a child. Uncle Mark was a doll, a peach. And his wife was lovely, ambitious. Very, very perfect.

Samantha always felt as if her own hair had to be messy and tangled, her blouse missing a button, her panty hose laddered with runs, whenever she was in Joan's presence. The woman didn't mean to make Samantha, or anyone, feel uncomfortable, but that perfection of hers could be intimidating to those who had to deal with her day to day in any official capacity.

To the public, she was just perfect. Pretty, friendly, articulate…even hip.

"Um…so…what does bring you down here, Aunt Joan?" Samantha asked when the silence became uncomfortable. For her, not for Joan. Joan was never uncomfortable.

"Well, dear, to tell you the truth, I just came to use the postal machine for some correspondence your uncle Mark and I want sent out. Is that what it's called? A postal machine? You know, that machine that marks envelopes with postage so that there's no need for stamps?"

"Close enough," Samantha said with a smile. "Would you like me to arrange to have one purchased for your home office? It would be more convenient for you."

"No, that's all right. I'm just as happy for an excuse to come see you and all our eager volunteers, dear. Besides, I have an appointment to have my nails done in a half hour." She reached into the lizard-skin briefcase she'd carried into the room with her and pulled out several flat, brown envelopes. "I'll just have someone stamp the postage on these and then I'll be out of your way."

"Oh, I'll do that," Samantha said, coming around the desk to take the envelopes from the woman.

"Really? Goodness, we don't pay you enough, dear. Thank you."

Samantha's heart was pounding as she accepted the envelopes.

And that's what they were. Envelopes, just envelopes. Four brown envelopes, the size needed to slip a typewritten page inside without folding it. Didn't all envelopes look alike? Of course they did.

Samantha put them on the desk behind her, then sort of blocked them with her body as she asked, "Is the president still deciding whether or not he'll be able to attend the fund-raiser next week?"

Joan rolled her eyes. "You know him, always trying to be the center of attention. Will he, won't he? I told your uncle Mark to announce that some Broadway cast, or one of those popular boy bands, or somebody like that would be there to perform. Entertainers always mean more media coverage. That would get Jackson to the affair, you could count on that, humming 'Hail To the Chief' to himself all the way."

"The whole world would want to be there if we could get that sort of entertainment, Aunt Joan. Even the opposition. But this isn't going to be that big a do, you know. Just two hundred of Uncle Mark's closest friends and supporters. Individuals. Nothing corporate.

Nothing to excite or upset anyone. We're just getting our feet wet.''

"Nonsense, Samantha. Your uncle has been raising funds on a daily basis for all of his three terms in the Senate. It's what has to be done. Only two hundred people? He doesn't need something small to get his feet wet. We're in fund-raising up to our ears, and have been since the beginning. You know as well as I that money for this presidential bid has been collecting in the proper accounts for almost two years. How else are we able to underpay you so badly, hmm? Now, who do you have for entertainment?''

"I'm...um...I'm still considering several options,'' Samantha said, desperately running through the file cabinet in her brain, wondering who she could call at the last moment, because she had not booked any entertainment.

"Well, good, then it's not to worry, is it?'' Joan said, getting to her feet in one fluid, graceful movement. "I must be off, I'm afraid. A stop at the salon, and then we have a dinner with several members of the party's California Primary Committee tonight at seven. We all know a candidate, to be viable, has to carry California. Have to plan ahead, right?''

"Definitely, and we're already polling well there, I'm happy to say,'' Samantha agreed, following Joan Phillips out of the office and through the central room that was loud with ringing telephones, clicking computer keys and the general babble of any office. "I'll...I'll be sure to get those envelopes in the mail for you, Aunt Joan. You said they were from both you and Uncle Mark?''

"Did I? Oh, yes, of course. Although we all know that, to your uncle, we're all errand boys, happy to do his bidding. Mine, his, ours, what does it matter? We must send out mail by the ton. Maybe I will take you up on that offer of one of those postal machines, dear. Except then I wouldn't get to see you so often, now, would I?"

With another exchange of air kisses, Joan Phillips was gone, and Samantha, after heaving a relieved sigh, was heading back into her office, carefully closing and locking the door behind her.

She spent the next two hours with a phone pressed to her ear, trying to round up some sort of entertainment that would follow the thousand-dollar-a-plate fund-raiser. As she dialed, then was put on hold, she pushed the envelopes Joan had left around her desktop with the eraser tip of a pencil.

She wanted to keep her distance, just in case one of them tried to bite her.

No return address, not on any of the envelopes. Just like the envelope locked in her bottom drawer. Computer-printed address labels, and all the addresses post office boxes, again just like the envelope locked in her bottom drawer.

Could she open the envelopes? Was that legal? There weren't any stamps on them yet, so it wasn't as if she'd be tampering with the U.S. mail.

Technically.

But it would be a breach of trust. Uncle Mark's trust in her. Her trust in him.

After two long, frustrating hours, Samantha had wrangled a gratis appearance at the fund-raiser out of a popular female country-music trio, promising their agent that the media coverage would be "substantial." Three very pretty girls; talented, and they wore skimpy costumes. That alone ought to make that thousand-dollar-a-plate rubber chicken go down easier.

But she still didn't know what to do with the envelopes. Five of them now. Fairly bulky.

No wonder her aunt Joan, known to be tight with a penny so she could spend lots of dollars, hadn't wanted to trust licking the correct amount of stamps. With only a post office box address, and no return address, the envelopes would end up in the dead letter office if the postage wasn't sufficient.

So much more efficient to use the postal machine in the campaign office.

Except that, Samantha knew, as a senator, Uncle Mark could send out all the official mail he wanted via his office, and at no charge.

So this wasn't official mail. Without the return address, it probably wasn't campaign literature, either.

So what was in these other envelopes? More of what she'd found in the first one?

It was that last thought, the one that had been nagging at her all afternoon, that had Samantha unlocking the bottom drawer and sliding the four envelopes into it, on top of the first envelope.

Jesse checked his watch for the second time in as many minutes. Was he already too late? He should have known he wouldn't get out of the office at a reasonable hour. Reasonable, in his line of work, meant anywhere between six and eight. Face it, reasonable quitting times, for those working in the West Wing, were a joke.

It was now almost nine, and he had chosen to jog over to Phillips's campaign headquarters rather than take his car and spend another twenty minutes hunting up a parking space.

He stopped outside the office building and looked up. Second floor. Yes, there were still lights on, which meant that Samantha was there, waiting for him.

Probably with her lovely slim, coral-tipped fingers drawn up into fists. Pacing, cursing him, second-guessing herself for having contacted him in the first place.

No matter what, he was pretty certain he wasn't going to be greeted as if he'd brought the flowers of May along with him. Not when she was so nervous about whatever the hell she thought was so important about the mail she'd discovered.

He walked past the elevator and climbed the stairs two at a time, stripping off his black raincoat and mussing his hair enough that, he hoped, he didn't look like a SSST—Stereotypical Secret Service Type.

The last thing he wanted to look was official on this visit, in any way.

He walked into the office, surprised to see so many people still there, talking on phones, licking envelopes and examining poll numbers chalked on a large board.

First, he thought with a small smile, you work your buns off to get into the office, and then you work your buns off to stay there. First the small, crowded office, the Styrofoam white boater hats with the red, white and blue ribbons on them, the campaign jingles, the stale doughnuts and sore ears from spending their lives on the phone. Then the win, and a move to the OEOB, or maybe even the West Wing, and even longer hours for less satisfaction, not as many wins.

And no nifty Styrofoam boater hats.

Campaign workers were like hamsters running on one of those endless wheels, always running, never really getting anywhere. They just believed they did.

A blonde badly in need of a dye job walked past, reading a fax, and Jesse put out his arm to stop her. "Excuse me, but is Ms. Cosgrove available?"

The blonde looked up, blinked, and then put one hand on her hip. "If she's not, I am. Bettyann Muldoon, at your service. And I do mean that literally."

Jesse smiled one of his aw-shucks grins. "Thank you, ma'am, but I really do need to see Ms. Cosgrove."

"Ma'am? Oh, boy, now I know I'm past it. What's next, I ask you, orthopedic shoes?" Bettyann said, grimacing. "Well, I guess I might as well start acting like I've read the latest memo, huh?"

"And I'll pretend as if I know what you're talking about, okay? In any case, go for it, Bettyann," Jesse said, still grinning.

"Thank you. Here goes." She stood up taller and said in a patently fake official-sounding voice, "I'm so sorry, sir, but I don't believe I got your name. Do you have an appointment to see Ms. Cosgrove?"

"Not an appointment, not in the penciled-in-at-nine sort of appointment anyway, but she is expecting me. Perhaps she mentioned me? Jesse Colton?"

"Oh, so this is *personal?*" Bettyann asked, looking

as if she might pull out a pen and paper and begin taking notes.

"You could say that," Jesse told her, giving her another grin. This one not so shy and boyish.

"Hot damn, it's about time that girl got out and about. You just stay here, Mr....um...Mr....oh, just stay here, okay? I'll go get her."

Jesse busied himself looking around the large, square room, admiring the huge, smiling-faced reproduction of Senator Mark Phillips's handsome, even distinguished face plastered on one wall from floor to ceiling.

Red, white and blue bunting was everywhere, along with the requisite number of flags, the autographed photograph of Phillips with the president, taken in the Oval Office, and another of the senator and his charming wife posed on a rocky beach.

The atmosphere in the room was barely controlled pandemonium, and Jesse decided that he could probably work in this office for oh, five minutes, before the top of his head blew clean off.

Into this mess strode Samantha Cosgrove, the dye-job blonde trailing in her wake.

Samantha looked like the calm in the middle of the storm, the serene princess who kept her cool while everyone else ran around bumping into each other like the cast of a *Three Stooges* reprise.

He could have kissed her.

Hey, wait a moment. Why couldn't he kiss her?

"Samantha," he said, stepping toward her just as she opened her mouth, probably to tell him to go away, come back later, when the madness had died down.

Fat chance.

"Hello, baby," he crooned as he drew her into his arms, and he got a quick peek at Bettyann just before he claimed Samantha's mouth.

The secretary's eyes opened so wide that if someone hit her on the back of the head, both orbs might just have popped out, rolled away on the floor.

But that didn't matter. What mattered was that Samantha's mouth was everything he'd dreamed of through a long, nearly sleepless night. Warm, soft. Like her body. Warm, soft.

Her mouth tasted so good.

How would the rest of her taste?

She began to struggle, but not obviously, so that someone would come to her assistance. Oh, no. Samantha Cosgrove was too much the lady to do anything obvious. What she did was put her hands up to either side of his neck, then push her thumbnails into the crease directly behind each of his ears.

It did smart. It definitely did smart. He'd have to tell the guys at Quantico about the move, and they could add it to their One Thousand Nifty Ways to Disarm an Adversary handbook.

He pulled back his head just slightly and smiled down at her.

"What in hell do you think you're doing?" she asked. But she whispered.

"I'm kissing you hello," he explained, also in a whisper. And then he kissed her again, on the side of the throat, so that he could be even closer to her ear. "Think, Samantha. Nobody can know I'm here on official business, right? I thought you'd be the only one here."

"Oh. I hadn't thought of that. Okay. But you can let me go now. Please?"

"I don't want to," he said honestly.

"Tough beans," she answered, and when he dropped his arms in surprise, she stepped away from him.

"I take it you know Jesse James here?" Bettyann asked Samantha, jerking a thumb at him. "Man. If I could keep a secret like that, I'd have to wonder why."

"Go away, Bettyann," Samantha said, but she smiled as she said it. "Oh, and why not take everyone else with you. There's really nothing more anyone can do tonight about those new poll numbers."

"Are you sure? We dropped six points. If the newspapers were to find out about our private poll...? I mean, are you sure?" Bettyann was still looking at Jesse.

"Positive. And there will be a new set of numbers next week. I've checked, and New Hampshire is known for doing this sort of thing, right up until the primary. I think they like the attention they get when the outcome is still up in the air. But they're savvy voters, Bettyann, very well informed, so the senator will win when the votes really count. But remember, those numbers are confidential, and not for public consumption, should anyone ask."

"Spoken like a true, loyal campaign worker," Jesse said, walking with Samantha toward her open office door. "Did he lose his lead? The president wouldn't like that."

"No, he didn't lose his lead, but he's dropped out of a double-digit lead for the moment. And you weren't supposed to hear *any* of that,'' she told him, closing the door behind them, then turned to look at him, shake her head. ''Bettyann seems to have this problem.''

''A problem?''

''Yes. Her mouth. She opens it *way* too much.''

''Filled peppers?'' Jesse asked, grinning at her.

''Exactly. She trusts everybody. She trusted your secretary, probably because she's one of those innocent-looking types. I mean, you wouldn't have used her if she would have come in here swirling her cape and looking like the female half of Boris and Natasha, now, would you? And now Bettyann trusted you just because you're gorgeous—oh, damn! Never mind that last part.''

''Are you kidding? I'm never going to forget it. So, you think I'm gorgeous?''

''No,'' Samantha said, rolling her eyes. ''Bettyann thinks you're gorgeous. She also thinks your name is Jesse James, so don't be too flattered, okay? Now, do you want to see what I've got or not?''

''Now *there's* a line I could interpret in many wonderful ways.''

''Oh, shut up.''

''Touchy. I probably have to feed you again.'' Jesse looked around the small, cluttered office. ''This place doesn't look anything like you. I'd pictured chrome and glass and...oh, I don't know. Order?''

''I work well in clutter,'' Samantha said, seating herself behind the desk. ''What I don't work well in is being the center of office gossip. You do realize that now that everyone thinks you're my boyfriend, all I'll get are questions about you? And then sympathy, once you're gone again. Just what I've always wanted to be, the lovesick gal dropped by the gorgeous man. I can hear Bettyann now, looking all sad-eyed and sorry, constantly asking if I want to 'talk about it.' Yippee.''

He walked over to one corner, peeked under the shade of a floor lamp. ''One public kiss makes me your boyfriend?''

''Around here, yes. Or have you forgotten that Washington is the birthplace of more gossip than even Hollywood? By tomorrow morning they'll have us picking out china patterns. It's disgusting.''

''So now we have to get married?'' Jesse asked, just because Samantha was blushing, and she looked really cute when she blushed. Not so sleek, so sophisticated. More touchable. Definitely touchable. He looked up at the ceiling light, an old-fashioned chandelier type, but fortunately very plain in its design. Nope. He didn't see anything there.

''Sure, why not,'' she said, pulling a small key from her purse. ''I'd like three children, I believe. Two boys and a girl.''

''Glad to hear you have this all figured out.'' Jesse went down on his hands and knees, ran one hand along the underside of a folding worktable stacked with manila folders and campaign bumper stickers.

He moved his hand slowly, carefully. And then he felt it. He stuck his head under the table, took a good look. *Bingo!* He stood up once more, moved away from the table. ''Two boys and a girl, you say? I'll have to work on that. Can we start tonight? I mean, hey, tonight's good for me.''

She was looking at him as if he'd just set his own

hair on fire. "You're impossible, as well as hopelessly optimistic. We're meeting here, Jesse, because I didn't want to meet you anywhere else. Understand? And what are you doing?"

He put one finger over his lips, then pulled a small notebook from his pocket and borrowed a pen from the cup on her desk. Scribbled a few words, handed the note to her.

"Do I understand? That's what you asked? If I understood?" he asked as she read the note. "I think *you* also need to understand, darling."

She looked at him as if he'd penned "There's a great big bomb in here and it detonates in five, four, three, two—oops, too late!"

He grinned at her as she continued to goggle at him, and then spoke again before she could so much as open her mouth. "Well, to be clearer, I think I do understand what you think you understand. To you, this is strictly business, your effort to turn me into a rabid Phillips for President advocate. It's probably going to take days, even weeks, before you'll admit how much you love me."

"How much I love you? What are you talking about? I want to talk about—"

He shook his head, kept talking. "Gee, that's too bad. And here I was, all ready to ask you if you wanted to tour the Georgetown mansion next Friday. That, and to convince you that you don't just want me as a Phillips supporter. You're hot for my body."

Samantha was still looking at him as she repeatedly pointed to the note he'd written. "You're kidding."

She hadn't even heard him make that hot-for-his-body crack. Pity. He would have liked to have heard her response.

"I said," she repeated, "you're kidding, right?"

He shook his head. "Kidding? I'll have you know, Ms. Cosgrove, that I am loyal, and trustworthy, very often discreet, and still suffer from that George Washington complex. No, I'm not kidding. The current tenants are leaving for new quarters, and the place will be empty next Friday, at which time I—good person who never lies—get the key. The key, darling. So, are you interested?"

She held up the key that *she* already had in her hand, then frowned at him in question.

Good girl. She was scared, but she wasn't slow on the uptake. She knew what he wanted, why he'd mentioned the key.

He nodded, and Samantha nodded back at him as he picked up the note he'd written and slid it into the pocket of his suit jacket.

She opened the drawer, pulled out a stack of brown envelopes and slammed them down on the desktop. "You know I'm interested. In the house, Jesse, not you. Whatever we had, it's over, gone, *kaput.* Do you hear me?"

As she said those last words, she spoke directly at the folding table.

He gave an exaggerated sigh. He had to keep this light, keep it silly, if possible. Just two young lovers having a spat; nothing anyone would spend much time listening to, or try to decipher. "Ah, sweetheart. There goes your membership in the George Washington I Cannot Tell a Whopper Club. I mean, when you were kissing a guy out there in the outer office? I was the guy. And you were interested.''

''Maybe,'' she said, sorting through the envelopes, pulling out the bottom one, the open one. She held up one finger, then all five, and looked at him questioningly. ''You *are* kind of cute, in a pathetic sort of way.''

He held up five fingers. Hey, she said one, but if she had more than one, he wanted all of them. ''Gorgeous. You said I was gorgeous.''

Samantha wet her lips with the tip of her tongue. She was nervous, sure, but she was also great. Coming along like gangbusters, as if she did this all the time. He smiled encouragingly at her. ''I did not call you gorgeous,'' she said. ''Bettyann did. I thought you smart guys knew how to keep your facts straight.''

''We also know how to bend the facts so that they sound good, better than they really are. So, what about me do you find gorgeous? My eyes? My chin? My engaging smile? My scintillating repartee? Tell me how you love me. Let's count the ways.''

Samantha stood up and glared at him across the desktop. ''Would you please stop that.''

''Not until you tell me that you love me.''

As he said the words, he pointed to the folding table just to remind her. Whoever could hear them had to think they were lovers not conspirators. ''Say it.'' He slowly, silently mouthed the words *I...love...you.*

She blinked, then swallowed hard as she absorbed those three words. ''I loved you yesterday,'' she said at last, opening her briefcase and putting all five of the envelopes inside, closing it again. "Today I think you're nuts."

"Ah, another of my sterling features. I'm nuts. Speaking of nuts, are you hungry? I sure could do with some spaghetti, or maybe some Chinese?"

"I've got leftover roast beef at home, and some garlic mashed potatoes."

"Beef good, garlic bad, especially with what I have in mind, darling," Jesse said, motioning for her to come out from behind the desk.

She did, but then she stopped next to the folding table, bent down and looked at the underside of the thing.

Two seconds later, she was standing again, and her gorgeous blue eyes were open very wide. "Did you— do you *see*—"

Well, there was nothing else he could do, was there? She'd been great, a real brick, but now she was having a minor meltdown, and she was going to blow the whole thing. He had no choice. He had to kiss her again.

It might not have been part of his training as an agent, shutting someone up this way, but he was always open to learning new things.

Chapter Three

Very high on Samantha's to-do list was getting Jesse Colton to kiss her again. Definitely.

But it wasn't number one.

It couldn't be.

The moment they were outside the office building, she grabbed his arm, half spun him around and whispered hoarsely, "A *bug?* My office is *bugged?* Who? How? *Why?*"

Jesse ran a fingertip down her cheek. "You're cute when you're panic-stricken."

"Oh, shut up," she said, rapidly walking ahead of him down the wide pavement. Then she stopped. "Wait. Where are we going?"

"That depends, I suppose. My car's back at the lot. Where's yours?"

"Closer. We have our own lot out back. I'll drive you to yours. And then we're going somewhere to talk."

"I thought I'd been invited home to dinner?"

Samantha frowned as they turned the corner, headed for the back of the building. "Did I do that? I can't remember much at the moment."

"You did it, sweetheart. I accepted the roast beef, rejected the garlic mashed potatoes. Ring any chords in your memory?"

No, she thought. She was pretty sure her memories would pretty much concentrate on his mouthing the words *I love you,* and then kissing her. Again.

Even more, her dreams would be haunted by his words when she told him to let her go: "I don't want to."

The man had a way with words....

She shook herself out of her definitely mushy mood. "Too bad about the potatoes, because I'm having them."

"In that case, so will I. Well, that's one problem solved. Now, where did you park?"

She pressed a hand to her forehead and looked around the parking lot. Where had she parked her car? She *had* driven to work, right?

Now, *there* was a thought she should have had sooner.

Samantha looked at him, felt her cheeks growing hot. "I remember now. I took the Metro this morning."

"Easy enough to forget," Jesse said, swinging her around so that they were heading in the direction of the parking deck where his sedan waited. "After all, you've had an interesting few minutes."

She nodded as she did a quick double-step to keep

up with his long strides. "Bugged. I can't believe this. Who'd do that?"

"Well, for starters, the bug isn't government issue. That rules out a lot."

"So I'm not under some federal investigation?"

"I don't think so. But that leaves some even more uncomfortable conclusions."

"Name one."

"Okay. The opposition. It's a stretch, but dumb has been done before. Then there's the question of who rented the space before you guys moved in. This could be a leftover bug, inoperative now, from someone who'd been listening in on the last tenants."

Samantha liked that idea a lot. "Yes, that could be it. That has to be it. A leftover bug, one they missed when they cleaned out all the other bugs. Do you think there could be other bugs?"

"You like that scenario, do you? It's Washington, sweetheart, so we'll say scenario. It sounds so official."

"Would you just shut up and tell me what you think, please?"

"Ah, the lady has a temper. Okay, okay, how about this one? Your own people have bugged their own campaign office. You know, just to keep themselves informed about everything that goes on?"

Samantha stopped dead on the sidewalk. "No," she said, her heart pounding. "Uncle Mark wouldn't do that."

"Which answers my next question. You're not going to ask him, are you?"

"Ask him! Are you nuts? Are you out of your mind? I can't *ask* him."

"Probably not," Jesse said as they entered the parking deck. "Besides, I really should check out the bug more, make sure it is active. We can do that tomorrow night, after hours. I just need a few pieces of equipment, especially since I want to check for more listening devices."

"Yes, that's another thing. Why did you check? Do you know something I don't know?"

"Volumes, darling, when it comes to this kind of stuff," he said, his smile taking any sting out of his words. "And I don't know why I checked. Just a natural response for someone with my training, I guess. Little kids check under the bed for ogres, and I check everywhere else for listening devices, hidden cameras, all kinds of goodies."

"Well...thank you. I think," Samantha said as he held open the passenger-side door for her and she slipped inside. This time she let her raincoat fall open and gave him a glimpse of knee. He deserved that, at the least.

He started the car and backed out of the parking space, headed for the exit. "You didn't answer me. Do you know who the last tenant was in your office?"

"I don't know, no, but I don't have to know, because I just remembered something else. I bought that table. It wasn't in my office when we moved in."

"That's not good news."

"Duh," Samantha said, rolling her eyes. "Oh, I'm sorry, I didn't mean to be nasty," she said a moment later. "I'm...I'm pretty stressed right now."

"And still very pretty, sweetheart," Jesse said, reaching over to pat her arm. "I kind of like how you forgot you took the Metro to work this morning."

She nodded. "Yes. I couldn't find my car keys. I have an extra set, but for some strange reason I keep those in my office desk."

"Is that so?" Jesse said, then shook his head slightly.

"Bugged," Samantha said in aid of nothing except her own inability to absorb this news.

They drove the rest of the way in silence, both wrapped up in private thoughts.

Jesse pulled into a clear spot a few doors down from her house and cut the engine, but when she moved to open the door he placed a restraining hand on her arm.

"What? Don't tell me you want me to wait for you to be a gentleman?"

"That, too, but first I want to ask you a question. Last night, when I brought you home, you searched in your purse for something, then rang to have your maid let you into the house. Why?"

Samantha sat back against the soft leather seat. "Why? Because I couldn't find my keys. I told you that."

"Okay, I was just laying background here. It helps me think. Now, tell me, what keys do you keep on that particular ring? House key, key to the car—anything else?"

She reached into her purse and came out with a burgundy leather key case that snapped shut over her ample store of keys, waved it at him. "Sure. The keys to the offices, the main one and mine. The key to my bike chain. The key to my desk drawers, the one to my files, the—oh, boy.''

"Exactly, sweetheart. Oh boy. But you had the keys tonight, right?''

She nodded. "I keep extra office keys, desk keys, hidden in Bettyann's desk, so I could work, but it was late this afternoon before Bettyann found my case on the floor next to the copy machine in the main office. I don't remember using the machine, but I must have, and then left them there.''

"Uh-huh.''

"What *uh-huh?* I don't think I like when you say uh-huh. Scratch that. I definitely don't like it when you say uh-huh. So, what uh-huh? What are you thinking?''

"Nothing,'' he said, but he said it too quickly for Samantha's comfort.

"Don't do that, Jesse. If you're thinking something, I want to know what something you're thinking.''

"Okay, here goes. Someone lifted your keys yesterday, and used them to get into the office last night.''

"To plant that bug?''

He shook his head. "No, I don't think so. That's probably been there for a while, maybe even since you first opened up shop. Maybe there's something wrong with the bug, and they needed to get in to fix it…or to plant something else. You didn't notice anything unusual, like on your desk, in your desk drawers? Did anything look out of place?''

She laughed without humor. "You *have* seen my office, haven't you? I wouldn't notice an elephant sitting smack in the middle of the room playing a fiddle.''

"True. They probably counted on that.''

"They counted on what? And who's *they?* Who counted on it?"

"Whoever borrowed your keys, Samantha. Don't panic, and stay with me on this, okay? Someone needed the key to your office, maybe even to your desk. They just happened to get your car key and house key, but what they probably wanted was your desk key. Tell me, have you kept those envelopes in that locked drawer all along?"

Samantha began biting on the side of her thumb, a nervous habit she thought she'd left behind her in the third grade. "Yes, that's where I put it last week. Those other envelopes just came in today, and I put them with the first one."

"I was going to ask about that. I thought you'd only said one envelope. Okay. So you took an envelope that was supposed to go out in the mail last week. The envelope doesn't arrive where it's supposed to, when it's supposed to, and someone comes to check out why. You with me so far?"

"Sort of. But what about the bug?"

"Amateur-hour stuff, I'm sure of it. The kind of thing you can buy mail order these days, when nobody trusts anybody else. We may be working with two entirely different things. Or just one person with a whacking-great paranoia problem."

"Uncle...you mean Senator Phillips? No, I can't see it. I just can't."

"You're loyal, Samantha, and that's nice. I, on the other hand, am suspicious of everyone. It's my training. That said," he continued, pulling the keys out of the ignition, "we're going into your house now, but we're not talking until I've at least given it a visual once-over for bugs. Your house key was missing all day and night, right?''

"Right. But I've got Rose.''

"She was in the house all day yesterday?''

Samantha sighed. "No. Rose is also a full-time college student. She had a full boatload of classes yesterday. She only wears the uniform once in a while, as a joke, and to get a rise out of me—like when she has to take out the garbage. She keeps calling me the czarina and herself a prime example of the oppressed proletariat laboring class. She's majoring in Russian history, you understand.''

"Cute. So she wasn't home? Still, we can't be sure. Do you have a security system?''

Samantha brightened. "Yes! We have a security system. How could I forget that? You have to punch in a code within so many seconds of unlocking the door and—oh, damn it!''

"Now, why do you suppose I'm thinking that the next thing you're going to say isn't going to make me happy?''

"This tears it. Mother and Dad find out and I'm home before I can pack. You know that, don't you? Juliet gets to run all over New York, and our brother is on his own at college, but not me. Oh, no. Not Samantha. Why do parents always pick one to keep on a shorter leash?''

He took her leather key case from her slack hand and opened it. "Oh, I don't know, Samantha. But if I were to hazard a guess, I'd say it might be because one of their kids just might think she's going to forget things like, say, a security code, and so she writes it down inside her key case with permanent black marker. How's that for a guess?''

"I hate you," she muttered, grabbing the key case from him. "If I give you a quarter, will you promise not to tell my parents?''

"If you give me a kiss, I won't even give you a lecture on security. At least not one that lasts more than about ten minutes. How's that?''

Samantha glared at him, then opened the car door. ''Come on. I want you to see if there are any bugs in my house. Then I'll feed you, and then I'll show you the papers. After that, hey, buying me one dinner and finding a bug in my office do not count toward kissing privileges. You didn't even kill the bug for me.''

''I knew she'd get around to saying that one at some point,'' she overheard him grumble to himself before he, too, got out of the car.

Jesse spoke with Rose for about twenty minutes, the same amount of time it took for Samantha to go from looking great but professional to great but touchable.

Oh, boy. Definitely touchable.

When she reappeared downstairs, dressed in soft burgundy velour slacks and an ivory angora sweater with a large cowl collar, her blond hair pulled back in a casual ponytail at her nape, he was in the middle of one last question to Rose…a question which he promptly forgot.

''Yoo-hoo, still in there?'' Rose asked with a grin, waving a hand in front of Jesse's face. ''Man, I wish I had that effect on men,'' the short brunette continued, making a face. "Heck, I'd settle for one man. And he could be bald, really. I'm not choosy."

"Oh, stop it, Rose," Samantha said. "I had to put a separate telephone line in here in order to be able to use the phone, because you get so many calls."

Rose beamed. "That's true. I'm a goddess. Okay, I'm fine now. It was a momentary lapse. I have those when she's around," she added, looking at Jesse while she hooked a thumb in Samantha's direction. "Hey, why am I telling you? You're one of the poleaxed, right? Because you sure looked it when she came down those stairs."

"Guilty as charged, Rose," Jesse said, winking at the girl. "She's a babe."

"Cut that out," Samantha protested, sitting down in a large green leather chair, tucking her bare feet up beside her on the seat cushion. "I can see Rose has found a kindred spirit in you. I probably should have a shield, or a sword, or something, just to make things even."

"Yeah, well, fun's fun and all that," Rose said, getting to her feet, "but the books are calling me. Rasputin. Now, *there* was a piece of work, let me tell you. Do you know how many times they had to kill him until he finally died? I mean, this is big stuff!"

"Go away, Rose," Samantha said, shaking her head, and Rose skipped out of the room.

"She's not really a maid, is she?" Jesse asked once the young woman was gone.

"Technically, she is. In reality, she rules me. But it was the only way Mother would let me move back here, so Rose moved in and earns her keep and I have someone to talk to, someone who'd call the police if I didn't come home one night and ask them to drag the river for my body. That sort of thing. My mother's a good egg, honest, but she has this tendency to think in potential tragedies.''

Jesse nodded. ''Mothers can be like that. I know, because I have one, too. Oh, and you were right. Rose was gone most of yesterday.''

Samantha leaned forward in her chair. ''Can we really talk here?''

''Yeah, it's okay, we're clear, at least in this room. Although you might want Rose to dust behind the couch if you don't think she'll give you a lecture on abuse of the working classes. I think the dust bunnies have begun to mate.''

''Funny.'' Samantha made a face at him. He loved when she did that. She went from looking like a sleek high-fashion model to being this cute, comic girl-woman. The kind who could make one hell of an entrance at a party in her designer gown, yet look just as good in a sweater and corduroys, rolling around in the fall leaves.

Man, he was getting hooked. He was really getting hooked.

''Anyway, I think we're pretty safe in assuming that nobody was in here. It's a lot neater here than in your office, and Rose didn't think anything was out of place. Still, I'll give it a much more thorough check tomorrow.''

''So whoever took my keys—if anyone took my keys—wanted them to get into my office, into my desk?''

"That would be my guess. Are you hungry?"

"Probably. But I'm still too upset. No, scratch that. I'm *angry*. I'm really, really angry."

Jesse understood. "The violation, right?"

"Yes, exactly. I feel as if I've been violated. Is that stupid?"

"Not at all. Now, how about we hit the kitchen and warm up those leftovers."

She got to her feet and led the way. "You don't mind leftovers?"

"Sweetheart," he said, "I don't mind any food that started out as home-cooked, trust me. I'd even eat it cold."

She turned to him in the narrow hallway leading to the kitchen. "Why do you do that?"

"Why do I do what?" She smelled good, really good. Like spring flowers.

"Call me sweetheart. Call me darling."

"I do?"

She gave him a small push in the chest. "You know darn full well you do."

"Hmm," he said as she continued into the small but perfect kitchen. "I'll have to think about this. Do you think it's subconscious?"

"No, I don't think it's subconscious," she told him, pulling containers of food out of the refrigerator. "I think you're very conscious of everything you do."

"In that case, should I stop?"

She hesitated, holding plastic containers in both hands. "Let me think about that."

Feeling pretty darn good about himself, Jesse took

the containers from her and she dived back into the refrigerator for two more.

"Sit," she said, taking the containers from him and motioning toward a heavy round oak table and ladder-back chairs. "This kitchen is too small for two people, or at least that's what Rose says when she wants to get out of kitchen duty."

Jesse decided that, where Samantha was concerned, he was nothing if not obedient. He sat down, cupped his chin in one hand and happily watched her swift, efficient movements as she loaded containers of food into the microwave, ripped some romaine for salad.

"You like to cook," he said, and it wasn't a question.

"I love it," she said, looking at him over her shoulder. "I used to haunt this kitchen, and then the one in Connecticut. The colors, the smells, the textures. Even the cleanup doesn't bother me. Rose is very grateful for that, and in exchange, she does all the washing and ironing. I think I got the better end of the bargain."

"I think Rose fell into a pile of more roses, myself," Jesse said, pulling two glasses from a glass-fronted cabinet and filling them with ice from the dispenser built into the front of the refrigerator. "Ice water? Something else?"

"There are cans of soda in the pantry—that long cabinet over there. I'd offer you wine, but I want to keep a clear head, and I think even a sip of wine, with me feeling the way I do now, would send me over the edge into full-blown hysteria."

Ten minutes later, they were sitting across from each other at the table, and Jesse was falling deeper into love. The roast beef was tender and tasty, the gravy thick and dark, and the garlic mashed potatoes were a gift from the gods he was glad he hadn't turned down.

"If your leftovers taste this good, tell me who I have to kill to be invited for Sunday dinner."

"I'm glad you like everything," Samantha said, looking both pleased and proud at his comment. "I'm a plain cook, but I'm a good cook, if I do say so myself. Now, how about we leave these dishes and go look at the envelope that first had me calling you for help."

"I thought you said you liked to clean up."

"No, sir, Mr. Colton, sir, I certainly did not say that. I said I don't mind. Nobody *likes* cleaning up. Oh, all right, let's do it. I swear, sometimes there are more dishes and containers just heating leftovers than there are in making a full dinner."

Jesse picked up his own dinner plate and salad bowl and headed for the sink. This felt good. Natural. Being in this cozy kitchen with Samantha Cosgrove. Doing simple, domestic things.

He suddenly wanted things he'd never wanted before. A home of his own. Kids sleeping upstairs.

Samantha.

He watched appreciatively as she bent over the dishwasher, loading the last of the dishes, then started the appliance. Some people might say Mount Rushmore had a great view. Others, the Grand Canyon.

He'd take this view, any day…

"So," she said, straightening, wiping her hands on a dish towel. "I guess we can't put this off any longer. Back to the living room?"

"Since I checked it out already, yes. And you know, you never told me what you found in that envelope."

"You never asked," she said, preceding him back down the hallway.

"That's because I figured you were overreacting, but if I found out you were, you'd say we didn't have to see each other anymore, and I wasn't ready for that. How's that for honest, sweetheart?"

She half stumbled over a Persian-style throw rug, then kept walking.

Once back in the living room, she removed the envelopes from her briefcase, handed them to him, and sat down in the green leather chair once more.

He picked the couch, a soft, chintz-covered affair that probably had been restuffed and recovered umpteen times. Good furniture was like that, he'd heard. Kept forever, recovered and restrung, and always as comfortable as an old slipper.

"This is a great room," he said, laying the envelopes in his lap. "Does that fireplace work?"

"It's gas, yes. Should I turn it on?"

Would he like to see Samantha's blond hair and clear features in firelight? Yeah, he could handle that. "I'll do it," he said, but when he was only halfway to his feet the fire had already gone on.

"How'd you do that?" he asked, subsiding again.

She held up a small remote control. "Magic," she said, and grinned. "Okay. Fire's on, room's been commented on. Can we get on with this before I burst?"

So she knew he'd been stalling. Hell, that wasn't a stretch. He'd already admitted why he'd been stalling. But, he would admit only to himself, there was also a part of him that couldn't wait to see the papers that had set off such an alarm in Samantha's mind.

"Do the open one first. That way, if it's nothing, we don't even have to look at the others, right?"

"Beautiful, a great cook, and logical, too," Jesse said, locating the open envelope and sliding out the ten or so pages it held.

He looked at the first page, then looked at Samantha.

Poor baby. She was staring at him, eyes wide, and biting on the side of her thumb again.

He looked back at the page, then turned to the next, quickly flipped to the next.

"Oh boy," he said at last, sitting back on the couch. "Do you know what this is?"

She nodded. "I do. At least I think I do. I think it's planned legislation for a possible targeted tax break to certain types of industries."

"It sure is. And it's committee-stage work, not for public consumption. Nobody knows about this yet. I mean, sure, the president probably knows, and the majority leader, and the committee heads, of course. But this is early stuff, supposition, trial balloon-type stuff. Sort of a feasibility test, to see if it could work, help the economy. If these industries knew what was being discussed in this memo, the lobbyists would be out in droves, covering the Capitol, wining and dining, hoping for votes."

"So it shouldn't have gone out in the mail," Samantha said, twisting her hands in her lap.

"Hell no," Jesse said, looking at the pages again. "These are internal notes, an internal memo, and just to the majority's side of the committee at that. I don't get it."

"Yes, you do," Samantha said, and she turned away from him, stared into the fire.

"Okay, yes I do. If I wanted to sell my vote to the highest bidder, I'd want companies involved in these industries to know I'm up for sale."

"Like, maybe, they could buy a friend in government by contributing, big time, to a certain senator's presidential election campaign?"

"Move that girl to the head of the class," Jesse said, shoving the papers back into the envelope.

"What are you going to do?"

Jesse was angry, and it took him a moment to realize that although Samantha might also be angry, she also had other problems. She worked for Senator Phillips. She was, at this point, a reluctant whistle-blower. Not anyone's favorite place to be in Washington, D.C.

"First," he said carefully, "I'm going to look at the rest of these envelopes, see what's in them. I see that each one is addressed to a different post office box. Five envelopes, five different cities and states. Maybe they all contain copies of that same memo?"

"Are you sure we can open them? I mean, aren't they U.S. mail?"

"Not yet. There are no stamps on them."

"That's splitting hairs, Jesse," she told him. "I did the same thing. But I have to tell you, I still feel guilty about it."

"Close your eyes, then, and don't look," Jesse said as he opened the first sealed envelope.

He opened the second, the third. Didn't bother with the fourth.

"Blank. Nothing but blank pages," he said as Samantha gnawed on the side of her thumb once more, realized what she was doing and immediately stopped.

"I don't get it. Why would Aunt Joan be sending out blank pages?"

Jesse laid the envelopes to one side. "Do the words *this is a test* sound at all familiar?"

"A test? Of who? Whom, I mean. I'm sure I mean whom. A test of whom?"

Jesse wasn't sure. He hated not being sure. "I don't know. A test of the delivery system? A test meant for you? Tell me again about Mrs. Phillips's visit today. Step by step, sweetheart, don't leave anything out."

She did as he asked, with amazing detail, all the way down to Joan Phillips's move with the discarded advertising copy, how she sent it winging into a corner of the room.

"Okay," he said when Samantha had finished speaking. "This is just off the top of my head, but here goes. One, Mrs. Phillips brought the envelopes into your office, walking past all the people in the outside office, the postage machine, you name it, to let you see the envelopes."

"That's true. She could have handed them to Bettyann. Or Rita. Anybody. She certainly didn't have to carry them into my office."

"Two," Jesse went on, getting into it now. "She diverted your attention throwing that paper airplane. You did follow its flight, right?"

"Right," Samantha said, nodding. "It was a short

flight, though, Jesse. I probably only took my eyes off her for a couple of seconds.''

"But she was sitting in the chair directly next to the worktable? The one with the bug stuck underneath it? It takes less than three seconds to place a bug, Samantha. They come with their own built-in sticky bottoms now.''

Samantha got to her feet, began to pace. "You think…you think Aunt Joan placed the bug under the table?''

"It's just one scenario, sweetheart, but yeah, it's possible. At the same time, she returned your keys, leaving them near the photocopier in the main office.''

"No. I don't get it,'' Samantha said, returning to her chair. "Why would she take my keys?''

"Samantha. If she's the one who brought the first envelope to the office, to have it sent from there, then she knows it didn't arrive at its destination, because whoever was waiting for it told her it hadn't arrived. So she comes back—was she at the office yesterday?''

Samantha considered this. "I don't—wait, yes, she was. Bettyann told me she'd stopped by while I was out. I think I was stalking you at the time, as a matter of fact.''

"Did you take your car, or walk?''

"I walked.'' She rolled her eyes toward the ceiling. "Yes. Yes, I'm sure of that. I walked.''

"So your keys were…?''

"In my desk?'' She shrugged. "I really don't know. But probably in my desk, because I would have used them to open my office, then my desk drawers. Okay, yes, they were on top of my desk not in it.''

"Where anyone had access to them?"

"Well, it isn't as if my office is a high-security area. Although maybe it should be."

"Good thinking."

"All right, so let's go with it. Your keys were there, you weren't there, and someone walked off with them. Agreed?"

"And you think my aunt Joan took them? I know you aren't saying that, but you're thinking it, aren't you?"

Jesse raised one eyebrow as he looked at her.

"I don't believe it, not for a moment." She sighed. "Okay, maybe for a moment. Tell me more."

"All right. If she did take the keys, she took them because she was looking for the envelope that was supposed to have been mailed from here last week. You're the head of the office, Samantha. She knows you oversee everything. So you'd be the logical choice, because Bettyann, or this Rita person, or anyone else, would probably just have mailed the thing. Agreed? She was looking for the envelope, some evidence of it at least."

"And she found it? The envelope, I mean. I don't want to call it evidence."

"No, I don't think she saw it. That's why she came back, with the faked envelopes as red herrings, to see what would happen to them."

"It...it sounds so...I don't know—Tom Clancy?"

"Sure. But now we're doing the hunt for another sort of red October."

"Don't make jokes. This is serious."

"This is also something I can't keep the lid on for very long, Samantha, you do know that, don't you?"

Samantha's stomach knotted. "But you can't! I mean, who would you tell? I didn't bring you in on this because I wanted to break some awful new political scandal. I brought you in on this because... because..."

"Because you wanted me to pat you on the head and tell you everything would be all right. Sorry, sweetheart, that's just not going to happen."

"No, I suppose not. But we can't be sure it was Aunt Joan."

"No. It could be the senator. Which is worse? Oh, wait, I know," he said, shaking his head. "It could be both of them. How's that for a scenario?"

"I won't believe it. Not Uncle Mark. He's honest. And he's really not all that ambitious. I mean, if it weren't for Aunt Joan, I doubt he'd even be thinking about the nomination. He's very happy in the Senate."

"Really? I didn't know that. Ambitious, is she?" Jesse was silent for a few moments.

"What? You have this *look* on your face. What are you thinking?"

"Nothing." Jesse knew it was time to shut up, keep his thoughts to himself. He also knew that Samantha probably wasn't above torturing him with whatever could be handy in the kitchen, to get him to say what he was thinking.

And how could he tell her that? Because what he was thinking was that her dear aunt Joan and uncle Mark were, in fact, planning on selling the presidential nomination to the highest bidder.

Chapter Four

Samantha had walked no more than two feet into the office the next morning when Bettyann came racing out of the coffee room and made a beeline for her.

"Talk. Speak. Utter the words. He is *who?* You met him *where?* He has a brother just my age? A cousin? I'm not hard to please, I'd take a cousin. This would be a good thing, Samantha, because I want to bear his children. My God, Sam, the man is a dream. And those cheekbones? I haven't seen cheekbones like that since…I don't know when. He could slice granite with them, I swear it. Where did you get him? And, if you're going to throw him back, where do I apply for rebound babe?"

"Would you stop?" Samantha said, throwing her purse on the desk and then walking behind it, all but falling into her chair. "Oh, I'm sorry, Bettyann. I've had a bad night."

Bettyann leaned her palms on the desktop. "Define

bad night. Would that be bad as in a you-ate-a-bad-burrito night, or bad as in the man kept me up all night, making mad passionate love to me until dawn, so now I really need some sleep?''

Samantha opened her mouth to deny either scenario—ah, scenario; she was thinking in D.C. talk. How…awful.

"The first one," she said at last, pretending an interest in the stack of national and local daily newspapers that were delivered to the office every day. "Have you checked these yet? Anything for our scrapbook? Anything that might need a press release before the next news cycle? Any mention at all of the senator?''

"Nope, none, and nothing. For the senator, at least. But Mrs. Phillips is on the society page in the local gossip rag. She was a guest at some kind of save-the-endangered-snail-darter fund-raiser, or something like that. Man, the camera loves her. I should look so good, and I must be thirty years younger than she is. Oh, okay, so maybe twenty.''

Samantha hadn't planned to say anything to Betty-ann, at least she hadn't a specific subject in mind, but since the woman had brought up Joan Phillips's name, she decided to do a little judicious poking. "Mrs. Phillips was in here yesterday.''

"Yeah, so?''

"Nothing," Samantha said, busying herself in pretending to look at the headlines above the fold in the many sections of the first newspaper. "That's two days in a row though, isn't it? I mean, I wasn't here, but I think you'd mentioned that she was here two days ago, too.''

"I did? She was? Oh, yeah, she was. She asked if she could make a couple of calls from your office while she was in town, and I said sure, since you weren't in anyway. That was all right, wasn't it?"

"Fine, no problem," Samantha said, her heart pounding. So it was possible. Aunt Joan had been in her office, where her keys had lain in plain sight. The evidence was mounting, even as Samantha's spirits plummeted, because she knew she had to tell Jesse.

"Good. Because we've got to really get to work on this thousand-dollar-a-plate deal for next week, you know. I'm still trying to figure out how we can serve chicken for that amount of money and still sleep nights. I mean, at the least, we should give them the plate to take home with them."

"Funny," Samantha said, rolling her eyes. Then she frowned. "You know, I sort of like that idea, Bettyann. Not for next week, because we wouldn't have enough lead time, but for other dinners."

"You're going to give them their dirty plates to take home? Gee, that's brilliant—not. Although the dish-washers at the hotel would probably give you a rousing cheer."

"No, no. I mean we could give each contributor a plate. A really nice one, dessert-plate size probably, with the state seal on it, the senator's name, the date of the dinner, that sort of thing. And a small stand to display the plate. What do you think?"

"I think you were telling the truth, and you really did have a bad burrito last night."

"Not funny. Okay, on to other things. Do you have the seating chart handy?"

"Right here," Bettyann said, pointing to her head. "I swear I've got the whole darn thing committed to memory after doing it so many times, in so many ways. Do it with the president there, do it without the president there. Do it with the president and the first lady there, do it with the first lady and not the—"

"I've got it, Bettyann, I've got it. You know the seating plan. Now tell me, where am I sitting? Did you leave a spot next to me for a guest, or am I to spend the whole evening making nice-nice with some heavy donor from North Dakota?"

"A guest? You want to bring a guest? What do we do about the thousand bucks?"

"I donate it?" Samantha shrugged. "Yes, it will be the standard donation. There's no problem with that, is there?"

"If you're bringing Jesse James? And we're all sitting at the same table? Couldn't possibly be a problem with that," Bettyann said, rubbing her hands together. "That hunk-a-hunk-a-burning-love in black tie? Hey, if you're running a little short, maybe I can chip into the kitty, because he'd be worth every penny."

"Are you taking hormones or something?" Samantha asked, laughing. "I mean, are you on estrogen overload?"

"We will not discuss my love life," Bettyann said with mock seriousness, "or the current lack thereof."

"You and Benny are still on the outs?"

"And Benjamin is definitely not a part of any conversation that I'm a part of. Oops, ended that with a preposition, didn't I? Okay, Benjamin is definitely not included in any conversation in which I also partake. Better?''

"Remind me not to let you proof any more press releases," Samantha said, shaking her head. "Now scoot, I've got work to do."

"So do I, so do I."

Samantha looked up. "What are you working on? Yes, yes, ending with a preposition. Whatever you've got, Bettyann, it must be contagious. So?"

"A couple of things. Updating and correlating mailing lists for Florida, for one. I wouldn't want to live there, sun or no sun. People keep dying there."

Samantha grinned. It was good to grin, after the long, sleepless night she'd had once Jesse had left with the envelopes. "People retire there, Bettyann. Sometimes retired people are actually *old,* and they eventually die."

"Oh, okay, that makes sense," Bettyann said, winking. "What else? I have to be busier than that. Oh, yeah, and Mrs. Phillips wants an updated list of corporate contributors."

Samantha's ears perked up as she sat up. "Corporate contributors? Why?"

"Mine is not to reason why, mine is but to print out and fax," Bettyann said, shrugging.

"Okay," Samantha said, trying to sound casual. "And, since Mrs. Phillips wants an updated list, I guess I do, too. Fax hers to her, then give me the printout copy."

"You got it," Bettyann said, heading for the door. Then she stopped, turned. "And you do, you know.

You've really got it. At least Jesse James thinks so, you lucky dog.''

''Oh, close the door and go away, in any order you want to do that,'' Samantha said, sure her cheeks were burning.

Once she was alone, the door closed, Samantha looked at the telephone, willing it to ring. She had Jesse's cell phone number, but she wasn't going to call him. No way. He had to call her.

He had to...

Jesse adjusted the badge clipped to his suit jacket and took a deep breath before knocking on the door-jamb. Bob Forrester always kept his door open. It was the chief of staff's open-door policy, or so the man said whenever he was asked.

Mostly, Jesse thought, it was because the man was in and out of the office a thousand times a day, and had gotten tired of closing the door.

Bob Forrester was an impressive man, in reputation, in intelligence and physically. Over six feet six inches tall, rail thin, and with dark hair and eyes, he was often referred to by the interns as Old Abe, after Abraham Lincoln.

But never within earshot of the man, that was for sure.

''Sir?'' Jesse said a moment later, sort of leaning into the room without actually stepping inside. To do that, he'd wait for an invitation.

''Ah, we quoth the Raven—Nevermore,'' Bob Forrester said, tipping back in his burgundy leather desk chair, referring to Jesse by his longtime code name. ''I was just thinking about asking you to stop by and see me.''

"Really, sir?"

The chief of staff sat forward once more, grabbing at some papers on his large, cluttered desk. "Yes. A new report just came in on security plans for the Phillips fund-raiser next week, as the president has decided to be there, lend his support. Personally, I think it's because he likes the desserts at that place, but who am I to question our commander in chief?"

"Yes, sir."

The Phillips fund-raiser? Could the president afford to be seen with Senator Phillips? What if all hell broke loose before the dinner, or after it?

No. Jesse sighed. He couldn't let that happen.

Yet, at the same time, he wasn't ready to betray Samantha's confidence, act without knowing all the facts. Careers in Washington could be ruined with a rumor, true or untrue. He had to know more before he acted.

"May I see the report, sir?" Jesse asked, an idea forming in his head.

"That's what I'd hoped. I know you're vetting national security for us now, but you used to arrange presidential security for events like this, and I value your opinion."

Forrester picked up a sheaf of different-size papers and handed it to Jesse in one big pile. "Here you go. Ingress route, egress route. From the White House to the restaurant, and back again. From the door to the dais. From the dais to the men's room, you name it. Positioning of Secret Service. On the nearby roofs, behind the usual potted plants. Floor plans, everything.

Go on, Jesse, sit down, read it all while you're here. Let me know what you think.''

Jesse sat. He paged through the very detailed plan and found absolutely no fault with it, then looked across the desk at the chief of staff. "I don't like it."

Forrester furrowed his brow—his furrowed brow was famous, or infamous, in the West Wing. "You don't like it? What's not to like? I thought this was going to be a peaceful morning around here. Not that I'd recognize one, because I've never had one. Okay, this is why you're here, to give everything to us straight, without political spin—so talk to me. What don't you like, Jesse?"

"Well, sir—" Jesse said, trying to be earnest, but not too earnest. Liars always tried too hard to be earnest. "It's the timing more than the plan, the fact that the president will be there at all, at this time of the campaign process. The plan itself is good. Very thorough."

"The timing," Forrester repeated, folding his hands together on top of the desk. "Go on. What bothers you about the timing?"

"I'm not very political…"

"Jesse, for crying out loud, no matter what we say or what we even believe, we're *all* political. You can't be in this town and not be political."

"Yes, sir. Okay, here goes. Senator Phillips is running around collecting money left and right now that he has formally announced."

"Agreed. So are the three other candidates from our party, and the five from the opposition. So what?"

"So, and I'm speaking hypothetically now, sir, if the

president has already publicly decided to back Senator Phillips, and something were to come out, come up, come whatever, then whoever he had to switch to next would look like just what he was, a second choice."

Forrester's eyes narrowed. "Why do I get the feeling I'm suddenly talking to the Raven, agent, instead of just to Jesse Colton, currently—and supposedly benignly—serving at the president's pleasure in the West Wing? What do you know? What the hell do you know?"

"Nothing I'm prepared to share at this time, sir, because that would be premature. Senator Phillips seems to be a good man, a good choice. But there are a few questions that have come up…"

"Damn it," Forrester bit out. "I hate this town. What is it? Rumors, right? Drinking? Women?"

You wish, Jesse thought, but said nothing.

"So, Raven," Forrester said, picking up a pencil and holding it at both ends, "when will you know?"

"Can you give me a week? I mean, the press secretary hasn't announced that the president will be at the fund-raiser, has she? Nobody's planned any leaks? Nobody knows yet that Senator Phillips is the president's choice, or that he'll attend this fund-raiser?"

"No. Not yet. We've got a leak planned, but we haven't given the final okay. It's the World Series, Jesse. If it goes to seven games, the president doesn't want to be listening to boring speeches, he wants to be here, popping popcorn and watching the game. We could tape it for him, but he says that's just not the same."

"Played college ball, didn't he, sir?" Jesse said, smiling.

"And some semipro," Forrester said, nodding. "And I don't blame him. You ever go to one of those thousand-dollar-a-plate dealies? I never knew you could put so much bad food in one dining room at one time."

Jesse laughed, then got to his feet, placed the papers back on Forrester's desk. "I'm sorry I can't say more, sir."

"You said plenty, son," the chief of staff said, picking up a memo, his attention already on the next piece of business. "Keep me informed?"

"Yes, sir, I'll do that," Jesse said, turning for the door.

"By informed, Raven, I mean I expect to be the first to know."

"Yes, sir, I knew that. Thank you, sir."

"Wait a minute," Forrester called after him. "You didn't come here because you knew I wanted to see you. You national security types are good, but you're not clairvoyant, at least I haven't been briefed that you are. So? What do you want?"

"Another time, sir. I can see that you're busy."

"Son, I work seven days a week, sometimes sixteen hours a day. My wife insisted I show her a picture ID before she'd let me in the house the other night. If you waited until I wasn't busy, we'd never speak again. Now come here, sit down and spit it out."

"Yes, sir," Jesse said, retaking his seat. "It's personal, sir, but as it might have an impact on the president if we can't put our own spin on it, I thought you should know.''

The pencil snapped in two. ''My day's just getting better and better,'' Forrester said under his breath. ''So it's not women or booze. Even the press is bored with those. It's money, right? That's the new thing, follow the money.''

Jesse nodded. ''That would be it, sir. Money. Although that part of it really probably would never come out. It's the other part...''

''What else is there, if it isn't money?''

''Property, sir.''

''Property? Jewels? Land? What?''

''The Chekagovian embassy, sir. I, we, my family, that is...we recently found out that we own it.'' Jesse took a deep breath as two broken pieces of pencil sailed into the air, and began to explain his words.

''Ten million dollars?'' Forrester said when Jesse finally finished. ''That's a nice piece of change.''

''Yes, sir, we think so, sir. Although we still don't know what we're going to do about it. We're talking about forming some sort of foundation.''

''Nice. Most people would be talking about yachts and fur coats and condos in Switzerland.''

''Not my family, sir,'' Jesse said with a grin, relaxing a little for the first time since he'd entered the room. It felt good to have all of this off his chest, even if the Senator Phillips problem was still boiling on the front burner of his brain.

''I know Joe Colton,'' Forrester said, sitting back in his chair. ''Good man. How'd he take the news that his father was a bigamist, that he and his brother were products of an invalid marriage?''

"He's fine, at least his oldest son, Rand Colton, a lawyer here in the District, assures me he's fine. It was the former senator's brother, Graham, who went a little crazy when he heard the news.''

"How so?''

"He hired some goon to find and destroy any papers that showed that my grandmother and his father had been married. The goon, obviously an independent thinker, went further than that, trying to burn down the town hall to destroy any records. Among other larcenies.'' Jesse grinned. ''But Rand says that Graham is very sorry.''

"I'll bet he is,'' Forrester said with a laugh. ''Joe is so honest he squeaks. He probably tore a couple of strips off his brother's hide for that one. But back to business. Your family owns the Chekagovian embassy, and you work for this president. Certainly nothing illegal about any of that, not that I can see. It's also not the sort of thing that looks good in the papers, son, but you already know that, or you wouldn't be here, telling me about it.''

"Yes, sir, I do. That's why I'm glad I'm also able to tell you that the ambassador and his family are moving out next week, to occupy newer quarters elsewhere in the city.''

"That was a stroke of luck. How long was this estate the embassy?''

"Sixty years, sir. But nobody in our family knew about it until recently. So, it's really not anything the newspapers could do much with, except if it's a slow news day or something like that.''

Jesse winced inwardly. There wouldn't be any slow news days in the District for months, if what he suspected about Senator Phillips and his wife were ever to become public knowledge.

"I think you're right," Forrester said, getting to his feet as Jesse watched. It was always interesting to watch the chief of staff slowly unfold his long body. The president was actually only five feet eight inches tall, so Forrester was always careful never to stand directly beside him, as people seemed to like their presidents to be tall, as if mere height lent more credibility to the man.

"Sir?" Jesse said, also rising so he could look the man more levelly in the eye.

"It's not really news. Okay, so it's juicy, the Joe Colton part at least, but I don't see any of this coming out if nobody talks about it. And now, with Ambassador Ritka, his family and the embassy staff moving out…? After next week, it's not only not really news, it's old news."

He put his long arm over Jesse's shoulder as they both walked toward the doorway. It was, Jesse thought, rather like being embraced by a giant California condor. "I'm still glad you told me, Jesse. I appreciate it."

"You're welcome, sir."

"And I'll appreciate it when I have the full report on whatever the hell it is you're watching with Senator Phillips. An *oral* report, Jesse. Nothing on paper. Not yet."

With a final nod, Jesse turned left out of Forrester's

office, while the chief of staff headed straight down the hallway to the press secretary's office, probably to cancel the leak that the president would be at the Phillips fund-raiser.

Jesse decided he wouldn't tell Samantha that piece of news, because she was smart enough to know that he'd probably had something to do with the cancellation.

This was getting dicey. He was falling in love with a woman who was loyal to a man who might be the next big political scandal—while he was the man who brought the senator down.

Not the greatest subject for pillow talk...

Samantha was staring at her telephone again, and gave a small, startled jump in her chair when it finally rang and the light for her private line lit.

"Hello?" she said into the phone, and when her mother's voice came back to her she slumped in her chair and said, "Hiya, Mom. How are you?"

Fifteen minutes later she knew how her mom was, how her dad was, how her sister and brother were, how the housekeeper was doing after her bunion surgery and how the lilac on the west side of the house was looking really pitiful and probably wouldn't make it through the winter.

That was the thing with Samantha's mother. You said "Hello," you said "How are you?" and the woman took it from there. Put a few "Wow, reallys" and a couple of "No kidding, he said thats" in there, and you were home free.

After promising she'd fly home for Thanksgiving—

she'd already promised that, twice, but obviously her mother needed to be really, really sure—Samantha was able to hang up, wondering if Jesse had tried to call her.

She pulled a small notepad onto the center of the desk and scribbled: Note to self—Have call-waiting option installed on private line.

"Here you go," Bettyann said as she walked into the office, holding out a thick printout. "Names and amounts, broken down by alphabet, and again by amount. I can do much more for you, master. I can break it down by dates of contributions, even by type of company."

Samantha looked up at the woman. "You can do that? You can break it down by type of company? Like, for instance, you could give me, oh, say, all the mining companies?"

"Sure, why not. This is the age of the computer, you know. A couple of quick keystrokes, and you'll get all the mining companies, conglomerates that have mining divisions, etcetera, etcetera, etcetera, to quote Yul Brynner in *The King and I*. I love that movie."

"I'd like to see that. The breakdown, I mean. I've seen the movie," Samantha said, tamping down her reaction that, if she'd let it loose, would probably mean she'd be dancing on top of the desk right now. "Let's see, let's try it. Mining companies, all right? And oil and gas. Companies that make rigging and drills and whatever for oil and gas companies. Hydropower. Nuclear power."

"Power, period. What you want is for me to give you a listing that includes everyone in the energy industry who already contributed to the senator's campaign, or that we believe will be coming through for us soon. Have I got that?''

''Yes, that's what I want.'' And then, because it seemed like a good idea, she also asked for something she didn't really need. ''And agriculture. I'd like all of those, too. You know, agribusiness? Suppliers, wholesalers, you name it. Is your computer software up to that?''

Bettyann folded her arms high across her chest and gave a quick, sharp bow of her head. ''Before you can blink, master, they are yours.''

''Thanks, Bettyann, I appreciate that. And then you can go to lunch.''

''You're not coming?''

''Not today, Bettyann, sorry. She's got a date,'' Jesse said from the doorway. ''Don't you, sweetheart?''

Samantha looked to the doorway, to see him lounging there, one shoulder against the doorjamb, his eyes twinkling as he looked at her. Her stomach dropped to her toes.

''Oh, hubba-hubba,'' Bettyann said, taking her time as she walked past him. ''See you around, Jesse James. Oh, and you can rob my bank anytime.''

''Sorry about that,'' Samantha said as he closed the door and walked over to the desk. ''She's just full of talk, that's all. She has a boyfriend. Benny. They just aren't speaking right now.''

''Lucky Benny,'' Jesse said with a grin. ''Are you ready to go to lunch, darling?''

Was she ready? She'd been waiting for his call, for him to show up, for hours. Hours that seemed like days,

days that stretched into years. But fat chance that she'd tell him that, or look too eager. "Oh, I don't know. I'm really pretty busy. Why don't we order in?"

Jesse pointed toward the worktable. "I'd really rather go out, sweetheart."

Samantha closed her eyes, nodded. "I'll just go get my coat."

He retrieved it for her, taking the raincoat from the clothes tree in the corner, then helped her into it. He rested his hands on her shoulders for a moment when she made to move away, then leaned forward and sniffed at her hair. "You smell good."

"Um-hmm," she said, quickly stepping away from him before she melted into one great big puddle on the floor.

He was so lovey-dovey here, in the office, where someone was listening. But had he kissed her good-night last night?

No, he hadn't. He'd been a perfect gentleman. And all business, from the moment he'd seen what was inside that first envelope.

So this sweetheart, darling, you smell good stuff was just for here, where the listening device was stuck under the worktable.

She had to remember that. Jesse was playing at being her boyfriend because it was a good cover for him. Nothing more. Because he worked at the pleasure of the president, and that's why he was here, to protect that president.

Her heart had to remember that.

Jesse carried Samantha's raincoat over his arm because the sun had found its way to the District and the air had turned warm once more. Just a beautiful October day.

He suggested that they grab sandwiches and drinks from one of the shops and eat them while sitting on a park bench, and Samantha had agreed, probably knowing that he was deliberately trying to keep their location as isolated from other people as possible so that they could talk more freely.

Real *Secret Squirrel* stuff, straight out of the secret agent handbook or something like that. He hated involving Samantha in all this cloak-and-dagger routine, but it was unavoidable.

They sat down on a green wooden bench, the bag of food between them, and Samantha began doling out the contents. He got the pastrami on rye, and she got the tuna fish on whole wheat. He got the tortilla chips, she got the potato chips. They both got bottles of soda.

She handed him a napkin as she said, "You slept last night, didn't you?"

"Fairly well, yes," he answered, and was rewarded when she made one of those scrunched-up faces that he found increasingly adorable.

"I hate you," she said, then took a bite of her sandwich.

"You didn't sleep well?" he asked, already knowing the answer. Not because she looked tired; she looked wonderful. But because she did look worried, and he'd like to tear Senator Phillips's throat out for worrying her.

He took a bite of pastrami, reminding himself he was a civilized man, not a lion on the prowl. No, not a lion.

A raven. Maybe he'd fly on over to the Capitol building and peck the man's eyes out. Metaphorically, that is, because he was a civilized man.

On a very short leash.

Samantha patted her lips with her paper napkin, her manners as refined as they'd be if she was sitting down to a table loaded with fine china and silver, with a crystal chandelier hanging overhead. "I thought about it all night. What did you do with the envelopes?"

"There wasn't anything incriminating in them, even anything to photocopy except for the envelopes themselves, which I did. Then I sent them out in this morning's mail," he said, then banged her on the back as she choked a little. "But not the fifth one—not the first one, I mean. Jeez, Samantha, I'm sorry. I didn't mean to startle you."

She used the paper napkin now to wipe at her watering eyes. "You could be a little clearer, you know. I almost swallowed my tongue. Why did you send them out?"

"Why?" Jesse wadded the waxed paper into a ball and put it back in the paper bag. "Mrs. Phillips brought those envelopes to you, and you said you'd put them in the mail. She was playing a sort of game yesterday, like maybe a game of tag, to see what would happen. If they didn't get into the mail? Hey, then tag, you're it. You're the reason the first envelope never got into the mail."

"Good point," Samantha said, picking up the second half of her sandwich, then looking at him. "You eat too fast. Don't you know that you're supposed to chew each bite twenty-two times, then swallow?"

"Twenty-two? Not twenty-one, or twenty-three?"

"Nope. According to my mom, the magic number is twenty-two. It aids the digestion, and you don't choke quite so often."

"I didn't choke, and my digestion's fine."

"Lucky you. Just don't tell my mom."

"I'm going to meet her?" Jesse asked, knowing he was teasing her, and liking it. Besides, he wanted an answer. He really wanted an answer.

"Maybe. Mom always likes it when we bring home lost souls for holidays."

"Now I'm a lost soul?"

"Maybe not, but you'll look the part if you don't soon tell me what you're going to do next about that first envelope and everything that's in it."

It was time to be honest, brutally honest, with her. "Samantha, I haven't the faintest damn idea what I'm going to do about it."

"Oh, that's great," she said, wrapping the remainder of her sandwich in the waxed paper and shoving it back into the bag. "That's really just great, isn't it? You do know you hold the next election smack in your two hands, don't you?"

"I wouldn't go that far, sweetheart," he said, shaking his head. "Senator Phillips doesn't have the nomination for his own party sewn up yet, let alone the results of next November's election."

"He's getting the president's endorsement at the fund-raiser next week, Jesse. A two-time president, still with his popularity numbers in the high sixties, entering the last year of his last term—which is pretty darn unheard of? With that endorsement, how could Uncle Mark lose? Unless you break this…this mess.''

"Which I can't do, Samantha. We aren't exactly loaded down with proof." He averted his face as he said this because he had the feeling he had the word *tattletale* branded on his forehead. If she ever found out he'd told Old Abe to keep the president away from the fund-raiser, hold back his endorsement, there was going to be a war between he and this woman he was falling for so hard. A big one.

She stood up, began to walk down the path. "Proof? Facts? Oh, wait, you're a Boy Scout, chock-full of ideals and principles and—no, not a Boy Scout. You're a Pollyanna, and everything's rosy, there's no ending except for a happy ending. Sure, right. And here I thought you lived here, worked here. Since when does proof mean anything around here? Facts? This is a lynch 'em, then listen later town, remember? I never should have called you. Never!"

Jesse took hold of her elbow, hoping to slow her pace. "But you did call me, Samantha. So if we're talking about Boy Scouts, and Pollyannas, let's not forget Pandora, all right? She opened the box, and there was nothing left to do but try to pick up the pieces. That's what I'm doing, Samantha—what you're helping me do. Pick up the pieces. Sort them out. Then act, because neither one of us may be happy about what we find, but we'll both be damned if we'll be part of some sort of cover-up. Am I right?"

She stopped, then looked at him. "I still hate you," she said, but he knew she didn't mean it.

He stepped a little closer, put his hand under her

chin. "No, you don't. In a town piled high with lies, let's keep this honest, okay, sweetheart? You don't hate me, and I damn well don't hate you."

"Oh, Jesse, I don't know if—"

He didn't want to hear what she might say next, so he implemented his latest "shut her up" ploy and lowered his mouth to hers.

Okay, so it wasn't a ploy. It was a hunger he couldn't fight, didn't want to fight. It was a need that burned deep inside him. To touch her, to taste her, to tell her without words that he was there for her, wanted to be there for her.

Wanted all of that...and so much more.

Chapter Five

Samantha sat across the table from Jesse in a restaurant she hadn't known existed until he walked her into it from the street.

The establishment was small, fairly dark, and there was a heavenly aroma coming from the postage stamp-size kitchen she could see through a pass-through the single waitress used to both order and pick up food.

"I know, less than classy," Jesse said as she spread her napkin in her lap…her paper napkin. "But the spaghetti is the best in town, I promise."

"You only say that because you haven't tried mine. One of my meatballs and you'd spill government secrets in a heartbeat just to have another," she said, keeping the conversation light, the way it had been all afternoon, as they'd slowly made their way through Jesse's favorite museum, sometimes even holding hands. For a while, she'd even forgotten the envelope and its damning contents.

"I'll take that bet," Jesse told her. "Is Saturday night good for you? I'll bring the wine."

"Sounds good, if I'm still talking to you by then. I think I like playing hooky, by the way. Are you sure you can do that when you work in the West Wing?"

He took a sip of water from the glass the waitress had plunked down on the table along with two ragged-looking menus before heading back to the pass-through shelf behind the counter to pick up another order.

"We don't punch in and out, if that's what you mean. Besides, Brenda's covering for me. My secretary," he added, when Samantha looked puzzled.

"Bettyann's covering for me, too. Did Brenda ask a million questions, most of them painfully personal, before she'd agree to cover for you?"

"Not Brenda. She knows not everything I do is the sort of thing you write down on an appointment pad. Man, that sounds all cloak-and-daggerish, doesn't it?"

Samantha leaned her elbows on the table. "I still don't know exactly what you do, you know."

"That makes two of us. I guess I'm sort of a…sort of a floater? I'm there to be objective, brutally honest, and lend my expertise wherever it's needed. The president's idea. He wanted someone other than just the usual lifelong politicians to advise him, most especially on national security. I'm it."

"That sounds so official yet so vague. You're not telling me everything, are you?"

His grin was endearingly boyish. "Nope."

"I didn't think so," Samantha said as she selected a bread stick from the lopsided basket the waitress had slammed onto the table. "I'm sorry, we've been talking, so we haven't looked at the menus yet,'' she told the woman who was now standing there, pad and pencil at the ready.

"That's okay," Jesse interrupted. "Two plates of Gino's special spaghetti with meat sauce, and two salads with the house dressing, please, Lulu. Just ice water, no wine. That's where we start, at least. Who knows where we'll go from there."

"Straight for the antacids, bucko," the waitress grumbled, then headed for the kitchen area once more.

"That was Lulu, the owner's wife. She's part of the ambience."

"Utterly charming," Samantha said, grinning as she took a bite of bread stick. "Mmm...this is good."

"Everything's good. So tell me, have you enjoyed your afternoon?"

"Translation, have I calmed down enough to talk rationally and unemotionally about the envelope and what it means? I'm not sure."

"Well, she's honest," Jesse said, rolling his eyes. "Okay, here goes. I've got the envelope, I've got the contents, both all locked up in a safe place. I sent the envelopes with the blank pages off in the mail, to divert attention from you. They'll arrive at the post office boxes in four different states right on time."

"You just send them off, and that's that?"

"Not really. I've already got people—very close-mouthed people I can trust—all set to watch the four post offices, to see who picks up each envelope, and learn where those envelopes go after that. By now the four recipients have been told that this is only a test of the delivery system, I'm sure of that, which is why my people will be watching those boxes for another week, after the first delivery, ready to intercept any other mailings. Flash a national security badge these days, and you can get in anywhere, trust me on that one.''

"You're very...efficient.''

"That's what it said on my last merit badge,'' Jesse said with a grin. "The fifth envelope, if we're lucky, will be chalked up to a problem with the mail. End of suspicion being cast your way. When and if the time comes, we'll find a way to keep your name out of everything.''

"I'm not worried about me, but thank you anyway for the thought,'' Samantha said, then realized she'd begun shredding her paper napkin.

"Sure, you're worried, you're in a tough spot. Senator Phillips is your dad's good friend, and you've known him and his wife for all of your life. You've got to be worried that you've opened a huge can of worms better left closed, betrayed a confidence and ruined a good friendship.''

"All right, yes, I am worried about that. Dad would be crushed to learn his confidence had been misplaced. But that really isn't the most important thing.''

Jesse sat back and waited as Lulu put huge bowls of salad in front of them.

Samantha admired the mixture of greens and tomatoes, green pepper, radishes, scallions, even sliced black olives. She didn't have to lean forward to sniff the garlic smell that rose from the bowl along with that of oregano and other spices. "I could make a meal just with this salad.''

Jesse picked up his fork, stabbing a cherry tomato.

"Don't. You have to leave room for everything else. So," he said, taking the conversation back to the previous subject, "what is the important thing?"

Samantha, her fork poised over the bowl, sighed. "You know what's important. The *process*. The sanctity, if you will, of the election process. Our way of government, our way of life, to get a little schmaltzy about the thing. We can't allow a presidential election to be bought. We just can't."

"Oh, good. Now we're superheroes, out to save the world?"

"I'll be Wonder Woman," Samantha said, trying to keep the conversation from sounding too much like a sermon on good government. "She had great hair."

"Okay then, you'll be Wonder Woman and I'll stay the Boy Scout. But seriously, Samantha, do you really see this as you and me against the corruption of a presidential election? That's pretty heavy, sweetheart."

"I know. But what else would you call it? If Uncle—if Senator Phillips is soliciting money from corporations, a whole industry, by showing that he'd favor them taxwise if he's elected, then he's not only taking money to buy an election, he's also selling himself to those corporations. They'd own him for his entire term in office."

Jesse sat back, looked at her. "You've quite a way with words, don't you? And it all starts with lousy glue on one envelope and a woman trying to go cheap on postage by mailing it from the campaign office. You do know that's usually all it takes—one stupid mistake and an accidental discovery? And then the walls come tumbling down."

Samantha chewed and swallowed another mouthful of salad. "A piece of adhesive tape over the lock on a door, keeping it open, and a curious security guard— like that?"

"Just like that. The mistake, the cover-up, the inevitable investigation, and the next thing you know, an entire presidency comes tumbling down. And it all started with a piece of adhesive tape. That, and a stupid idea."

"This is a stupid idea, isn't it?" Samantha asked, already knowing the answer. "Oh, I mean it could work, but it's still a stupid idea. Stupid because Uncle Mark is already pretty much assured of getting the president's endorsement. Then the party will quietly endorse him, and he'll coast through the primaries, have all the money he needs for the general election. I mean, the presidency already is pretty much his to lose. Why would he do this? It doesn't make sense."

Lulu cleared away the salad plates and replaced them with even larger bowls of spaghetti crowned with a generous serving of meat sauce.

"Some people can't believe in a sure thing, I guess," Jesse said, shrugging. "Hey, you can twirl?"

"Of course I can," Samantha said, neatly selecting another few strands of spaghetti noodles with her fork, then using the round spoon to brace the fork tips against as she neatly twirled everything into a neat little package. "I'm Wonder Woman, remember?"

"And I'm impressed. First time I came in here? I started cutting up the spaghetti, the way I did at home in Oklahoma, and Lulu grabbed the knife out of my hand and taught me how to do it right."

"She is a commanding sort of woman," Samantha agreed, looking at Lulu as the waitress tucked a napkin into the collar of a rather corpulent gentleman sitting across the room. And the man was smiling.

"She could probably lead troops into battle," Jesse said with a grin. "Okay, back to the subject. You want to know what I'm going to do with the envelope and its contents."

"Part of me does. Another part of me wants you to put it all through a paper shredder and forget you ever saw it."

"I can't do that, sweetheart. The wheels are already turning."

"I know, I know," Samantha said, losing her appetite. "And you know what *I* have to do, don't you?"

He shook his head. "No. What do you have to do?"

"Talk to Uncle Mark." She closed her eyes for a moment, trying to picture that interview, and her stomach did a little flip. "I have to take that envelope to him tomorrow, no later, and show him what I found, and ask him if he knows anything about it."

"You can't do that," Jesse said, putting down his own fork and spoon. "Sorry."

"What do you mean, I can't do that? Jesse, I *have* to do that."

"Other than the fact that I'm doing my best to keep your name out of it, the envelope and its contents are evidence now, sweetheart. I can't let you have them back."

Samantha felt her eyes growing wide...and probably wild. "You never said that when you had me give it to you last night. If I'd known that, I never would have—''

"Exactly. Sorry, I don't always play fair."

Samantha got to her feet. "Neither do I," she said, just before she dumped the remainder of her spaghetti and meat sauce into his lap, then followed it with his own serving before she stomped out of the restaurant.

Jesse rang the bell, then waited for the door to open, fully prepared to sacrifice his foot to keep that door open when Samantha tried to slam it in his face.

But it was Rose who opened the door. "Ah, dead man ringing," she said, grinning. "I was told to say that Samantha's not at home if you showed up. So, you've screwed up, then shown up. Sorry, she's not home."

"The security system in this place was one I cut my teeth on, not to mention that I've memorized the code. Close that door, Rose, and I'm in there anyway in five minutes, and that's stretching it."

"You're being a bully," Rose said, wagging a finger at him. "Shame on you."

"Rose, she spilled two plates of spaghetti in my lap an hour ago. Bully does not even begin to describe what I can be. Now, are you going to let me in, or am I going to let myself in? I'm game either way."

"Spaghetti? Two plates? Meat or marinara sauce?"

"Meat."

"Oh, wow. I'll bet you had a fun ride home."

"First I had a fun twenty-minute walk to my car, then I had a fun ride home. And that was only after Lulu, the waitress, tried to wipe me down with a dishrag. Did you know that *lap* becomes *crotch* when you stand up?"

By this point, Rose was leaning against the door, choking with laughter. "You…you had a real *Lulu* of a time, didn't you? Oh, come on, come in. Please understand that I'll have to tell her you put a gun to my head."

"Tell her anything you want. Just make sure she's downstairs—unarmed—and ready to go to her office with me in five minutes."

"Masterful, aren't you? I like that. Excuse me while I drool."

"Would you just go get her, please?" Jesse said, but he laughed.

He stood in the small foyer, cooling his heels, and listened as he heard voices coming from upstairs. He couldn't understand the words, but he recognized the tone.

He damn sure recognized the slamming of a door.

"Okay, that tears it," he said out loud, heading for the stairs.

Rose was on her way down. She stopped on the fifth step from the top and spread her arms, blocking his progress. "No, wait, you can't go up there. I mean, sure, she said no, but you still can't go up there. She's—"

"Out of my way, Rose. Please."

"Gun to my head again?"

"If that works for you."

"We'll pretend it does. Go ahead. It's not my funeral, but you might want to tell me which tie you want the undertaker to put on you for the services. Excuse me now, I want to go find my camera.''

''Your...oh, the hell with it.''

Jesse took the remaining stairs of the narrow, steep flight two at a time, then hesitated for only a moment before turning to his left at the top of the landing, heading for the one closed door in the hallway.

It was locked. He'd expected it to be locked.

One credit card and thirty seconds later, he was inside Samantha's bedroom.

Nice room. All cherry furniture and white eyelet drapes and spread. Even a canopy over the four-poster bed. Dark green walls with big purple cabbage roses climbing all over them. A dressing table loaded with cut-crystal bottles; the uniquely flowery smell of Samantha's perfume dancing lightly in the air. Family photographs everywhere.

But no Samantha.

He opened a door to his right, closed it again when he saw clothing hanging inside on double racks.

That left one more door.

It wasn't locked.

''Samantha?'' he said as he opened the door, walked into a large, old-fashioned bathroom with small black and white tiles on the floor, a freestanding white porcelain sink...and a huge, claw-footed bathtub.

Samantha was in the bathtub, sunk in bubbles up to her chin, her blond hair piled high on her head, her eyes about as wide as they could get.

''You!''

''Me,'' Jesse said quietly, putting a hand to his forehead, sort of shielding his eyes as he turned slightly away from her. "Rose didn't tell me you were—"

"Why should she? A *civilized* person would have taken a no for a no, and gone away. Humor me, Jesse, pretend you're civilized...and *go away.*"

"I can't," he said, lowering his arm. He wondered, just for one mad second, if Rose had found her camera, not that he needed any reminders of this scene. It was already burned into his brain. "We have to go to the office."

"Are you crazy? I wouldn't cross the street with you...you...you double-crosser."

"Ah, there we are," Rose said a split second after a sudden flash lit the room. "Student pays tuition selling photo of senator's campaign manager and White House bigwig to tabloids. Headline? How about Bubbles Cosgrove and Her Wicked West Wing Lover?"

"Get...out!"

"You'd better do what she says, Rose," Jesse told the girl, who was busily snapping more photographs. "Remember, I can help her bury your body where no one will ever find it."

"Yeah, yeah, I'm so scared. Okay, just kidding. I don't have any film in this darn thing anyway. Shall I lay out fresh clothes for you, madam? I am, after all, your servant."

"Jesse, get her out of here, and go with her. These bubbles are beginning to disappear."

He fought the urge to push Rose out, then lock the door, with him still inside the bathroom. But he was a gentleman, and the women in his family would have helped Samantha string him up if he forgot their training, even for a moment.

"I'll be downstairs, Samantha," he said, one hand on the doorknob. "And no kidding, sweetheart. We have to go to your office tonight. Either that, or I do it alone, and I'd really rather not break in when you can let me in."

"Oh, please, go there yourself. Then I can alert the police and have you arrested and sent to some maximum-security prison."

"You wouldn't do that," he said, grinning at her. "Now, come on, get dressed. Oh, and Lulu says to tell you she doesn't want to see you in her restaurant for at least six months. When I left, she was on her hands and knees picking up spaghetti noodles. She was not a happy woman."

"I'll send her an apology tomorrow, and flowers," Samantha said, sinking lower as the cooler air coming in from the bedroom made those bubbles dwindle even more. "But if you're expecting an apology, you can just forget it. You're lucky I didn't pour the spaghetti over your head."

"There is that, I suppose, sweetheart," Jesse said, and left the room.

Samantha unlocked the office door, then stood back and glared at Jesse.

He turned the knob, pushed the door fully open, then motioned for her to precede him, whispering, "Lady conspirators first."

"Darn right I'm a lady," she said, then began to

sweep past him, planning to turn on the lights. "And I'm loyal, and honest, and trustworthy, and—"

He pulled her back out of the office, and halfway down the hall. "Wait a minute. If you're going to be the Boy Scout now, the Superman, I refuse to be Wonder Woman. I think the outfit might pinch. On top of that, I don't want you to talk in there. Not until I've swept the place for bugs. You are to tiptoe, make no noise, okay? Now, if you have anything else to say, sweetheart, say it now."

"Just one thing. Go to hell," she said, brushing off his hand and heading for her own office—on tiptoe, damn him—to open that door as well. But that was it, that was all the help he was going to get from her. She'd already *helped* him into probably destroying her uncle Mark.

She watched as he made his way around the outer office, holding some sort of James Bond-type instrument and turning in circles, watching the needle on a small meter.

He repeated this action in the small lunch room, in the tiny alcove where the photocopier and three fax machines were kept.

Then he moved to her office.

She followed after him, wanting to see what the needle did when he pointed the gadget at the worktable. Sure enough, the needle jumped, and she looked at Jesse just as he turned to look at her.

"Live," he mouthed, then put a finger to his lips just in case she hadn't understood.

Samantha nodded, biting her lips together to keep from talking. She'd had no idea how difficult it was to keep silent when it was so important not to say anything.

Any more? she scribbled on a piece of notepaper, which she handed to him.

Jesse shrugged, and continued turning in slow circles, watching the needle.

And then he did something she most certainly had not expected.

He reached under the table, removed the bug and *stepped on it.*

"Okay, that's done," he said, smiling at her.

"That's it? You *stepped* on it? Why would you do something like that? I thought you'd want to feed false information into the thing now that we know someone is listening—*was* listening. You know, sort of set up a sting operation, or something like that?"

"Read a lot, do you, huh?" Jesse asked, picking up the squashed "bug" and slipping it into his pocket. "See a lot of movies?"

"You mean it's not like that?"

"It could be. Except that we don't have time for a lot of games. I've got a friend who owes me a favor, and he's going to be part of your staff, starting tomorrow morning. Geoff Waters. You hired him."

"I did?"

"Trust me, you did. Geoff will watch your office, make sure nobody comes to check on why the bug isn't working—and report to me if he sees anything and anyone suspicious. I've got someone else who should be outside right now, and he'll be here every night until this is over."

"Another friend who owes you a favor? Like the

men watching the post offices in those four cities where the envelopes will be delivered? Tell me something, how many people owe you favors?''

''A couple.'' Jesse sat down on the edge of the desk and looked at her. ''Okay, Samantha, the bug's gone. We could go home now, except that you're still mad at me, and I don't want you mad at me.''

''I don't want to be mad at you,'' she admitted, sitting down beside him, her hands on either side of her, holding tight on the edge of the desk. ''But you lied to me.''

''By omission, yes.''

''It's still a lie. It still goes in the angel's black book.''

''Or, as my great-grandfather would say, 'It is difficult for the Raven to speak clearly with a forked tongue.'''

Samantha turned her head sharply to look at him. ''You're kidding, right?''

''Nope. Not at all. My great-grandfather—George WhiteBear being his Americanized Comanche name—is one of those grand old men who likes to say obscure things and have us all believe they have some deep meaning.''

''And Raven? What does that mean? Is that you?''

''Yeah, that's me. He's the one who originally gave me the name, and when I needed a code name, I chose Raven for that, too. I'd like to think my great-grandfather picked it because of my black hair, but I'm pretty sure he was thinking more of my nose resembling a beak.''

''You have a wonderful nose,'' Samantha said before she could think, then quickly added, "I mean…there's nothing wrong with your nose."

"It's a throwback, just like my cheeks, and my hair, too, I guess. To my Comanche blood."

"I didn't know. Oh boy, if I tell Bettyann you're part Comanche, she'll go nuts. She's already waxing poetic about your cheekbones."

"Gee, I'm flattered," Jesse said, making a face.

"You said your family owns the Chekagovian embassy. Would that be the Comanche side of your family?"

"It would," Jesse said, shifting his weight on the desktop. "It's a long story."

"Yes, one you were going to tell me, remember? Now seems like a good time."

"I don't know where to begin."

"Try beginning with once upon a time. That's usually a good place."

"Okay," he said with a decisive nod of his head. "Once upon a time there was a lovely young woman named Gloria WhiteBear."

"Her Americanized name, right?"

"Right. I called her Grandmother. Anyway, Gloria and her family lived in Black Arrow, Oklahoma, where there weren't a lot of opportunities for a pretty young woman, especially one whose burning desire in life was to bring home money to help her struggling parents."

"When was this?"

"Just before the war. World War Two. Anyway, she left home, went West, and ended up working in a casino. A gambling palace, if you will. And she fell in love with one of the guests. He was young, like her, came from here in the District, and had plenty of money, not that Gloria cared about that. She was in love, or so she thought at the time. She'd never seen anyone like this man, never experienced the wiles of a sophisticated man bent on getting her into bed, to be frank about the thing.''

''He only wanted to take her to bed?''

''That's my assumption, and my great-grandfather's, but nobody can be sure. Anyway, one thing led to another—and pretty damn quick, or so I'm told—and the two of them got married within two or three days of their first meeting. She woke up the next morning, and he was gone. From there, I'm pretty fuzzy, except that she somehow found out he had to get home here to Washington—to see his fiancée. He could do that now that he'd gotten what he wanted from Gloria, even if it had taken a marriage license to get it.''

''Ouch,'' Samantha said, wincing. ''She must have been heartbroken.''

''You could say that. She ran back to Black Arrow, and that would have been the end of it, except that she soon discovered that she was pregnant.''

''Oh, dear.''

Jesse picked up the paperweight that depicted the Washington Monument and turned it in his hands. ''Gloria knew where her husband—if you can call him that any way but legally—was, and went to see him. She felt he should know about his child. That's all, just know about the child. Except that her husband panicked. He was sure she was there to blackmail him.''

''Blackmail? I don't understand.''

''It's simple. The husband had married that fiancée,

the daughter of very rich parents. He saw his cushy world ready to come crashing down on him because of what he considered nothing more than a one-night stand with some dumb, innocent Indian girl who should have had the good sense to go away now, leave him alone.''

''You're angry about that. I can hear it in your voice. And I don't blame you.''

''Yeah, I guess I am. He told her the marriage wasn't valid—although we all know differently now. When he told Gloria that his wife was also pregnant, he did it to make her understand that he couldn't be a husband to her, and then he realized that telling her only made things worse. Now she could really put the screws to him.''

''I don't think I like this man,'' Samantha said. ''You haven't given him a name.''

''No, I haven't, have I? We'll get to that another time. For now, I just want to tell you Gloria's story. She was appalled that her husband had betrayed her, that he had impregnated another woman. All she wanted was to go home to Oklahoma, which she did. She had the marriage license, she knew her child would be legitimate, and she told everyone that her husband had died. My great-grandparents stood behind her one hundred percent. That should have been the end of it. But the man couldn't believe that was the end of it.''

''He followed her?''

''No, not that. What he did was set up a trust for his unborn child, letting Gloria know that the trust would be abolished if she ever told anyone the truth.''

"Let me guess. The Chekagovian embassy was part of the trust?"

"Give that lady a cigar," Jesse said, smiling wearily. "Most of the trust was cash, and the rest was the house—the mansion—which was rented out for the past sixty years, all of them to the Chekagovian embassy. And, for all of those sixty years, the trust was managed by very good lawyers who built it all into a damn nice fortune."

"I won't ask how much."

"You don't have to, because I'm going to tell you. It's over ten million dollars. We just found out, and let me tell you, we're still reeling."

"You never knew?"

"No, Gloria never told anyone, and never touched a dime of that money. She raised her boys—the baby turned out to be twins—strictly on the income from the family's feed and grain store, and never told anybody about the trust. I doubt she even believed it existed. She's gone now, so what we know now is all we'll ever know."

He took a deep breath, let it out slowly. "So, that's it. That's how my family came to own the Chekagovian embassy, which is soon to be vacated. I've been charged by the family with looking over the property, deciding what to do with it. I asked my great-grandfather what I should be looking for when I go inspect the property. He said that the mind will know what the heart tells it. I've got to tell you, that wasn't a lot of help."

"No, I suppose not. What else does your great-grandfather say? I'd really like to hear."

Jesse sighed. "Well, let's see. There's so much. Okay. Last time I was home? He's big into hearts and feelings right now. He took me aside just as I was leaving and said in that profound way he has, 'The raven who seeks will find the heart's truth.' How's that?"

Samantha was quiet for a few moments. "I don't know. The heart's truth? That can't be what you seek now. You're seeking now to uncover who is behind leaking information in that envelope you're keeping from me. Your heart has nothing to do with any of that."

"It doesn't?" Jesse asked, putting a finger beneath Samantha's chin, turning her face toward him. "That envelope led me to you, Samantha."

She lowered her eyelids, not wanting him to see what would be so obvious if he could see into her eyes. "That's…that's stretching things, don't you think?"

He leaned in closer. She could smell his aftershave, feel his heat. "I don't know, what do you think?"

She opened her eyes once more, and the intensity of his gaze sent a sharp stab of white-hot lightning straight through her. "This is…this isn't why I'm…I mean, we really should be…"

Thankfully, before she could completely tie her tongue into knots, he lowered his mouth to hers and kissed her.

His arms slid around her as he moved to stand up, take her along with him, and she went, willingly, her arms slipping up to his shoulders. She clasped her hands together behind his neck and held on for dear life.

His lips brushed against hers softly, slanting, withdrawing, touching her lightly once more. He teased her bottom lip with his teeth, slid his tongue over her softness, then finally crushed his mouth against hers, plunged inside her, took what she had no choice but to offer him, no wish but to offer everything to him.

Their bodies were pressed tightly together as she went up on tiptoe, needing to be closer, longing to be closer. She felt his strong fingers skim her sides, moaned low in her throat as his hands cupped her breasts.

Just when she was ready to give him anything, anything at all, everything and more, he put his hands on her arms and slowly moved her away from him.

"We probably should go now," he said, and she envied him his composure, even as she felt the first niggling rise in her temper at the way he could turn her on, then turn himself off with such seeming ease.

"That…that would probably be best," she said, stepping away from him, turning her back to him as she struggled to regulate her breathing.

"I don't want to," he said, and she shivered as he laid a hand on her shoulder, "but my friend outside is going to be stopping by any time now, to check the doorknobs, stuff like that. We left the front door unlocked, remember? I don't know about you, but I don't want to see Billy come crashing in here, his weapon drawn."

"Billy? Oh, another friend who owes you a favor. I forgot. All right," Samantha said, nodding her head, although she still kept her back to him. "We probably should leave."

"Do you want to go home?"

No, she didn't want to go home. Not unless she was going to *his* home, to be with him.

"I think that would be smart," she said, heading toward the main office. "I'm still angry with you for taking me out of the game. That is what you've done, isn't it? Taken me out of the game?"

"You call what just happened a game?"

"No, not this, although you sure can turn it off quickly, can't you," she said, turning to him, cupping a hand on his cheek. "I mean the business with the envelope. Isn't that what you call it—what they call it in books and movies? Being in or out of the game?"

"What's going on is no game, sweetheart, but yes, I've taken you out of it. From here on in, it's my game."

"The Raven's game," Samantha said, then she sighed. "I wish I'd never brought you in on this."

"If you hadn't, we'd never have met, so I can't wish that, Samantha. I really can't."

"Even if you know I'll never be able to forgive you, or myself, if Uncle Mark is destroyed because of what I've started, what you might do next?"

His expression turned dark, almost frightening in how handsome he looked, definitely frightening in how sincere he looked. "Even if you never speak to me again, never see me again, never let what might happen between us happen. My first duty, Samantha, always has been and always will be to my country. I can't turn away, can't let this go, even if I know it means losing you."

"You think the contents of that envelope are that damning? That dangerous?"

"Don't you?"

She bit her lip, nodded. "That's the hell of it, isn't it, Jesse? We both do. Maybe…maybe it would be better if we didn't see each other quite so often for a while. Just for a while? I mean, this has been pretty intense, hasn't it? I…I need time to sort out my feelings, learn what is and is not connected to that horrible envelope and its contents."

He took her hand in his, lifted it to his mouth, kissed her fingertips. "We'll give it the weekend," he agreed. "I still want you to see the house, and I get the key on Monday. It wasn't going to be available until next Friday, but my cousin left a message with Brenda today, to tell me the place is already vacant. In the meantime, I'll stay away."

"I'd…I'd like that," Samantha said, knowing she'd be crying like a baby in a moment, just with the prospect of not seeing Jesse for four days.

Which just proved how much she really needed *not* to see him for the next four days….

Chapter Six

Jesse sat at his desk in the West Wing, holding the house key in both hands, looking at it as if it was the missing piece to some puzzle he was having considerable difficulty putting together.

He'd been to Rand Colton's office earlier, and his newly discovered cousin had some additional information for him. Nothing much, just that Graham Colton, the former senator's brother, was still moaning and groaning and insisting that he meant no harm when he'd sicced some goon named Kenny Randolph on the Oklahoma Coltons.

Sure. Right. He meant no harm. Guys like Graham Colton never mean any harm. To themselves.

Now he was singing every tune he could, to get back in his brother's good graces, to get off with a fine and a suspended sentence in the ''small matters'' of arson, breaking and entering, aiding and abetting, conspiracy before the fact—just to name a few of the man's "small" indiscretions.

What a guy. And Jesse was related to him? Gee, that was comforting.

At the same time, he now knew he and his family were related to Joe Colton, that same former senator, and one hell of a good man.

Did it balance out? Jesse thought it had to. After all, was there any choice? Pick your friends, sure, but you can't pick your relatives.

Not that he'd had much time to think about the California branch of the Colton family, or their wealth and many enterprises. They'd all been invited to Prosperino, to the Colton family ranch, and they'd probably all go at some point.

For now, their only connection was one dead son of a bitch grandfather Jesse couldn't punch in the mouth for what he'd done to Gloria WhiteBear all those years ago, and the firm conviction that what they'd learned was private, and definitely not for public consumption.

His family could handle keeping things quiet at that end, in Black Arrow, especially if this Kenny guy could be found soon, handed a deal of his own if he'd plea to lesser charges and keep the Colton name out of everything. Rand seemed pretty confident he and their mutual cousin, Bram—sheriff of Black Arrow—could handle everything.

If they couldn't, then the Raven could pay Kenny a little visit in the Black Arrow jail. He knew he could be very…convincing.

"Except when it comes to Samantha," he said out loud, then sighed.

How did he convince her that he was only doing his duty? That she had only been doing hers? It sounded so…hackneyed, he guessed. "I was only doing my duty." Sure, that's what they all said. Just like the Graham Coltons of this world said, "I didn't mean any harm."

But this *was* different, damn it. This wasn't protecting a family from some old scandal. This was preventing a corrupt candidate from assuming the loftiest office in this land, becoming the corrupt leader of the free world for the next four years, maybe eight.

That was heavy…stuff.

Jesse put down the key and sat back in his chair. He wondered how Samantha had been over the weekend, and was human enough to hope she'd missed him even half as much as he'd missed her.

That was a real kick in the head, too. He'd never been serious about anyone before, and never really thought he was the romantic sort, the kind who could fall like a ton of bricks for a warm smile, a pretty face.

Although it was the spaghetti in the lap that had sealed it for him. God, the woman had spirit. Loyal, yet independent, a class act, and yet with a temper that was all her own. He was crazy about her.

Or maybe just crazy. There was always that.

He leaned forward, picked up the phone, punched in the numbers to Samantha's private line. He might as well get this over with, then go jump off the White House roof if she asked "Jesse *who?*"

"Samantha?" he said after her brief, rather distracted hello.

"Jesse," she said, actually recognizing his voice.

That was good. Wasn't that good? He thought it was good. After all, it had been four days.

"I've got the key," he said, picking it up just as if she could see through the phone lines. "I thought…is one o'clock good for you?"

"I can meet you then, yes," Samantha said, then lowered her voice. "Anything new?"

"Just my blue slacks. Seems my former best pair somehow got tossed in the trash after a fatal meat-sauce accident."

"Oh. Sorry. One o'clock?"

"I'll bring lunch, and we can have a picnic in those gardens you told me about."

"Jesse, it's raining."

"Details, details. I'm still bringing lunch. Tuna fish okay?"

"Tuna fish is fine. Look, I've got to go. It's a madhouse around here this morning. What? Jesse, excuse me a sec."

Jesse pressed the receiver closer to his ear, but couldn't make out more than a few words, although he thought he heard his friend's name.

"Okay, I'm back. Sorry about that. Geoff was just telling me that he got the copier unjammed. He's wonderful. I may not give him back, you know."

"I don't think the campaign could afford his salary," Jesse said, smiling.

"Probably not. Uh-oh, here comes Bettyann, and she looks loaded for bear. She still thinks I brought Geoff in to replace her. Bye. Gotta go."

"Bye," Jesse said to the dial tone, then held the

receiver a few moments longer, as if trying to maintain contact.

God, he was in trouble, and falling fast.

"You free?"

Jesse looked toward the door, put down the phone and quite automatically stood up as Bob Forrester walked into the office.

"Yes, sir. I was…I was going to stop by this morning, but I was called away."

"No big deal, my legs still work," Old Abe said. He closed the door, then walked over to the desk, lowering his long, lanky frame into a chair made for a smaller man. "God, these miserable government-issue chairs had to have been made for the average-size man in 1780. Bought my own, you know, when we moved in here. It was either that or work at my desk all day with my knees jammed up under my chin. Sit, sit. And then talk to me."

"I really have very little to report, sir," Jesse said. Which was true. The only thing he could report, for certain, was that one Samantha Cosgrove had come to him with incriminating evidence that, by rights, he should have shown to Forrester last week.

"Then let me help you, son," the chief of staff said, shifting in his chair. "Joan Phillips is a pain in our collective butts, right?"

"Excuse me, sir?" Jesse worked hard to keep his expression neutral.

"Oh, come on, hark the Raven, don't play dumb. Mark Phillips is such a straight arrow I'm surprised there aren't feathers sticking out of his—well, never mind. He's a good man. Not an inspired man, I'll grant you, not a walking-talking genius like our current fearless leader, but a good one. After eight years of our current commander in chief, he'll be four to eight years of status quo, which ain't a bad thing, because we'll be leaving quite a legacy. He won't rock the boat we built, understand?''

"Yes, sir, I do," Jesse said, waiting for the other shoe to drop. The other shoe being Joan Phillips.

"Now, his wife? There's a different kettle of mackerel. She's ambitious. Damn ambitious, and she doesn't want anyone else telling her husband how to run, how to win, how to govern. She sees strings attached to an endorsement from our president, and she's right, there would be. So she keeps pushing us all away, making her own plans. Oh, she's not above using us, she just doesn't want us to use her. President Joan, I think that's how she sees it.''

"Interesting, sir. I didn't know any of that." Interesting, hell! *Damning,* was more the word, knowing what Jesse knew.

"I don't like the woman, that's no secret. I applaud ambition, be it in a man or a woman, so that's not it, I'm not some closet misogynist. It's her tactics I don't like. She's got a lot of bodies hidden, you know. People she stepped on to get her husband where he is today. And Phillips? I don't know. The man must wear blinders where his wife is concerned.''

Jesse said nothing, but just kept his own counsel. At times like this, silence was always safest. Besides, the longer he remained silent, the more Old Abe would talk. He knew that from experience, working with any-

body he was trying to get information from, bad guy
or good guy.

Forrester sighed, then continued: "But hey, bottom
line? Phillips is a good man. The man we want. We're
all set to endorse him, show up at the fund-raiser, give
him our blessing—and then you come waltzing in, tell
me to back off a while. I had to ask myself—why?
What does the Raven know that I don't know?"

"Probably not much," Jesse said, suppressing a
smile. "You seem to already know most of it. You've
had me followed, haven't you? I must be getting lazy,
because I never thought of that, or picked up on the
tail. Shame on both of us."

"Smart-ass. And, yes, I did have you followed. I've
even got pictures. The girl? Lovely. You in spaghetti
sauce? Not so lovely."

"Samantha Cosgrove," Jesse said, sighing. So much
for keeping Samantha out of it.

"Yes, that's the name. Pretty name. She's in charge
of the local office of the senator's election campaign.
Not the top dog, not nationally, but a good worker, and
loyal. And then there she is, one minute being cozy
with you, so we think, okay, the Raven's got himself
a girl, good for him. And then the next minute? Hey,
the next minute she's dumping food in your lap.
There's also after-hour visits to the office, and a report
that you're cashing in favors and having the place
watched day and night."

"Man. I'm either getting very sloppy, or you guys
are very good."

"A little of both, I'd say. Anyway, I hear about all
this, stack it up against you telling me to hold off on

endorsing Phillips, and I've got to ask myself—why? What's going on here? Then I figured, no, I've got to ask Jesse. So Jesse—why? What's going on here? In fact the only thing I don't have to ask myself in any of this is *who*. Because it has to be Joan Phillips. She's been trouble for us before, and I'm betting she's being trouble for us now."

"I've kept this very close to the chest, sir, working with people I can trust, and totally off the record. No leaks. I can assure you of that."

"Good. And, considering this town usually leaks like an old iron pot shot with buckshot, very encouraging. You trust these men?"

"Men and women, sir, and yes, I do. Let me show you what I've got, what I've done so far, and then I can tell you the rest."

Jesse went over to his file cabinet, the one with the combination lock on it, and opened the bottom drawer. He lifted out the envelope, sealed in a plastic bag, although it was a little late to hope for fingerprints, and tossed it to the chief of staff.

"Samantha Cosgrove found this by accident in the outgoing mail last week. The envelope had come open. Because she brought in more envelopes just like it later, we're sure Joan Phillips left it in the office, to be mailed. We just didn't know if it came directly from her, or if she was mailing it for the senator. I think you just answered that question, sir."

Forrester looked at the plastic bag, then at Jesse. "It's all right to touch?"

Jesse nodded. "Not even any saliva for DNA on the address label. It's clean, and useless for any more forensics, as both Ms. Cosgrove and I handled everything pretty extensively, I'm afraid, before we knew what we had. Standard computer printout, almost untraceable unless we had the machine and could make one-on-one comparisons, and even that would be dicey to prove in court.''

"Court?" Old Abe looked at him. "This goes nowhere near a court, son. It goes nowhere, period. We neutralize Phillips, and whatever is in here means nothing.''

"Neutralize, sir?''

"Oh, sorry. In your previous line of work that means something different than it does in mine. Remove him from any power, that's what we're going to do. If we're not too late. If we are, then we can't stop it, can't sit on it, and it all hits the fan, big time. I don't want to even think about that scenario.''

Jesse waited while Old Abe opened the bag, slipped out the contents. He pressed a button on the intercom and told Brenda to hold all calls, cancel the remainder of his morning meetings. And he waited, while the chief of staff looked at the ten-page memo, page by page.

"Do you know what this is?" Forrester asked at last, stabbing a finger at the pages.

"Yes, sir, I think I do."

Forrester let out a low string of down-home cusswords that had even Jesse's ears burning.

"Where did she get this?" he asked at last, tossing the pages back onto the desk.

"Ms. Cosgrove, sir?"

"No, no, I can pretty much figure out where she got

it. The question is, where did Joan Phillips get it? Answer? From Senator Phillips. Next question. Did he give it to her? My gut answer? No way in hell. She just plain took it.''

Jesse leaned his elbows on the desktop. ''So you're saying Senator Phillips has no idea this is going on? Has no idea what his wife has done?''

''I'm saying I'm hoping like hell that's what it is. But I have to go to the president with this, Jesse, without delay. So, what else have you got for me?''

Jesse filled in the chief of staff on what else he had done. The operatives watching the post offices for the other envelopes. The bug. The operative inside the campaign headquarters, the one who had the night shift outside those offices—although the chief of staff already knew about Geoff and Billy.

''Blank pages? Damn, the woman's crafty, isn't she? Good work, Jesse. I think you've covered Ms. Cosgrove fairly well, have kept her name out of this. I'd like to think we can do the same. With her, and with the senator as well. Even Joan, much as I'd like to feed that interfering woman to the wolves in the press.''

''Yes, sir,'' Jesse said, relieved about Samantha, and damn glad he wasn't Joan Phillips.

''You know, my wife gardens, volunteers at the hospital, plays canasta and runs her own travel agency. She's glad when I succeed, stands behind me, but she'd never interfere, just as I'd never try to tell her how to run her company, or where to plant her roses, for that matter. Why couldn't Joan Phillips be more like her? No, Joan Phillips has to be a big fan of Machiavelli, damn it.''

He stood up, slowly unfolding his body, and grinned at Jesse without mirth. "So, who do you like for the party's nominee for president next spring, now that Senator Phillips is out of the race?"

"He's out of the race, sir?" Jesse asked, also getting to his feet.

"What do you think, son?"

"Yes, sir," Jesse said, nodding his agreement. "I knew that."

"I'll just bet you did. But nobody else will, not yet. Stick around, and keep Ms. Cosgrove handy—and in the dark—until I can set up a meeting for all parties involved. That won't be until those other four envelopes have arrived at their destinations. I want all the ammunition I can get so that the senator's wife can't wiggle out of this one, and so that the senator understands exactly what happened."

"I'm on top of it, sir."

"Good. Now to keep the pretty spaghetti lady in line and in the dark, huh? That won't be a walk in the park, son, I'm sure of that. Good luck, and keep reporting to me. In person. No paper, all right?"

"Yes, sir," Jesse said, sitting down heavily when the chief of staff left the room.

Samantha stood outside the former Chekagovian embassy, glad the rain had stopped. She looked at the huge redbrick mansion with something definitely approaching awe.

So impressive, and yet welcoming. A home, not a house. A mansion, yes, but still a place where it would not be impossible to visualize children running across the lawn, or a baby carriage parked at the front door.

It was one of the few buildings in the area that had any real land around it, although that wasn't much, not by Connecticut standards, where her parents' home was located on five acres of rolling grass and heavy trees.

This was a city house, yet a country house. Three floors of rooms that had seen so much history.

She rubbed her arms because she'd begun to shiver.

Because it looked like...home.

"Hello."

Samantha turned around quickly, startled, to see a young woman approaching along the pavement. Blond, quite tall, she had huge blue eyes that dominated her face, and the walk of someone—although young—who knew who she was, and where she was going. Her smile was friendly, almost welcoming.

"Hello," Samantha said in return. "I...I'm waiting for someone."

"Yes, so am I. Jesse Colton?"

Samantha's polite smile faded. What had the man done—set up tours? It's Monday, so this must be Blondes On Tour? "Why, yes, that's right. Jesse Colton."

The other woman nodded. "Then I'm right, and you're Susannah Cosgrove?"

"Samantha, yes," Samantha said, relaxing a little, but not much.

"Oh, I'm sorry. Samantha, of course. I wrote down the name, but then left the note back at the embassy." She put out her right hand. "I'm Eva. Eva Ritka."

Samantha took her hand in hers, shook it. "The former ambassador's wife?"

"His daughter, actually. We moved out in such a rush that I've been discovering things missing as I unpack. Mr. Colton was nice enough to agree that I meet him here, take another look around to see if I can find anything. Although my father swears things are lost in every move, as if goblins carried them off, never to be seen again."

"I agree with your father," Samantha said, laughing. "I lost my entire treasured collection of colored hopscotch chalk in our move to Connecticut, but didn't realize it until a few years later, when I decided to give it to my cousin's daughter. Oh, here comes Jesse now."

She watched as he parked his car—only one back-up, which really annoyed her, because it had taken her three in this town built for a million people and two automobiles.

"Hi," he said a few moments later, walking toward them. "Samantha," he continued, nodding at her rather quickly before turning to Ms. Ritka. "You must be Ms. Ritka. I hope you can find what you're after."

"Oh, so do I," Eva said as the three of them walked to the front door. "There are a few things we can't find, but one is very important. It's a music box that's been in our family for generations. Hand-carved wood, with the Nativity depicted on it. Not exactly a priceless work of art, not in the usual sense, but it's definitely priceless to us. I can't understand how it got left behind."

"Well, then I doubly hope you find it," Jesse said, pushing open the door and punching in the security code, then standing back to let Samantha and Eva enter ahead of him.

"Oh my goodness," Samantha said, stopping just inside the foyer. Her voice echoed in the empty house. "It's just as I imagined—and yet so much more."

"Pretty, isn't it?" Eva said. "The chandeliers? These lovely floors. I slid down that banister, you know. Just once, and was punished by my nanny, but it was fun, and well worth the scolding. Excuse me now, please. I'll just run upstairs and begin checking through the closets and cupboards. There are a thousand of them in this place."

Samantha only nodded, already walking into the expansive living room, blinking back tears at the beauty that unfolded in front of her.

"So solid. So…eternal. This house was built to last, Jesse. Can you see it, can you sense it?"

She turned to look at him, only to see that he was looking at her.

"What?" she asked him, feeling uncomfortable.

"Nothing. You just look…I don't know. You just look *right* in here. I feel like an interloper, like I should be knocking at the back door while kicking the mud off my work boots."

"Oh, no, no," she said, taking his arm. "This house welcomes everyone. How can you say that?"

"Because you've never seen Black Arrow?" he suggested, grinning. "I think we could put half the town in here, and have room left over for the feed and grain store."

"You make it sound as if you came from the back of beyond, Jesse. Your family is in Oklahoma, that's home to them. Washington is different, I grant you, but a home is a home, no matter what it is or where it is. Because it's *people* who make a house a home.''

"People with a whole big bunch of furniture. I think we could set up a bowling lane in that last room,'' Jesse said, looking around as they walked through the downstairs, their heels clicking on the hardwood floors. "How many rooms are on this floor?''

"About eight, so far,'' Samantha said, taking his hand. "And we've yet to find the kitchen. I can't wait to see the kitchen.''

When they found it, there were two of them. A small, cozy family kitchen, and a much larger industrial one with acres of countertops, a huge eight-burner stove and two deep refrigerators.

"Excuse me while I try to catch my breath. I think I'm in love,'' Samantha said, opening cabinet doors to find specialized racks for cookie trays, tablecloths, pot lids—everything and anything that could be organized.

When she opened a set of large double doors and saw a huge walk-in pantry with rolling shelves, she said, "Scratch that. I *know* I'm in love.''

"You'd cook in here?'' Jesse asked her as she reluctantly left the pantry and rejoined him on the ceramic-tile floor of the kitchen.

"Oh, yes. The smaller kitchen, the family kitchen, is lovely but cramped, the way that sort of kitchen was constructed when this house was originally built. I'd make the whole thing into a much larger breakfast room—those windows facing the gardens are perfect—and use this as the real kitchen for the house. It just needs some…oh, I don't know. Some *humanizing*. You know. Pretty curtains, copper-bottom pots hanging over that wonderful stove, strings of garlic and onions and other vegetables hanging with them, a ceramic-pig cookie jar..."

"Pardon me?" Jesse said, laughing.

"What?" Samantha was lost in her dream.

"A ceramic-pig cookie jar? Tell me, where did that one come from?"

"I don't know," Samantha said, blinking in surprise. "I just said it. I don't have one. I don't think I've ever even *seen* one. But it would be perfect in here, trust me."

"Excuse me?"

Samantha and Jesse turned to see Eva Ritka standing in the doorway.

"Any luck?" Jesse asked her.

"Some," Eva said, sighing. "I've found a blouse I was missing, and a crystal candle holder on the top shelf of one of the closets. Some hangers, which I left, if you don't mind. And one of my father's dress shoes. Just one. I can only hope its mate made the trip with the movers."

"But no music box?" Samantha asked her.

"No, no music box," Eva said sadly. But then she brightened. "I probably overlooked it in one of the boxes we've stored in the basement of our new residence. It will probably take me weeks to find it."

"Well, if you don't," Jesse said, "please feel free to call me and we'll look again."

"Thank you so much, and I'll do that," Eva said, smiling. "I'll let myself out. Enjoy your tour, Samantha. But be careful. This is a wonderful house, and you might just fall in love with it.''

"I already have," Samantha answered honestly, "and I haven't even seen all of it yet."

"That can be remedied, you know," Jesse said once Eva had gone. "If we can find our way back to the foyer and stairs, that is."

"We don't have to. I saw a second set, near the study, or at least what I'd call the study. There were enough bookshelves in there to open a branch library. We can go up that way. Come on, let's go exploring."

She took his hand and led him toward the servants' stairs, and within moments they were standing in the wide upstairs hallway.

If the downstairs had Samantha falling in love, the upstairs nearly brought her to tears.

Window seats, deep enough for cushions and books and cups of tea and long winter afternoons, were in every bedroom.

There were nooks and alcoves and curious little turns that led to one architectural marvel after another. Detailed woodwork, magnificent wallpapers from another age, high ceilings, huge windows, magnificent vistas outside those windows. She felt like a kid set loose in a candy store.

"Look," she said, leaning on one broad windowsill that overlooked the gardens. "Chrysanthemums. The garden is drenched in chrysanthemums for the fall. Aren't they gorgeous? Oh, look, and there's a gazebo. I'd forgotten about the gazebo."

"You're enjoying yourself, aren't you?" Jesse asked, coming up behind her, so that when she turned around they were standing so close together she could make just one small move and be in his arms.

"I'm sorry," she said, ready to back away to where it was safer for her heart. But she couldn't. Physically, she was up against the wall. Emotionally, she couldn't move if her life depended on it.

"I've missed you like hell," Jesse said, his voice low and faintly rough.

She lowered her head, unable to look in his eyes because they were so hungry they nearly scared her. "It...it has been a long few days, hasn't it?"

"Rome was built in less," he said, putting his hands on her shoulders. "You look good here, Samantha. Like you belong. I like that."

"Here? Don't be silly. This place is *huge*. I'd rattle around like a marble in a huge bucket."

"We could put down carpets," he said, his hands inching to the sides of her throat, his thumbs beginning to lightly massage the sensitive skin just behind her ears.

"What are you doing?" she asked, wetting her suddenly dry lips with the tip of her tongue. "I mean it, Jesse, what are you doing?"

"I don't have the faintest damn idea, sweetheart. Maybe I'm finally finding my heart's truth," he said, and then he kissed her.

"Rand? I hate to bother you again today. It's Jesse Colton."

"Jesse, hello. You're not bothering me, you're rescuing me. I've about burned my eyes out reading a brief that could keep Rip Van Winkle asleep for another twenty years. Did you go see the house?''

Jesse adjusted the cell phone at his ear as he headed toward the parking garage, stepping around two tourists taking pictures of the White House. "I did, earlier this afternoon. Great place.''

"I didn't think it was a prefab knockoff of a Georgetown mansion," Rand said, and Jesse could hear the amusement in his cousin's voice.

"Yeah, well, what I want from you now, Rand, if you don't mind, is the name of a good appraiser if you've got one. Is that what they call them, appraisers? I've never bought a house, so I'm not sure.''

"A real estate appraiser, yes. But you don't have to do that. I've got the latest appraisal here, thanks to the trust. We had a new appraisal done for you the moment we found out about the house. Hang on a second and I'll find it.''

Jesse made it to his car while waiting for Rand, and had his hand on the door handle when Rand read him the figure, which otherwise might have been enough to knock him off his feet.

"Wow," he said, his hand frozen in place. "It's true what they say about Georgetown, isn't it? Pricey.''

"Are you planning to recommend that the family sells it?'' Rand asked as Jesse opened the car door, slipped into the driver's seat.

"Yes, that's exactly what I'm planning. I mean, we could continue to rent it out for the income, but I think the family wants the assets of the trust to be all in funds so it's easier to handle. This is the only real estate, and it kind of messes up the works, you know?''

"I can probably help you out, then. I mean, all you have to do is put out the word and you'll have buyers lining up. One of my associates can handle the title search—you need one, even if we know it's a clear title—and the closing when the deal is done."

"Thanks, I'll take you up on that," Jesse said, backing out of his space. "The title search and the closing, that is. I already have a buyer."

"You work fast, cousin," Rand said.

"I'm an easy sell," Jesse said, smiling at his own small joke.

"What? Do I understand this correctly? *You're* going to buy the house? But you already own the house."

"*We* own the house, cousin, my whole family owns that house. That's why I wanted the appraisal, to make sure I'd be offering the full market value less only my share, as my parents have already decided each of us kids gets one share, and one vote in what we do with the trust."

"Nice. I like your family, and I've yet to meet most of them."

"Thanks. As for the price? I got really lucky with a few little security gadgets I dreamed up over the years, so I can afford it, although I'll probably have to work until I'm eighty to pay off the mortgage. But that's all right. You see, I need a house. I need this house. I'm getting married."

"No kidding. That's terrific. Your fiancée must be over the moon if she's seen the house."

Jesse pulled to the exit of the parking garage and stepped on the brake, not wanting to pull out into traffic while still on the cell phone. "Definitely crazy about it. Now to get her to be crazy about me."

"Excuse me? What did you say? Are you saying you haven't asked the woman yet?"

"That would be it in a nutshell, cousin. Probably because she might hate me once I tell her everything I have to tell her. Still, it wouldn't be fair to ask her first and then tell her the bad news. Wish me luck?"

"Sure, even if I don't have the damnedest idea what you're talking about. Keep me informed, okay? Man, I've got to meet all the rest of my new Colton relatives, if you're a sample of them. I think you'll all fit in very well with our branch of the family. Believe me, we're all just a little off center when it comes to romance and marriage."

"We'll have to swap stories one day," Jesse said.

"I'll bring the wine and the crying towel. And good luck to you, cousin."

Jesse thanked him and cut the connection.

He was buying a house. His family would approve, he was sure of that.

Getting Samantha to agree, however, was going to be—as Old Abe might say it—a whole different kettle of mackerel.

Chapter Seven

"No, everything is fine, really. I would have called you otherwise, you know that."

Samantha listened with only half an ear, because Rose was always on the phone. Always, and with everyone. Adding another line just meant that she could talk to more people at the same time.

With call waiting, Samantha figured that Rose often spoke with four different people at the same time, on two different cordless telephones.

Other than Rose's extensive knowledge of Russian history and her ability to grow her nails long enough to stick small decorative decals on them, Samantha most envied Rose her mastery of keeping four different conversations going without breaking a sweat.

"...and then she told him if he didn't agree with her theme statement, he could just blow it out his ear. Can you imagine her saying that? To a *professor?* No wonder she's changed majors three times."

Samantha snuggled deeper into the comfortable couch and smiled as she turned a page in her book, *Political Campaign: Strategies for the New Millennium.*

"...so I told her, I said, Sarah, if you want to wear pink, wear pink, but then, for God's sake, get rid of the orange lipstick..."

"Rose," Samantha called out, leaning her head back on the arm of the couch so that her voice would carry into the dining room, "could you please do me a great big favor and go upstairs to—"

"Yes, I know she shouldn't have dumped the spaghetti in his lap, Mrs. C., but I think she's calmed down now. Come here? You want to come here? Well, I—"

Samantha, who had nearly done a flip as she jack-knifed off the couch, grabbed one of the telephones from Rose's hand. "Mom? Samantha here. Mom, no. You don't have to come here. It was an accident, and he deserved it anyway. And it was only spaghetti. It wasn't as if I'd beaned him with a brick or something. So really, you don't—"

"Wrong phone," Rose said, handing her the other one, the one that had been stuck to her right ear. "You just told my friend Cynthia about the spaghetti caper, which you didn't have to do. She already knows. Trust me, everybody knows. Here—Mrs. C.'s on this one."

"Mom? It's me," Samantha said into the phone while glaring at Rose. "I...I didn't know you had called. Rose didn't tell me."

What followed was a solid twenty minutes of Samantha's mother talking, and Samantha saying the occasional "Uh-huh" or "I know, Mom, really I do," while glaring at Rose, who'd popped popcorn and sat there watching and listening—and grinning like the Cheshire cat.

By the time Samantha could convince her mother that, yes, the bridge tournament to benefit a local summer camp *was* more important than flying to Washington to explain, yet again, that *ladies* do not resort to physical violence, she was exhausted enough to actually thank Rose for putting a bowl of microwaved popcorn in front of her.

"I suppose this is your idea of a peace offering for betraying me to my mother, telling her all my secrets?" she asked her live-in Benedict Arnold. "Um...extra butter. Okay, I forgive you."

"Boy, you're easy. Anyway, you should forgive me," Rose said, curling up on one of the chairs, her own half-eaten bowl of popcorn in her lap. "I talked her out of it, even before you grabbed the phone."

"Oh, really? You're such an innocent do-gooder, Rose, always with my best interests at heart. So? Who do you suppose told her I dumped the spaghetti in Jesse's lap?"

"A little birdie?" Rose suggested, throwing a piece of popcorn in the air, then deftly catching it in her mouth. "So, you saw him again today, right? What's he wearing tonight? Beef Wellington? Moo-goo-guy-whatever? I'm keeping a journal, you understand, and since your life is loads more interesting than mine, I borrow stories once in a while, changing the names to make me look like I have a life at all."

"You're crazy. How you got past the interview with my mother without her figuring that out is still a major marvel to me—and thank God you did, because I really enjoy having you here.''

''Beats talking to the walls, huh? Besides, if I can't get a good job with my Russian history major, I may try doing a little stand-up comedy. Hey, you never know. So, answer the question—how did it go today?''

Samantha leaned her head back and closed her eyes, melting inside with the memories of a perfect afternoon. ''It went…well. Really, really well.''

''Oh, kootchie-mama, I want details. Lots of details. Consider it charity work to a shut-in, since I haven't had a date in three weeks.''

Samantha opened her eyes, sat forward and clasped her hands in her lap. She had to tell somebody or she was going to burst. ''Okay, here's the thing. I think I'm falling in love with him.''

''Hot damn! Talk slowly, I want to commit this all to memory, okay?''

''Nothing *happened,* Rose,'' Samantha said, hoping she wasn't blushing as she told that whopper. ''I mean, okay, he kissed me. I kissed him back. We…kissed some more. And then I had to go back to the office for a meeting with a women's voters group from Indiana, and he had to go back to the West Wing to save the free world. Although, if we hadn't both had appointments…?'' She let the sentence hang.

''What kind of kisser is he? I mean, there's all kinds, a lot of them pretty darn sloppy. Is he sloppy? He doesn't look like he'd be sloppy. So, what kind of kisser is he? Rate him for me.''

Samantha rolled her eyes. ''On a scale of one to ten, you mean?''

"Exactly. On a scale of one to ten."

"Okay." Samantha grinned. She couldn't help herself. "He's a fourteen."

"Oh, wow. Oh, wow oh wow oh wow! A ten. Even a twelve. But a fourteen?"

"Maybe a fifteen. Or a ninety-seven. In a league all his own, Rose. Definitely."

"Oh, stop, you're killing me here. Can I be you in my next life?"

Samantha laughed, but then her smile faded. "I don't know what's going to happen next, Rose. I mean, he seems serious. Heaven knows I'm serious. But…but this is all moving so quickly, except for the four days I didn't see him. Those were the longest, hardest, loneliest days in my life. How do you not know a person exists one day, and then not be able to imagine your life without him the next?"

Rose pulled her glasses off the top of her head, positioned them low on her nose and looked at Samantha through slitted eyelids. "Ze girl, ze iz smitten, *da?* No need iz there for ze crystal ball, ze tea leaves. I zee a wedding gown in ze future. Ze man, dark and handsome. Ze little childrens, all of them laughing, happy, *da?* Ze picket fence—"

"No picket fence," Samantha interrupted. "But there is a gazebo. A white one, with climbing roses on it. They're all done blooming for the year, unfortunately, but I'm pretty sure they'll be red. Red roses look so lovely against white. Although yellow is pretty, too."

Rose shoved her glasses higher on her nose. "You

made up a gazebo? You have been giving this a lot of thought, haven't you, Samantha?''

"I didn't have to make up anything. I saw it. We met today at a house Jesse and his family own in Georgetown. It used to be the Chekagovian embassy.''

"Get out! You're kidding me, right? The Chekagovian embassy? That's a mansion.''

"It is large,'' Samantha conceded. "But it's still a home, really. You can just *feel* the welcome when you walk inside the door. It's vacant right now, and Jesse told me the family is going to sell it. Oh, and I met Eva Ritka today, too. She's the youngest daughter of the Chekagovian ambassador. She came by to look for something the movers missed when they packed up all the Ritka belongings.''

"What was she like? I've never met an ambassador's daughter.''

"She was very nice. Very pretty. I wish she could have found what she was looking for, but Jesse said she could come back anytime, to look again.''

"I wish I could see this house. You seem to be fascinated by it.''

"I'm more than fascinated.'' She was quiet for a moment, then shrugged. "Can I swear you to secrecy and really believe you won't go running to tell the world? Oh, and world translates to my mother. Understand?''

"Sure,'' Rose answered quickly. "I only tell unimportant stuff. You didn't swear me to secrecy about the spaghetti, so I'm guessing this is important?''

"Yes, it is. All right, here goes. Jesse's cousin, Rand Colton, is a lawyer here in town, and he knows all about it. Jesse's related to him, you understand. He told me a lot more about his family this afternoon. I...I phoned him when I got back to the office. Rand, that is.''

Rose sat up straighter, tucking her legs under her. ''Wait a minute. You talked to his cousin—about the house, right? Why?''

Samantha took a deep breath, let it out slowly. ''I...I think I want to buy it...with my trust fund money, and give it to Jesse.''

Rose's mouth dropped open for a few seconds, and she blinked rapidly before saying, in some awe, ''So much for all your mama's teachings. You're going to buy it, give it to him as a gift? Tell me, Samantha, would this be before or after you propose to him?''

''I'm not going to propose to him. I wouldn't... couldn't do that. I mean, if it never goes that far, if I'm wrong, and he doesn't feel the way I do, then I'd just never tell him I bought it, and sell it again. But what if it got sold before he gets around to asking me to marry him? It's *our* house, Rose. I could feel it as we walked through the rooms.''

''As you and Mr. Scores-Ninety-seven-on-the-Kiss-o-meter kissed your way through the rooms, you mean,'' Rose corrected with a grin, then wrinkled her nose in thought. ''But wait a minute here. Won't he know if you buy it? Your name would be on the offer, right?''

''Mr. Colton—Rand—says that can be handled. In fact, he was really quite nice. He asked if I had just been to the house with Jesse, because Jesse had told him about the house, and about someone he'd taken there today.''

Then she frowned. ''He kept...laughing. I don't know why. He said the house couldn't possibly even come onto the market for another month. But he said he'd help me, keep me informed. We're having lunch next week because he wants to meet me.''

''Sure, he'll meet you, feed you, then push you straight into a rubber room,'' Rose said, sighing. ''Lord knows, this is going to sound strange coming from me—the original Miss Impulsive—but aren't you sort of rushing things?''

''Sure, I am. I know that. But did you ever know...I mean, just *know* that something was right? I mean, there are a few problems Jesse and I still have to sort out—something to do with work—but Jesse's special. What I feel for him is special. And I think he feels the same way about me.''

''You *think* he feels the same way about you?''

''All right. I *know* he does. The heart...well, not to sound soppy, but the heart just *knows*. Please don't ask me to explain how, because I can't tell you. I don't understand it, I just *know* it.''

''Someone should call your mother,'' Rose said, hunting in the nearly empty bowl for one of the few remaining popped kernels of corn. Then she lifted her head, grinned at Samantha. ''But it's not going to be me.''

A few days later, after two long, intimate dinners in two more of Jesse's and Samantha's favorite restaurants, after two lunches taken together on park benches...and quite a few kisses...Jesse walked into Samantha's office and sat down, his expression determined, and noncommittal.

He didn't even kiss her hello.

"Your dog just die?" Samantha asked, looking at him across the desktop.

He looked at her. How he loved her. How he hoped she felt the same way...and that their love would be enough to get them through the next couple of days. "That might be easier. We have to talk, Samantha."

She frowned. "You're going to refuse to wear a monkey suit to the fund-raiser Friday night?"

He cracked a small smile. "I'll have you know that I look very good in a monkey suit. Better than very good. Splendid, even. Women faint in my path when I walk past them in a monkey suit."

"Probably when they get a glimpse of the tail," Samantha retorted, balling up a piece of typing paper and tossing it at him.

"Maybe. Or maybe it's the little red hat that gets to them, or the tin cup?"

"Would you please stop," Samantha said, laughing. "Why do they call a tuxedo a monkey suit anyway?"

He knew she was stalling. She had sensed that he had bad news for her, and she was stalling...and he was more than willing to stall along with her.

"Is this going to be a philosophical discussion," he asked her in mock seriousness, "or do you really want to know? Because I can grab Bettyann's computer from her, go online, and probably have an answer for you in ten minutes."

"No, that's all right," Samantha said, leaning back

in her chair. "Okay, I guess I've stalled enough to get my heart rate back down to normal. What's up, Jesse? You said we probably couldn't have lunch together today because you'd be too busy, remember? So why are you here, and why are you looking like a man bearing bad news?"

He reached into the inside pocket of his suit coat and pulled out a typed sheet of paper, folded in half lengthwise. "They've all been delivered."

He watched as Samantha wet her lips, then folded her hands in front of her on the desktop. "The four envelopes?"

"That would be them, yes. The always unfathomable United States Post Office being what it is, naturally we had to wait an extra day for the envelope going to Saint Louis to arrive, although the one for Sacramento, California, showed up yesterday. Go figure."

"And they were all picked up from their post office boxes? Already?"

"The Chicago guy was hanging around the post office waiting for the boxes to be loaded. Everyone knew the envelopes were expected."

Samantha picked up a large paper clip and began unbending it, her eyes on her task and avoiding his. "Your people were there? To photograph everything? To follow the people who picked up the envelopes?"

"Photos, following, the whole nine yards, Samantha. And do you know what we discovered?"

She put down the paper clip. Looked at him levelly. And shocked the hell out of him.

"Yes, I think I do. Saint Louis? That would be PDE, Incorporated, an alternative energy company. Chicago?

Paul Manners and Sons, a large, privately owned company, also energy. They design nuclear power plants, which is not exactly a booming business right now, but could be if the federal government did something about it. Sacramento has to be First Hit Mining, and Butte, Montana, is either Hasbrook Energy or Sullivan Mining and Engineering. So? How'd I do?''

Jesse shook his head slowly as he stared at her. "How? It was Sullivan, by the way, but—how? How did you know? We didn't know, not until we followed the pick-up guy back to each headquarters.''

Samantha unlocked the bottom drawer of her desk and pulled out a green and white printout, then handed it to him.

"Bettyann made up a list for me of all contributors involved in mining and any other energy business, from alternative sources to coal, to gas, to nuclear power. The first pack are those that already contributed, and the second is our list of hopeful contacts for the future. Mrs. Phillips pretty much has the same lists. She asked for them.''

Jesse paged through the printouts, shaking his head. "So, since you knew the cities involved from the address labels, you just went down these sheets picking companies? I thought I said you were out of this, sweetheart.''

"Exactly, Jesse. *You* said I was out of this. I never said so. Oh, and you'll see from the printouts that there are four possibles for the address on the first envelope. That's as far down as I can get. Sorry.''

"That's okay, I think we can take it from here.'' He held up the printouts. "May I keep these?''

She shrugged. "I suppose so. I was pretty sure today would be the day you'd get back to me on the envelopes. I've already typed up my resignation, effective immediately, and will take it up to the Hill and hand deliver it to the senator later today in his Senate office. All I need to do now is to put today's date on and print out a fresh copy. Friday night will be my last day, right after the fund-raiser. I might as well go out with a bang. Besides, I bought a new dress for the dinner."

Jesse was surprised. He hadn't expected her to resign. He got up, walked around the desk and helped her to her feet. "Are you sure about this?"

"How can I stay, Jesse? I have to admit that, until you walked into the office a few minutes ago, I was still hoping this was all some grand mistake, even a bad dream. But it isn't. I can't stay here. I can't be a part of this, because it isn't honest, and because I've chosen up sides, and I'm on your side, not Uncle Mark's. That's confidential information I've given you, about corporations on our wish list of contributors at least, even though all actual contributors become public information at some point. So, yes, Jesse, after Friday night, I am out of the game."

He looked at her for several moments, watched her eyes cloud then clear again as her chin went up, her resolve, it would seem, hardened into granite. She was being so damn brave, as all her dreams of serving President Mark Phillips, of serving in the West Wing, went down the circular bowl. He wanted so badly to hold her, to comfort her.

"Let's get out of here, sweetheart," he said, grabbing her raincoat from the clothes tree and taking her hand, leading her to the door.

"My goodness, going out, Samantha? I'd hoped to go over a few things about the fund-raiser on Friday. And who is your young man?"

Jesse felt Samantha's hand tighten warningly in his. He knew that face, that beautiful, well-preserved, smiling face. Mrs. Mark Phillips's face appeared on the pages of his morning newspapers at least twice a week.

He squeezed Samantha's hand reassuringly in return, then let it go, and smiled broadly as he extended his hand to Joan Phillips.

"Ma'am," he said with an exaggerated drawl as she looked at his hand for a moment, then offered hers as well. "I'm Joe Carter. I was in college with Samantha, although three years ahead of her. Prettiest little thing in the freshman class. I just got into town from Alabama a coupla weeks ago and decided to take a chance, look her up. We've been sight seein' ever since. What a pretty little town, this Washington, ma'am. She's going to take me to see the Lincoln Memorial this afternoon. Aren't you, Samantha?"

"I...well, I—yes, I am. Unless you need me for something, Mrs. Phillips?"

Joan was intently looking at Jesse. "Joe Carter, you said? But—but I do believe Bettyann told me your name was Jesse. Jesse James." She rolled her mascaraed eyes. "I should have known. Bettyann is horrible with nicknames. Jesse James was that outlaw, wasn't he?"

"Yes, ma'am. Outlaw or folk hero, depending on who you ask," Jesse said, looking out toward the main office, to see Bettyann standing in the middle of the room watching them. Odd thing about Bettyann—she was always watching, wasn't she? "I'm supposin', ma'am, that you and Samantha have bunches of things to talk about, so I'll just go step outside and give you some privacy."

"Well, thank you, Mr. Carter, and I appreciate it. You're very nice. I won't keep her long, I promise."

"Joe, please," Jesse said, wishing Samantha had been able to suppress that small whimper. He leaned over, kissed her cheek. "I'll be waitin', sweetheart. No rush. Oh, and I'll tell Bettyann what you wanted her to do."

"What I wanted—oh. Oh, yes. Thank you."

Good girl, Jesse thought as he left the smaller office, closing the door behind him. Thankfully, he'd retrieved the page he'd brought to show Samantha, and had rolled up the printouts she'd given to him. The last thing any of them needed now was for Joan Phillips to see either item of evidence lying on Samantha's desktop.

Now to get rid of Bettyann. Samantha had picked up on that one fast enough, bless her. Jesse didn't want the woman and her loose lips anywhere near Joan Phillips, asking questions about "Joe Carter."

"Bettyann?" he said, then coughed, because her name came out in a sort of drawl. It was time to get back to his usual speech patterns. "Samantha asked me to tell you that she really needs you to go up to the Hill right away, up to the senator's office."

Bettyann looked toward the glass-topped door to Samantha's office. "Me? Why?"

"To pick up something that was supposed to have been sent here," Jesse told her, improvising easily. "Something for the fund-raiser dinner."

"Can't...can't I send someone else? Geoff could go. I mean, Mrs. Phillips was going to tell me about her dress for the fund-raiser. Some designer thing."

Jesse gave a little jerk with his head. "Gee, I don't know, Bettyann. Whatever this is, Samantha seems worried about it, and said she definitely wants you to go get it. Oh, and then you can go straight to lunch from there."

Bettyann brightened. "What am I complaining about? With any luck, I can stretch this into a two-hour project, and I do need new panty hose for Friday night. Okay, I'm gone."

"Thank you, Bettyann," Jesse said before he pulled out a desk chair and sat down, his back to Samantha's office and his eyes on the large exterior window that reflected the interior of that same office.

He could see Samantha sitting behind her desk, Mrs. Phillips sitting in the chair on the other side. They were talking. Nothing more, just talking. Samantha seemed composed, collected.

"Hello. May I get you a cup of coffee?"

Jesse looked up to see Geoff Waters smiling at him. "Sounds good," he said to his friend and former co-worker at the National Security Agency, "but I can get it myself. If you'd show me where you keep the pot."

"In the staff lounge. I'll be happy to show you where that is," Geoff said, leading the way then closing the door behind them.

"What's up?"

"Well," Geoff said, leaning his rangy frame against the edge of an old table, "I've got four paper cuts, and I've learned how to put a new roll of black film in a fax machine. I've discovered a pretty good little café around the corner—great grilled-cheese sandwiches— I've talked to at least five hundred people who either want to give money to Phillips or have him burn in hell...and I've found a mole. That's probably the part you want to hear about, right?"

Jesse, who had been in the process of pouring himself a cup of coffee he didn't really want, turned his head to look at his friend and fellow agent. "Who?" he asked, holding out the full coffee cup, hoping he didn't already know the answer to his question.

Geoff took it, took a sip of the hot coffee. "Bettyann," he said then, wincing as the coffee hit his tongue. "She's Mrs. Phillips's eyes and ears in here. Nothing, and I do mean nothing, that goes on in here isn't reported to Joan Phillips. I sure hope you didn't do one of your infamous good ole Alabama boy Southern routines in there, bucko, because Bettyann has probably reported everything but your shoe size to Mrs. Phillips by now. So? Think she made you?"

"Damn it!" Jesse put down the cup he was going to fill for himself and sat down. "Great information, Geoff, but a little late. Oh, yeah, she made me. Which means she made Samantha. She knows now, for sure, who took that first envelope. Damn it! I've got to go get Samantha out of here."

"What about me?" Geoff asked, following him. "Do I stick here?"

Jesse paused, his hand on the doorknob. "Can you give me until Friday night?"

"It goes down then?"

"What goes down then, Geoff?" Jesse asked, looking at his friend.

"Oh, come on," Geoff said. "Mrs. Phillips has eyes and ears, and so do I. Besides, Billy and I talked about it at lunch. Mark Phillips is dirty in some way, isn't he? Him and the missus. And you're going to take them down."

"Go wash your face," Jesse said tightly. "You've got ink on your nose."

"Hey, I was just asking is all, bucko," Geoff said, holding up his hands. "Is she…is she in any danger? Your whistle-blower?"

"No. No danger. But you are, old friend, if you let anything slip."

"Consider me mute, bucko," Geoff said, then rubbed at his nose, just in case there was ink on it.

Jesse opened the door, immediately looking to his left, toward Samantha's office. Joan Phillips was just getting up from her seat, and Samantha rose as well, walking around the desk to give her "aunt" a kiss on the cheek.

How hard had that been for her? Probably pretty damn hard.

Moments later, Joan Phillips walked through the office, calling a cheerful goodbye to "Joe," and then she was gone.

"How'd it go?" Jesse asked Samantha once they, too, were outside the office, heading for the park.

"Fine, actually. She just wanted to know the final

seating chart now that the president is definitely going to be there—the man changes his mind so often I wonder how he can run the country so well. And she questioned my choice of table linens. I told her it was too late to change the color and she said that was fine. And that's it.''

Jesse only nodded. "You're excited about the president being there, aren't you?"

She goggled at him. "Are you kidding? I can't *stand* that he's going to be there to put his seal of approval on Uncle Mark. When he finds out what Aunt Joan has done? The president, the whole White House, the whole party, is going to be standing there with egg on its collective face. Can't we stop this?"

"That's up to Bob Forrester," Jesse said, taking her hand as they crossed at the corner, entered the small pocket park and headed for "their" bench.

"The chief of staff? It has actually gone that far?"

"I'm sorry, sweetheart, but yes, Old Abe knows. I had to tell him. And with the information we got today, the names of the companies...?"

Samantha pressed the heels of her hands against her eyes. "Do you know yet if Uncle Mark is involved, or just Aunt Joan? I don't want it to be either of them, but most especially not Uncle Mark. I...I've always looked up to him, you know. What happens Friday night, Jesse? Please. Tell me."

"I can't, sweetheart. I really can't. The only thing I can tell you is that you're out of it, you're safe, and nobody can involve you if this news breaks out, becomes fodder for the press."

"I don't *care* about that," she said, putting her

hands in her lap, squeezing her fingers together. "Oh, I wish there were some…some *graceful* way out of this. Some way that wouldn't be a scandal."

Jesse put a finger beneath her chin, tipped her head up to his. "Do you trust me, Samantha?"

She blinked, then sighed. "Yes. I trust you, Jesse."

"And you'll do anything I say between now and Friday night, and most especially Friday night?"

"I'm not robbing a bank for you," she said, summoning a weak smile. "But, yes, I think so."

"And then, when this is all over, will you let me ask you a question, Samantha? A very important question?"

She took another shaky breath. "You…you could ask it now."

He pulled her into his arms, her head resting against his shoulder. "Sweetheart, I'm going to have to do my duty Friday night. It might work the way Old Abe and I planned it, and it might not. If we screw up, if something goes wrong, you'll always know that I'm the guy who brought Senator Phillips and his wife down, disillusioned your parents, and got your name dragged through the mud."

She sat up, looked at him strangely. "Wait a minute," she said, her voice steady, no longer hesitant or nervous. "Let me see if I've got this straight, okay? You're planning something big for the night of the fund-raiser. If it goes well, you'll ask me an *important* question—a *very* important question—afterward. But if it doesn't, if it all hits the fan—you're not going to ask the question?"

Jesse shifted his eyes right, then left, sort of mentally

hunting through his words to figure out why they sounded so stupid when she repeated them to him. "That had been how I thought about it, yes. But—"

Samantha stood up, glared down at him. "You're such a *jerk,* Jesse Colton. What do you think I am? Some…some *shallow* person? Do you think I wouldn't be able to handle a little trouble?"

"Being a witness at televised congressional hearings, being subpoenaed by a Special Prosecutor, having your entire life put under a microscope by the tabloids, who would just love to make you their latest political pinup gal—that's not my definition of a little trouble, sweetheart."

"Oh. Wait. I get it now. You don't want your name linked with mine if that happens, right?"

Jesse stood up, feeling his own temper rise with him. "That's bull, Samantha, and you know it. I've got my backside hanging right out there with yours, you know. Okay, Old Abe knows now, but he didn't, not in the beginning. I set this thing up on my own, and I probably didn't have the authority to do that. If we hang, we hang together, and that's fine by me—where you stand, I stand beside you, period. But that doesn't mean that you'll like me, now, does it?"

"I don't like you right now," she said, turning her back on him.

Jesse put his arms around her waist, pulled her back against him. "Do you think either of us is making any sense here, sweetheart?" he asked, kissing her hair.

"No," she said quietly. But she didn't fight him, try to get free of his arms. She just leaned the back of her head against his shoulder and sighed.

"So, if I apologize for being an ass, will you understand that I'm on some shaky ground here, and have been ever since we met and I figured out that you were going to be the most important person in my life?"

"Really?" she asked, turning in his arms, sliding her own arms up and around his neck. "I felt the same way. You have a very powerful effect on people, Jesse."

He went forehead to forehead with her, looking deeply into her eyes. "It's all for show, where you're concerned. Inside, I'm sixteen years old, asking for a first date with the prom queen, and scared out of my socks that she'll turn me down. Maybe even laugh at me."

"I wouldn't do that, Jesse," Samantha said, her voice little more than a whisper. "But you're probably right, and you shouldn't ask me that important question until everything else is out of the way, and we can concentrate on both your question and my answer."

"Okay," he said, kissing her, then moving away from her, taking her hand as they walked back toward the street. "But I will tell you one thing now, if that's all right."

"About Friday night?"

"No. About the other afternoon, after I got the go-ahead from my family. I bought the house, Samantha."

When she stopped dead and stared at him, he smiled and repeated, "I bought the house. My cousin Rand called and told me there was another bidder—how anyone found out it was going to be put up for sale baffles me—so I had to move fast."

"Another...another bidder? Imagine that." Samantha started walking again. "And it was your cousin who told you about the other bidder—obviously an anonymous bidder, because you didn't give me a name."

"Yes, you're right. Why?"

"Oh, no reason," Samantha said, smiling at him. "So you bought the house. What are you going to do with it?"

They stopped at the corner, waiting for the traffic to clear so that they could cross the street. "I'll tell you…Friday night."

Chapter Eight

Jesse sat in his office in the West Wing, staring at the telephone.

Did he dare? And, if he did, would his sister be able to keep her mouth shut, not tell their parents until he told them himself?

Sure she could. Sky was a good egg.

His pretty little sister was also one first-rate jewelry designer.

"Okay, for better or worse, here goes," Jesse said out loud, reaching for the phone, punching in the number of his sister's shop in Oklahoma.

"Hi, sis, make any nose rings lately?" he asked when she answered on the third ring.

"Jesse! I didn't expect to hear from you until we all got together at Thanksgiving. What's up?"

"Pretty much, actually, but I don't want to get into that right now. What I need to know from you is—do you have any engagement rings in stock? I know you do mostly custom work, all that turquoise stuff, but I figured maybe you had a couple of regular engagement rings just sort of lying around there somewhere…''

He let the sentence dangle for a few moments, then said, ''Sky? You still there? Help me out here, Sky.''

''I'm here. I was just hunting up a stool so I could sit down before my knees gave out,'' his sister answered. ''You want a *ring,* Jesse? I mean, I'm on the portable phone, and sometimes it goes a little wonky…but you really said you want an engagement ring?''

''I know, I know, it all sort of comes as a shock to me, too.''

''You didn't say anything when you were in Black Arrow, Jesse. When did you meet her? Where? What's her name? Do you love her so much it hurts? Will I like her?''

''You'll be crazy about Samantha.''

''Samantha. Nice name. What does she look like? How does she live? What does she wear? Talk to me, Jesse.''

''Why do you need to know that?''

''Because I do have some lovely engagement rings here, but I'd have to know something about her to fit the ring to the woman. That's important, Jesse. Does she like modern stuff? Avant-garde? Or traditional? Maybe a simple solitaire? Maybe she's a knuckle-to-knuckle person—you know, wide band, maybe even three rings total?''

''Damn, Sky, I didn't know it would be this hard,'' Jesse said, sighing.

''Not hard, Jesse. But this is important. She's the one who has to wear it for fifty years, look at it for fifty years. She might not want one from me just because I'm your little sis, the jewelry designer. So tell me.''

Jesse leaned back in his chair, closed his eyes. "She's…she's sleek, Sky. By that I mean she's one of those graceful blondes who looks like she should be on the cover of some magazine.''

"I'm thinking not *Popular Mechanics,* right?'' Sky asked with a laugh.

"No,'' Jesse agreed, shaking his head. "How do I explain Samantha? Sophisticated yet touchable. Beautiful in a classic sense, but she loves fun, isn't afraid to make faces, look silly. She wears lots of fuzzy sweaters and soft slacks at home, suits to work. Her suits always have skirts, and she has fantastic legs— not that you probably need to know that, but I enjoy them. Oh, and she always wears the same thick gold chain around her neck. Does that help?''

"It helps me know that she likes gold. Would you call her traditional, Jesse? Would that be the word? You know, big soft couches, cherry woods, stays away from the trendy, the latest fads?''

"Yes,'' Jesse said, sitting forward. "You've got it, Sky. That's Samantha. I bought the house for her, you know.''

"What house?''

"The one Grandmother Gloria never told us about, along with everything else. I spoke with Great-Grandfather George and Bram, a few others, and they okayed the deal. I'm paying full market price, less what would be my share. She's crazy about the house, Sky. I figure it's my ace in the hole when I propose, then tell her about the house.''

''Tell me about the house, Jesse. If she likes it, I'll be able to tell even more about her. As it is, I've already got my mind down to three possible rings I designed a while ago, in one of my sentimental June-bride phases. I'm such a romantic. Man, I can't believe this. Jesse, getting married. Am I the first to know?''

''Even before Samantha,'' Jesse told her. ''Oh, and before we talk about the house, I need one more favor from you if I can. I have to have the ring by Friday afternoon. Can you ship it that fast?''

''If you're getting married, I can *fly* it there myself. Seriously, Jesse, this is great, just great. And I think it's wonderful that this is all happening so fast, really I do. I don't believe in wasting a day when you've found your happiness. What did Great-Grandfather George say about you the last time I called home? Oh, I remember now. Something about the raven seeking, and finding the heart's truth. Is this Samantha your heart's truth, Raven?''

''Yes, Sky, she is, which means that Great-Grandfather George is going to be spouting even more of his obscure wisdom now that I've proved him right.''

''Oh, he already is, Jesse. He wants to call Billy overseas, as a matter of fact, to tell him something about how danger lurks in the big city, and that the night is always darkest before the dawn.''

''That sounds like Great-Grandfather George, all right. Poor Billy, he's in for it now, isn't he?'' Jesse said with a grin, then told her about the house. His and Samantha's house...

Samantha walked down the stairs, careful to hold the banister because the bottoms of her new shoes were still a bit slippery, then stopped at the bottom to inspect her reflection in the long mirror on the lower landing.

She'd chosen black, although this was far from a dress anyone would pick to wear to a funeral...even if she was going to the death of a candidacy.

Turning slightly to her left, Samantha admired the way the soft, swingy skirt resettled just at the middle of her knees, leaving her legs exposed in almost nude stockings. The scoop neckline, front and back, was almost like an off-the-shoulder cowl neckline, with a large fold-over of black silk that skimmed her breasts, her arms, and all the way across her back. And her waistline didn't look so shabby, either, encircled with a slim self-fabric belt with a small golden buckle.

"Oh, wow," Rose said, walking in from the dining room, licking at a double-decker mint chocolate chip ice cream cone. "Hot mama."

"Thank you," Samantha said, leaning forward slightly as she skimmed a hand over her hair that she'd pulled back in a classic French twist. "Now, tell me the truth, Rose. Do I look professional yet friendly, competent yet approachable, sincere yet—"

"You look fine, Samantha," Rose said, shaking her head. "And since when are you nervous about this stuff, anyway? You could pull off one of these dinners in your sleep."

Samantha took a deep breath, trying to believe Rose. But, then, Rose didn't know what she knew...which wasn't much. All she really knew was that tonight could be a success or a disaster. And that, either way, this was the last night of Mark Phillips's short run for president of the United States.

She went to the hall closet and pulled out her black raincoat, the one that went down nearly to her ankles, and slipped it on. It took her three tries to get her left arm into the sleeve. "Jesse should be here by now."

"I hope he brings a basket with him, because you're going to need one. I mean it, you're a real basket case, Samantha. Here—your purse. You'll need it."

Samantha took the purse from Rose. "Thanks. Oh, there's the bell. He's here. Gotta go."

"I'll keep the home fires burning," Rose called after her as Samantha ran toward the foyer. "Go get 'em, Samantha. Break a leg. 'Ray, team, and all of that! Bye!"

"What's she saying?" Jesse asked as Samantha opened the door, practically barreled into him.

"Who knows," she said, taking a deep breath.

He looked magnificent. Black tuxedo, obviously custom made. Snow-white shirt with small pleats running down the front. Simple yet elegant black onyx studs. A perfectly tied bow tie—no clip-on for the Raven. A soft white wool scarf draped around his neck.

"You look…good," she said, sighing.

"You look like you're wearing a raincoat," he said, kissing her cheek. "Are you going to flash the thousand-dollar-a-plate crowd, or is there a dress under there?"

"Very funny—not."

"Sorry, I was just trying to lighten the mood. Are you okay?"

"No, I'm not okay," she said as he helped her into the passenger seat of his car, then got in on the driver's side. "You've kept me totally in the dark for days,

Jesse, when you know exactly what's going to happen. Did you really think I'd be okay?''

He pulled away from the curb, heading for the Watergate Hotel, the site of the fund-raiser. She'd tried to make a joke about the location at one point, but it had fallen flat, just like her mood every time she thought about what might happen this evening.

''Is the president still going to be there?'' she asked. ''Can you at least tell me that? I mean, I've got to do some big changes with the seating arrangement if he's not going to be there.''

''He'll be there, with the first lady and the chief of staff. In fact, he's probably going to arrive in about twenty minutes.''

''No, he can't do that, Jesse. We're only going to the hotel now because I have so much to do, to check on. The dinner doesn't start for another two hours. The president is scheduled to arrive just in time for a small meet-and-greet, then sit down to dinner.''

''Well, you know what they say about the best-laid plans of mice and men,'' Jesse said, reaching over to squeeze her hand. It was only then that she realized that she'd been unclasping and clasping her purse like some madwoman.

''Okay, okay. You're having fun with your big secret plan. Just tell me this—are the president and first lady going to be staying for the dinner? Or are they just showing up to say something terrible to Uncle Mark and then leave again?''

''They'll be at the dinner. I understand the president even has a speech prepared. A few remarks.''

''Oh, God,'' Samantha said, sinking low on the bucket seat. ''Please tell me he's not going to take over the night. Our president doesn't know the meaning of *a few remarks*. He'll talk for an hour, while the desserts made up in perfect little American flags of blueberry, pineapple and strawberry sherbet melt all over the kitchen while the staff waits to serve them.''

''Sherbet flags? Your idea?''

She shot him a level stare. ''Do you really think that? *No-o-o*,'' she said with great emphasis on the word. ''They were Aunt Joan's idea. She actually talked a chef into making up slice-and-serve American flags.''

''I didn't think it was your style,'' Jesse said as they pulled up to the valet entrance of the hotel. ''Well, we're here. Promise me something, Samantha. Whatever I say or do, just follow along, all right? No questions, no hesitation, just follow my lead.''

''I'd like to say no to you on that,'' Samantha told him honestly. ''I'd like to say that no, I'm not only going to be standing back and watching Uncle Mark's dreams be ground into dust, but I'm going to help with the grinding. But I can't. I trust you, Jesse. I trust you not to let him be hurt any more than he has to be hurt.''

''If he's unaware of what his wife has done, that's a deal, Samantha. Everybody likes Senator Phillips. But if he's in on it? Then all bets are off, and I have nothing to say about any of it.''

''I understand,'' Samantha said as one of the valets opened her door for her. ''Okay, let's go get this over with before I chicken out and go lock myself in a closet somewhere.''

Samantha had really outdone herself. The ballroom had a lot going for itself, just from an architectural standpoint, but Samantha had used the tables and other furnishings, the chandeliers and dais, to great advantage with some inspired decorating.

No red-white-and-blue crepe-paper bunting, no tacky blowup photographs of the candidate. Nothing that looked like election night in the local fire hall in Black Arrow.

This was class, all class. Silver sparkled, crystal caught the light. Fine china rested on dark navy linen tablecloths. Flowers were everywhere.

"Looks good," he said, not bothering to say more because he doubted Samantha even heard him. She was too busy checking on the flower arrangements, making sure the twenty-five musicians were fed before they took up their instruments, checking the individual table place cards against her master list and the seating chart.

"You know," she said during a break in the controlled mayhem that seemed to rage all around them, "this is a whole lot of work for nothing if this dinner doesn't come off. But you said the president is staying?"

"Five times," Jesse said, then saw the tall, thin form of Bob Forrester out of the corner of his eye. The chief of staff motioned to him, a prearranged signal. "Uh-oh, show time. POTUS is in the building."

"Where?" Samantha swung around, looking for the usual contingent of Secret Service agents, and for some sign of the commander in chief.

"I understand there's a sitting room down the hall. That's where we're going. The senator and his wife are probably already there, at Old Abe's request. Are you ready?"

"Yes. No. Wait, I need Bettyann. She needs to take

over if I'm going to be out of the ballroom.'' She looked around the room once more. ''I don't understand. She should have been here an hour ago.''

''Bettyann won't be here, Samantha,'' Jesse said, knowing he'd just taken the first step toward everything else that would happen tonight. ''She's decided to move back to Ohio.''

''O-what? She can't—she wouldn't—she *what?*''

Jesse quickly put his hand at Samantha's elbow and began walking her toward one of the exits into the hallway. ''Remember how calm and cool you were going to be, sweetheart? Now's the time.''

Samantha smiled at one of the waiters, then asked him to make sure the staff knew they were not to serve the fruit cocktail until everyone was seated. ''Nobody likes warm fruit cocktail,'' she told him, then kept walking. ''There, how was that? Calm enough for you?''

''Very good. And you're right. Nobody likes warm fruit cocktail. Now, about our friend Bettyann. She worked for Joan Phillips.''

''Well, of course she did. We all do. We—wait a minute. *How* did she work for Aunt Joan?''

''Didn't you ever wonder why she asked so many questions, sweetheart?''

Samantha shrugged her elegant bare shoulders. ''I thought she was nosy.''

''So did I, at first. But, according to Bettyann, she kept Mrs. Phillips informed about everything that was going on at the campaign office. All about you, all about everyone. And she also volunteered, after a few more questions, that she did some private mailings for the lady. Got lists together, printed up computer labels, everything. And then intercepted any mailings that came into the office that were addressed to her directly and had Personal written on the bottom left-hand side of the envelope. Oh, and she planted that bug in your office, Samantha, for her employer.''

"Bettyann? I can't believe this. Did she *know* anything? I mean, did she know what she was doing was wrong?''

"We're pretending she didn't. She swears she didn't. Even as she was delivering those *personal* envelopes to Mrs. Phillips twice a week, unopened, and picking up her extra pay for services rendered. She was going to get teeth braces and a new car with her extra earnings.''

"But, if Bettyann was doing the mailings, why was that envelope there for me to find?''

"The stupid mistake, Samantha. When we pressed her on it, Bettyann remembered that her ex-boyfriend Benny called her to say he wanted to come over, get the rest of his clothing out of her apartment, and she got upset, wanted to intercept him before he got there because he still had a key. She mailed the rest of the envelopes—yes, there were more we're still trying to track down—and left the one with the damaged envelope to deal with the next morning. She figured you saw it, as you were still at the office when she left, and put it in a new envelope, mailed it for her. Stupid mistakes, Samantha. They always happen, sooner or later. And then, as we've said, the walls come tumbling down. All right, here we are.''

They stopped outside heavy wood double doors guarded by two agents in black suits and earpieces, and were asked to show identification.

"You're on the list, Mr. Colton," one of the agents said. "You, too, Ms. Cosgrove." He handed Samantha's purse back to her after inspecting its contents, then reached over and opened the door. He closed it after they passed inside the small room that held the leader of the free world.

"Samantha, hello there. Joan, look who's here, our wonderful campaign organizer. Excuse me a moment, Mr. President," Senator Mark Phillips said, putting down his wineglass as he stood up, held a hand out to his wife. Together, they walked over to kiss her cheek. "Ah, and this must be your young man? Joe, isn't it?"

"Jesse, Senator," Jesse said as they shook hands. Mark Phillips was a handsome man, with a genuine smile and a firm handshake. Not that any of that meant he couldn't also be, as Great-Grandfather George said, crooked as a dog's hind leg. "Jesse Colton. I work in the West Wing."

"Is that so, is that so," the senator said, still energetically pumping Jesse's hand. "Well, Joan, looks like you had that one wrong. Not Joe, Jesse."

Jesse looked at Mrs. Phillips, who had begun to go pale under her expertly applied makeup.

"You're not Joe Carter? Where's your Southern drawl? The West Wing? I don't understand. Were you deliberately making fun of me the other day, young man?"

"No, ma'am," Jesse said, motioning for everyone to go back across the room, retake their seats. "I think you'll understand everything shortly, ma'am, Senator."

"Hello there, Jesse," President Jackson Coates said from his seat beside his wife on a red-and-ivory-striped satin couch. "And you must be Samantha Cosgrove."

The president got to his feet, extended his hand. "I expressly asked Jesse to include you in our little group tonight. It's a distinct pleasure to meet you, young lady."

"Thank you, Mr. President," Samantha said, then stepped back a pace and looked at Jesse.

"We'll sit over here," he told her, taking her hand and leading her to two chairs fitted into a corner of the room, on either side of a square wood and brass table.

Jesse sat down, then looked toward the center of the room, to see Joan Phillips looking at him over her shoulder. Glaring at him over her shoulder. Glaring at Samantha.

The woman knew. She had to know. It was over, all over.

"Mark," the president said, sitting down once more, "I'm afraid I have some bad news for you."

"Mr. President?" the Senator said, immediately looking at his wife. Not hard to tell who was the power behind the throne in that relationship.

Jackson Coates crossed one leg over the other and also looked at Joan Phillips. "Where to begin? Ah, Bob, thank you, yes, that's probably the best place," he said, taking the large manila envelope the chief of staff handed him. One of *the* envelopes. He slid out the contents, the internal memo that had started it all.

"What's that, Mr. President?" the senator asked, and the president handed over the pages. "Why…why this is…" He looked at the president. "I don't understand. This is internal information, even speculation. Committee work. But in the wrong hands—how did you get this, sir?"

The president raised one eloquent eyebrow. He

might not be a tall man, but he was an impressive man, with a presence that made him seem larger than life. "We thought so. You don't know, Mark, do you?"

"Know what, sir? What's going on? Did someone break into my office?"

Jackson Coates cleared his throat, folded his hands in his lap and looked at Mark Phillips's wife. "Joan? Do I tell him, or do you?"

Twenty minutes later, it was over and everyone stood up, even shook hands.

Joan Phillips wiped at her eyes, for she had cried, just a little, before getting herself back under control.

She'd tried to explain away what she'd done, tried to call it nothing more than smart campaigning. She'd even gotten angry when the president told her that special interests would *own* her husband if he got into office.

"Don't be silly, Jackson," she'd said. "Once we were safely in office, they could all go hang. We just need them to *get* there."

The woman was a real piece of work, Jesse decided as he watched them all leave the room.

"So that's it?"

He turned to Samantha. "That's it. Dinner's in ten minutes, sweetheart. Are you hungry?"

"Not really, no. I still can't believe what happened, what I heard, what I saw."

"It's for the best, Samantha. Your uncle Mark is a good man, with a foolish, ambitious wife. But, luckily, bottom line, there's been very little actual harm done. With the senator leaving the race—for health reasons, an ever-popular reason—any money that's already come in can be returned once Mrs. Phillips tells us the details, and nobody has bought anybody's influence or vote.''

''I can't believe Uncle Mark is going to resign from the Senate.''

''It's the only honorable thing to do, Samantha. He and your aunt can go home, take it easy, and she can run for president of the local town council, or something.''

''She could, you know,'' Samantha said, sighing. ''Mom used to wonder why Aunt Joan didn't run for office instead of Uncle Mark. She seemed to enjoy it all more. The campaigning, the celebrity.''

''Don't forget the wheeling and dealing, sweetheart. So it's all over. The senator announces he's dropping out of the race, the president gets to make a very nice speech about the senator's long years of service to his country, and the contributors get to donate their thousand-bucks-a-plate to the party if they want to—and I can't picture any of them asking for the money back, can you?''

''Not when they can say they were the first to hear that Senator Mark Phillips, the top contender, has dropped out of the race, no. I guess I don't have to give Uncle Mark my letter of resignation now, do I? After tonight, the whole office staff is out of a job.''

As they walked back down the long hallway, Jesse heard the orchestra striking up ''Hail to the Chief.''

''We can't go in now, not until the president is done making his entrance, shaking hands with everybody from captains of industry to the waiters.''

''That's all right. I don't really think I want to stay, if you don't mind. I'm certainly not hungry.''

''I know where we could go,'' Jesse said, taking her

hand and heading toward the cloakroom to get her raincoat and his scarf. "It is Friday night, and I do have that question I want to ask you."

She smiled at him, her eyes bright, although still faintly shadowed with pity for her uncle. She stepped closer to him as he put an arm around her shoulders. "I think I'd like to answer that question. No matter how the rest of tonight had gone."

Samantha held her hands clasped together in front of her as they walked into the Georgetown mansion, Jesse leading the way, turning on lights.

The chandelier in the foyer was magnificent at night, and Samantha's eyes began to sting with tears as she looked at the wide, winding staircase and saw, in her mind's eye, laughing children running down those stairs in nightgowns and pajamas, to see what Santa had left for them under the huge Christmas tree in the living room.

"All mine and the bank's," Jesse said, spreading his arms wide as he walked back to her, his broad smile almost sheepish. "Can you imagine what it takes to heat this place in the wintertime?"

"There are plenty of fireplaces," she said as he took her hand and led her through the house. "How good are you at chopping wood?"

"Better than you'd expect. I chopped a lot of wood in my days back in Black Arrow. Come on, I've got something to show you."

"I thought you were going to ask me a question," she said, but kept walking, because he was half pushing her forward.

"I decided you already know what it is, so I did something else."

She shook her head as he took her hands, pulled her into the large kitchen. "Would you stop? You're like a little boy."

"I don't feel like a little boy," he said, taking her in his arms and waltzing her around the large center island of the kitchen. "Little boys don't get to do this," he said, kissing her eyes, her cheeks. "Or this," he said, and stopped dancing, slanted his mouth against hers.

Just when she was melting quite nicely, he put his hands on her shoulders and put some space between them. "Okay. Enough of that for now. I've got a present for you. Look," he said, pointing toward the countertop.

She looked. She saw.

And she burst into tears.

"Jesse! Where...where did you find this?" she asked, stroking the fat ceramic-pig cookie jar. "I can't believe you found this."

"Neither can I. It took three hours on the Internet and a really quick trip to Maryland early this morning, but I've got it. Probably the last surviving ceramic-pig cookie jar in captivity. Do you like it?"

"I love it," Samantha said, wiping at her eyes with a tissue she'd found in the pocket of her raincoat. "I love you," she said, sniffling.

His smile was so sudden, so bright, that she had to press her fingers against her mouth to hold back a sob.

"I love you, Samantha Cosgrove," he told her. "Marry me?"

"Do...do I get to keep the pig if I say no?" she

asked him, because if she didn't say something silly she was going to turn into one big watering pot of happy tears.

"Nope. We're a package deal. Oh, and you haven't looked inside. There's something inside."

"Cookies?" Samantha asked, lifting the lid. She bent over the jar, peeked inside. "No, no cookies. It's empty."

"Look harder," Jesse said, standing close beside her.

And there it was, sitting on the bottom of the jar, in a small ivory velvet case.

"Oh, Jesse," she said, taking out the box but not opening it.

"My sister, Sky, she made it. She designs jewelry back in Oklahoma. She says if you don't like it you can pick out anything else you like better, but she's pretty sure she picked the right one. Go ahead. Open it."

"No, you open it," Samantha said, handing him the box. "I'm afraid I'll drop it."

Jesse did as she asked, removing the ring that, through her tears, she saw only as a mass of rich gold and a sparkle that she could swear lit half the room.

And then he went down on one knee—right there in the kitchen, dressed in his tuxedo—and slipped the ring on her finger. Kissed her hand. "The pig is yours. And the ring. And the house. Will you marry us?"

"Yes. Oh, yes. I'll marry you. I'll marry all of you."

She held out her arms to him, longing for him to stand up, for him to hold her, but he stayed where he was. He raised a finger and said, "One more question."

She knelt down and slid her arms around his neck.

''When? Anytime. Tonight. Tomorrow. Next week. I'll marry you every week if you want.''

''No, that's not it,'' he said, pulling her close. ''I have a special request. I want to know if we can serve spaghetti and meat sauce at the reception.''

''Oh, Jesse, I love you,'' Samantha said, and pulled him to her for a kiss.

* * * * *

Don't forget to look out for
A Colton Family Christmas
in November 2003 from
Silhouette Books.

SILHOUETTE®
DESIRE™ 2-IN-1

AVAILABLE FROM 17TH OCTOBER 2003

THE WILL TO LOVE   Lindsay McKenna

Earthquake survivor Deputy Sheriff Kerry Chelton looked into
rugged rescuer Lieutenant Quinn Grayson's eyes and felt a powerful
attraction. But could Kerry break down the walls around Quinn's
heart so he could love again?

THE RANCHER, THE BABY & THE NANNY
Sara Orwig

Wyatt Sawyer knew he needed a nanny for his five-month-old niece.
He just hadn't known that the nanny would be the lovely Grace
Talmadge. Whose bone-melting kisses were a dangerous temptation
to a committed bachelor...

TAMING THE PRINCE   Elizabeth Bevarly

For royal escort Sara Wallington, errant bachelor Shane Cordello was
hardly the regal and serene prince she was expecting. He was too tall,
too handsome, too...*everything* to be the missing heir...wasn't he?

ROYALLY PREGNANT   Barbara McCauley

Though Emily had planned to seduce a prince, she soon discovered a
man she could love behind the playboy persona of Prince Dylan of
Penwyck. But what would her prince do once he learned she carried
another secret?

A LAWMAN IN HER STOCKING   Kathie DeNosky

Feisty, sophisticated and lovely, Brenna Montgomery was the type of
woman Dylan Chandler normally avoided. Except despite his best
efforts he couldn't get her out of his mind. But was he prepared to
pay the price of his soul-stirring seduction—marriage?

HER TEXAN TEMPTATION   Shirley Rogers

Mary Beth Adams wanted nothing to do with love-'em-and-leave-'em
old flame Deke McCall. She was too busy trying to save her home.
Yet Deke's tempting kisses and heated caresses were just too hard to
resist...

THE COLTONS

A Colton Family Christmas

JUDY
CHRISTENBERRY

LINDA
TURNER

CAROLYN
ZANE

On sale 17th October 2003

*Available at most branches of WHSmith,
Tesco, Martins, Borders, Eason, Sainsbury's
and all good paperback bookshops.*

SILHOUETTE® INTRIGUE™

proudly presents

a brand-new trilogy from

RITA HERRON

NIGHTHAWK ISLAND

This is one place where you won't want to fall asleep...

November 2003
SILENT SURRENDER

December 2003
MEMORIES OF MEGAN

January 2004
THE CRADLE MISSION

1103/SH/LC73

SILHOUETTE SPOTLIGHT

Two bestselling novels in one volume by favourite authors, back by popular demand!

Tall, dark and dangerously tempting. These men can't be tamed by just any women!

Available from 17th October 2003

Available at most branches of WHSmith, Tesco, Martins, Borders, Eason, Sainsbury's and all good paperback bookshops.

1003/064

♥ SILHOUETTE®
DESIRE™

is proud to introduce

DYNASTIES:
THE CONNELLYS

Meet the royal Connellys—wealthy,
powerful and rocked by scandal,
betrayal…and passion!

TWELVE GLAMOROUS STORIES IN SIX 2-IN-1 VOLUMES:

2 FREE

books and a surprise gift!

We would like to take this opportunity to thank you for reading this Silhouette® book by offering you the chance to take TWO specially selected titles from the Desire™ series absolutely FREE! We're also making this offer to introduce you to the benefits of the Reader Service™—

- ★ FREE home delivery
- ★ FREE gifts and competitions
- ★ FREE monthly Newsletter
- ★ Exclusive Reader Service discount
- ★ Books available before they're in the shops

Accepting these FREE books and gift places you under no obligation to buy, you may cancel at any time, even after receiving your free shipment. Simply complete your details below and return the entire page to the address below. *You don't even need a stamp!*

YES! Please send me 2 free Desire books and a surprise gift. I understand that unless you hear from me, I will receive 3 superb new titles every month for just £4.99 each, postage and packing free. I am under no obligation to purchase any books and may cancel my subscription at any time. The free book and gift will be mine to keep in any case.

D3ZEE

Ms/Mrs/Miss/Mr ....Initials.................................
BLOCK CAPITALS PLEASE

Surname ....

Address ....

....

....Postcode.................................

Send this whole page to:
UK: FREEPOST CN81, Croydon, CR9 3WZ
EIRE: PO Box 4546, Kilcock, County Kildare (stamp required)